THE DEAN OF DI$

CANED

AND ABLE

By

Dee Vee Curzon

ISBN-13: 9798841898122

CONTENTS

CHAPTER 1

MELANIE IS TEASED, GETS EVEN,

GETS PUNISHED!

The overweight student stood before him with tears running down her cheeks.

"I am so sorry, I really am. I know I shouldn't have done it, I am so sorry. I have never done anything like that before, I just got so fed up and I lost my temper just for a moment. Please don't send me home, Professor, it would break my mother's heart, I am so very, very sorry."

Stones, ever the poker face, just stared at the blubbing girl as she blustered on. Not as hard-hearted as he always liked to appear, he had plenty of sympathy for this transgressor. Bated and teased over her weight, Melanie Thorpe had finally snapped in the dining hall a couple of evenings ago and had pushed another student's face into her dessert. Unfortunately, she had probably not realised the strength her surplus pounds gave her and aside from mashing a rather slight fellow student's face into her meringue and cream, she had given her a nose bleed and a bruised cheek. Having heard the full story from staff and students present, Stones was well aware that the offensive student, a Prascilla Guptil, had been quite cruel in her jibes and that a complaint from Melanie of bullying would probably stand its ground under investigation. However, Melanie had made it clear that she did not wish to pursue this path, albeit Stones had pressed her on the point. He had decided that this would not release Prascilla from any comeback though, as after an initial chat with her he had suggested that she might like to reconsider her earlier thought of filing a formal complaint against Melanie for assault.

"This is a violent act causing actual, bodily harm, Melanie. I do hope that you realise that I cannot let this incident pass without the strongest and most thorough punishment. Might I suggest that you take a moment to gather yourself and then apply a little bit of thought as to how I could consider an alternative punishment to dismissal from our ranks of the finest and most privileged of your sex? You should perhaps spend a moment to reflect on just exactly how lucky you are to be stepping out amongst the hallowed halls and formidable cloisters of such an august college. You might also like to consider exactly as to what exactly you feel you should undergo to receive redemption for such behaviour. Indeed, what punishment could be seen to be of such a severity that would punish you sufficiently for carrying out such a heinous act? Into the corner with you, hands on head. Quickly, now."

The professor ushered the confused and distraught young woman into the corner of the room, placing her close to his cabinet of punishment implements. Having deftly unlocked the door, he opened up the cabinet to the trembling form beside him and smiled in delight at Melissa's sharp intake of breath as she espied the arrangement of whips, canes, crops, straps and paddles hanging before her.

"In five minutes time I will give you one opportunity to suggest a route that could lead to you remaining on site as a member of our esteemed institution rather than being drummed out in disgrace. This route will necessitate you undergoing an extreme punishment befitting your crime and one that you will request that I consider most convincingly. Are you understanding me, girl?" He snapped, knowing full well that he had his fish already about to nibble at the bait offered.

As Melanie's eyes filled with tears, Stones turned away to leave her to stew in her dilemma. In his experience, it took a moment or two for his subjects to run through a variety of emotions before usually realising that the opening he was steering them towards was actually the only escape route on offer, however unpalatable it may appear.

As it happens it took almost an hour before a quivering, timid Melanie found her voice. To Stones' amusement, she had half-turned and opened her mouth on several occasions before she finally found the backbone and spirit to request with the utmost politeness if she could have permission to speak!

"Ah, yes, I had almost forgotten you were still here, my little reprobate. Well, get on with it. I presume that you have come to your senses and wish to offer to undergo whatever punishment it takes to clear your slate. Before you speak, I would like you to consider very carefully what you propose. I am not in the habit of giving counsel to timewasters, young lady. I expect you to acknowledge your disgraceful violation of the rules of civilised society and put forward an appropriate request."

"Um. I think so, sir. But I will change it to whatever you want if it's not good enough."

"Child, you really do need to consider ways to improve your self-assertiveness and confidence in your own actions. I will send a note to your pastoral care tutor here and we will see if we can get you on one of the courses we send some of you shy, docile, timid little flowers on. Oh, but you slammed one of your fellow students faces into the dinner table, did you not? So maybe not quite as shy and retiring as you act, are you? Well, I will tell you what, before I peruse your request for an alternate form of punishment fitting for the crime committed, I will give you a further few minutes to rewrite your little script. I suspect that you have skirted around the issue, so this will be your final opportunity to volunteer yourself for a suitable solution to our problem with you. To help you focus, you will now remove your clothing…"

Stones got no further as the student burst into tears and crumpled to her knees before him, a strange primal howling sound coming from her mouth.

"Desist that awful racket this very instance, young lady!" For a man of his age and considerable build, he often moved with pace and dexterity that caused surprise, and, as in this case, shock and fear. A terrified Melanie found herself hauled upright, her flowing dress raised high up her back and within seconds she felt the impact of the professor's huge hand slamming into her substantial knicker-clad bottom.

"Clothes off, folded neatly and placed on the chair, now!" Stones thundered, correctly adopting the persona that he judged would cause the response he required.

"Oh my God, I don't believe it! I am so sorry, sir!" With quivering lips and tear-flooded eyes, she looked at the professor's angry face; he could see the realisation of her situation finally hitting her. "Oh dear, oh no. Yes sir, of course, sir, I am so sorry sir. Yes. Yes. Take my clothes off. Yes. Yes. Yes."

The naked student soon stood before him, one hand between her legs, shielding her groin, with the other arm across her large, pendulous breasts.

"Legs apart, hands on your head. Come on girl, move yourself. That is better, everything on show. Now, let me have a proper look at what you have to work on. There's no need to be embarrassed about your weight or shape with me, young lady. I certainly do not do fat-shaming or body form taunting. All I am really interested in is the application of the most suitable method of improvement." He prodded her buttocks, squeezing a handful of flesh and moving his spread hands over both cheeks while Melanie whimpered and trembled at his touch.

"Yes, these beauties, and they are beautiful buttocks, Melanie, don't doubt that, will withstand an awful lot, I suspect. Now, why don't you come with me and see if we can select the right tools for the job before you rewrite your little piece suggesting the form of justice that needs applying to the issue."

He took her hand and Melanie gripped it tightly, suddenly seemingly spellbound and submissive. In the tone of a true supplicant, she spoke the words that caused Stones to smile in approval, causing her own face to lighten and revive.

"Oh sir, yes sir. Of course, sir. I am so sorry, sir. Of course, of course."

"Now, Melanie, if you had to select the two implements you wanted to be used to thrash your backside that would best suit the occasion and help ease your conscience for the heinous crime of violence you committed, which do you feel most appropriate?"

His voice was delivered in his most hypnotic tone and it gave him much self-satisfaction to see Melanie stand before the display of punishment weaponry giving due thought and consideration to words that she would probably have never thought she'd hear even in her worst nightmare!

"Can I touch them?" Melanie's query was of no great surprise to him; he had often found that once a student had accepted that the punishment was inevitable then part of the fear left them. His intention was to give Melanie a severe thrashing; her instinctive act could be deemed understandable but that sort of violence was not acceptable in college life and, regardless of her reasons, she had used her weight and strength to her advantage to cause facial damage to another student. It was certainly in the arena of gross misconduct, wherein expulsion via the college process known as 'sending down' was an outcome that would fit the crime. Stones' challenge with a girl carrying excess weight such as Melanie was that by nature of her size, she had considerable padding on most parts of her body, particularly her backside. As he gave her the go-ahead to handle his wicked but beloved – by him, at least – array of 'improvers', he stood back to look at the fleshy buttocks that would face his application. The hand marks of his quick slapping were already fading, barely pink outlines still visible, and he knew that a lot of force would be required to ensure that she truly suffered the sting and lash of his tools. A message to Jamie, the college porter whom he called upon when assistance was required, loomed and he suspected that this could be another opportunity for Emily Govans to join them and experience another session as support student to a punishment victim. Emily, in her role as student support, would be perfect for Melanie, he mused, and he knew that she would appreciate the chance to be a part of another's correction. He enjoyed the company of this attractive, stoic and very independent-minded student, and he felt that she deserved a treat after her performance and involvement in bringing to account the dreaded Seven Sisters gang. Her acceptance and keenness to take a beating, as well as her nonchalance concerning nakedness and displaying her gorgeous body along with her completely open obsession with him meant that he had learned to have much trust and faith in her loyalty and obedience.

To Stones' surprise, Melanie continued to handle and seemingly appraise each of his 'improvers', piece by piece, methodically feeling the texture, weight and thickness of every item. Her face was a picture of concentration, with no obvious fear or trepidation apparent.

"Well, young lady, you seem rather enraptured with my collection. Do you approve, and is anything taking your fancy?" Stones decided the teasing approach was called for. As Melanie removed a cane and, taking an end in each hand, bent the rod flexing it in its centre, he could see her eyes open in wonder. His words snapped her out of whatever was playing though her mind and she immediately coloured, quickly replaced the cane and dropped her eyes to the floor.

"Oh, do not be ashamed, Melanie. It is a pleasure to have someone who seems to have an appreciation of the tools of my trade. It is a fine collection, although this is only a selection; I have many more that I would be happy to show you but perhaps on another day. I could probably do with a test and sample student if you would like to be considered for the position?"

Melanie's face was Stones' perfect reward. In almost comic fashion, her eyes blinked and her mouth started to open and close soundlessly as she clearly struggled to find words for this situation. Stones decided to enjoy himself further at her expense. He did not consider this a malicious act but more a part of the humiliation process he liked to put each errant student through. Before Melanie, whose red blush had now travelled down her neck to the tops of her monumental breasts, could bring forth the required ability to put words together into a sentence, Stones pursued his belittling rhetoric.

"Now, have you chosen the ideal implements that you feel would best serve the purpose of allowing you to return to civilised society feeling as though you have atoned for your sins and learnt a valuable lesson? I would be interested in our opinion on the best way to deliver the corporal punishment that your disgraceful, thuggish behaviour deserves. I think you will be a student who will truly appreciate the relief when the weight of your disgrace, the shame and mortification, has been lifted from your substantial shoulders after our joint enterprise. I am very much looking to working in combination with you to aid your reintegration into civilised college society."

Melanie's face was a picture of perplexity as she processed his words. Stones allowed her to wallow in her own confusion and could see that she was desperately attempting to come up with an answer that she would be happy with as well as satisfactorily answering his question.

He tapped her buttocks with the back of his hand.

"Come on, girl. I do not expect to be kept waiting when I ask you a question. I know that was a lot of words to consume there but you are supposedly one of our elite young ladies on her path to a successful career. Try and keep up. Your buttocks. My weaponry. Remember, we were trying to marry the two together. Chop chop!"

Melanie's hands grabbed at a cane, knocking several implements to the floor. As she scrabbled to pick them, Stones' voice froze her as she bent to retrieve them.

"Slightly unusual method of selection, Melanie, and I did say two not five. However, I am happy to bow to your wishes."

"No. No. No, sir. I didn't mean that I wanted all of them. It was an accident. I am sorry, sir. I am just so clumsy." Melanie's protestations dried up as she looked at the expression on his face and the hand reaching out for the fallen items.

"I think realisation is dawning. My methods and processes may seem irrational and unfair to you now, Melanie, but one day soon I believe that you will see the light and understand them fully. So, we have a thin, whippy cane, a split-end tawse, a medium cane, a thick cane and a riding crop. They should do the trick – harsh but fair. If you are going to assault people and cause physical pain to others, then you can hardly complain if you receive treatment in kind. You may now go over to that desk and sit down and write me a one-page essay detailing your misdemeanour and appalling behaviour; specific but concise, please. You will then request a punishment of the severity that is in accord with your own foul act, naming these implements which you can take over to the desk with you. You should nominate your own amount of strokes that you think you wish to receive to help ease your conscience and guide you down a more righteous path. To save you going through any more conflict and disquiet in your mind over whether or not you dare ask for my opinion on the number of strokes, I advise you to listen carefully now as I will not repeat myself without a requirement for you to double the punishment as an aide-memoire. My thoughts are that to serve you best you require a thorough spanking to warm those mighty cheeks up and get them prepared for what will follow. Two hundred slaps is a good start, generally." He paused to take in the look of absolute horror and astonishment that had appeared on the clearly stricken student's face.

"Oh, don't you think that's enough? Did you want to add some more, per chance?" The challenge and scorn in his tone was evident even to a newbie entrant into the corporal discipline environment, such as she was.

"Oh no, sir. Sorry. Sorry. Sorry. I just don't know anything about these matters. Did you really mean 200, sir? Sorry to ask, sir."

"Actually, I think you're right, that is a bit lenient; well done, Melanie. Good girl. Let's raise that to two hundred and fifty."

Melanie finally learned to maintain her silence but a single tear trickled from one eye and gently ran down her cheek; she looked scared witless.

"One tear, I will allow. Now, wipe your eyes; you are not in pain.

Yet." He passed her a tissue from his desk. "But if you are going to blubber at this point, then I will take it upon myself to give you something to really cry about. Save your tears for when it's appropriate – when your backside is feeling like it has been flayed by barbed wire and then set on fire, just to give you a heads-up. Actually, young lady, just bend over, legs apart fully so I can gauge exactly what level of application we might need to employ to get the job done properly."

Taking a deep breath in, Melanie complied, stretching her legs as far apart as she could while keeping her balance, her hands grasping her shins. Stones moved behind and first ran his hands around her quite taut cheeks before taking firm grasps and squeezing tight. To her credit, Melanie stayed still although Stones could feel the tension in her buttocks as he worked the fat of the cheeks between his fingers. Abruptly, he yanked her cheeks wide open, digging his thumbs in and exposing the student's anus and lower vagina.

"Damn well stay still, you minx! The dog needs to see the bone. I hope you are nice and clean in your nether region? I do not deal with unhygienic trollops."

Melanie tried to stand and twist away from his probing and he used all his strength to force her down to her knees with her flanks raised high.

"Head down and smell the carpet, bottom up, legs apart. You are already in big trouble for not adhering to a simple instruction to stay still, so do not make it worse. Now do I need to shower you down first or are you relatively clean down below?"

There was a large gulping sound of anguish as Melanie tried to pull herself together and out of the nightmare he had foisted upon her. His iron grip held her neck down to the floor as she felt the power and strength that he still possessed despite his age.

"Oh, my lord, sir. I cannot believe that you are saying such things!

Is this normal? It does not feel appropriate, sir, I have to say, sir, sorry sir, sorry. However, I showered not long before I came to you, sir, but could you please not look at me down there? It is not appropriate behaviour, sir. It is, in fact, disgusting, sir. I am sorry, sir, but I will not allow myself to be demeaned in this manner, it's just not appropriate."

Melanie's whimper as he'd begun his response suggested that she may have realised that she hadn't perhaps taken the right tone or chosen the right words in her reply.

"Well, bravo to you, found some backbone, have you? However, I very much doubt your victim with her face smashed into her plate in front of the rest of the guests at formal dining thought that *your* actions were appropriate, did they? Since we are making speeches, let me give you a little bit of information to digest. Listen carefully as I may ask questions! The college call this retribution or payback. We call it learning and improvement by education. We call it the use of emotional intelligence and behavioural psychology. We look closely at the four main behavioural types: optimism, pessimism, trust and envy. And we use the emotional information to guide thinking and behaviour. We look at curbing and resolving behavioural anger of which there are three types basically, that shape the way human beings react in a situation when their ire tends to become awakened. These are passive aggression, open aggression and assertive anger. We do not include the right to use corporal punishment just to amuse ourselves, although I do indeed find most aspects pleasing; we believe that it assists us in producing fully formed, emotionally adjusted, strong-willed and strategic thinking young ladies, ready to take on the wider world for the benefit of all. This is information that was freely available to you and your guardians, in your case your mother and your aunt, whom I remember very well. They signed a contract, witnessed and counter-signed by yourself, accepting the methods of this revered and renowned institution. Do I really need to continue or would you like to quickly get dressed and leave my office while I make a telephone call to your lovely aunt? It was agreed with your mother's blessing that any issues were to be raised with her older sister prior to informing your mother herself, as she has always handles disciplinary matters in your upbringing, as I understand."

There was a rather forlorn sounding groan now coming from Melanie, who had ceased her resistance to his force and was now supplicant, her forehead touching the floor and her flanks raised as he had demanded albeit, Stones noted, with tightly clamped thighs.

"Please don't call Auntie Wendy, sir. I am sorry about what I said."

The professor sighed dramatically, as though reluctant to carry out something that he felt a necessity. He was well practised at this, never wanting to appear eager to dispense punishment, always presenting it as a matter of regret, a necessary evil, so to speak, though he suspected that it did not fool that many of the wretches he dealt with.

"Oh, get up, girl, you look quite ridiculous in that position!"

Melanie hauled herself to her feet to face him, her cheeks flushed with the effort and her eyes full of tears.

"I am so sorry, Professor Stones. I have just failed some sort of test, haven't I? I am so sorry, I do realise that my behaviour was unacceptable and I do accept that I have to take punishment. I just wasn't ready for the, you know, the other stuff. The showing you my intimate areas. I just did not realise that this would come into it. Nobody has ever really looked at me like that, sir. Oh God, I am just talking rubbish now, sorry, sir."

Stones took pity on her; he had read her the pastoral tutor's notes that assessed her on the more non-academic performance and demeanour in the university and knew that she was deemed an earnest, polite and honest young member of the college. His expression softened and her face immediately brightened in response.

"Think on what I have told you, young lady. I rarely waste time dispensing wisdom if I feel the recipient does not warrant the effort, so take that on board as a positive. For the record, if I ever ask you a question, to adopt a position or to perform a task, regardless of what it is and definitely regardless of what you think, then I expect instant acquiescence. No matter what. Do you understand?"

"Yes, sir, I do, sir. Thank you. Thank you so much, Professor." Melanie was holding herself to her full height now, her confidence restored by his words.

"Good. So, if I command you now to turn round, bend over, open your legs and pull your cheeks wide apart, to open up your intergluteal cleft and show me the orifices hiding beneath, what would your response be?"

Back came the facial flush as the naked student found herself once more on the end of one of Stones' renowned curve balls and change of directions.

"I... I... I... I would do what you asked, sir?" Her voice was reduced to a mouse-like whisper as her eyes resumed their study of the carpet.

"Just to be clear that we are in accord, please tell me exactly what this would consist of, my dear?" he coaxed.

"Oh no. I mean yes, sir, sorry, sir. I would turn around to present my rear to you, sir, then I would bend over before you, sir, with my legs wide apart and then, then, then ... I'm sorry, sir. Then I would put my hands on my buttocks and pull my cheeks apart so that you could inspect my privates, sir. Is that alright, sir?"

"Good girl. Now, proceed."

With that instruction, Stones dawdled over towards the desk

where the canes, tawse and crop were sitting on the paper ready for Melanie to show her writing prowess. His back was to her deliberately, knowing full well that this would add confusion and discombobulation to Melanie's thinking. Out of the corner of his eye he watched as she slowly turned to present her back view to where he had been standing. She quietly sighed and then wearily bent over, her legs apart; her large hands took substantial handfuls of her cheeks in each hand. With a sob, she pulled the crack of her bottom wide apart and then stayed motionless.

Keeping his back to her but a sly eye to the side, Stones flexed and swiped the implements through the air and was impressed that there was no visual or audible reaction that he could tell. After several minutes virtually ignoring the lewd display from Melanie, he replaced the tools of his disciplinary trade, his beloved 'improvers' with which he liked to taunt his victims, before wandering across his room and standing behind her.

"So what exactly do you think you are doing?"

"Beg your pardon, sir?" was the not altogether wise response.

"I do not like repeating myself. I asked you a simple question!" Stones snapped back. "Now explain to me in detail exactly what you are doing at this very moment."

"Waaaaaah!" was not the response he expected as the student hit a new level of utter despair.

"Oh, my goodness, oh my, oh my, oh my. Sorry, sir. Of course, I am so sorry sir. I am bending over, my legs wide apart and am proudly and obediently showing you my intimate places by pulling my bottom cheeks apart, sir. I am ready for you to inspect my private parts, sir. Oh my, please sir, I hope you will be satisfied with my display. Oh dear. I don't know what else to say, sir, thank you, sir."

"Oh yes, good heavens, stand up you look absolutely ridiculous holding your behind stretched wide open like that!"

A loud gulp was the response before Melanie released her cheeks which sprang back into place which such force they created a resounding splat. So unexpected was this that Stones burst out laughing.

"My apologies, my apologies. That is something that I have never heard before but, my dear, please don't look so ashamed and horrified, it was a thing of beauty not one of shame. Now to the desk and your chosen punishment implements. Get writing, get writing! No excuses now, I will expect a perfect script, full of remorse and a clear proposal to enable your conscience to be cleansed of guilt and shame for the atrocity you committed. Move girl, out of my way now, you have made me late and I do have other business to attend to."

Melanie went to the desk and sat down to begin her task, a giant sigh escaping from her.

Minutes later, Stones was nodding his approval at her efforts. Melanie had made a few queries as she worked but Stones could see that the student had applied herself to the task as if she'd been set a piece of written work for a university supervision.

His complimentary words had brightened Melanie up considerably and she was looking very self-satisfied when the buzzer sounded at the professor's door. Melanie froze in shock and moved towards her clothes.

"Stand where you are! What the devil do you think you are doing? Put that dress down now and stand in the corner, hands on head. In fact, I think you need a little lesson now so that you are a little bit more aware of how you damn well behave in my rooms."

Stones pressed a button releasing the door lock before moving across to Melanie and slapping her unprotected buttocks with his open hand. As Prascilla Guptil entered the room, she was presented with the sight of a gyrating and naked Melanie Thorpe, her massive buttocks being pounded by the Dean of Discipline while she howled in distress.

"Ah, Prascilla, welcome, do come in," said Stones as he pushed Melanie into the corner.

"Just giving young Melanie a little taster of what you get if you don't behave at St James'. Now eyes front, my dear. We have things to discuss, do we not?"

Stones looked at the young Indian girl before him. Her face still showed signs of Melanie's act of violence and retribution, mild bruising in particular around her eyes and a small healing cut on her forehead. It was highly unusual for any of the students from the Indian subcontinent to be called to his office for disciplinary reasons. In fact, Stones had often bemoaned at the college's monthly council meeting, the council being the governing body of the college, that if they wanted the level of obedient, studious and respectful students to increase then they needed to attract as many young ladies as possible from outside of the British Isles. 'Familiarity breeds contempt' was a much-used refrain from the Dean of Discipline, dutifully supported by Celia Ford, the senior tutor, and he advocated annually for the college to increase its percentage of undergraduates from Asian countries. Respect for authority and their elders was paramount, and Stones hated disrespect for authority more than anything, making him the ideal person to dispense justice, right wrongs, and dispassionately and objectively dispense and deliver physical retribution to transgressors.

Stones always enjoyed the moment when a reprobate came to his room, misguided in her presumption of innocence. There was always a lightbulb moment when the person under investigation actually realised that they were possibly in trouble. Prascilla's confidence was visibly draining away as her eyes flicked between the naked figure of Melanie, and her large bright red bottom, and the unblinking stare of the Dean of Discipline.

"Now, I just need Melanie here to finish off her duty and she can get her disgusting self out of my sight until her punishment day that will take place in a few days' time."

Prascilla's smirk, which seemed to suggest that she thought that she was on safe ground, was duly noted by Stones, and he made a decision to give her the rope needed to hang herself!

"Right, Melanie, fetch your essay of contrition for your appalling act of violence towards young Prascilla here and the items you have chosen to be punished with. She will be back here soon, Prascilla, for the serious business – those rosy cheeks were just a gentle admonishment for some minor disobedience in front of me today." His smile embraced Prascilla totally and she reacted in kind although her eyes conveyed a definite disturbance of her calm exterior as she espied the contents of Melissa's hands.

"Right, young lady, let us hear what you have to say. I very much hope I am not going to be disappointed in you further as that would mean further remedial work today and I really need to get on."

Melanie's face reddened a further deep shade as she contemplated the words of the professor and tried to avoid Prascilla's eyes, who was not making any attempt to hide her fascination in her naked body.

"Have I got to read it out, sir?" Melanie looked between Stones and Prascilla frantically as though she expected to have a say in the decision. Stones just laughed and Melanie gulped and continued:

"Of course, I have to, sorry to question you, sir." She took a deep breath.

"I, Melanie Thorpe, would like to express my sincere apologies for my act of mindless violence towards a fellow student in the dinner hall. I behaved in a manner unbecoming to any member of this college, or indeed wider society, and can only ask for forgiveness and to be allowed to make amends. To this end, I propose that I undergo severe physical punishment at the hands of the Dean of Discipline to ensure that I have paid the debt which I owe the college for my actions. I am truly sorry that I reacted to what was just childish taunting and insults in a disgraceful manner and hope that you accept that I am truly apologetic and full of remorse. I therefore propose that I be subjected to a spanking on my bare buttocks and that 250 spanks be applied. I also request that I receive ten strokes each from the canes, the tawse and the crop which I have selected for the purpose, to therefore give a total of 300 blows in total. This, I truly believe, will teach me a lesson in controlling my temper and serve me well in my future time at the college and beyond."

The professor gave her a subtle bow of approval.

"An excellent piece of work, my dear. Acknowledging guilt and acceptance of appalling behaviour, showing remorse and a willingness to make amends, a proposal to correct wrongdoing and a clear and voluntary offer to submit to, and select, the means to do so. Textbook, don't you think, Prascilla? Wouldn't you say that young Melanie has taken the appropriate steps to begin to clear this matter up and have it consigned to history, a mere blot on the landscape, a momentary lapse, serious though it was, in an otherwise exemplary student and rather gracious and pleasant human being? Don't you agree, Prascilla? As the person who suffered physical harm in this incident, are you satisfied that the intended flogging of her bare backside, for which Melanie has most humbly and eloquently volunteered, is the appropriate response?"

Stones raised questioning eyebrows at the rather perplexed and somewhat uncomfortable looking student. He could see she had enough about her to sense a possible trap set in his words but was also showing that she possessed a level of arrogance that she simply had not realised that her role in Melanie's situation was anything but as the innocent and injured party.

"Oh. Um. Yes, sir, I think it would be entirely appropriate, sir. I am happy with your decision and thank you for dealing with this, sir."

Stones spotted the sly grin that made Prascilla's lips twitch upwards as she stole a quick glance at the naked Melanie, who was staring motionless at the floor, her face a picture of pure misery.

"Excellent news, Prascilla. Melanie, you can cover yourself up. Yes, yes, get dressed and get out. Seems like your mother is going to be spared the upset of your disgrace. In some ways a pity; I would have enjoyed the opportunity to catch up again with your Aunt Wendy. I have some pleasant memories of her time here. She was truly appreciative, I can promise you, of my methods to cure misconduct and delinquency and is a great advocate of the expression 'spare the rod, spoil the child'. Never mind, time to move onto the next little issue. Seems like I have some more work to do concerning young Prascilla here."

Prascilla's body jolted and as she saw the sternness return to the professor's face, her confident manner visibly began to drain away.

"Sorry, what do you mean, sir?"

Stones smiled the smile he had developed over many years that chilled the blood of the unfortunates he was about to sentence. Prascilla now wilted before him, the earlier evidence of an assured young woman now assigned to the past.

"Bullying! That's what I mean, you miserable excuse for an acceptable member of the human race. Bullying! A despicable act, a form of behaviour that I am trying to eradicate from this college. Bullying! A form of coercion that I absolutely abhor. What do you think of bullies, Prascilla? Do share with the room."

Prascilla's mouth hung open. A despairing glance was thrown at Melanie, who had frozen halfway through dressing, her bra affixed underneath her huge breasts as she stood transfixed.

Stones slammed his hand down on his desk.

"Speak child or by Christ I'll upturn you now, rip the trousers and pants off your skinny little backside and give you the spanking of your life!"

"Oh, sir. No, sir. We were just joking, sir. It was never bullying, sir. More a bit of fun, sir."

Silence hung in the room before Stones gave a long sigh and reached one arm out towards Prascilla, who yelped.

"No, sir, please, sir, I didn't mean anything by it. Melanie, tell him, please, Melanie. I'm so sorry, Melanie. I didn't mean it. Honestly, sir, it was just a bit of playful joking – perhaps it got out of hand and maybe we just went a little too far, sir. Just got carried away in the moment, sir. I never intended to upset you, Melanie. I am sorry if we went too far."

The Dean's giant hand grasped Prascilla's arm and spun her round to face Melanie, who was still struggling into her final pieces of clothing.

"I have investigated this incident fully, I have spoken to the Head of your previous school and the tutors here, and I am happy to discuss this with your parents. Do not speak until I ask you to!" he thundered as Prascilla tried to interrupt. "The conclusion I have come to is that you undoubtedly *did* tease Melanie to quite a degree. That teasing did very much border on bullying, and what I have heard subsequently leads me to the conclusion that you have indeed crossed the line and I am satisfied that you provoked Melanie, therefore causing this incident to occur. I am not overly interested in hearing you dispute this or deny it in any way. As far as I am concerned, you are guilty of low-level bullying and I want you to consider whether you would like to take the responsibility for that?"

Prascilla's dilemma was written all over her very expressive face. Not in a million years would she want him to be speaking to her parents. Stones knew Prascilla's mother, Adena, from her time at the college and he was absolutely certain that the studious, quiet and kind woman would be devastated to discover the circumstances that had resulted in her only daughter being stood before him. Her eyes were skittish as she struggled to form the question and her features almost gurned in her efforts to compose an inquiry without unintentionally accepting blame. Stones waited her out and, as he knew she would, she finally pieced a proposal together.

"So, sir, I do accept that my taunting could be perceived by Melanie as bullying although it was never intended to be so and I am upset that you have perceived it as such. However, there is no need to contact my parents, sir, as it would indeed very much upset my mother. Sir, I would like to offer my sincere apologies to Melinda and, of course, to you, sir, for causing you to have to deal with this. I would be happy to carry out a punishment of any tasks in the college that you see fit to make amends, sir"

The professor sighed and looked at Prascilla with such disappointment in his eyes that she started to tremble in response.

"Oh dear. Oh dear. Oh dear. How very sad. I feel let down and disillusioned to realise that you just have not grasped the real situation here. Never mind, I am sure that once Adena and I have chatted things through, the issue will be resolved to my satisfaction. You can go. Goodbye."

Prascilla's face was now one of absolute horror.

"Oh no, please don't. Please sir, no. I am so very sorry, sir. What do I need to say to put things right, sir?"

Stones let her stand fretting for several moments before speaking.

"Last chance saloon, young lady. You will go and sit at the desk there and write a similar piece to the one you heard from Melanie. For goodness sake, girl, why do you think I made her read it out in front of you? How many clues do you need? Now, apply some of the thinking prowess that got you your place here and try and remember what I have said about your offence of proven bullying and how you think that should be punished. I'll spell it out if you like as, unlike you, I have a good memory. I will expect a perfectly scripted piece of work that shows clear remorse and offers to enable your conscience to be cleansed of guilt and – hopefully – the shame you feel for your heinous act. You are guilty of body-shaming, belittling and offensive behaviour, and to assist you with feeling the effects of that, you will write this piece naked. So, clothes off, neatly folded on the chair there, and then get yourself over to the desk. You have 15 minutes to complete and hand over a perfect request. Please take note of the word *request*. This is going to be you volunteering to be subject to appropriate punishment to atone for your sins. So close your mouth, keep it shut and get moving this instance or I will assist you. Clothes off, now!" Stones shouted the final words and with tears now streaming down her face, Prascilla's resistance slipped completely away and she pulled her top over her head immediately.

Stones gave her no respite and stood close to her, watching her divest herself of each item. The gulp as she unhooked her brassiere to reveal her small breasts with surprisingly attractive dark, wide aureole, Stones thought with appreciation, was quite comical. With a quick swish of her arms, her knickers joined the rest of her clothes and, as she hesitated naked before him, one arm across her breasts and the other reaching down to her groin, Stones grabbed her by the shoulders, spun her round and with a lusty blow to her small tight buttocks he sent her yelping to the desk.

"Please, sir, may I be permitted one question?"

Stones was happy to allow this and the situation looked like it was going to go as planned. The clothes had come off with far less resistance than he had anticipated and he suspected that Prascilla had been hoping to get away with her act rather than really expecting to. He was pleased that she was on the road to accepting responsibility and softened to her request.

"Sir, do you consider my behaviour to be as bad as Melanie's?" Prascilla stuttered through the last words and the fear in her eyes warmed Stones' heart.

"Interesting question, Prascilla, that shows you are thinking along the right lines and accepting your guilt fully at last. What, however, I would like to know is, do *you* think it was?"

"Oh, sir. Um. Maybe not quite as bad as she was physically violent and my bad behaviour was verbal, but I do understand that I was being cruel, sir. Um, sir, I am so scared and so sorry. Do I have to be caned, sir?" Once more the tears flowed although, as always, the professor paid them no heed.

"You are rather missing the point – that it is up to you to be volunteering yourself a punishment to fit your own particular misdeed. On this occasion, as you are clearly struggling, I will advise you that 100 spanks of your bottom over my knees and twenty hard slaps of a wooden paddle might be considered appropriate in your case, Prascilla."

The first reaction he noted was one of relief, the fear of the cane apparently trumping all others in Prascilla's mind, but then came the dawning realisation that the punishment was still a formidable cross to bear and her face dropped in apprehension.

"Time is running out, girl, so I would get on with it if I were you. A short, hard spanking today is available as a free sample if you do not complete your task to my satisfaction in the time allowed. I am happy to dispense this as the soreness of Melanie's bottom testifies, so jump to it!" Stones grinned as she did actually jump before quickly returning to her sheet of paper on which he could see little evidence of commitment to the task set.

It was almost 20 minutes later before Prascilla raised her hand to indicate her completion of the task. Stones beckoned her over.

"First thing, young lady, is that you do not cover yourself with your arms when you are naked in this room. Hands by your side unless I have told you to place them on your head."

Prascilla squealed theatrically as she stood ramrod straight to attention in response, her face once more beginning to redden in embarrassment.

"That's better; you see, now you are shamed and completely uncomfortable which I hope you are learning to appreciate is a punishment in itself. Also, it allows me to see those rather delightful aureole and nipples you possess; very pretty I must say." Stones gave her a big smile as his eyes flitted from her face, now with bright red cheeks, to the main object of his attention which were conveniently for him at just about eye level as he sat before her.

"Yes, lovely pair of breasts, I must say, it's not all about size, is it? Melanie's and your bosoms may not be comparable in size but they are in beauty, do you not agree? Lovely, lovely. Now, where was I? Ah yes, secondly, you were tardy, your timekeeping was poor, and you ran over the limit set, and thirdly, you have failed to write down the number of blows that I thought we had agreed and I do not quite feel the commitment in your words that suggests full contrition and wholehearted belief in your proposal. This is supposed to be you volunteering to undergo chastisement, as you feel that not only do you thoroughly deserve it, but also you appreciate that it would serve you well. So, a little rewrite is in order which sadly means you will be way over your dedicated time and therefore you now need to add a couple of lines on the bottom ... oh no, that's my job." Stones broke off into a guffawing laugh at his own play on words that did nothing for the demeanour of the naked girl now trembling before him.

"Not that funny, eh? Perhaps not, but regardless, you do need to consider a footnote of apology for wasting my time and failing to obey implicit instructions properly and in a timely manner. You should also request an immediate, appropriate punishment so that in that aspect at least your behaviour will have been dealt with and you will have learned a lesson. Off you go; the longer you take the more severe the punishment, but do make sure that I will not need to make you rewrite it again. I have a cabinet of improvers over here that I can bring into play very quickly if you are going to continue to be so troublesome and lacking in alacrity."

Once more, she was accompanied back to the desk with a hearty swipe of her buttocks. A squeal and the first tears to run down her face were the response. Stones meandered over to the wall-mounted cabinet that housed the majority of his collection of punishment implements and opened the door wide as though in contemplation of the display, although in reality it was for Prascilla's benefit.

"Oh, my goodness, oh my, oh no. Not now, sir, oh my, they are so scary. Please do not beat me, sir, I am hurrying." Prascilla's face was a perfect example of the phrase 'eyes popped out' as she stared in horror at Stones who rearranged his improvers to rehouse the items accidentally selected by Melanie and her clumsy fumbling.

"You may have a hand spanking only today if your work is completed to my satisfaction shortly. But any further outbreaks or interruptions like that and we will be doubling the figures you have finally managed to scribble down, as well as making a selection from my little beauties here to aid your application and compliance for the present time. Now, eyes down, the clock is ticking and my spanking arm is restless!" With a gesture of his head he dismissed Melanie, who scuttled from the room.

Prascilla's resistance had gone and minutes later Stones was reading a scruffily presented but almost perfect essay of apology, remorse and regret, an acceptance of punishment due and a request for strong and firm application to ensure lessons were learnt and humiliation was complete.

"Very good, albeit rather delayed. I agree that a damn good, bare bottom spanking followed by 25 slaps of the wooden paddle will suffice, and well done, I have noted that you have chosen to increase the number, all credit for that. I agree with you that this would seem a fair and appropriate punishment and accept your words of contrition. The sentence will be carried out in a few days' time; you will receive an email requiring you to arrive here with minimum belongings, no mobile device, freshly bathed and thoroughly cleansed on the inside and out, empty bowels and bladder, of course. The cane is not prescribed for you on this occasion unless I hear anything else detrimental about you or you add to your misbehaviour in any way. Anyway, I repeat that that includes your demeanour in this room whether while you are being punished or otherwise."

Prascilla's fortitude that had developed whilst writing her script and the ridiculous thrill of pleasure that had spread through her body as Stones had responded to her piece now left her. As expert as he was at manipulating these students, it still gave Stones a frisson of satisfaction when his words built these recalcitrants up and then ripped their souls away. He smiled his smile of victory and triumph, watching it chill her to the bones, accepting that Prascilla had never really been a challenge but having enjoyed the session with her immensely.

"Right, my dear, let us finish off. We must not forget that you felt that a quick sharp lesson now might help you focus on following simple rules and instructions. I have a nice, swishy, leather round paddle that should be the perfect accompaniment for the task. I will save my hand for the more onerous task ahead when I have both of you over my knee. Let us have you bent over in the transitional manner, hands on your ankles, legs wide apart, full display, and your anus pointing at me, please."

The power of words, thought Stones as an absolutely shell-shocked young Asian woman froze in terror for a few seconds before her shoulders slumped and she turned around and lithely presented her bottom to him.

"Excellently displayed, pert little buttocks, small dark crack and a very tightly clenched little anal slit I do spy." Stones did not let up on her sensing that his highly personal wordplay may well be punishing her more than a few swats with the reasonably flimsy paddle.

"Try and keep your balance – this will be quick but firm."

He was true to his word and unleashed the punishment in double-quick time, Prascilla just about managing to hold her position as she wailed, wriggled and sobbed throughout.

"Well, that has brought a nice contrast of colour to your dusky skin, my dear, but frankly far too much unnecessary fuss. Goodness alone knows what sort of din you will produce when the wooden paddle is applied. This thing is just flimsy in comparison and produces one of the mildest punishments I distribute. You'll need to toughen up, girl. Up you get, please, nice though the limited view of your vaginal lips is. I think that you have shown enough of yourself to me for now. I will have a longer and more detailed inspection when you return for your spanking and paddling."

Prascilla did not look too much like someone who felt that she had just had an easy time. The tears were flowing freely and she was frantically rubbing her red bottom as though able to wish the pain away.

"A nice 'thank you for my punishment' note would be most welcome, Prascilla. You may write it standing up and bending over so as to present your smacked bottom to the room, if you would be so very kind. I do like to look at my work sometimes and your bottom is looking particularly delightful, I must say: light brown, blossom-tinged with pink – lovely. Thank you so much." Stones thoroughly enjoyed this 'belittling by compliments' approach as it so bewildered the recipients of a good walloping. Prascilla obeyed to the letter of the word, ridiculously over-praising and thanking him for her punishment.

"Good girl, well done. A perfect example of how to write an appreciation of a job well done. Good job. Now put your clothes on and be on your way, my dear. Time moves on and I have things to do. Chop chop! It will not be long to wait before we will have you buck naked again for your proper chastisement."

Prascilla rather scurried away and Stones returned to his laptop, happy in his work.

CHAPTER 2

IN WHICH SARA AND JENNY ARE

REUNITED

Sara and Jenny stood side-by-side before Professor Stones and Celia Ford, patently avoiding looking at each other, the awkwardness of their closeness in this situation so obvious. Sara had just been dressed down cold-heartedly by Stones, making it crystal-clear where he thought that the blame for their predicament lay. She was now shaking in total fear and apprehension as this second reckoning began.

"Yes, sir, I let myself down, I let you down, and most importantly, I let the college down. I behaved disgracefully and I will regret that forever, Professor Stones," she said.

Stones pointed a thick long finger at her.

"You also placed the college in an unacceptable position: you risked our reputation and standing and you could have given fuel to our detractors. So, Celia, just refresh Sara and Jenny here with some salient details – what do we do in this institution when we commit a heinous offence against the rules?"

Celia, her eyes averted but her back straight, gave a clearly spoken response.

"We admit our guilt, we show our remorse, we seek contrition, we request punishment, we beg for forgiveness and we thank the college for our guidance and improvement."

Stones was never going to let her off the hook that easily.

"Do expand please, Senior Tutor. How did you resolve this behavioural abomination yourself?"

Celia gulped but Stones was confident that she would bow to him as she always did.

"Yes, sir, sorry, sir. I … um, er. Oh. Yes. Yes. Sir, I asked for the most severe corporal punishment available to assist me in correcting myself and improving my conduct in the future. At my request, you thrashed me several times, you treated me like the wretch I was, sir. I suffered fear, degradation and total humiliation, my indignity heightened by being punished in front of others, and my beating caused me phenomenal pain for many days. It was absolutely correct and appropriate, sir, and I will be forever grateful to you for my re-education by chastisement and for your mercy, sir."

There were tears in her eyes but she had raised her chin to meet his gaze.

"Sara, you have admitted your guilt in this disgraceful episode. You accept that you took advantage of a vulnerable student and abused and misused the faith and trust placed in you by the governors, the fellows and your senior colleagues. You have already requested and taken severe physical chastisement for your totally unacceptable behaviour and I think it would be appropriate for you to display your buttocks now so that we can assess the recovery, to ensure that you are in a position to move onto the next stage of your rehabilitation. This will, of course, consist of further corporal punishment and hopefully we can reach the stage where we are all assured that you have learned your lesson, abated your guilt and paid your just dues. Jenny will need to forgive you for the trauma you have put her through, as well as Celia, your line manager, being convinced that you have earned the right to be trusted to continue in your role. Come along, skirt off, knickers down, and bend over. Full display, please."

Stones could see that Sara had patently come prepared and was quite psyched up for this moment; she immediately disrobed, turned, bent over, and, placing her hands on her buttock cheeks, she eased them apart to fully display her anal rosebud.

Stones might respect her fortitude but, as always, he was keen to discombobulate his miscreants and take away any sense of composure they brought to the occasion.

"Well, your buttocks look as though they have repaired themselves splendidly: blemish-free, nice and clear, all set for your next dose. Jenny, as the one here who had most intimate knowledge of Sara's body, perhaps you would have a good look and sniff to make sure she has come properly prepared, please."

"Of course, my pleasure; thank you, Professor." Jenny, eager to please, and just as eager to add to any humiliation of her former lover, knelt behind Sara and placed her face right into the open cleft before taking in an overly elaborate, deep breath.

"Oh sir, she smells as lovely as ever. Melon Fresh – her favourite body lotion, I believe, sir. Good enough to eat, let alone flog, sir."

The tightening of Sara's buttocks rather gave away her nervousness at Stones' ploy but she held position.

"Excellent, Sara, good behaviour, well done. It seems like *some* lessons are being learned at least. Now, Jenny, your turn. Get beside Sara and adopt the exact same pose, please."

Jenny beamed at him and conducted a far more alluring striptease, pouting at the professor before turning and displaying herself, copying Sara's performance perfectly. Stones and Celia exchanged lustful grins as they viewed the two exquisite exhibits before them.

"Well, Celia, what a pair of scrawny little backsides we have here waiting to be striped and roasted. Right, Sara, fair's fair after all; your turn to inspect. Up you pop and let us know that you think of Jenny's hygiene, please."

Sara rose quickly and, without a word, bent to Jenny's parted buttocks and took a far more discreet inhalation of her nether regions.

"She smells thoroughly cleansed to me, Professor – a fruity fragrance noted," was her response.

"Good, good. Let us proceed with the main feature then. Sara, to the flogging desk, please. Pubic bone to the mound, bend over, legs splayed, ready to be fastened securely. Jenny, you may have the pleasure of securing her so that she can be thrashed without interruption and any nonsense."

Another big beaming grin from Jenny as she rose and, in a rather perfunctory manner, took Sara's arm and marched her over to the desk and more or less pushed her over the professor's flogging desk and table arrangement. She roughly kicked her legs apart and bent to secure the ankle cuffs and then moved over to Sara's compliantly stretched arms and strapped her wrists to the top of the legs on either side. Going back behind Sara, Jenny put one hand between Sara's legs, making a show of checking that she was correctly placed with her pubic bone on the raised hard plastic mound which helped lift the buttocks and open the bottom cleft further. Stones was quick to note a finger straying into her vaginal folds.

"That will quite do – you are securing her for punishment, not giving her a thrill. Get your slippery fingers away from her sex, please, Jenny. I think you would be wise to remember that you are here for dual purposes, young lady. Yes, I have agreed that you may watch and participate in this part of Sara's chastisement but please do not forget that you have agreed that your role was pivotal in developing this into a major incident and that you have admitted attempting, and failing rather spectacularly, to threaten and issue demands that could have been damaging to our reputation and good standing. You are therefore to be thrashed in punishment at a level suitable to your misdemeanour. So, to ensure that you do take this seriously I will start by paddling your backside. Against the wall, please Jenny. You can see the metal rings, which I have exposed, between the books. The intention is to lower your upper body so that your buttocks are the high point of your body, your head below at hip level. A firm grasp on the rings, please, step backwards until you are almost bent 90 degrees, legs apart, buttocks up, cheeks apart. Yes, that is fine – now hold that pose."

Jenny turned back to look over her shoulder coquettishly, a slight smile, an alluring look that chilled Stones' blood. He handed the round leather paddle to Celia, meeting Jenny's eyes with a cold stare.

"Celia, you can start things off. As many times as you like until that smug expression is wiped off her face."

Stones walked over to Sara, placed his hand on her head and gently ran his fingers through her hair as the first sharp slapping sound followed by a small yelp from Jenny rang around the room, quickly followed by others as Celia swung her arm back and forth in perfect time.

"Just try and enjoy the sounds of that young scoundrel experiencing some minor repercussions of her appalling behaviour. It will be your turn soon enough, my dear, so make the most of this peaceful time as your bottom will soon be on fire." As he spoke, he let his fingers trail down her back to the base of her spine before drumming them against her tailbone.

"Harder, Celia, please. Make some effort for goodness sake, it is a beating not a tickling session. I want to hear her squealing more than that." He put his hand on Jenny's neck, twisting her face so that she was forced to look at him as she felt and reacted to each of Celia's blows now being delivered in anger at his belittling words.

As the slaps continued, and Celia focused on the sensitive tops of Jenny's legs, the effect became far more noticeable with Jenny struggling to hold her position, tears falling freely down her face and the cries becoming more desperate and plaintive. Celia knew only too well that even the hardiest and experienced submissive tended to favour their buttocks as the target, the sexual element of a beating more emphasised by the nature of the taboo of the buttocks as an erogenous zone. As she tried to turn her body away, Stones pulled her away from the wall, twisted her round and down, forcing her head between his thighs, his hands going to her hips and holding her bent over and fixed into position with her buttocks facing Celia.

"Fetch the long-handled, round-end paddle, Celia, the one that looks like an extended bath brush. That's the one, a real stinger. Take a step back, my dear, and really swing."

The paddle landed with a resounding slap and after a split-second delay, came the responding screech from Jenny. Again, Celia swung enthusiastically and once more Jenny screamed and tried desperately to move.

"Faster, Celia, let's have her hopping. Batter those buttocks for me, I want that smile permanently wiped off that smug face. Do me proud, Celia."

Stones knew exactly the buttons to press to invigorate Celia and he was rewarded as she slapped Jenny's squirming and extremely red cheeks. Thirty slaps and howls later, Stones released the sobbing young woman who collapsed to the floor, her hands rubbing her sore buttocks frantically.

"Oh, fuck, oh, oh, oh, oooooh!"

Stones nudged her with his foot.

"Lost the cockiness, have we? Good, as it is time for your caning now. Up you pop. Come along, let's have you strapped down opposite your old friend Sara." Stones led her round to the opposite end of his spanking desk and table combination, Celia moving quickly to fasten the cuffs as he bent a now very pliable and obedient Jenny over.

"Now, Sara, you must be feeling left out. Don't worry, we will soon fix that. Celia, please give your junior here a good dozen with that paddle as it was so effective on young Jenny."

Sara, whose shoulders and back had tensed up as the conversation carried on around her, now slumped as she displayed total surrender. Stones nodded to Celia and the dozen strokes rained down hard and fast, accompanied by Sara's sniffling sobs and yips of protest and pain. Stones came around the table, inspecting the bright red circles covering Sara's buttocks.

"Backs of her legs are rather white, aren't they? Such a contrast. I think we should have them matching, Celia. Five on each, please, nice and hard and as quick as you like."

Sara's sobs, as the words sunk in, were soon replaced by full on screaming as the resounding splat of the paddle hitting the backs of her upper legs sang around the room. As her arms tugged against the cuffs, Stones saw Jenny reach out – the design allowed the victim's hands to meet and the two women interlocked fingers. Sara's shaking head stilled to lock eyes with the young woman whose jealous and malicious actions had led them to this day. As Celia raised and swung her arm with the paddle for the tenth and final time, Sara howled into Jenny's face before her head slumped again to the wooden desktop.

"See, you two are making up already. We will soon have you best friends again, although maybe without the previous benefits!" Stones taunted, then went to his cabinet and removed his thick leather strap and his knotted, braided lash. He went over to one of his cupboards and returned with a three-foot bamboo cane, swishing it through the air as he returned to the two fastened women who were twisting their heads to follow his steps.

"After much thought, and taking into account punishment already received, I pronounce your sentence to be the following ..." He was enjoying his moment as the two were held spellbound, their fate in his hands, literally!

"Jenny will receive a dozen with the bamboo and a further six stripes with the knotted lash. Sara will receive the same one dozen with the bamboo plus twelve with the braided lash and then a final flourish of six with my favourite heavy strap."

Sara let out another heartfelt sob, Jenny breathed in deeply but appeared unperturbed to Stones. He had suspected her of true sadomasochistic tendencies previously but now was coming to realise that the college graduate was definitely more advanced in the field than that! He vowed to give her his best shots, much as he recognised that Sara was the main transgressor in their dalliance as far as the college went. He was aware that in reality Sara had been sucked in by a determined and devious young lady who was far more accomplished in the sexually specific arts of seduction than the more naive, albeit older, Sara.

The long bamboo cane had a particularly painful strike due to its length and wide arc before contact, and, as he stood behind Sara, he took careful aim and pulled his arm back, ready to whip with the cane.

"Prepare yourself, Sara. I will do you proud and help you redeem yourself through your penance and acceptance of contrition chastisement; no mercy to be given as you undoubtedly expect and desire. I will apply the cane to you alternately, ladies, so you can share the joy of your painful redemption. And so we begin."

The cane swept through the air and landed high on Sara's taut buttocks, flattening the skin as it bit deep and causing her to scream as the pain hit home. As the scream came to an end, the only sound was the swishing movement as the cane whipped down onto Jenny's bottom, the strike hitting centrally and creating a perfect cross on her flanks as it traversed her tightened cleft. There was no scream from her, just a quiet, rather unladylike grunt, and little movement in reaction. Only the clenching and unclenching of her buttocks for a few seconds gave any sign that there was any real discomfort felt and Stones knew that he was going to have to up his game. The caning continued in that fashion for several strokes, Sara's screams more subdued as she embraced the painfulness of the searing impact. While she showed some fortitude, Jenny's response remained muted with just her subtly rotating hips and continual clenching signalling acknowledgement of the severe impression on her bottom cheeks made by the bamboo. As the ninth stroke landed on top of a previous stroke and the welt blistered, Jenny finally let out a yelp, and before he moved back to deliver Sara's tenth, Stones paused to take in the sight of Jenny's bottom. It was a view he decidedly admired as she relaxed her cheeks and opened her crack before him.

It was a gorgeous bottom, delectable and most definitely kissable, and he savoured the moment as he knew that this was a bottom he was unlikely to see again. Jenny's labial lips were wet, glistening almost, her arousal impossible for her to contain and for him to forbid, or deter, her gentle movements betraying her sexual desire and licentiousness. He could tell that she was building towards an orgasm and Stones could only feel a certain amount of respect for her open promiscuity and wanton behaviour.

"You are a little hussy, aren't you my dear? I will be back in a moment to help you along the road a bit further. I think I will give Sara a nice finale with my bamboo and present her with the last three together. At least with you, Sara, I can see and hear that you appreciate that you are being punished rather than being supplied with masturbatory material like your old lover here."

He didn't give Sara time to think about that before once more her screams ripped through the air as the cane struck her lower buttock cheeks, and finally, with a real swing, he cracked it down on top of the previously delivered strokes for a twelfth time. It caused a visible ridge of a raised weal, one that he sincerely hoped she would feel every time she sat down for the next few days. Sara's howl turned to banshee proportions as she almost raised the table legs in a flurry of activity, her whole body shaking and twisting to deal with the intense pain.

Stones marched back behind Jenny and swung hard and low, cracking the bamboo against her red, sore upper thighs, the pain making the young woman pause in her hip rotation as she ground her pubic bone hard against the table.

"Fuuuuuccckkk! Yes, I'm fucking coming, yes, yes. Fuck it!" she yelled unwisely as her climax hit, and had cause to regret it as Stones immediately placed two sharp strokes on top of the previous one.

"Those two are punishment strokes for foul language and these next six are for sexual misbehaviour while being punished. These should, and I repeat *should* because I can always continue, be your last strokes of the cane."

The unforgiving bamboo cracked hard across the centre of her cheeks three times and then harder still, thrice more, across the tops. The screeching cries of pain brought a smile of satisfaction to Stones' features, the clenching and unclenching of Jenny's buttocks along with the swaying of her torso giving support to his presumption that he had landed some perfect strokes with his last efforts. The sensitive skin across the top of her cleft had formed into a savage-looking, raised red welt caused by a combination of the strokes which created a perfect T-junction effect on her bottom. He could not resist running a finger tenderly across the raised, swollen mark, causing her to flinch in anticipation of further pain.

"Relax and hush for now, my little rascal; you may take a break now and enjoy the sounds of this treacherous rapscallion receiving her dozen with the braided lash. A wicked little bugger, this lash, as you will both come to appreciate, the added knots intensifying the fire across your skin like being prodded with a multi-pronged, red-hot poker, I am told. So, Sara, do you think initiating sex with young Jenny here in contravention of strict college rules was such a good idea now?"

"Oh, sir, no, no, no, of course not, sir! It was abominable and shameful behaviour of which I – yaaaaaaaaaaaar!" Stones interrupted her with the first of twelve ferocious strokes. He was quick, accurate and unrelenting in his application as he applied the whole twelve lashes with no restraint, hesitation or mercy. He watched fascinated as her bottom transformed before his eyes. Little, raised blemishes from the knots pebble-dashed her skin, and her screams and gyrating body gave him a deep satisfaction, confirmation that this chosen implement of punishment had completed its job as anticipated and hoped for. The gasps of breath and continuation of her writhing fascinated him and he filed away the information in an objective manner, always keen to reassess the attributes, or indeed shortfalls, in his armoury of weapons of improvement. Heartfelt sobbing was the next stage and Stones was pleased to hear and see the compassion induced in Jenny as she held Sara's hand tightly and whispered quietly to her former bedroom partner. Celia, however, was leaning in enthusiastically to have a close-quarters look with hungry eyes and flushing cheeks. Stones raised his eyes in an unspoken question and Celia nodded back, licking her lips, her eyes sparkling, confirming her desire to taste the sting of the wicked lash at a later date. Her lust excited him and he could feel his erection grow as his mind drifted into realms of his own personal hunger, and he fought to bring his focus back to the matter in hand as he moved round to position himself behind Jenny.

"I think that I will save my strength for Sara's strapping, Celia. I do so want to do her justice and not let her down in her quest to pay her just dues." Sara's whimpering groan suggested that she might not quite appreciate the professor's dedication to the task, or his ironic asides and commentary to her denouement. Jenny, however, raised her head, showing a pouting expression, clearly not cowed enough to be grateful as she watched the handing over of the lash from her main tormentor to his female assistant.

"Oh look, Celia. Our young, good-for-nothing scoundrel is sulking because Daddy is handing the naughty stick over to Mummy! Well, Celia, now is your opportunity to show these two that you have a good whipping hand and the stamina to match. Forget the six strokes – lash the little madam until she begs for you to stop and apologises for being so offensive about your ability to give a good thrashing. Hard and fast, wipe that arrogant and haughty look from her naughty little face."

Stones held her under the chin with one huge hand and spoke right into her face.

"Let her damn well have it; whip her to purgatory! I want to hear her suffer, Celia. Go!"

Celia drew her arm back, her eyes fixed on the tight buttocks and the hirsute cleft exposing the winking, dark arsehole at its centre. Jenny's body barely moved as the first stroke landed but, as she held his stare dispassionately, Stones had the knowledge from Sara's dozen to know that the knots caused a slightly delayed reaction in their deep burn effect. He was confident that the intensity, once multiple strokes had landed, would surely defeat even one as resistant and embracing of the pain of punishment as Jenny. It took five hard slashes before her body jolted and her eyes filled with tears, her mouth dropping open as she began to struggle to keep her cool composure. Still, Stones held her chin, forcing her to meet his gaze, his expression icy and daring. He was confident that her discomfort would be heightened in her knowledge that he was watching not only her suffering, but also the dismantling of her truculent defiance.

"Release her hands, Sara. She deserves no such support and succour; just watch her face with me as we witness close hand the breaking down and belittling of this wicked imp. Enjoy her suffering, Sara. You may have transgressed severely and your chastisement may be warranted, apposite and justly deserved, but she reported you through malice and selfishness with devilry in mind and, as such, her castigation is truly merited and has been my pleasure to dispense and oversee."

Sara's face showed no pleasure in viewing Jenny who was now contorting in pain, but Stones was well aware that Sara's bottom was causing her a lot of distress and that her concentration on Jenny's discomfort was not foremost in her mind!

Celia continued to slash at Jenny's ravaged buttocks, swiping them from her lower back to the tops of her legs, a spatter of bright red spots rising everywhere. Stones could not fail to be impressed with Jenny's resolve and he was beginning to wonder if Celia would tire before the resilient woman cracked when at last the lash caught an already ultra-sore mark and Jenny screamed into the faces of Stones and Sara.

"Ah, that's better, Senior Tutor. Give her a few more in that area. Looks like you've hit a sweet spot!"

Sara grimaced as Stones revelled in the moment but he recognised that in her empathy there was forgiveness for what Jenny had brought forth, and he was further convinced that Sara was showing true remorse and contrition for her abdication and dereliction of duty. As Celia followed his wish and whipped down without mercy on the tender spot discovered, Jenny thrashed in her bindings, screaming and begging for the cessation of her beating. Sara's head went down, but she once more grasped Jenny's hands and kept her fingers tightly entwined in her own, seemingly suffering with her former lover.

Eventually, with Jenny screaming and wailing hysterically and begging Celia's forgiveness wholeheartedly, Stones signalled the end of her suffering and Celia stood back, breathing deeply, her face flushed. Stones studied Jenny's bottom with a detached expression, viewing the lacerated buttocks calmly, touching some of the most raised marks with his fingertips as she slumped, sobbing in total surrender, a beaten young woman, all fight gone, broken in spirit.

"There is just your strapping to go then, Sara. Well, let us not keep you waiting. Celia, please hand me my favourite thick leather strap."

Sara was motionless as Stones positioned himself beside her, standing slightly forward of her in line with her upper hips, his position for the optimum impact as he swung the strap, catching the receiver in full flow and creating the most severe point of contact possible. He held the strap over his head and behind him, deliberately holding this moment in time, watching Sara's twitching buttocks as she strived to keep still and hold her position correctly. He began his swing, picking up speed as it travelled through the air so that by the time the heavy leather smashed into her waiting cheeks it was at full speed and so landed with maximum impact. The noise was like a whip crack, both globes fully flattened by the force, before Sara registered the pain that seared into her consciousness and howled in agony as the deep heat burned into her. Stones waited patiently for her distress to lessen and some sort of decorum to be restored before once more raising the strap and swinging his arm with real force. The collision between leather and soft flesh was loud, the delivery savage. Once again, Sara howled, tossing her head frantically and calling for mercy and absolution, screaming into Jenny's reawakening face, and, for the first time, he heard her apologising to Sara and regretting her actions that had spelt so much trouble for them both.

Stones waited now as Sara took on board her pain and began to connect with the words of repentance being voiced by her former loved one. Once Sara seemed to have absorbed the torment of the previous stroke, he whipped his arm down again. He laid the strap on hard; it was important for him to ensure that she truly recognised that her crime was of the worst kind for one of his team to commit, and he was determined that the punishment was acknowledged as fit for the occasion. He very much liked and admired Sara, and as such felt that her betrayal, albeit a betrayal of her heart as much as her mind, had to be subject to the most severe punishment. Celia had felt his wrath when she had lost an inner turmoil between her lust and her duty with Emily Govan, and it was important to Stones that she should witness him apply the same standards of disciplinary action that he had forced her to submit to. Sara received the fourth stroke in near silence, her breath driven out of her, her body seeming to tighten all over, and Stones saw Jenny grimace as Sara's hand squeezed her fingers almost white for a moment. A low guttural moan came from deep within her as another thick red stripe landed across her battered bottom. This fifth stroke virtually completed the covering of her compact bottom with thick red tramlines from the top of her crevice to the tops of her legs. Her arsehole winked repeatedly and lewdly at him as her loud sobs wracked her body and her legs trembled uncontrollably.

"I think I will give you two more, Sara, if you do not mind." It was not a question and he did not expect an answer. "Good girl, you are taking them well. I hope you appreciate the effort we are taking to bring you to book, and back into line."

Sara took a deep breath and spluttered a response.

"Oh yes, sir, thank you, sir, I do, sir, please, sir, thank you, sir. I am so sorry."

Her rambling was cut off as the sixth stroke sped through the air to land diagonally from the top right to the bottom left with a fearsome whack. Landing across already sore and throbbing marks, the impact caused Sara immense distress and she screamed at banshee level, her bottom writhing dramatically as her intense pain bit in.

Stones moved behind her, his fingers tracing the lines of the strap.

"Final stroke to come, my dear. Let's have some decorum, please. Calm yourself and point that pert little bottom up, please. Show those lovely labia that so alluringly taper up to that charming, exposed little anus. How sweet you look! She is a delight, is she not, Celia? You can understand why young Jenny here found her hard to resist, can you not? Such a gorgeous sight. Celia, please do take a look."

Celia held her silence and did his bidding, affording him a knowing look. Stones was using Celia to turn Sara's embarrassment levels up a notch and Celia would know that no response was required.

He resumed his position and with all his strength whipped the strap down on the opposite diagonal, the table jolting with the force as Sara's beleaguered body reacted to this further, almost unbearable, torment. Again, she screamed, her face now just a wet mess, and Celia moved in to wipe her eyes, nose and mouth with tissues as she shook her head, bouncing her forehead against table-top.

Stones returned the strap to his cabinet, instructing Celia to relocate Jenny to the bathroom and the relief of his iced bidet to squat in.

"No ice or respite for you, Sara. I want you to suffer completely for as long as possible. You can stay there in distress and on display for as long as I feel is adequate. Obviously, it will be a talking point when any visitors call but I will leave you to explain your shame if anyone asks."

The despairing sob response from Sara rather indicated to Stones that she wasn't exactly appreciative of handling that scenario but she was not to know that there was only one expected visitor – the college mistress, Dorothy, and that it had been prearranged as part of her punishment. Her gentle weeping continued throughout the time that Jenny soaked her sore buttocks which were then dried and moisturised by Celia's very attentive hands. Once dressed, Jenny was given a firm reminder of the repercussions that would befall her if there was any repetition of the behaviour that had resulted in the double thrashing, and then, with a rather lustful but pensive last look at Sara's ravaged open buttocks, she bid her farewells and was escorted from the dean's rooms by Celia.

It was almost an hour later when Stones greeted Dorothy into his rooms, causing an almost sleeping Sara to snap into full consciousness.

"Well, young lady, you are certainly a sight for sore eyes. Although to be fair, it is your poor bottom and legs that seem to be rather sore, and maybe your pride as well? I sincerely hope that you have learned a valuable lesson. I am sorry that I missed it."

"Oh, that can soon be remedied, Professor Winslow-Bellingham," soon remedied," interjected Stones.

Sara was now sobbing openly in pure shame and total embarrassment, shaking her head and struggling to respond to the head of the college.

"Mistress, I am so sorry and ashamed of being seen like this in front of you. I am so thankful to have been allowed to keep my position at the college … thank you, thank you, thank you."

Stones unbuckled the distraught young woman from her bindings and pulled her to her feet to be able to direct her words to the mistress, face-to-face.

"Well, to be honest with you, young lady, it is Professor Stones and Dr Ford you need to thank. They strongly argued your case as a valuable member of staff who would serve the college well in the future. I do so hope that they are proved correct. Do you think it would serve Sara well if she was to watch herself taking her comeuppance with us, Edward?"

Stones smiled while Sara gulped and looked absolutely horrified at his words. Seconds later, a screen dropped down into place, Sara positioned standing between, and just in front of, the now seated pair of most senior academics, and Celia standing to one side, as images that Sara really did not want to dwell on filled the screen. Tears fell down her face as she watched herself pulling her buttocks apart for Stones and Jenny to study and discuss the fruit flavours they could discern between her cheeks.

"Really suffered waiting, didn't she, Edward? I imagine being strapped down helpless while your young former partner had her paddling was a bewildering time, Sara, knowing that you were going to be getting the same treatment?"

Sara swallowed noisily before answering, any hope that this

thoroughly demeaning situation could pass by without her having to contribute having evaporated with Dorothy's words.

"Yes, ma'am, it was awful but nothing that I did not deserve for my disgraceful behaviour, letting you, the dean and the college down in such an appalling and shameful way."

Dorothy leaned forward in her chair and stroked Sara's beleaguered cheeks, her fingers straying down her crack, and Sara automatically tensed as the intrusive touch was accompanied by Dorothy's next seductive words.

"Come on now, Sara, we know you are not shy. Open up and share. I don't see why I should not have access, seeing that everyone else has. Are you really denying me? Are you sure, my dear?"

Sara risked a look back, clearly unsure as to whether or not the mistress was teasing or testing her. The professor was delighted to hear her choose the wisest course and play safe.

"Of course, Professor Winslow-Bellingham, I am so sorry. It would be my honour to allow you to touch me anywhere you wish."

Sara opened her legs wider and bent forward slightly to give Dorothy the opportunity to touch her intimately if she so wished. Stones raised his eyebrows quizzically at his companion; he was unsure as to how far Dorothy wanted to go with this but perfectly happy to see where things led. He was not expecting Dorothy to sink to her knees behind Sara and begin to plant light kisses on the battered buttocks before her, but was finding this development decidedly erotic and had an erection that proved that sometimes the unexpected was a bigger turn on than leading the play down a prescribed route.

"Well done, Sara, your acquiescence is admirable although perhaps we should not ponder on the fact that your pussy is quite wet and almost irresistible. You are also very lucky to have such a lovely bottom, quite lovely indeed, even with the disfigurement that the dean has applied. However, you can straighten up, my dear, I will not be taking advantage however gorgeous your lower regions are, although you do seem quite keen. More importantly, young lady, have you learnt your lesson? Are your days of seducing students over?"

Sara resumed her standing position before them and Stones thought she was probably very grateful that she was facing forward, especially as the screen was now showing Celia paddling her buttocks.

"Thank you for your kind words, Mistress. I can assure you that I have definitely learned my lesson and you will never hear of me stepping outside the college regulations again. I am so sorry, Mistress, Professor, Dr Ford, so very sorry for everything I did wrong. Please forgive me."

Stones flicked his fingers against a red cheek.

"Silence now, Sara. Forgiveness may be a long way off. Let us enjoy the rest of your chastisement in peace and quiet please."

The next few minutes caused Dorothy to grimace a fair few times as Sara's ordeal on screen continued. The bamboo cane, braided lash and strap were applied to Sara's thoroughly tormented backside, although both Celia and Stones were more captivated by Sara's bottom tensing and tightening sporadically right in front of them as she relived her anguish.

"Beginning to realise what a naughty thing you have been, Sara?" sighed the mistress as the final blow was relived and the tension started to leave her body. Stones prodded her bottom to prompt her to respond.

"Oh, Professor Winslow-Bellingham, Professor, Dr Ford, please, you must know how sorry I am. This has been a most awful experience to go through, especially in front of my senior colleagues. I cannot stress enough how regretful I am to have let you down so badly. Thank you so much for punishing me so thoroughly, Professor. I do hope you have not found it too onerous and distressing. I appreciate the efforts you have made to correct and improve me, sir." Sara illustrated her nous and realisation of the language that she had come to accept was the appropriate tone for his miscreants to take with this formidable man and Stones could tell how carefully she was picking her words.

Stones allowed her to stand and stew for a few seconds before he applied his finishing blow.

"For now, Sara, for now. Yes, satisfaction has been achieved, I believe, and the college will welcome you back into its fold and embrace you. Chastened and humbled you may well be, a sore and throbbing bottom you have endured again to push the message home. Some serious bruising to look forward to, hopefully causing you some uncomfortable reminders of the journey you have undertaken to earn redemption. However, I have discussed with Jamie a further step that I would like you to volunteer to take to complete your absolution and seal my faith in your understanding of your role and your position amongst us. Turn around and face us, Sara. I presume that you will accept my considered option as a just finale to this episode?"

Sara took a shuddering breath in.

"Sir, it would be my absolute honour to do anything, anything at all, whatever the cost to myself, to be given the opportunity to have your faith in me restored."

She dropped to her knees in front of him before continuing.

"Anything, sir, please, there is nothing I would not do for you all to regain your trust and respect. Please, sir, please forgive me."

Sara was openly weeping now, the shame and disgrace that she had suffered over the last few weeks bursting forth as her body became wracked with sobs, her head bowed as tears dropped onto the carpet before them.

"Good girl," said the professor in his most patronising tone. "But do turn around and put your head down and your bottom up. We really do not want to have to look at your childish weeping and snotty nose. Celia, fetch a tissue and wipe and blow her nose quickly, please."

Sara was to stay in that position for over an hour, with no option but to listen as the professor amused the other two by replaying Sara's first punishment at the hands of his spanking machine for their entertainment on the giant screen. She eventually left the room chastened and subdued but Stones suspected that she was keen to talk to Jamie to discover what exactly the two of them had been discussing.

CHAPTER 3

IN WHICH SARA RECOVERS ENOUGH

Sara came into the lounge wearing bright red underwear.

"My bottom is touchable now, my love, would you like to fuck me?"

His eyes were already fixed on her breasts so sexily displayed in the push up brassière. He smiled up at her, his eyes lowering to the bright red panties. He moved quickly, pulling the briefs down and off in one slick movement and threw them across the room. Then his hands closed around her breasts and he kissed her deeply, one hand slipping around her back to deftly unbuckle her bra. She took hold of the bottom of his T-shirt and he raised his arms as she pulled it off, her lips lightly kissing his large chest. They kissed passionately again and, feeling his hardness pressing against her, she slid her hands over his body down to his belt and dropped to her knees in front of him. Her fingers were deft and within moments his trousers and underpants were at his ankles and Sara was delicately running her fingers up and down his throbbing, ten-inch shaft. Jamie's eyes closed as she tenderly licked his helmet before she very affectionately kissed the tip. As he took a long shuddering breath, Sara gently ran her wet lips around the twitching head of his throbbing penis before she plunged her mouth down and engulfed most of him. As he gasped and entwined his hands in her hair, she reached around and scratched his taut muscular buttocks fiercely with her long fingernails. Looking up, she could see that he was totally in her control, effectively rendered powerless with pleasure. She stopped, with his cock pulsating between her lips, her tongue encircling the tip. His face was a picture, and she knew that he was torn between anguish at her sudden lack of movement and ecstasy at the thought of what she might be planning to do next.

At first, she made no motion, his cock quivering between her lips. His desire was shining in his eyes and, looking up, she could see the tormented desire. He tugged on her hair but she shook her head and pushed his hands away. Taking his sex deep into her mouth again, with one hand she encircled his balls and caressed him gently, dipping the fingers of her other hand into her mouth before, with a wet finger, she tickled his arsehole. She felt him relax his sphincter to allow her to slip her finger inside him. With very gentle and soft sucking motions, her probing finger searched for his prostrate, making him buck and groan.

As he instinctively started to thrust into her mouth, she sucked hard, matching his movements both with her mouth and her twitching finger. She waited until he neared climax and, judging it perfectly, pulled her finger out of his arsehole whilst she wrapped her other hand around his straining cock and squeezed hard.

"Kiss me, my darling, kiss me." Sara's voice was husky and wanton.

His cock was still stiff and ready in her hand as he bent towards her breathing deeply. She had to still him, make him wait, make him treasure her, make him earn her. Their kiss was long, tender and loving, his passion under control now with the pace of their union slowed. His tongue running along her lips drove her own mounting desire and she pressed against him, both naked now, skin against skin, her nipples erect and hard, her pussy moist. One hand tweaked a jutting nipple, a little pressure to begin with, then gradually harder, her legs almost buckling, but a strong arm had now reached her bottom and she felt his fingers exploring the bruised and still raised welts.

"Poor baby," he whispered huskily. "Poor, naughty baby, beaten for being such a naughty, naughty little girl. Worse to come as well when you get taken to the society."

Sara froze momentarily, remembering the pain and utter humiliation of the two savage thrashings she had received. She had, of course, agreed to the professor's stipulation that she joined the bondage and domination club, BADS, that Stones and Jamie both belonged to, but was trying hard not to think about what that might entail. Stones had told her that she would need to take whatever was on offer on her first day as the final part of her punishment, although after that she would have free-will to enjoy herself! That being on condition of her behaving correctly and compliantly enough to earn her right to be a full member, of course. However, for the moment she had another full member to take care of. Jamie had said little to reprimand or sympathise with her after her beatings and their relationship was still in the early stage of finding mutual trust and faith in each other. She had not betrayed him in her ill-judged dalliance with Jenny Goldman as this was before they had begun their partnership in earnest and she had ceased seeing the graduate student after she and Jamie had first kissed, but she knew that he still felt uneasy that the affair with another female had been so long and of such intensity. Sara knew that she was in love with Jamie and was confident that he felt the same way but she had put a hurdle in their path and needed them to skip easily together over it. She moved his cock between her legs to rub against her swelling labia and her ever-developing wetness.

"I want your tongue, my darling, and then your gorgeous cock, please."

Jamie pulled back from her, his manhood swinging free, pre-come lightly seeping from his tip.

"So, what did you want me to do with my tongue and my cock, sweetheart?"

Sara raised her eyes to his briefly before demurely dropping them.

"My love, my body is totally yours, whatever you wish, wherever you wish. Do what you want, my love." Sara had remembered that Jamie had said, weeks ago, that those words were the sexiest words a woman could say to her lover. The twitching of his large cock showed his appreciation, his large hands hoisting her up and over his shoulder as if she was made of paper. He marched into the bedroom and laid her down across the huge bed. With Sara lying there, her eyes closed in total acquiescence, Jamie moved between her legs and hooked them over his upper arms, splitting her wide apart. He moved his mouth to her mound, little kisses around her pouting, wet pussy lips. He pushed his nose into her intimacy, licking down at the lowest divide of her swelling sex lips. His nose rubbed against her hard, erect clitoris, his tongue delving below and lapping at her juices as they began to flow. He slurped as he raised his mouth to the top of her pussy and sucked hard before he dipped again, causing her to groan and whimper in passion. He had learnt by now what she really liked, those little touches or soft caresses that made her squeal and gasp, her fingernails that would dig into his back or shoulders, always the sign that she was appreciating his efforts. He drove his tongue inside her, setting off another long, shuddering moan that was music to his ears. Sara surrendered to his manipulations and became lost to his dexterous and gifted fingers on her nipples, his magical tongue and lips nuzzling her pussy. His touches drove her to distraction, the most basic of lust-driven sounds of raw sexual satisfaction and intense pleasure escaping her lips. He plundered her honey pot with his ravenous mouth, the loud slurping noise making her more rampant. She reached down, scratching his shoulders and pulling his hair, trying to force his head further into her crotch. As her juices dribbled down beneath her into her arse crack, she almost lifted her bottom off the bed in her desire to encase his mouth with her pussy. Releasing her nipples, he brought one finger down and under her, to the rude open entrance to her anus and slid it smoothly into the welcoming entrance. He thrust his finger deep inside of her, making her buck her listing body frantically, his tongue buried deep inside her, his nose rammed against her clitoral nub. Sara yelped as he withdrew his tongue and replaced it with his thicker thumb, thrusting it hard into her dripping wet sex, twisting and curling it until she screamed with the intensity of the passion he was generating. As he pumped his thumb and finger simultaneously inside her intimate orifices, he forced a second finger up her arsehole before he withdrew his thumb and brought his other hand down to slide four fingers effortlessly into her open gash as he bit hard into a breast. She shuddered and thrashed underneath him, her arms flailing against his head and back, fingernails scratching deep, her legs pulled back over her body as she stretched herself wide to allow his digits full access to drive into her body. She shrieked and shrieked as she came, her body convulsing as though an electric surge was pulsing through her. When he finally slowed to look into her eyes, he saw her hair was a wild tumble, her breathing erratic and her face glowing.

"Fuck! Fuck! Fuck! Oh, you fucking beauty, fucking shit! Yes! Yes! Yes!" Sara's orgasm went on and on, sweat pouring down her flushed, bright red face.

She screamed again as he slipped his fingers from her holes unceremoniously, her pussy belching out air that he had pumped into her, her arsehole stinging in protest from his rough anal probing. Sara embraced the discomfort; as much as she was loathe to admit just how much being mastered and basically abused by a lover turned her on, she knew it was obvious. In general, and in normal society, she found violence abhorrent, not really a fan of combat sport or violence as entertainment in any form, but, when bedded, she knew she could be savage and, to her chagrin, welcomed a lover's ferocity in sexual congress and the sexually charged pain it could cause.

As Jamie threw her roughly over onto her face, Sara found herself fantasising that he would beat her far from recovered sore buttocks before sodomising her, forcing his large cock up her arsehole.

"Open your legs, my darling, and get ready to take more tongue in your pussy and my nose up your arse. You are all mine. Your tits are mine, your mouth is mine, your arsehole is mine and your cunt is most certainly all mine."

Sara spread her legs and raised her bottom lewdly as he crawled up behind her. She held her breath as his lips caressed her rather engorged folds and his tongue flicked out, licking droplets of her intimate juices.

She pushed herself back, her fingers screwing up the sheets in her frenzy. He spat into her arse crack before plunging his head down, his tongue driving into her pussy, his nose now embedded into her arsehole. He started to thrust himself into her, his arm snaked around her hip, his fingers finding her slippery clitoris instantly. She came again loudly, cursing and shouting obscenities.

He flipped her over and climbed up her body to kiss her passionately. She could smell the earthiness of her arsehole and the sweaty juices of her pussy on his face. She reached down to hold his cock.

"Take your weight on your elbows and knees, big boy, Sara is going down!"

Down she wriggled and slid beneath him until her eyes were feasting on the open eye of his prick. Her tongue snaked out and she left a trail of her saliva around his tip. Her hands went round to the hard, taut muscles of his toned buttocks and she dragged her nails down fiercely, hearing the grunt of pain and pleasure that she had come to know and love. Her lips subtly circled the head of his cock and he whimpered. She adored the indistinct little sounds of his response, his sensitivity and passion that showed a timidity and susceptibility in her lover. She so wanted to satisfy and please him; she wanted his unadulterated love, his adoration, his acceptance of everything that she was and most of all she wanted understanding and forgiveness. She was not keen to try to fully understand the conflict between loathing her helplessness and vulnerability with a man, and embracing the submissiveness and acquiescence that she seemed to desire.

Sara wanted to please him so much. She knew that there was nothing that she would not do to keep this man, who she acknowledged had been the best thing to happen in her life ever. She wanted him to know her devotion, she wanted to love and reward him with all that she had, her whole being, her entirety, to give him everything he had ever dreamed of or aspired to. She was fearful of the doubts that she knew she had raised in his mind. The ambivalence he showed towards her when she had returned shamefaced, beaten and in a lot of pain from her thrashing and degradation at the hands of Professor Stones was steadfast, but was not totally convincing. On the first occasion, as she had told him about the spanking machine and the 500 lashes she had received, he had immediately stripped her naked to inspect her lacerated buttocks and upper legs. The intake of breath had made her realise the damage that had been done was visually as great as the agony of the burning fire she felt. Uncomfortable as it was to be touched in any way, she was so happy when, after planting kisses all over her striped bottom, she had felt him release his hard cock. He had masturbated frantically, his hand and cock juddering behind her before she had soon heard his groan of climax and the feel of his come splattering over her sore cheeks. He had then smeared his ejaculated offering all over her tender behind before fetching towels, tied full of ice cubes, to ease the swelling and throbbing, and laid alongside her, holding them against her wounded flesh.

Now, as she licked and sucked his massive penis, Sara marvelled that this magnificent monster was hers to feast on. She stroked its whole length with long, slow and tender licks, her tongue curling around his sensitive tip, the small cries and moans he generated making her so proud that she was of service to this man, *her* man, her life, her everything. She sensed from his rapid panting that he was struggling to hold onto control of his body, and it was no surprise at all when he suddenly began to thrust into her mouth, grunting and groaning, the tenderness now over as his muscular body slammed down on her, brutal and savage. Sara knew that this was partly a punishment fuck, his anger at her sexual shenanigans having been openly discussed, an anger that had been brewing, and she had been prepared to accept his sentence for her crimes. His hand beneath her effortlessly lifted her up and his middle finger penetrated her arsehole again; he rammed it into her and began to alternate the thrusts of his cock and digit. He was not taking any care and there was no gentleness now; she knew that she would be sore afterwards but cared not a jot. His action in her mouth was quite brutal and she knew that she must decide whether to surrender to a harsh mouth fuck to show her subservience or to curtail his motion and move his cock down to her wet and wanton pussy.

The decision was taken from her as with one smooth movement he lifted himself off her, slid down her body, his hands now gripping her buttocks as he tossed her over. Roughly he pulled her onto her

CANED AND ABLE

knees and slammed his cock into her easily and with no resistance. Her breath was forced out of her as, with a grip of iron, he drove her flanks back and forth as he thrust his cock hard and deep into the centre of her very being. One hand reached around and pinched a nipple, the other sought her slippery, hard clit. At no point did his systematic pumping of force pause or falter; Sara's body was putty in his hands, like a rag doll, as he continued thrusting. Then the hand on her nipple was gone and she screamed as it came down with sudden and unexpected force on her still sore bottom. He pulled back, his cock head twitching in her entrance as he began to spank her rhythmically, fast and ferociously, her bottom burning as she shrieked and struggled at the relentless beating. Then his cock was out of her pussy and his fingers replaced it, three or four curving themselves into her as his mouth came down onto her bottom and his tongue invaded her most secret and taboo hole. Sara knew where this was leading but never for a moment thought of anything other than to submit and to accept that he would use this as a way of asserting his dominance and authority over her. His machismo must be supreme in that way, something she had learnt that all men placed so much importance by. She had neither the willpower nor the strength to thwart him or deny him. She subconsciously, and without his awareness, gave him the right to exploit and abuse her body; she understood and conceded that this was her doing and – rightly or wrongly – she would accept her fate at his hands. The tongue was removed and without preamble the slow and quite painful insertion of his large phallus began. He nudged his tip through the tight barrier of her entrance without allowing it to yield naturally and continued with the slow penetration. Sara's eyes were squeezed tightly shut, her mouth hanging open, saliva dribbling from one corner as she took the brutal invasion with fortitude and total submission. Sara accepted

59

that this was her doing, her fate, as she hung her head down in submission and acceptance. Just when she thought that his cock couldn't possibly still be inching its way inside of her, he stopped and she heard him speak softly.

"No, my love, this is hurting you. I do not want that."

She felt him start to withdraw and instinctively grabbed the sheets with her hands and pushed back hard, forcing his cock to go to its full length up her rectum.

"Oh no you don't, my love, this is what you want and this is what I am going to give you. Take me properly, own me, my darling, take my arse, make me yours entirely, please, please fuck me."

They both groaned loudly, hers as much in discomfort as she was sure that his was in pleasure. She willed herself to relax and allowed her body to accept the intrusion and yield to the enormity of his size. To her delight, she felt the first twinges of pleasure as her resistance slipped away and she fully encompassed his giant girth inside of her bottom. Suddenly, her juices began to flow and she pushed back, sucking him in deeper and deeper with each stroke.

"Fuck it, my darling, fuck it hard. I want to be reamed and creamed, my sweet. Ram that motherfucker of a dong up my sweet little arse. Fuck it, Jamie, fuck me hard!" Sara yelled, surprised at herself once more by how much she meant it and how much she wanted it.

As he pulled out and then eased back in again, she yelped and then her tunnel was emptied; as she turned to look over her shoulder, he pushed her head back down as he leaned over to retrieve the tub of lubricant. He pushed two covered fingers deep inside of her arsehole and the squelching sound of the gel application to his cock nearly gave her an orgasm it turned her on so much. Then her back tunnel was full once more as he drove in to the hilt easily with the route made so silky and smooth by the lube. Soon her head twisted from one side to the other and her hands again gathered up the soft sheets at her sides into knots. It seemed her whole body was flushed and afire as his fingers found the rock hard nipples of her swelling breasts, the heat between her legs intensifying as the fingers on his other hand slid between the moist folds of her wanton sex to gently frig her. The cheeks of her bottom were stinging pleasantly now as she embraced the agony that her buttocks had endured. Jamie sunk his teeth into her shoulders and she welcomed the pain and the pleasure. Sara felt that she could no longer tell the two apart as his thrusting cock seemed to drive the breath up from her innermost void through her mouth. She panted like a wild animal as she lost all sense of control and decorum. He nibbled her neck and ears, making her scream out in pleasure, those intimate tender touches combining with the crude hammering in her arsehole, the alternate pinching of her nipples and the tweaking of her clitoris sending her into a long, shuddering, noisy climax. She felt the hot fluid between her legs as she coated his twiddling fingers that worked her frantically, and in that moment she loved him beyond words as his concern to please her appeared paramount. As her orgasm subsided, she squeezed her internal muscles to encourage him but then he found (whether by luck or judgement, they would never discuss) the place inside her vagina where his fingers were able to touch his cock embedded inside her arse. This orgasm was instant and explosive; it felt like a lightning strike inside her head, electric shocks seeming to hit her everywhere. Her body tremored as she felt the most intense orgasm and she screamed out in her ecstasy. It was enough to push him finally to the brink, a quick flurry of thrusts and a loud long groan as he unloaded and Sara could feel the stream of spunk deep inside her.

"I love you so much," he whispered in her ear. "Please be mine forever."

It was all she needed to hear as he slipped out of her anus and she felt her body readying itself to eject his deposited load. To her chagrin, she had no control and with a loud slurping she emptied her bottom of his sperm and his creamy load bubbles. He laughed as he scooped his own liquid mess from her arsehole and wiped it down his chest.

"I love your spunky farts. Now, lick me clean," he demanded.

Sara knew then that her depravity had no bounds as she sucked up the creamy goo and opened her legs wider as he continued to scoop cum out of her. The thought flashed through her mind that maybe that evening, which she was supposed to spend at the fetish club, would be less arduous than she had imagined. Maybe she had to accept that she was a truly wanton and depraved woman, a lustful and sexual creature, a woman with rampant desires that must be fed. These were the thoughts that played through her mind as she entwined her limbs with her exhausted lover and slipped into the sleep of the sexually satisfied and exhausted.

CHAPTER 4

IN WHICH MIRANDA RETURNS   TO

COLLEGE

A week after her return to the college, Miranda had finally received her summons to the office of the Dean of Discipline to undergo 'atonement for her acts of sinfulness by means of improvement and correction in a manner befitting her behaviour'. Having previously, and cringingly in the company of her distraught parents, stood before Professor Stones and suggested the punishment she felt would be appropriate, she could have no doubt as to her fate. His tongue-lashing of her as her mother stood crying behind her had been agonising, his description of her behaviour and her forced acknowledgement of her crimes a memory that she was sure would never leave her, and the discussion of the implements that would be most suited to chastise her had been horrific. The broken face of her father as he stared at the floor when agreeing to her denouement was a sight she would have hoped never to witness. Her shame was absolute, her humiliation complete, and her embarrassment unequalled. However, she had still not had a finger laid on her and, to her shame, she had begun to wish it, so that her guilt could be eased, her contrition completed and her dread relieved. The email from the Dean of Discipline calling her to attend his rooms did not take much interpretation but she had replied immediately, accepting his invitation and now stood terrified and quaking before the seated man. She waited in silence as he operated his laptop, then the lights lowered and a screen quietly and slowly dropped down from the ceiling above. It flickered into life and she watched, transfixed with horror, as the professor addressed a small audience of college personnel as they settled down to watch. His voice boomed from the speakers.

"Miranda Booth is deemed to have been a reluctant and generally non-active member of this little gaggle and as such will be allowed to return to complete her third year as any normal student. However, and this has been agreed and signed up to, she will be subjected to corporal punishment of the highest severity when she returns a few days ahead of the rest of her year in October, her crimes being by association, and therefore still of major concern. But for now, please enjoy the sight of five very naughty, naked girls, bottoms up high, legs apart, while my wonderful machine flays the living daylights out of them."

Miranda gulped loudly as Stones stared at her with intensity; her eyes teared up as the sight of five of her former friends filing into the room filled the screen. At the college's request, and with her parents' insistence, Miranda had broken off all contact with the other members of the Seven Sisters gang which had formed in her first weeks of college. The professor had taken a lot of time and effort to establish the history of the group, noting the signs and flags that might assist the college to ensure that never again would a student collective be allowed to become so influential and powerful within the institution. His investigations had led him to realise that the initial purpose had been a reasonably harmless gaggle, originally known as the Secret Seven, with the intention of merely pushing boundaries and getting up to fairly harmless mischief. It had gradually turned into a malevolent force, mainly due to the influence of Chloe Tang and Zoe Taylor, who had harassed, bullied and frightened many of the college's less confident students. He had soon realised, with the aid of Emily Govan's input, that Miranda had been uncomfortable and reluctant with much of the gang's latter activities. Her fear of standing up to Chloe and Zoe had resulted in her taking the option of going with the flow rather than rocking the boat. Stones did not forgive her at all for this and although she had escaped the worst stricture of being exiled from the ground of the college for the majority of her remaining time, he was determined that her corporal punishment should be delivered on a par with the other five who had already been dealt with. Hilary Brook-Taylor, the seventh member, had had her punishment deferred until she was deemed medically and mentally fit to return to college, albeit that it had been made clear to her and her parents that any return would come authorised only on the condition that she accepted whatever punishment the college and her parents agreed was acceptable. Miranda, however, had already signed all the paperwork necessary, handing over all authority and decision-making to the mistress of the college and the Dean of Discipline's sole control. Stones intended to make her verbally acknowledge this throughout her chastisement to ensure that there would be no doubt she accepted that the punishment handed out was at her own request, fully merited and delivered in the most humiliating way possible.

Stones noted the look of horror on Miranda's face as she watched and listened to the five subdued miscreants read out individual statements accepting their guilt and taking responsibility for their actions. Her face showed particularly alarm at seeing the chastened figure of Zoe, with tears running down her face, asking that no mercy be afforded them, and that they should receive the most severe corporal punishment possible. Miranda visibly wilted as the camera panned the room showing the watching faces of Emily Govan, Senior Tutor Dr Celia Ford, Chief Academic Administrator Sara

Morgan, Head of Health, Elizabeth Young, and Head Porter, Ronald Beaumont, as they coolly observed the young women stripping naked before them. Stones showed little interest in the screen, his attention focused on Miranda's face which illustrated the range of emotions she was experiencing as Stones' spanking machine lashed the bare bottoms of her associates one by one. As Chloe was shown being summarily bent over and strapped down for her turn, Stones decided to up the ante for Miranda a bit more.

"Seems a tad unfair that you are allowed to stand their fully dressed while your friends are so exposed. Can you please take your clothes off in preparation for the flogging I have planned for you? Do not be shy now, Miranda, you had better get used to the idea as I can assure you that your private areas are going to be the focus of much attention soon!"

Without pause, Miranda complied and within seconds had placed her clothes on a chair and turned back to face Stones naked with her fingers entwined on her head.

"Please, sir, I am ready for any discipline you wish to dispense. I fully understand that my behaviour deserves the need for severe punishment, sir, and would be happy if you would allow me to show how sorry I am, sir, by accepting any penance you wish to mete out. Would you like me to bend over your lap for a spanking, sir?"

Stones contemplated the expectant student before him. His intention had been to make her wait until she had seen the fully edited highlights of her compatriots suffering before laying a hand on her. He sensed that her offer was a reflection of the mental anguish she was experiencing as he made her wait for what she knew was inevitable. However, the request was tempting as she was a very pretty brunette, with full breasts, a tight, flat stomach and a neatly coiffured pubic bush. Most importantly, her bottom, the soon-to-be focus of his attention, was a nicely proportioned and symmetrical pair of full, but not too fleshy, buttocks, and he was decidedly keen to have a closer view.

"It was not in my plan for a while yet, Miranda, but as you have asked so nicely it would seem rude to refuse you. I can certainly find time to give you extra punishment if that is what you so wish. But to kill two birds with one stone, so to speak, I will run the video and you can have the pleasure of watching young Chloe receive her mechanical thrashing while I give a nice rosy hue to your bottom cheeks that you have so politely requested."

Miranda's sigh and slumped shoulders were a perfect response and as she processed the words, she realised that she seemed to have inadvertently increased her punishment, but with a more stoic look on her face, she leaned forward and draped herself over his knees.

"Lovely, lovely," said Stones as he begun to pat the cheeks gently while using one hand to force her legs wider apart.

"That's it, legs apart, bottom up, cheeks open, let your anus and vagina get a bit of fresh air."

A gulp from Miranda indicated his words had hit home but she did as he requested. Stones took a moment to enjoy studying between the legs of the sixth member of the gang of seven to meet their fate.

"Ah yes, I remember, I remember. You were the first to take a whopping with my belt when we caught you conniving ratbags in full flow with poor Emily. Up straight away with your hand I do recall, very keen to have your bottom walloped, were you not?"

There was a shy cough from below him before she spoke.

"Yes, sir. To be honest, sir, part of me was relieved to have been caught as it had all got out of hand. I was almost pleased to take the thrashing, sir, as I knew that what we were doing was all wrong. It does not excuse me at all, sir, but I truly regretted my involvement in most of what the Seven Sisters got up to in the second year. It had all started as a bit of fun, just jokes initially, a bit of teasing. Then it sort of snowballed, sir. The jokes became tricks and not quite so funny japes, and there was a strange feeling of power as people started to be a bit in awe of us, sir."

Stones gently stroked the tensed buttocks pointing up at him as he encouraged her to continue her monologue.

"Do go on, my dear, it is all very interesting and does add to the intelligence."

"I suppose that as second years there is a sense of seniority over the new intake, sir. I know it sounds horrible and as if we were all bullies, sir, but it really did not start out like that. We were just thrown together, and to be honest Chloe and Zoe were the alpha females and sadly we all looked up to them and vied for their approval, I suppose. I am not particularly blaming them, sir, because I think that we were all equally culpable … Ouch! Yowzah! Ouch! Ouch! Aarrgh!"

Five meaty slaps from the professor brought Miranda up rather short.

"Oh no, please do not stop, Miranda. I rather thought that we needed to get started, but just think of it as a minor interruption every now and then. Remember that this is just a warm-up spanking as you requested, nothing serious. Now, pray continue with your blood-letting."

Miranda's voice was now shaky as, lured into a false sense of security by his stroking hand and quiet demeanour, she had fallen into a mildly serene state of mind as her confession developed. The explosion of stinging pain to her bottom cheeks had stunned her somewhat.

"Oh my. Yes, sir, I will try my best, sir. Oh, we were so under

Chloe's spell really, all of us including Zoe looked up to her and just sort of fell into doing her bidding. Yaargh! Yow! Yow! Noooo! Yaargh! Oh shit! Christ! Fuck! Ooooooh!"

"That is your one free, allowed, blasphemous outburst, Miranda. This is a 100-stroke spanking, and each further episode of foul language will earn you five additional strokes. Oh, get a grip, young lady, this is a taster of what is to come, a tickle in the grand scheme of what is planned for this sweet little derriere. Fair warning, please note. The next delivery will be ten strokes."

Tears were flowing now as Miranda took deep breaths in before continuing.

"Oh my, thank you, sir, sorry, sir. I will try my best to take my punishment better, sir. Oh, it stings, sir."

"I am afraid that you are losing my attention somewhat now. I think I told you to continue with your little story."

Stones' voice hardened but Miranda failed to react and seconds later was to regret it.

"Yaargh! Yaargh! Yowzee! Ouch! Ouch! Ouch! Aaargh! Noooooo! Yaargh!"

The ten slaps were hard and quick, and all landed on her right cheek. As Miranda took a spluttering breath and grasped the chair legs with all her strength, the onslaught was repeated on her left cheek at greater speed, Miranda failing to draw breath between slaps.

"Yeeeeeeeeeeeeeeooooooooooooooooouuuuuuuuuuuu!"

One long scream of pain as the ten spanks cracked against their target.

"Sir, sir, sir. I am so sorry. Yowzee! Let me continue please sir. Oh my, oh my."

"Speak!" barked Stones.

"Sir, most of us knew we were doing wrong, sir. I cannot pretend that we did not. I tried to help Emily as much as I could, sir, but I was scared and weak, sir. I did not want to fall out with Chloe, sir, and if we were all to be honest, sir, I think we were all just a little bit in love with her, sir. She was so magnificent, sir, so confident, never flustered, always in control, no one ever got the better of Chloe, sir, oh my god, sir, she was just majestic. Yow! Yikes! Ugh! Ugh! Yaargh! Yaargh! Yaargh! Nooo! Oooooer! Yaargh! Oh my word, sir, sorry, sir, thank you, sir."

These ten strokes were delivered to the tops of the backs of her legs and the new target caused a fresh burst of sobbing.

"You are making a bit of a fuss, girl. I am going to give you the next 60 in two doses so please try and quell your mouth and take them with a bit more dignity. Obviously they are going to hurt more as there is no fresh white skin left to target, so the rest of your spanking will be on already sore cheeks. So take a breath, tighten your grip and hang on for dear life!"

Stones launched into a ferocious delivery, a well-rehearsed sequence that had shocked many a student who thought that being designated a mere spanking as their punishment was not going to be such a big deal to endure. He doubted that there was a single student on the receiving end of a spanking from him who had retained that viewpoint when they left his room. His hands were large, he was an exceptionally fit and powerful man for his age, and the action of a hard spanking was something he had perfected over the years.

For several seconds, as the avalanche of blows landed, Miranda managed to hold her breath, pushing her head down hard against the carpet, her lips clamped together. Stones was impressed at her attempt to obey him and hold her noise but as he neared the end of the onslaught, she let rip with an ear-piercing scream. It was at that point that his buzzer sounded to indicate visitors at his front door.

As the last of that particular grouping of resounding slaps was delivered, he rose without warning, tipping Miranda off his lap onto the floor, where her hands immediately went to her ravaged buttocks before the realisation of what the door buzzer indicated. As Stones clicked the relevant keys on his computer that released his entrance doors, Miranda's eyes widened and a look of fearful apprehension formed on her tear-stained face as she knelt in an ungainly state.

Stones was back on his chair before the second door had opened, impatiently pulling her without pause back over his knees.

"Position yourself and pull yourself together for goodness sake, Miranda. I keep telling you that this is just the warm-up act – no need to make such a fuss. Do not be such a baby in front of my guests, please. There will be time enough for that shortly." His hand slammed down again and the final 30 strokes of the spanking were underway as Celia, Jamie and Emily entered the room to be greeted by a wailing, tossing head as the bright red cheeks were pummelled by the flashing hand of Professor Stones.

"Already underway, Dean? Was this wretch impatient or is this just a bit of fun before we get underway with the serious stuff?"

Stones smiled at Celia's words which he knew were a poorly disguised criticism and that she was not happy that he had started without her. He finished off the final slaps to the backs of a writhing Miranda's legs and then held tightly onto the sobbing young woman as he addressed Celia.

"What I choose to do when punishing our scoundrels, and when I chose to do it, is not something that I am aware that I need to run past you first, Senior Tutor. Or do you have a view that contradicts that?"

His icy tone belied his smile and Celia's face registered her mistake; she was quick to apologise.

"Apologies, Professor Stones, no, of course not. Just envious that I had missed out on any suffering young Miranda was undergoing."

His steely gaze left Celia in no doubt that she needed to watch her words in front of others. He was becoming more conscious of her growing confidence to speak out and wondered if it would soon be time to remind her of her place. He allowed her a lot of leeway due to their relationship when they were alone but he had warned her many times that speaking out of place in front of others would see her duly cut down.

By this time, the recording of Chloe's thrashing at the hands of his device had ended, the supposedly invincible girl now howling in distress, and the film switched to the second half of the day and Stones' address to his colleagues.

"As you are aware, Celia, Elizabeth, Jamie and Emily are not with us – I am sure you will have guessed that they are with our reprobates in the garden, awaiting the next stage. To save poor young Emily any embarrassment, please be aware that the treatment I am about to apply now is in response to the gang putting her through a similar process. So, it is not a random act of sadistic pleasure for no reason; it is entirely justified and totally apt, even if not perhaps to everyone's taste."

As Stones indicated that the trio took a seat alongside him, a weeping Miranda was pulled to her feet and, with true acquiescence, automatically put her hands to her head and stood with her feet apart.

"Now, Miranda, no seat for you. You can enjoy the rest of my little film show standing or you can come and sit on my lap. What is it to be?"

"Sir, I am happy to stand, sir, thank you."

As Stones' eyes twinkled Miranda realised her mistake.

"Obviously as you have chosen to stand then you would rather not sit on my lap as an alternative. Now, how rude is that? I am mortally offended," Stones laughed as he teased the forlorn-looking Miranda whose body language suggested she was already prepared for the instruction that was to follow.

"It is a punishment, so clearly you do not get to choose; that was me just having a bit of light-hearted fun with you. On my lap now, my dear. Don't be shy. Join us in watching your erstwhile friends as they are shown the error of their ways, and then taught a damn good lesson. Not too uncomfortable with that bright red bottom, is it?"

Miranda's face illustrated exactly how uncomfortable she did in fact feel at that point as she tentatively settled her naked body on the professor's lap, his arm stretched around to hold her firmly around the waist, his fingers resting inches from her pubic mound.

Stones, Celia, Jamie, Emily and Miranda watched the screen as it showed the professor leading Martin, Annabelle, Shirley, Ronald, Sonya and Sara through to the garden to join Emily, Elizabeth, Celia and Jamie. Miranda gasped with a choking sob as she saw the series of wheeled tables with the variety of straps and attachments sprouting on all sides, her five fellow gang members naked and restrained. Strapped down on their backs, legs akimbo and pulled back towards their shoulders, attached to poles rising from the table corners, their buttocks were lifted clear of the surface so to present their opened legs and cheeks to the full view of their audiences. Tears rolled down Miranda's face and her body began to convulse with sobs.

"There, there, my dear. Pass the tissues please, Dr Ford. We appear to have a scared little weeper on our hands here. Now, blow your nose, and wipe your eyes, Miranda. You can save those tears for when you feel some real pain."

"*Oh excellent, Edward, we're giving the rascals an enema are we? Oh first class, Edward, first class!*"

The rather victorious and approving words of Professor Martin

Flanagan brought the apparatus beside the young women to Miranda's attention and a shudder of realisation went through her whole body as the fate of the five dawned on her. Stones' next words intensified her trembling and he tightened his grip as he sensed her ready to fall from his lap in her despair.

"These malefactors, these villains, this bunch of bullies felt it would be a fun thing to do to young Emily. So today they are going to find out how much fun it is. Two litres of a warmed saline solution will be forcibly introduced into the rectums of these reprobates by insertion of a rubber tube into their anuses. Sorry, Charlotte, I'm using you as my model although I am sure my guests can see where your anus is since you are presenting it so well."

The sight of a distressed Charlotte as Stones pushed a fingertip into her arsehole caused Miranda to squeeze her eyes shut, much to Stones' disapproval.

"Eyes open at all times, young lady. This show is principally for you, remember."

Miranda reluctantly opened her eyes to stare at the sharp images on the screen, her unease increased at every utterance as the scenario continued to unfold.

"Each of our five will be lubricated with gel; actually, Emily, would you like to don a pair of Nurse Elizabeth's surgical gloves and give them each a good dollop before we tube them?"

"Oh sir, it would be my absolute pleasure, are they all a bit tight at the moment sir?"

Miranda glanced sideways at Emily, her mood not made better at the sight of her obvious enjoyment of the re-run, which clearly matched the beaming and triumphant student on screen. The rather callous inspection and probing of the young women's bottoms by Professor Stones was adding to Miranda's already heightened sense of foreboding, much to Stones' approval. The psychological torment was, in his mind at least, a perfect alternative to the proposed enema that poor Miranda was obviously convinced was heading her way!

As the professor continued, on screen, to describe the planned enema and flushing out of the five pairs of bright red and badly marked buttocks, Miranda's stomach grumbled loudly as the turmoil in her mind racked her physically. She winced as Stones forced a finger into Chloe's protesting backside, further tears falling as his words hit home once more.

"Oh dear, very dry, and you being such a fan of penetration of other peoples' rear holes. But plenty of room up there for a tube and a lot of warm water. Emily, over to you for the preparation and then Isobel can slide in the tubes. It's a simple process, my friends — two litres of our saline solution injected into the colon via the rectum and then our performers will be spun around to face the garden fence and encouraged to unload and relieve themselves. They are all aware that this is part of their punishment and have been advised to take the necessary steps to ensure they do not disgrace themselves any more than they already have done. So, no breakfast or lunch for them today although they have been well hydrated so we may see number ones added to the fun!"

Miranda's distress had heightened considerably and Stones could see her struggle at the sight of a rubber-glove-donned Emily liberally smearing lubricant into the back portals of the five distraught students on the screen. As the tubes of the equipment were slid into protesting bottoms, Miranda began to tremble uncontrollably, the ridiculous and demeaning spectacle adding pure horror to her contorted facial features. As the tables were spun around so that the women's rear ends were directed at Stones' garden borders, he flicked a switch to pause the film.

"Well, Miranda, do you understand the torment Emily would have been going through after being told that this was what the seven of you intended for her? So, I imagine that you, being a fair-minded person, would agree that you abysmal wretches should duly suffer a similar fate? This is what justice looks like, young lady, when it is applied quid pro quo. Cause and effect, Miranda, cause and effect."

Stones' raised eyebrows snapped Miranda into a response. A glimmer of hope fleetingly passed across her face as she seized the chance to beg for mercy.

"On my word, Professor Stones, I wanted no part in what they had planned. I am so sorry I was too weak to do anything about it. I did not want to hurt Emily at all. Emily, I am so sorry. Professor Stones, I beseech you, please do not do this to me. I am so sorry, so truly sorry …" Miranda's pleas were lost in her uncontrollable sobbing.

Stones was aware that Emily was looking to him for a merciful reaction; he met her eyes and without words conveyed the message to her not to speak. She looked away and he knew that she had accepted that he would play this out as he desired and would remain obedient and adhere to their pre-determined plan.

On the screen, the pumping action could be heard as Professor Stones was shown walking along behind the group, taking occasional swipes at the prominently positioned buttocks, tubes comically protruding, before he then subjected the five once again to a lecture. Unknown to his victims, of course, he was just prolonging their anguish and then turning the screw that notch further by suggesting that they apologise to Emily. Seconds later, after they had been reduced to pitiful squirming in their apologies, came the exchange the students would have been dreading between Stones and Elizabeth. The order to proceed with the enemas was given as the mistress made her timely appearance.

Stones allowed the silence to drag out as the screen showed a close-up of the distressed and conquered faces of the five students.

"Well, ladies, I have news. There is to be no flushing, no enemas, no internal cleansing. I just wanted you all to have a taste of the ordeal that you thought so entertaining to have planned yourselves. Not such an amusing activity when you are on the wrong end, is it ladies? Take the tubes out please, Elizabeth, and we will content ourselves with washing them down with some freezing water from the hosepipe."

The laughter from his audience at hearing his pronouncement was matched by the trio in the room as Miranda almost fell from Stones' lap in her amazement at the reprieve.

"Steady yourself, Miranda. Yes, as you have witnessed, mercy was shown. I will not bore you with the cleaning regime that followed, although rest assured that the use of anti-bacterial liquid certainly added a bit of zest to the procedure." Stones broke off, chuckling at his own memories, whilst Miranda's expression illustrated that she was not yet convinced that her worst fears would not be realised.

As the screen's image changed to show the five young women now strapped down and bent over, Stones pushed Miranda from his lap, and Celia and Jamie moved quickly to propel her to the table to be similarly fastened.

"Head up, watching the screen at all times, Miranda, otherwise punishment strokes will be added."

The recording showed Jamie, Ronald, Martin, Emily and Stones taking practice strokes with long bamboo canes as the professor's words filled the room.

"Twenty strokes of your finest to each of the reprobates' bottoms, and then move on to the next. On my word, Jamie will thrash Helen, Ronald will begin with Zoe, Martin takes Chloe, Emily has the pleasure of Charlotte and I will pay homage to Saffron's beautiful bottom. On my word, my friends. Cane!"

As the instruction was aired on screen, Stones nodded to Emily who moved forward and applied the first stroke to Miranda's rounded buttocks.

The cacophony of sound as Miranda's screams joined her on-screen companions was married to the swishing canes and impact sounds of bamboo hitting flesh and became all-encompassing over the next few minutes. Stones stood close to Emily as he instructed and guided her strokes, since she was the least practised of the caners, but he was all smiles when she held up the cane once she finished her task.

"How was that for you, Emily?" queried Stones.

"Most enjoyable, sir, thank you for the opportunity. Least ill-minded of the group definitely, but she still deserves this without doubt."

"Miranda, presumably you have something you wish to say to Emily?" said Stones as he ran his fingers over some of the most raised fiery red welts on Miranda's backside.

"Oh what, oh yes, of course, Professor Stones. Yes, thank you Emily, thank you and I am so very sorry for all the hurt and distress that we caused you. Thank you for caning me, Emily, it was truly deserved, thank you." Miranda's head twisted around as she desperately tried to see Stones' face to confirm that she was taking the right path with her rather pitiful attempt to apologise, win favour and make amends.

"Hmmm," said Stones. "We will see, young lady, we will see. Celia, thrash her soundly please, my dear. Do your worse, let us hear her sing."

Celia took the cane, swished it through the air a few times close to Miranda's head and then marched to her flanks and whipped the bamboo down across the raised buttocks.

"Waaaaah! Waaaah! Waaaah! Waaaah! Waaah! Waaah!"

The first six strokes were delivered in rapid succession, grouped closely together on the more fleshy, lower cheeks of Miranda's bottom, and the student thrashed about in her bindings as she hollered in pain at the unrelenting assault. Stones was well aware that although Emily may have had reason not to lay on her mightiest strokes, Celia, he was confident, would hold no such reservations. There could be no doubting the ferocity of the college senior tutor's application to the task, her wide grin a sign of the pleasure she was taking in the student's suffering.

Twenty seconds later, the table was rocking, its stability tested as the final biting strokes were administered to the same expanse of flesh, which had turned purple and blistered under the concentrated attack.

"Job done, I would say, Dean. Seems to be screaming like a baby now. I hope you are satisfied."

"More to the point, Senior Tutor, is our *recipient* satisfied that you have done a worthwhile job? Or perhaps she would like you to apply a few more to make sure. Eh, girl, how did you find those?"

There was no response to Stones' words other than a continuation of wailing and groaning from the writhing body.

"Oh dear, looks like you have not made the mark you thought, Senior Tutor. Such a rude young woman not to answer a simple and polite question. Here, take this back and give her another half a dozen to teach her some manners," said Stones as he handed the cane back to Celia.

Celia's look of delight rather illustrated her sadistic tendencies as she quickly took aim, keen to apply more punishment to the distraught student. The first stroke landed on the narrow, tender strip right at the top of Miranda's bottom cleft before she had time to register and respond to the ominous conversation behind her.

"Waaah! No! No! No! I am sorry, I am so sorry. Professor … Waaah! No! No! Waaah! Oh stop please. Waaah! I am so sorry, Senior Tutor. Waaah! Oh no, oh help me! Waaah!"

Miranda's belated response cut no ice with the smirking Celia, her face ablaze with glee at the effect of her punishing strokes on her victim. She leaned in, running her fingers over the raised flesh, causing Miranda's to flinch.

"Oh, I did enjoy that. Have you had enough yet, or would you still like some more, my sweet?" She taunted Miranda who spluttered out her answer at lightning speed having realised exactly what any delay would bring forth.

"No! I mean, thank you, Dr Ford, Senior Tutor, Madam. I am so sorry for my behaviour, please no more, thank you for my caning, thank you, thank you, thank you. Please no more, no more."

"Music to my ears, my dear," said Stones. "That is exactly the sort of gratitude I would expect from a contrite student, full of remorse for their disgraceful actions. Much better, you do actually now sound as though you appreciate the efforts made here today to address your evil ways and improve you considerably. My turn now, my dear. I think the middle of this lovely bottom seems fertile ground for a good 20 taps with the cane now. Are you ready to receive my contribution, young Miranda?"

There was a choking sob, a desolate sound which conveyed a broken spirit and vanquished foe, as Miranda gasped out her response.

"Oh no, no. Sorry, sorry, sorry. I mean, yes, please, Professor. Oh no, sorry, yes please, sir, please cane me."

Stones took his time; his was a slow methodical delivery. A harsh 20 strokes all tightly gathered together in the central high point of the buttocks bent over before him. He waited until Miranda's previous scream had died down and she had ceased struggling before he applied the next one.

Halfway through, with the screen still showing close-ups of the five in turn as they suffered through the 100 strokes each received, the view alternating from a bottom to an anguished face, Stones gave Miranda a reminder.

"Unless I see you paying a bit more attention to what is being played out for your viewing, I will up your punishment from the 80 originally planned to the same 100 your chums received. So head up, eyes on the screen, and a little more resilience and fortitude to be displayed, please."

"Oh my heavens! Oh Lord, but it hurts so much, it is so hard to concentrate, sir. Oh, yes, of course, sir, sorry I did not mean to answer back, sir, please do not give me any further extra ones, sir. I'm watching, I'm watching, sir."

Stones did not bother to continue the conversation. In truth, she would have needed to have a tolerance of pain far beyond what was apparent to be able to focus on the video that played. As usual, he was just adding more pressure as he broke Miranda's spirit and tested her ability to take punishment, intent on ensuring complete compliance purely for his own satisfaction.

Finally, Stones stood back to take a look at his work before once more furthering Miranda's humiliation and shame by prodding and pulling her battered cheeks as he inspected his work.

"Now, Jamie, can you give her your best 20, please? From the backs of her knees working all the way up to run across the top of her bottom cleft. Hard and true. Hold tight, my dear, my friend here is somewhat stronger than the rest of us and his strokes are a bit more challenging. However, I have not heard you thank me yet, so maybe I need to think about taking back the cane for a while."

"Oh no, no, no, no. I am so sorry, sir. Yes, yes. Thank you, thank you, thank you. Yes, sir, I have been well and truly beaten, sir, and I am so sorry about everything, and I apologise to you, to Emily, to everyone, sir. Yes sir, thank you, sir, please do not beat me anymore, sir, please, sir. I think I have had enough now, sir." A sobbing, desperate Miranda was now reduced to a despairing plea of mercy which received the scant attention that she must have expected.

"What, and not truly punish you for your sins? You clearly do not mean that, Miranda. I am sure that was just a moment of madness. Remember that this is the punishment which you yourself requested in order for you to come to terms with the foul and despicable actions you have owned up to. Surely you would not want us to go back on our commitment to give you some self-esteem and dignity, to improve you and help you with your true remorse? Please confirm that you wish to complete your just and deserved chastisement."

As Miranda's sobs subsided, she took a deep breath and spoke the words that put a smile on all four faces standing behind her.

"I am so sorry. I do wish you to complete my punishment, sir. I am sorry to have spoken so pathetically, sir. Of course I should be beaten some more, sir. Thank you, sir. I am sorry to have made such a fuss, everyone. Please continue with my beating."

Her words garnered a smile of approval from an impressed Stones and Miranda regained her composure and fortitude. Not that it stopped him from signalling to Jamie who immediately delivered a fearsome blow to the back of Miranda's knees.

To a cacophony of screams from Miranda and the background of the wailing five sufferers onscreen, Jamie worked his way, slowly and methodically, up the backs of Miranda's legs to her bright red, severely marked buttocks. As the last wicked blow of the bamboo cracked down across the top of her crack, accompanied by a piercing scream, the screen above dimmed and a new scenario unfolded. Stones moved to pause the picture before going across to the loudly crying student and lifting her tear-streaked face.

"I will give you a minute to pull yourself together, young lady, and then we will address the issue of how I dealt with the appalling and vindictive act of maliciousness that you had planned with a thorn-covered branch. Oh, I can see by the look of horror on your face that you well remember the little treat you had stored up. Before you start with your entreaties about how you were not part of the plan and how you wanted no part in the horrendous torture planned, you might want to have a look at how your companions were punished for their part in this endeavour."

Stones released Miranda, indicating her to stand beside him, and let the recording continue. On the screen he appeared in front of the five, woeful-looking young women, their faces full of dread as he spoke.

"One of my bags contains a plentiful supply of dock leaves; can anyone guess what the other one contains? Oh and please feel free to leave now, my friends, if this makes you feel a bit squeamish. But, and this is a big but, as opposed to the delightful array of not so big butts on display, ho ho, we have good reason for proceeding down this road. Our lovely ladies, five here presenting their naked bodies for our entertainment, threatened Emily with a thorny bramble in her vagina and anus. Think on that, my friends. Dominated and totally overwhelmed by their number, Emily was beaten, abused and subjected to rape threats with the added menace of the threat of prickly plants in her most intimate places! So, we have five double cracks and openings here awaiting five fresh and lively stinging nettles to torment and add anguish to their day. I say they deserve it. Emily I see is nodding, Celia too and, of course, Sara agrees."

The pain from the cane seemed almost forgotten as, with gasping sobs, Miranda began to beg for mercy for herself and her impending punishment.

"Sir, no please, sir. My word, sir. This is just awful, oh no. Please no, sir, please sir, no. please do not do that to me."

Stones ignored her as the story unfolded on the screen before them, and each of the five, with the exception of Zoe, made the choice to have the nettles applied to their arseholes rather than their pussies.

"Be quiet and just watch what your friends endured before we decide what to do with you," snapped Stones.

Tears cascaded down Miranda's face as she watched the suffering of her former cohort. As their ordeal ended with the five compelled to display themselves lewdly for the watching audience, Zoe being most harshly punished and humiliated after her most unwise act of rebellion, Stones turned from the screen to face Miranda.

"I hope that you appreciate the leniency we have showed you, young lady. I have accepted that you showed reluctance to take part and did your best to assist Emily through the disgraceful trauma conducted by your spiteful, nasty little gang. However, I think you should just watch the final moments that Chloe went through during this during this monumental effort to punish, correct and improve her before I come to a decision about any further work required with you."

Stones fast-forwarded the recording to the point where just Chloe, Emily, Celia and James remained with him in the room. Miranda had frozen, horrified, when, retaliating to the taunting from the college mistress, Chloe had launched an expletive-ridden mouthful at the most senior figure in the institution.

"Well fuck you, Mistress and fuck you, Professor. Fuck you and your fucking college. I fucking hate you all, you and your bunch of arse-licking cunts!"

The words of the defiant Chloe hung in the air and Stones could see the look of dread on Miranda's face as she waited to see the response the offensive diatribe brought forth. He chuckled.

"Got some spunk, hasn't she? A very worthy opponent in some ways, your chum. Now let's all watch and see what extra treats I had in store for the feisty young thing, shall we?"

On the big screen, Chloe, bent over and held in place with her head between Emily's legs, received the first savage stroke of the thickest cane Miranda had ever seen on her already scarlet backside. The thudding crack as the cane hit its target made Miranda yelp, her hand going to her mouth in horror. To her obvious amazement, however, Chloe took 15 mighty strokes of the wood before she finally succumbed and let loose a short cry, and then tears began to trickle down her face. Miranda whimpered as Chloe's screams and wails finally started to reverberate around the room when Jamie took over the mantle and laid on fast, hard strokes. Miranda's legs appeared to develop a mind of their own, twitching and flinching in sympathy with each stroke landing. She stared at the screen as the camera panned in to show the look of pure anguish and despair on Chloe's face, the pain she had suffered so evident for the watching audience to see.

The film skipped forward to the sights of a sobbing Chloe now reduced to begging for mercy as she was strapped to the fearsome trestle table, with her legs spread apart and her buttocks lifted clear of the cushioned top. Miranda gulped as her eyes met Stones' and he grinned at her, before leaning forward and slapping her left buttock.

"Eyes to the front, Miranda. Don't want you missing anything, do we now?" he said as his own voice boomed once more from the speakers.

"Welcome to my form of hell, Chloe Tang. It's time to make you repent."

On the screen before her, Miranda watched as Stones stood holding a thin cane, the thick leather strap and his braided, knotted leather lash in his hands. Miranda stared transfixed at the sight of the erstwhile powerful group leader, the seemingly never flustered and totally hard-nosed Chloe screaming and howling, her legs akimbo, her most private and sensitive body parts displayed crudely as she thrashed and jolted under a fusillade of strokes from Professor Stones' whippy cane. Miranda flinched and whimpered as each stroke struck close to Chloe's prominent pussy lips before Stones discarded the cane and lashed down between her legs with the fearsome knotted lash. Her eyes widened as the cruel weapon whipped down into her bottom cleft and the scream became a banshee's wail of agony. A second stroke brought a similar response and Stones observed Miranda dispassionately as the watching student clenched dramatically at Chloe's reaction once again. A sob escaped her lips as, on the giant screen, the camera zoomed in to show in minute detail Chloe's pussy and arsehole as the lash's knots hit home again. A piercing screech emitted in response from the frantically writhing student, her whipped orifices vivid red and seemingly swelling before the audience's eyes.

"Dear God, please stop. No more, no more please. I am so sorry about everything. Please stop, Professor. I am so sorry, Professor Stones, so sorry."

"Emily, sooth her brow and wipe her eyes and snotty nose – she's a mess. I'll give her a moment to compose herself and then I'll apply my lovely, thick strap to those blistered buttocks."

As the image panned across the tabloid of horror, Miranda was shocked to hear the words of a visibly exhilarated Dr Ford and then the whispered words of the professor to her that caused a look of pure malice to appear on the senior tutor's face. Stones could see that Celia's response brought her terror and fear levels to a new high point, and caused her to glance in absolute horror at the woman beside her.

"Oh, Edward, yes, that should be fun. If she doesn't piss herself, I'll take my hat off to her!"

The film then skipped to the sight of Professor Stones raising the thick strap above his head before he delivered the first of five tremendous blows to Chloe's bright red, mottled and badly marked buttocks.

As the images showed Stones handing over the strap to Celia to continue Chloe's torment, Stones could sense a newfound fear of the Senior Tutor developing in Miranda's contorted face as she seemed to suffer the blows herself as they landed on Chloe's writhing bottom. Her body twisted dramatically in horror and disbelief in Emily's direction at Celia's words as she finished her viciously laid-on five strikes.

"Do you think that you can go harder and get a louder scream? Be my guest, I challenge you, my dear."

The rather loud and forced throat-clearing from Stones brought Miranda quickly back to attention, her focus back on the screen as she watched a smiling Emily take Chloe to a new level of high-pitched squealing as the strap landed on the lower and upper cheeks of the distressed student whose face was shown racked in pain. The video switched to the final strokes that Stones slammed down with clear relish before he finished with a vertical stroke flush on the cleft of Chloe's bottom.

"Quiet now, sweetheart, it's done. We have just a little detail to finish off, do we not?"

"Ladies, let's wheel her into the bathroom and have a little chat about whether or not she now has a full bladder."

"Oh no," whimpered Miranda at the image of Chloe's face as she stared at the strange contraption that Stones held in his hands, before he gave Chloe the chance to have it placed in her mouth or her pussy. As the tableau played out before Miranda, Stones smiled in satisfaction as the horror of Emily's proposed revenge became clear.

Miranda looked at Emily in absolute terror and incomprehension as she went through the pretence of using Chloe's fixed, open mouth as a toilet bowl.

As the subterfuge became apparent with Chloe evacuating her bladder as Emily squatted over her face, Miranda found herself red-faced and furious, and, to Stones' glee, directed a look of pure hatred and disgust at Emily.

"As you can both see and hear, Miranda, Emily's actions were just a tease. A tease that resulted in the rather successful outcome of Chloe demeaning herself completely by voiding her bladder before us. More concerning for me is the fact that you still feel empowered and in control enough to direct such villainous looks towards my companion here. Who, might I remind you, was subject to the most foul bullying behaviour ever to have been witnessed in this institution. So, young lady, you will now bend over and place your hands on your ankles and your head between Jamie's strong thighs while Emily has the pleasure of applying a good six of the best to your buttocks with my thickest and heaviest strap!"

He handed his favourite instrument of punishment to Emily who allowed a slight tremor to run through her body as she met Stones' eyes and a shared moment passed between them in memory of Emily's own taming by the wicked leather. Stones allowed the film to run so that the sound of Chloe's weeping, as she was forced to clean up her ablutions, was the only sound other than the movement of Emily who moved into position and laid the strap across Miranda's cheeks as she took her aim.

Thwack! Miranda's head jolted between Jamie's legs as the strap landed flush across the centre of the already inflamed buttocks. It was a second or two before the fearsome burn of the strap hit home and Miranda's scream brought a smile of satisfaction to Stones' face and a sadistic chuckle from Celia who was watching intensely.

Having learned from being on the receiving end, Emily earned herself a nod of approval from the professor as she waited until the impact of the first stroke had been fully absorbed and coped with before she raised the leather again.

Thwack! The underside of Miranda's buttocks took the next stroke, the echo of the contact barely dying before her scream filled the air. Jamie found himself having to hold her arms fast as the suffering student tried to fling them back to shield her ravaged buttocks. As her sobs and pleas for mercy fell pitifully on deaf ears, Emily's arm was raised again.

"No more, please, no more. I am so sorry. Please, I beg you, no more. I can't take it."

Thwack! High across the very top of her cleft came the next vicious blow, the tight, thinly protected skin turning white for a split second before beginning to almost glow crimson as Miranda howled once more.

"If it meets with your approval, Professor Stones, I will repeat the strokes to land on top of the first three. Hopefully these will be memorable for her."

Stones grinned and nodded his assent.

"Emily, no please, no. Aaaaaaarrrggghhh!"

The fourth stroke struck home just off centre but the effect was just as devastating for the recipient who screeched once more.

"Concentrate, Emily, and line up the strap so it lands horizontal; don't over-swing but control the direction with a firm wrist." A tutting Stones leaned in to inspect the awry stroke as he re-enforced his words, mimicking the action he was advising.

"Celia, fetch me the knotted lash. I think we are almost ready for the end game, so to speak."

Even in her agony, those words permeated into Miranda's head and she stiffened and let out a choking sob.

"Nearly there, my dear. Just a couple of final points to go. Soon you will be feeling the benefits of this. You will be a wiser, contrite and enormously improved young woman, thankful for our efforts in aiding and assisting you along the route. Emily, finish off with a flourish, my dear. I do so love a flourish."

Stones chortled away as Miranda desperately clenched her maimed buttocks in expectation of receiving the final two swinging blows from Emily.

Emily, well tutored by Stones, was, however, waiting for the moment of relaxation before she swept in at speed and landed a full-blooded blow, hitting the despairing student's fleshy lower cheeks exactly as before.

"Yaaaarrrrghhh! Noooooo! Fuck! Fuck! Fuck! Ow ow ow oooooo. Maaaar!"

"Language, Miranda," was the rejoinder from Stones. "You do not want to earn extra strokes for having a foul mouth, now, do you?"

With an almighty effort, Emily unleashed her final stroke across the top of Miranda's split cheeks, overlaying her earlier stroke precisely, much to Stones' approval as he clapped his hands in appreciation of her accuracy. Less appreciative was Miranda whose screech of pain lasted several seconds although she did manage to heed the words of warning and restrain from adding any swearwords to her lament of anguish.

As Miranda's screams slowly began to reduce to a gentle moaning and copious weeping, the film flickered on.

"Pull yourself together, Miranda, up you get now. I would like you to watch Chloe's final embarrassment with us. You need to see how quickly one can fall. Fearless leader to conquered foe. A princess of meanness to a snivelling wretch grovelling on her knees, begging for mercy. How the mighty have fallen, eh girl?"

Miranda stood, face awash with tears, a bottom as red as ever it could be as the professor's demeaning voice emitted from the speakers and Chloe's shame was played out.

"Actually, I was thinking that we would have Emily here escort you back to your room. However, just to make an example of you, I am thinking that you should remove your knickers and carry them in your hands and we will have your skirt pinned up at the back so that anyone around can see that I was true to my word and that you have the battered backside to prove it."

Stones watched Miranda's face intently as the sight of a distraught and wailing Chloe appeared on the screen. She dropped to her knees and threw herself towards the professor before actually wrapping her hands around his legs. Miranda's face was a perfect picture of disbelief as she seemed transfixed by the spectacle before her, her mouth dropping open at Chloe's pleading words.

"Oh no, sir. No, sir. Please, sir. I beg you, sir. I have learnt my lesson, sir. I am truly sorry, sir. Please, sir, I beseech you."

"Well, I haven't been beseeched for a long time but when I ask something, I expect compliance. I am hoping that you have learned that at least today, young lady. Now, get up off the floor and do as you are damn well told!"

Stones was pleased to see that Miranda seemed frozen by the scene playing out, even in her own torment, as, with tears again streaming down her face, Chloe rose then stooped and removed her knickers before she turned towards Celia, who had produced a safety pin so that her skirt could be lifted up high and pinned.

"What a lovely sight to behold. Most proud we can be, ladies. Good job, good job. Emily, you can have the pleasure now of parading Chloe through the college and back to her room. The walk of total shame, the thrashed villain returns, head bowed, bottom bright red and stinging. Swollen and throbbing, clear cane strokes

marking the fallen scoundrel's golden buttocks. The queen of nothing, the nasty strumpet and bully brought down to earth, disgraced, humiliated and bloody well flogged to within an inch of her life. On the plus side, you took it very well. Now, get out of my room, worthless wretch."

There was otherwise silence in the room as the film showed Chloe's defeated body language while she waited obediently for her final humiliation. She took Emily's proffered hand and, with head bowed, turned to Stones and Celia. Prompted by Emily's squeeze on her hand – of this Stones was certain – she spoke quietly through her weeping.

"I would like you to please accept my apology for my behaviour and my thanks to you for taking the time and effort to correct me and show me the error of my ways, sir and madam."

"Good girl, well said. Let's hope that the next few months will evidence that and you will return here to take your examinations and graduate later. Now, turn around and present that lovely bottom for me once more. Put your knickers back on and Emily, take that pin out and make her presentable. That was just a little test at the end, Chloe, I was never going to make you do such a walk of shame. Straight back to her room, Emily, no hanging about please. Of course, if Chloe is stupid enough to issue a single word, a glance or a gesture that offends you in any way, Emily, please bring her straight back and I will strap her all over again. Otherwise, the rest of your evening is free, Emily. Thank you for your help today."

Miranda was then taken into the bathroom and helped to settle, once she had recovered from the initial shock, onto the ice-laden bidet by Emily.

"Emily, give her face a good wash as well, please, and wait with her for 15 minutes, then you can bring her back in here for a last inspection before you ladies take your leave. The door will be open and you two will conduct yourselves in silence unless you wish for me to have to spend more of my valuable time thrashing both your backsides!"

As was his way, Stones became totally dismissive and matter-of-fact once a punishment was completed. From the terrified look that Miranda gave Emily, Stones was confident that his order would be obeyed to the letter.

Celia, however, as Stones was well aware, was clearly aroused and excited and he knew that she was hoping that she would still be in the room with him once the students had left.

"Yes, Celia, you can stay. You will make us a cup of coffee but first go to my cabinet and select a good strong paddle and leave it in full sight on the table by the door."

His voice was strong and clear and undoubtedly would have carried into the bathroom as he intended. Celia's eyes betrayed the annoyance that he was giving Emily the chance to guess what would be happening once they were alone, but her awareness of his penchant for playing these little mind games, that usually involved a level of embarrassment for her, made her swallow her objections and obey him. He smiled the smile of the victor as she met his eyes, nodding and accepting her price for his attention.

It was half-an-hour later, with a note of pure contrition and remorse for her own actions and gratitude for his actions, that a chastened Miranda left the professor's room, swiftly followed by a dismissed Emily. Stones saw the look that passed between Emily and Celia, Emily almost pouting and Celia looking rather triumphant, but he let it pass. The friction between the two suited and amused him and he was happy to allow it to develop to see what direction their rivalry would take. He had hopes that it would lead to a situation that would be of his liking and certainly under his control. He was a patient man and he could bide his time. He saw Emily's final gesture to score a point back at Celia as she very deliberately ran her fingers over the displayed paddle before smiling at Celia as she turned and left.

CHAPTER 5

A LITTLE WHILE LATER

Emily arrived at Miranda's room 30 minutes later, carrying a small backpack. Miranda let her in, and their arms automatically went around each other's necks, and they kissed deeply and passionately. As they broke apart, Emily held Miranda at arm's length and took hold of the cloth belt that held Miranda's robe together.

"I knew that you would come, I knew, I knew," whispered Miranda.

"I see you have had a quick shower for me then, darling." Emily pulled at the belt as she spoke, with no resistance from Miranda.

"I so knew that you would come. I believe that we have unfinished business, do we not?" Now naked as Emily pushed the robe from her shoulders, Miranda closed her eyes and her tongue slid out and wet her lips seductively.

Emily discarded her backpack before stripping naked, and moved back into close quarters before very gently licking Miranda's lips. Their tongues met and the embrace turned more passionate as Miranda wrapped her arms around Emily and pressed her body hard into hers, their groins and breasts meeting perfectly together.

"Let me love you, Emily. Just lie back and let me be nice to you, let me enjoy you, let me love you properly, my darling."

Emily lay back and willed herself to be compliant to her new lover's request. She closed her eyes as Miranda ran her fingers down from her shoulders to her ankles, and then up again, then back down. Emily's flesh tingled all over at the gentle scratching that set her senses alight. She stretched like a cat, relaxed in her supine position, almost purring at the mild pain as her pale skin began to show the red lines of the fingernail marks up and down her body. She met the lustful gaze of Miranda, saw the want, the passion and desire and blew her a kiss. Miranda parted Emily's legs and slid between them, her eyes dropping to the blonde growth of her pubic mound and the labial lips that Emily could feel were moist and swollen. Her hand slid down her own body and her fingers ran over the top of her pussy, gently working the wetness into herself, tweaking the growing hardness of her clitoral hood. She sighed, her body arched in her wantonness and she slipped a finger inside of herself.

"Your turn, sweetheart, I have oiled the door for you, you just need to push to enter."

Emily watched as Miranda's head tantalisingly lowered and she began to place delicate little kisses on the insides of her legs. She moaned and thrust her torso up, desperate to feel the wet tongue on her swollen lips. Emily gasped with desire as she felt the tongue slip inside her pussy, bucking her hips to meet the welcome intrusion. Miranda's hands pushed her down, but she shook her off and raised her head.

"Just relax and enjoy, my darling, just relax and enjoy."

Fingers replaced her tongue as Miranda continued her administrations. Emily's pussy throbbed with lust as she moaned and bit her lips in her growing desire. Miranda worked her way back up Emily's body, kissing and biting her skin gently before fixing onto a nipple and sucking hard. As Miranda's teeth grazed her erect nipple, Emily gasped and entwined her hands in the hair of her paramour, encouraging her. Miranda swapped to her right breast and sealed her lips around the nipple, her left hand squeezing her left breast hard while her other hand continued to delve and tantalise her pussy.

Emily was in ecstasy, fully appreciative that it was another woman who had found the right places and the right pressure to apply at the right moment in a way that no man had ever done with her.

"Oh my, yes, yes, yes. Fuck! Fuck!" Emily gasped as Miranda delved deeper, harder and faster.

"My word, Emily, you are so wet. You are literally oozing from your pussy. God, you taste so sweet. Hmmm, nectar from the heavens. So wet and sweet, my love."

Emily wanted her to fill her, to fuck her, to take her totally.

"I need you to fuck me properly, Miranda. I need to be bloody well shagged, my love. Please fuck me."

Miranda's face appeared above her.

"So, are you saying you are ready, my darling?"

"Yes, fuck me, yes. I have never been so fucking ready."

Emily felt so alive, so hot, and so ready for some pure, hard sex. She closed her eyes as she felt Miranda's weight shift from her and the sound of her scrabbling to pick up whatever she had secreted in preparation. Emily knew that she was not that fussy about what was coming as long as Miranda filled her gaping pussy with something long, hard and thick. She felt Miranda climb back on top of her, probing her with something that was sliding straight into her. She groaned as it went in further and further, Miranda skilfully using her knuckle to rub Emily's prominent clitoral nub.

Miranda's tongue, fresh from its exploration of the depths of her sex, tasted glorious to Emily. Her arm was pumping fast now and Emily's hips rose to meet the unknown object as it went deep into her inner being. She felt electrified, desperate now for her orgasm. She sucked on Miranda's tongue, her hands grabbing the other's buttocks as she was taken to her climax. Their eyes locked, lust met lust, desire mirrored desire, love sensed love.

Their nipples rubbed against each other and Emily's mind noted the intense sensations that the contact invoked as she began to come, her legs wrapping around Miranda's pounding arm. Emily came, screaming obscenities mixed with words of love and adoration. Her body shuddered and convulsed as she yielded and succumbed to that unstoppable force. Then it was over. She lay supine, breathing heavily, sweating profusely but fulfilled and satisfied.

Miranda kissed her gently, stroked her face as she murmured into Emily's ear.

"You have been a very naughty girl today. Do you think you deserve a spanking, young lady?"

"Do you think you have the balls for that?" Emily smiled innocently.

"Fetch me a belt and a hairbrush and we will see which one of us has any balls, shall we?" Miranda face hardened.

Emily smiled but dropped her eyes.

"Yes, of course, Miss. I have been a very naughty girl. I am so sorry and my bottom does need to feel your wrath. Beat me hard, Miss, beat me like I deserve to be beaten, please." She handed Miranda the hairbrush and belt.

"Over my lap, Emily, let's paint those delicious cheeks of yours bright red."

The thrashing began and Emily lay still, her teeth gritted hard together, her buttocks clenched as Miranda rained down hearty blows that stung and burned but which she found arousing rather than painful. Emily started to grind her pubic mound against Miranda's as her desire mounted. She could hear the change of breathing from Miranda and knew that she was as excited by her dominant role as Emily was by her submissive one. The brush was thrown down and Miranda tipped her off her lap.

"On your knees on the bed, arms and head down, legs apart, that naughty bottom up high in the air demanding it receives its just desserts," Miranda instructed as a compliant Emily moved into position obediently.

"I am so sorry that I have been so naughty, Miss Miranda. What can be done? Can you help make me a good girl?"

The belt swung down and cracked loudly as it connected with the taut buttocks. Emily sighed as the first sting registered; the second forced her breath out and the third garnered a slight moan. This was enough to spur Miranda on and six fast slashes hit the same spot, causing Emily to gasp and groan out loud at last. Learning from this, Miranda now assaulted Emily's upper legs and lower buttocks again and again. Emily could no longer hold back the whimpers and yelps, her bottom beginning to sway as the onslaught continued, the narrow tender strip at the top of her cheeks now taking the beating. She started to cry out, struggling to hold position as the pain began to override the sexual thrill. Then it was over and hands were on her bottom as she felt Miranda's face between her legs and a probing tongue tickling her pussy. As a wet nose plugged her arsehole and fingers reached round and grabbed her breasts, Emily was in ecstasy as the throbbing sensation from her beating merged with the sensation of her erogenous zones all firing up under Miranda's administrations.

Her legs were suddenly forced further apart as Miranda slid under her, legs first, and Emily found the slippery moist lips of Miranda's gash in her face. Her own tongue now mimicked the action of her lover and the only noise in the room was the sound of the two craven women as they slurped and sucked at each other's quims. Emily eased her fingers in to the dripping cavern and sealed her lips around the prominent bud of Miranda's clitoris.

The reaction was intense from Miranda, and Emily knew that she had found her sweet spot and increased the pressure. The response was everything that Emily wanted as Miranda gurgled loudly and began to shudder all over as her approaching climax was signalled. Her legs clenched hard around Emily's frantically pumping fingers and a hand grabbed her wrist, pushing her deeper as she writhed wildly. Emily sat back, engulfing Miranda's face with her bottom and thighs as she came.

As her passion subsided, Miranda pushed her buttocks up and forced Emily above her, with no resistance, and slid three fingers into the available pussy.

"You dirty cow, you are dripping all over my face, you dirty, dirty cow."

Emily held herself still as most of Miranda's hand was now inside of her and she felt herself stretch to accommodate the hard bones. Feeling teeth bite hard into the tender skin of her anal cleft, she submitted to the building orgasm, the toxic moisture of pleasure and pain bringing forth the masochistic tendencies that she could no longer deny. With a piercing scream as Miranda's hand slipped completely inside of her, she came long and uncontrollably, screeching and swearing in her release.

The bodies eventually parted. The two of them slumped head to toe on the bed, for the moment sated and exhausted. Minutes passed as the two slowly recovered before sighing and stretching, sexually fulfilled and fully relaxed. Emily roused herself from the bed and tugged on Miranda's arms.

"On your hands and knees then, my petal. Time for me to give you a portion, I believe."

Miranda raised herself onto her haunches and Emily crawled behind her, pretend noises of shock and outrage spoken as she placed her hands on Miranda's hips and lifted her bottom towards her.

"Oh my, someone has been a naughty girl then. Look at the state of your arse. How on earth did that happen? You must have been so naughty," Emily teased Miranda as she ran her fingers along the scarlet ridges and discoloured patches of her raised globes. She dipped her head and began to kiss her battered cheeks.

"Blimey, your delightful little bum hole smells very strongly of mint, Miranda. Have you shoved a polo up there?"

Her reward for her crudity was a sharp squeeze of Miranda's thighs which only succeeded in ramming Emily's face into her cleft. Not one to miss an opportunity, Emily slipped her tongue into the wet folds and nuzzled Miranda's arsehole with the tip of her nose.

"Emily, you are so crass sometimes. Jeez! Oh, that's nice. Yes, yes, it is a minty cream. Oh yes, oh yes. Strangely enough, I felt it important to smell fresh and clean in my more private areas, knowing what was likely to happen. I was pretty sure that I was not going to be wasting my time ensuring that I was clean and ready for you! Oh yes, do that, do that. Oh my days, that's good."

Emily's tongue had been joined by her thumb that was rubbing in a circular motion around Miranda's clitoris. She dipped her nose down into the wet and welcoming pussy, engulfing it inside of the wetness before slipping it out and up, sliding it effortlessly into the winking dark orifice above her. As her tongue probed once more, the pressure of her thumb increased and her nose pushed deep into the musky back entrance. Emily felt the tremors of Miranda's approaching orgasm. As the intensity grew and the first wave pulsated through her shaking body, Emily pulled away and snatched up the strap-on from the floor. As Miranda moaned in compliance, her own fingers delved to replace Emily's manipulations as her body shuddered to a climax, and Emily thrust into her hard with the huge appendage now attached to her midriff.

"Aaaaaarrrrrghhhh!" Miranda screamed as the thick leather penis plunged into her. "Fuck, that's so big, Emily. It feels like it is half way into my chest. Oh my days, oh my goodness, oh, oh, oh."

Emily smiled and pulled her hips back.

"Hold on tight, sugarplum. That was just to pave the way. It was only halfway in. Take it all, baby, take it all!"

She thrust herself back and slammed her groin into Miranda bottom, sinking the appendage into the deep inside of Miranda's pussy, grinding and pumping alternatively, her fingers digging into the passive woman's thighs as Emily enjoyed the experience of fucking someone in that masterful and dominant position. The appeal of the position for a man became totally obvious to her as she fixed on the glistening wet cock, pulling it almost completely out before bucking her hips and ramming it inside of Miranda again. She could feel her own climax starting to build once more as she feasted her eyes on the savaged buttocks of the thrashed beauty at her mercy, watching fascinated as Miranda's arsehole opened and closed in response to her actions. Now she understood that it really was not an insult if your lover did not want to face you during sex when this view was so utterly delicious. She totally acknowledged that it was a power trip, the dominance and control being completely in the hands of the giver, but even without the sensation of a man's cock that, as a woman, she could only ever fantasise about, she got the turn-on that doggy style generated. With one hand reaching under to press on Miranda's clit while the other one held firmly onto a hip, she accelerated her thrusting to mimic a man's lovemaking and pounded into Miranda as she began a high-pitched and lengthy squeal to signal her climax. With the artificial cock still wedged deep inside of her lover, Emily slipped her fingers down to her own dripping vagina and quickly brought herself to a finish, gasping and shuddering. Miranda slumped down, causing Emily to slip out and fall beside her, their arms reaching for each other in a passionate and joyful embrace as their lovemaking came to its conclusion, their desire sated, their needs met for the moment.

*

Not far away, Celia bit hard into the pillow, gasping loudly as Stones slammed down with the thick wooden paddle and her thoroughly reddened cheeks squeezed tightly together. Again and again his arm rose and fell. He hit first one cheek repeatedly before moving on to the other. Her screams began to fill the air as he tested her by speeding up his delivery, his power and strength not letting him down as the paddle rose and fell over 100 times.

"Keep that arse up in the air; you know you want this!" Stones snapped.

Stones battered Celia's rosy cheeks until she collapsed onto the bed, and her hands finally succumbed and covered her beaten flanks.

"No more, please, Edward. Fuck me, my darling, fuck me hard."

His response was to take both of her wrists in one of his huge hands while the other one continued with the onslaught on her purple buttocks, no trace of white left as he applied the paddle from every conceivable angle to every bit of exposed skin.

"You get fucked when I decide you get fucked, you filthy, wanton slag!"

Another avalanche of strokes landed on her ravaged bottom before he grabbed her by the hips and pulled her up, slipping a hand with force along her slippery, sodden vaginal crack.

"Who's a wet, randy little cow, then? Answer, bitch, I am not talking to myself!" he snapped, slapping her bottom with a huge hand.

"I am, Edward, I am. A soaking wet, randy little whore. Your randy little whore, who wants your lovely, big cock now. Fill me up, my lover, my master, my hero, my mentor. Fill me up, please. Fuck me, Edward, fuck me, please."

Stones stripped his clothes off as Celia replaced his fingers with her own and began to lustily frig herself.

"Dirty little wanton slag!" snapped Stones as he thrust his erect cock into her mouth and taking her shoulders began to pump inside the warm wetness. With one hand wrapped around his stem to stop his huge cock from choking her and the other moving in a blur, she reached her first climax, struggling not to bite down on him. He pulled himself out of her and laid on the bed, manipulating her over him and facing him cowgirl-style. She slipped him in easily, in a well-practised manoeuvre, and came again immediately as his girth filled her pussy.

"Fuck me, Edward! Fuck me, my love," she yelled into his face as he raised his haunches and slammed into her, taking her weight with his strong hands so she was suspended in the air as he rammed himself hard inside her. With a grunt, he pulled her down, his giant hands grasping her sore buttocks as his speed increased and he began to search for his moment of release. A finger found her arsehole and he rimmed her, opening her up as he just enjoyed the feeling of having her ready for whatever he desired, the power of touching her most secret of places, the sense of owning and completely mastering her.

"Yes, yes, yes, yes, yes, yes, yes," was Celia's response as she gave herself to him, rubbing her pubic bone against him as she strove for her third orgasm.

His spunk exploded into her as he groaned in ecstasy, the air filled with Celia's little high-pitched yelps and his masculine animalistic roar of sexual completion.

They kissed deeply and with total love and affection as they came down from their glorious trip into that unmatched paradise of sexual oblivion and minutes later were dozing, entwined in each other's arms.

CHAPTER 6

MELANIE AND PRASCILLA RETURN

FOR THE REAL DEAL

orty-eight hours after Melanie and Prascilla had discovered their fates, Jamie and Emily had joined Stones in his office for a pre-session discussion and were enjoying a pot of coffee. The bell sounded and the CCTV monitor in front of the professor showed an anxious-looking Melanie in a flowing, flowery dress, her hair in ribbons, looking the picture of innocence on his doorstep. He buzzed her in and watched as the joint expressions of puzzlement and apprehension fought for superiority on her face when she saw the other two present. Puzzlement appeared to win the fight, at least in voicing her concern.

"Oh, sir, mmm, are you busy?" she queried but with more hope than expectation.

"Just with you, my dear, just with you," Stones replied.

"As you can see, Jamie, we have plenty to work on here. This will be a good challenge; her buttocks are more substantial even than those of our mutual friend, Pres."

Stones knew that this oblique reference to the head of the fetish club they both belonged to would go over Emily's head, although he could see that she had made a mental note and wondered whether she would be a possible guest at one of their meetings in the future. Much as he was becoming somewhat attached to the seemingly very devoted, rather striking blonde, he was never going to break the code of conduct concerning liaisons of a sexual nature between staff and students. Not that this seemed too much of a barrier to Emily who had made it quite clear that Stones' age and position held no such concerns for her!

"Er, OK. What should I do now please, sir?" Melanie's voice was compliant and subversive.

Stones loved her honest and respectful tone and was warming to her the more he spent time in her company. Unlike many who had trod her footsteps before, she had accepted the presence of Jamie and Emily and just moved on. He had a lot of sympathy for the position she found herself in and felt that, so far, she had handled things in a most impressive way.

"You may go to my cabinet and bring me the items you selected earlier when you asked me to carry out the punishment that you decided you deserved."

Melanie swallowed noisily but walked straight to the cabinet and picked out the thin, whippy cane, the split-end tawse, the medium cane, the thick cane and the riding crop.

"Well remembered, my dear. That does at least save you the additional punishment any memory loss would have brought to your door. Now, young lady, what was the exact chastisement that you chose be delivered to your bare buttocks to aptly serve as a form of correction and atonement for your disgusting and barbaric behaviour?"

Stones did not give the student time to acclimatise. Melanie had arrived knowing that she was to be thoroughly thrashed but, as often was the case with these errant young women, she had turned up with just that little bit of hope in her eyes. Surely by now, Stones thought, the word would have permeated around the college that he was a man without a heart when it came to discipline. His reputation was that he was a monstrous ogre, maybe, but he was also subject to respect for being a man of his word and it was reluctantly accepted that he was a fair man. Once a punishment had been designated and accepted in principle, and usually in writing, there was next to no chance that he would have a change of heart or decide to be lenient.

Melanie reddened, her hands going to the hem of her virginal-looking, mainly white, dress with its little flowery insignia, but she managed to speak the words which had been maddeningly running through her mind all morning.

"If you please, sir, it was a 250 stroke spanking on my bare bottom, then the whippy cane, then the medium cane, followed by the crop, and then the split end tawse and the heavy cane, sir."

"Excellent, of course! You are a greedy girl with your need to be punished. However, we must remember that you were very, very naughty, so I suppose you must have such a severe beating. It certainly is severe for a first-timer, but you do have a meaty and ample bottom to target with some good substantial padding so maybe it is fair. We are all looking forward to seeing you present those formidable buttocks for our delectation."

The young woman's face had displayed a fair shade of pink the moment she entered the room, but this had progressed to red and now it had gone a deep crimson as Stones used demeaning words to belittle and humiliate her.

"Melanie has asked for ten strokes each from the fearsome five; we must ensure that we don't disappoint her, Jamie. My thoughts are that I will take the first with the small cane and end with the tawse; you take the middle ground with the other two canes and the riding crop. However, let us play this one by ear and see how things go after she has had a damn good spanking. Now, 300 wasn't it, Melanie?"

She blinked. There was a second's hesitation before she spoke clearly.

"Yes, sir, 300, sir."

Stones beamed and almost hugged the well-natured student who was so eager to please.

"Oh Melanie, you are a delight. No, it was 250 and because you are so honest then that is where we will stay."

She smiled gratefully in response, and Stones marvelled at her acquiescence and longing to please him.

"Tally ho! Shall we get this show on the road?" Stones moved his chair clear of the surrounds, sat down and patted his thighs. He raised his eyebrows as he looked at Melanie.

"You still seem to have your clothes on, my dear. Do you need help undressing, or are you just a bit slow to understand and a little dense?"

Melanie now turned into a gibbering wreck.

"Oh my days. Oh no. I am sorry. I didn't know ... I thought ... Yes, yes, I'll take my clothes off."

To be fair, Stones mused, she reacted quickly then, her dress over her head, sandals off in a thrice, the bra unfastened and off, the voluminous bosoms released to his delight, and no hesitation or turning away in modesty as she scurried to whip her panties down and off. *Wonderful*, Stones thought as she turned her back to the three of them, bent over and pulled her enormous buttock cheeks apart exposing her cleft and arsehole nestling there.

"Presenting myself for checking, sir," she said in a clear voice.

He could not fail to be impressed with her charming efforts to please him and decided he would oblige her and carry out her wishes.

"Yes, good girl, that's a perfect display – let me just breathe in your aroma for a moment. Ah yes, very much citrus fruits, possibly grapefruit, I would hazard. Lovely and fresh. Well done, thank you. Jamie, Emily, have you both seen enough? Well, you could hardly see less, ha ha! Beautifully displayed, thank you, Melanie. Oops, there is a stray pubic hair blotting the landscape, let's get rid of that. Hold still while I pick this little blighter from your anus … there, that's got it! What do you think, Emily? You seem to be drinking the sight in. Have you any observations to make? Please feel perfectly free to comment unreservedly."

Emily looked excited at being able to openly speak her mind.

"Wow! Sir, it *is* awesome! I have never seen anything like it; her bum crack is sooooooo long and there's just so much of her bottom. However, amazingly her bum hole is very small and neat and tidy. I thought it would be like a cavernous crater, sir. Her pussy slit is long and she has loads of folds but her butt hole is tiny. It's weird, sir."

Stones loved the way Emily could just say what she saw; it was a double-edged sword for her though, as he was well aware that she could come out with something suspicious as well as something objectionable.

"Interesting, Emily, but put your tongue back in, I promise you can have a role later on that will be a treat. Now, Melanie my dear, at my side, ready to take the position, please." Melanie moved into place.

"Yes, sir, and you are absolutely correct, sir, grapefruit body cream all over. I hope you like it, sir."

She turned to Jamie and Emily saying, "I am so sorry about you having to see all of this, I know I look disgusting."

Stones swung back his arm and backhanded her buttocks with a stinging blow.

"No more of that sort of talk, Melanie, we are not having self-deprecation from you and certainly there will be no body shaming from us. Right, my lovely girl, let us see if we can find a nice, comfortable pose over my knees as you will be there for some time. I have got a nice round hairbrush here in case my hands get too hot and stingy, so I think we are about ready to roll. Over you go, hands on the ground, bottom up, legs apart. Emily here will help you stay in position and give you words of advice if you need them. So, let the spanking commence."

This was to be one of Stones' favourite spankings. He loved spanking large, fleshy bottoms, and Melanie's was the largest student he had seen in the flesh. He thoroughly enjoyed the sensation of the flattening impact before the buttock reformed, rounded once more, the handprint so clear on the expansive surface, the beautiful symmetrical cheeks presented and enhanced by the over the knee spanking position. Melanie was a perfect recipient, maintaining her posture, letting out little yelps and showing no resistance, just perfect acceptance. Emily had little to do as Melanie was stoic in her acceptance of the agony she was enduring and there was no fight or defiant struggle apart from minor tremors that passed through her expansive upper thighs.

After 150 hand spanks, Stones paused; he would have had no problem completing her punishment but wanted to up the ante and cause the tremendous buttocks a bit more discomfort before moving onto harsher implements.

"Think I'll move on to the back of the hairbrush now. What do you think, Melanie?"

She continued with her overly polite compliance in response. She was gently weeping but otherwise showing fortitude and total subservience.

"Of course, sir, indeed if that is what sir thinks is required, then I am happy for my bottom to receive any punishment you see fit, sir. I am so deserving of my walloping, sir, and thank you for what I have received so far."

Stones exchanged glances with the ever-eager Emily, her wide eyes and ruddy cheeks showing her fervour for the whole process as she dabbed away the tears that rolled down the beaten girl's face. The blows came thicker and faster now, Melanie's yells increasing in volume and her body starting to wriggle and writhe. The flesh was really bouncing now and thoroughly reddened all over the massive expanse of her large behind. The deep stinging of the harder blows from the hairbrush broke any resolve Melanie had begun with to retain a sense of composure; words of apology and cries for mercy were interspersed with screams of pain as the relentless onslaught continued. Then it was over and Stones cast the brush aside and began to gently stroke the strikingly red cheeks of her still jerking bottom.

"Hush, hush, now, that bit is over. Of course, the best is yet to come but for now, my dear, just try to calm yourself down and embrace the throbbing and be thankful that correction and its consequential improvement is taking place. Your improvement is well under way and looks very much like being a successful process."

Not words actually intended to sooth or reassure Melanie, who was noisily trying to catch her breath and failing miserably, but part of Stones' mind games with those being sanctioned. Stones allowed Emily a few moments of encouraging words and supportive entreaties, which she delivered enthusiastically as always.

"Right, Emily, take her over to the caning table and strap her down. We shall see how she enjoys my little friends here. Jamie's turn to shine coming up, Melanie. This should be interesting as I have set him the task of really making you suffer and holler. All for your own benefit, of course!"

Stones waggled the instruments of her coming chastisement in her face as he signalled Emily to take Melanie over to her next position.

Minutes later, Stones, Jamie and Emily stood in silence, admiring the sight of Melanie's magnificent buttocks which fully benefited from the design of the professor's punishment desk: the wooden legs raised high, the rubber mound forcing her crotch up and out, the hand restraints pulling her stretched across the desk. With her legs wide apart and her body stretched over the top of the desk, her buttocks were as rounded and taut as never before. The substantial flab of her cheeks was no longer so apparent and Stones felt that here was a fine and glorious figure that Melanie should be proud of, regardless of her low self-esteem and poor sense of worth.

"To her head, Emily. She may take some holding I suspect but I hope that we will beat the fight out of her quickly. Just a moment to wait and ..."

He was interrupted as his bell rang and he moved to buzz the door open after glancing at his laptop screen. In walked a very apprehensive Prascilla Guptil.

"Good girl, perfectly on time. As you can see, we have warmed Melanie up but saved the main event so that you can join in the fun! Now, say hello to my partner, Jamie, who assists on applying corporal punishment to students of this college. Unless you behave impeccably, young lady, he will step in to apply any additional beating you earn with a cane to your scrawny naked backside, so you have been warned. Stronger than me, you see, so he can apply more muscle to the swing, more grit to the mill, and more pain to your buttocks, more's the point. So bear that in mind if you think about misbehaving or being disobedient during your punishment."

Stones went straight for the jugular and Prascilla was sobbing pitifully before he had finished speaking, clearly shaken by the presence of others and the sight of a prostrate Melanie, her bright red bottom in the air. The instruments about to be used on Melanie which were in the professor's hand certainly seemed to be adding to her distress as she kept glancing at them.

"Oh dear, this is a bit ridiculous and disappointing. What a mess! For goodness sake, girl, get a grip. Your backside has not been introduced to anything yet. Emily, take her into the bathroom, sort her out and bring her back to the room naked within five minutes, please, and she can assist you with holding Melanie while she meets the small cane. Oh, and if she is not ready in five, you can take her place for her paddling. The clock is ticking so get on with it, Emily. You have complete freedom to achieve this in any way that works, my dear, as long as she is out in time and her bottom is still unmarked, mind you. That pleasure will be mine to begin with."

Emily certainly did not hold back. As Prascilla attempted to back away from her, she grabbed her by the shoulders, spun her round and unleashed a stinging pair of slaps across the backs of the distressed student's trouser-covered legs. Seconds later, she was in Stone's bathroom and those same trousers were round her ankles, with Emily sharply and loudly pointing out to her that she needed to get her shit together unless she wanted her punishment doubled. Prascilla hastened in removing her underwear.

To no one's surprise, a red-faced but totally naked Prascilla stood, head bowed and trembling, before Stones within the specified time.

"You can stop trying to hide your shame and protect your modesty. Very soon every little bit of you will have been shown to the occupants of this room. Right, off you go with Emily and enjoy watching Melanie take her strokes with this little devil. Stings like buggery but only for a few seconds. To be honest, ten is hardly worth having. But enjoy, and remember that this is basically your own doing."

Prascilla seemed in a daze and the sneaky little glances she directed at Jamie indicated why. Stones was well aware that he had hit her with a double whammy; not only was an agile and powerfully built, good-looking man possibly going to give her a caning, she was also completely naked in front of him and that was a far different ballgame to being naked in front of your crusty old Dean of Discipline! To her credit, he heard her whispering apologies to Melanie as she took hold of one cuffed hand following Emily's lead, which indicated to Stones that she was indeed on the road to improvement.

"Still awake young Melanie? Don't worry, we haven't forgotten you. These beauties will be getting some attention now." Stones ran his hands quite lovingly over the large cheeks.

"I'm afraid that we are not getting to see those lower slits of yours really, Melanie; seems a bit unfair that you are able to hide them away from us particularly as they are so joyous to the eye. But for once we will make an exception and allow your vagina its moment of privacy. Let us get on."

With that, Stones brought the small whippy cane down savagely, striking the same two spots on each cheek repeatedly, in very quick time. Melanie yelped but Stones was not convinced that this was that much of an ordeal and would be glad to move onto a heavier implement to, hopefully, make more of an impact. Nodding to Jamie to continue with the medium cane, Stones moved away and fetched his wooden, bat-shaped paddle.

Melanie's body jolted as she felt the force of Jamie's powerful arm for the first time. A small cry escaped her lips, followed by a deep intake of breath. Again, he struck the huge cheeks savagely. Melanie cried out in real pain and then louder still as his third strike hit low on her fleshy under cheeks. He repeated the next three strokes exactly as before and Melanie howled as the second wave of strokes stung her. Stones was aware that she would never have experienced pain like this before, but Janie showed no sympathy or reserve, he was pleased to see. With the last four, Jamie went for the top of her bottom crack, slashing the cane down on the less protected area to a crescendo of screams from Melanie, who, Stones suspected, was wondering about the excellent protection that the layers of fat were supposed to be giving her! The truth, he knew, was simpler than that. She was a good girl who had rarely been spanked or hurt physically and although it might take a lot to mentally hurt her as she was hardened to the teasing and taunts about her weight, she had no built-up resistance to the pain of a hard caning and Jamie was certainly giving her what for.

"Your turn now, Prascilla. I think I shall give Melanie a break to process that little tickling she has just received. The sting of the cane does have an after burn that is worth savouring for the true sense of a caning to be experienced. Look what I have got for you. Come along, over here by my knees now. It's time for your walloping."

Prascilla seemed frozen to her spot beside the sobbing Melanie, and tears began trickling down her own face. Stones watched her as she tried to process this alien world into which she had inadvertently entered and put some kind of order into the mayhem happening around her.

"Oh, for God's sake. Emily, give her a nudge over here please before I double her punishment."

Emily spoke quite harsh warning words to Prascilla that jolted her into action and she quickly took her place by his side.

"In your own time then, obviously?" Stones snarled, virtually ensuring that any resistance was broken before he had laid a finger on her.

"Now, what is it you wish me to do now, you naughty little thing?"

"What? I mean I'm sorry, sir, er, um, what do you mean?"

Stones gave one of his most theatrical sighs.

"Looks like this one is going to need your pastoral support, Emily.

Not too quick on the update, are you, my precious princess? I am really not sure how some of you ladies ever pass our admissions process."

Emily ceased her stroking of Melanie's forehead, gave her eyes one more dab with a tissue and came and stood opposite the confused and shivering Prascilla.

Emily took Prascilla's hands in her own. Stones could see her tensing then she spoke slowly to Prascilla, as if talking to a school child.

"Now, sweetheart, you know what you are here for so let's clear your mind of any nonsense. There is no hope of a knight in shining armour riding to the rescue, but there is, however, the possibility that things could get so much worse than you could ever imagine. *Why do I know? Who the fuck are you?* Apologies for language, Professor. *Why are you helping him?* Now, these could be fair questions going through your mind and the answers are simple. You requested your punishment in writing as a means of accepting blame and ownership; you believe in the college's ethos to correct and improve its students; I am a person who has been beaten extremely severely because I thoroughly deserved it and I assist those who need to be disciplined to carry out their acts of restitution and contrition via corporal punishment. Simply put, I will help you through the chastisement you have chosen. Now, just for the professor to know that you are true to your promise, remind him of the punishment you proposed for him to deliver."

Two tears, one from each eye, almost hypnotically rolled down either cheek of Prascilla's doom-laden face as if in a race to be second rather than first. Her eyes glazed over but fixed into a vacant stare at Emily.

"I would like to be spanked and then paddled please, sir. Thank you," she whispered in a robotic monotone.

"Cheer up, my dear. Absolution and redemption are on the horizon waiting. Emily, give her a little tug, please, she looks rather reluctant for some reason. Jamie has not got much to do at the moment so if she wants a taste of the cane she only has to ask." Stones was enjoying the little cameo between the two students and he always enjoyed Emily's dedicated assistance at these moments. Her hushed next words to Prascilla, and Stones only caught the emphasis on the pain of the cane, produced a new lease of life and a spurt of energy from Prascilla and she suddenly seemed keen to lay herself across his lap.

Stones stroked the pronounced and rather bony buttocks, running his fingers along her crease and flicking either side of her crack to encourage Prascilla to open her legs.

"Wider, dear, wider. Show me your little pink anus and let us see those labial lips, please. I haven't had a smell check to make sure you are clean, so lift your bottom up and let me have a good sniff, please."

Prascilla groaned but complied as she struggled to get into the most undignified position she had ever been in. She held her breath as Stones delved with his nose between her cheeks.

"Ah, lovely, very nutty, most pleasant. Good girl, well done. Happy to work with that, good job. Jamie, as you are redundant at the moment and I do not think we want Melanie getting bored, why not give her the ten with the riding crop? It is a leather-covered, fibre glass crop, Melanie, so very flexible, very swishy and very stingy! Enjoy, Jamie. I'll spank while you whack."

Stones went straight to it and his hand landed hard and fast, over and over again, on the light brown skin of the Indian student's small buttocks. As Jamie followed his lead, the riding crop flew through the air, and in a moment the room was full of the competing cries of the two delinquents being thrashed. As Jamie applied each stroke of the crop every ten seconds, Stones felt there was a majesty of sound as

Melanie's long, banshee screams and Prascilla's wails combined. He bounced his beefy, flat hand off the twin taut rocks of her taut writhing buttocks at pace. By the time Jamie put the crop down, Stones had landed over 150 slaps and Prascilla was sobbing hysterically.

"Please, no more, Professor Stones, I can't do it. It hurts so much, no more please, sir."

Stones chuckled, and stroked the now bright red cheeks.

"Shush now, dear. Be a good girl and you will just take a good paddling and then it will be over and you can watch Melanie take her final ten. Now, up you hop and we can get you cuffed up opposite Melanie and we will see if we can get you two talking."

He led the sobbing, defeated Prascilla over to the desk opposite Melanie who was whimpering quietly while Emily moved to her side, leaning over her back to stroke her face. As Prascilla obediently spread-eagled herself over the table top, her slim body stretched taut, her buttocks protruding so starkly now that they were raised by the mound and the slant of the desk, her red cheeks wide apart, emphasising the extra darkness of the inner skin of her crack and the bright pink of her arsehole.

"Cute," said Stones, always keen to ratchet up the embarrassment levels of his vanquished rascals, as he ran his hand over her back. "Such lovely colour combinations we have produced. I'll fetch the thick wooden paddle to be ready for your grand finale. Jamie, please give Melanie her ten with the thick cane and warm her up for the sting of the tawse. Prascilla and Melanie can interlock fingers while we beat them together and perhaps they can take the opportunity to have a little chat between strokes."

Stones stood with the paddle raised and met Jamie's eyes across the two prone girls. The contrast was extreme: the massively overweight, pale-skinned blonde and the slim, dusky Indian. The only thing they had in common was the bright red sore bottoms. With a nod from Stones, they brought their implements down together, Prascilla screeching as the paddle bit hard into the point where her upper legs met her lower cheeks and Melanie groaning deeply as she banged her head on the table while she tried to absorb the pain. As Emily leaned over to pull Melanie's hair back, Melanie flinched her giant shoulder and tossed Emily off, who lost her footing and crashed to the floor.

"You stupid, fat fuck!" Emily yelled and then came to a sudden halt. "Oh my goodness, I am sooooo sorry, Melanie, Professor Stones. I don't know where that came from, I really didn't mean it."

Stones moved round to where she was pulling herself to her feet.

"How dare you. Have you learned nothing? I keep thinking we've made progress with that temper of yours and then you do something like this. Well, come on, what are you waiting for? Get your damn clothes off!"

Emily, to no surprise, did not hesitate.

"Yes sir, of course sir. Absolutely. Melanie, please forgive me. I am so sorry."

Melanie seemed confused by the fuss.

"Oh it's alright, it's alright. Not a problem. Let's face it, I am what you said."

Stones took the paddle round behind Melanie and slammed it into the backs of her legs, unleashing a torrent of ferocious blows.

"No. No. No. Melanie you will not take that line, you will not accept that is who and what you are. Right, Emily, get those knickers off quickly. Jamie, hook her up on top of Melanie as she is now going to take Melanie's remaining nine cane strokes and you are going to give her your very best efforts. I want those beautiful buttocks blistered."

Jamie and Stones lifted her up and on top of the shuddering Melanie whose body was wriggling about as she tried to twist and turn to ease away the biting pain from the paddle. Stones was more interested to see that Emily appeared far more concerned about being spread and exposed so blatantly in front of Jamie than the fact that she was about being caned.

"Come on, get those legs spread wide open, push those buttocks up and you can point that anus at Jamie. You are way past the point where I care one hoot about your dignity or pride. Hold onto Melanie's shoulders and you and Prascilla can both keep telling her how sorry you are. Your little respite is therefore over, Prascilla. Let us beat them both, Jamie, beat them hard, and do not worry about counting anymore just cane these backsides true and proper."

As Jamie slammed the heavy cane down hard across the rounded buttocks of the beautiful young blonde, Stones picked up the paddle and cracked it against Prascilla's bottom.

"I cannot hear a word from either of you. Melanie, listen."

Prascilla and Emily immediately started spluttering apologies but were interrupted as the cane and paddle struck again. Prascilla had nowhere near the resilience and forbearance that Emily had developed in these situations and howled each time Stones landed the paddle. Emily, facing Stones, was stoic, and gave a little guttural grunt as the cane bit into her cheeks her words of apology to Melanie, whose face looked mildly bemused, albeit that confusion was clearly competing with the pain from her throbbing legs, were clear.

Stones brought Prascilla's punishment with the paddle to an end but stood and watched Emily's suffering for a few strokes more before he signaled for Jamie to stop.

"Emily, get yourself off Melanie, pull yourself together and stand in front of our friend Jamie. Thank him very much for your excellent thrashing and apologise for your behaviour. Hands on your head, and as you do, please face him full frontal and with respect."

He saw her cringe, but she did as she was instructed, tears running down a face that was almost the same colour as her bottom with the embarrassment of facing the handsome and grinning porter, knowing the intimate display that she had just given him.

"Thank you so much for my caning, Jamie, um, sir. It was very much deserved and excellently applied. I am so sorry that I had to put you to the effort of delivering it. I apologise for my behaviour, sir."

A nod from the smirking porter as his eyes drifted over her firm breasts and down to her blonde curly mass covering her sex caused Emily further embarrassment, much to Stones' delight.

"Into the corner now to think about your behaviour, you naughty girl. Jamie, I would very much like Prascilla to experience the cane, to ensure that she never feels the need to act in a way whereby she would have to receive multiple strokes. One nice and hard should do the job."

By now, as he knew she would, Prascilla was pleading for mercy, promising never, ever to be mean to anyone or misbehave in any way again.

"Be quiet, you scoundrel and retain that position, nice and still please. It can be six strokes as easily as it can be one. When you are ready, Jamie, an extra hard stroke to make sure she gets the message, please, my friend."

His words had the expected effect and Prascilla froze in position. The cane flew through the air, the unprotected, bony cheeks producing a sharp, thudding sound rather than the fleshier, slapping sound of Emily's and Melanie's bigger buttocks. The scream from Prascilla paid tribute to the strength of the strike as a thick, raised crimson line appeared across her cheeks.

Stones moved across to his cabinet and selected the split end tawse, not as thick as his thickest strap but the ends did have that extra cut due to the tiny gap between the strips of leather that landed slightly independently of the rest of the tawse, giving a feeling of receiving strokes from two different implements.

"Almost seems a waste of an opportunity to beat just one when there are three naked bottoms available. What say you Emily, Melanie? Do I need to educate and improve the two of you further?"

A wide-eyed Melanie was stunned into silence, whilst the sobbing Prascilla just howled in response. Luckily Emily's voice was even and controlled.

"Sir, if you or Melanie think that I deserve more punishment then I would gladly take it. Melanie has paid her dues, I feel, and I would be happy to accept further punishment in her place. I will happily take any further punishment in Prascilla's place also, sir, as she seems to have been beaten to her limit."

Getting some points back, thought Stones.

"Not your call, really, but I can see that having blotted your copybook you are most willing to make amends. Good girl, good girl. Melanie's call, I feel. Melanie, sweetheart, I think I do need to ensure that you have learned a lesson. There are three options: you can have your ten all on your own bottom or we could let Emily share the ten, so five apiece, or you could have ten each or you could nominate Emily to receive all of them. However, if you take the third option, then Emily will have to take 20 strokes on her own. Prascilla, I am still wavering over the question of whether or not she has been punished enough to learn her lesson. Your call, Melanie, although I can tell you that I would love the opportunity to give Emily a thorough tawse whopping."

Emily's head dropped but she stayed silent whereas Prascilla was yet again reduced to a further outburst of sobbing. Stones suspected that she had realised that he was deliberately testing Melanie without ever believing that the good-natured and kind young woman would allow someone else to take what was due to her. Melanie passed admirably.

"Oh sir, no. It was my bad behaviour, sir. I should be punished alone, sir. Emily and Prascilla have received their punishments, sir. I have forgiven then both, sir, and am happy for you to beat me alone, sir."

Stones smiled and looked at Emily who played along and her knowing eyes told Stones that she acknowledged his ploy and accepted the challenge.

"Professor, I think that we both recognise that we are naughty girls and that we both need punishing, so may I suggest that we be given ten strokes each, sir?"

Stones nodded in approval, his smile aside to Emily rewarding her for her understanding of the role-playing that was taking place. What Melanie was not to know was that his intuition told him that Emily's sado-masochist tendencies, that he was tuned into, meant that she had a desire to know what the tawse would feel like.

"Excellent decision – accepted, ten strokes of the tawse each. Prascilla can be released, Emily, and can stand facing the corner for now."

As Emily led a weeping but thankful Prascilla over to the corner, Melanie interjected in the most submissive and apologetic manner possible.

"Sorry, Professor, sir. Being a nuisance and all that, so sorry, sir. I do rather need to have a wee I am afraid, sir. Is that possible?"

"Yes, of course dear. Emily, Jamie, unstrap her, please and then come and take the circle seats. Melanie, the door will open on my touch here, and you can trot along and empty your bladder."

As others before her, Melanie entered the professor's lavish bathroom and assumed that the door would close on her pull and looked confused that it did not budge. Stones followed her, ushering her in and walked across to the toilet roll.

"Come along, Melanie, sit your bottom down and get on with it. I am ready to wipe the drips."

Stones pulled off a few sheets and folded them over as though this was the most natural thing in the world. Melanie stood by the toilet bowl and looked across to see that Jamie and Emily were sitting in clear view of the toilet and would be able to watch her doing her business. The student looked devastated but once again was quick-thinking enough to realise that this was her fate, humiliation and pain was her punishment, and she seemed to have little resistance to the intricacies of the professor's process of degradation and dismantling of her spirit. A sigh and then compliance followed and Stones knew that he had conquered this one totally. Melanie settled herself, adjusting her bottom to find a position that was close to bearable, considering her throbbing buttocks, and immediately rattled the porcelain as she unloaded her obviously full bladder without hesitation.

"Done, sir," she said in a voice that illustrated abject surrender.

Stones leant in between her legs and, to her consternation, dabbed her vagina gently, her head drooped in absolute resignation.

"Up you pop, good girl, oh yes that looks a healthy colour, does it not, my dear?" Stones indicated that he wanted Melanie to join him in perusing her deposit in the bowl.

"Yes sir, thank you, sir."'

Stones steered the totally embarrassed and crestfallen student out of the bathroom and back to stand before Jamie and Emily.

"Well done, Melanie. All emptied; presume you are not going to need to request any further breaks, toilet-based or otherwise? No, then let us move on. Excellent performance today, Jamie, thank you. Once you have strapped her back down and given me my target, I think you can leave these two to me to finish off. Lovely, all tied down and displayed, Melanie, and as a last task can you escort young Emily to the other side and strap her down too, please? Lovely, lovely, drink in that sight, Jamie. Hasn't she got a lovely set? Beautiful breasts and nipples, an hour-glass figure, an art class perfect vagina and a marvellously constructed anus in the middle of that perfect bottom? That is excellent, all tied down and displayed properly for a last tribute. Well done, Jamie, thank you. Have a good rest of the evening and I'll be in touch soon."

Jamie left the room, leaving an extremely red-faced Emily in his wake. Stones knew damn well that he would, on one hand, have embarrassed her to an extreme with his description to Jamie of her most private parts, whilst on the other hand his complimentary words about her body would have touched her besotted heart. He moved behind her and ran his hands over the exposed, wide-apart legs, touching her lower buttocks as he assessed the target area for the split-end tawse.

"Nice and relaxed cheeks now, young Emily. I know you are secretly looking forward to this. I am going high and low to put you to the test if that's OK with you, my dear?"

"Of course, sir. Aaaaaaeeeeeeeooowww!" Emily screeched as the tawse landed across the tops of her cheeks and the split ends wrapped around her thighs to slap into her hip bone.

Stones paused and then hit the same spot again, causing another ear-splitting scream. No relief was to come as he went a few inches lower and then repeated the stroke before bringing the tawse down diagonally across the bright scarlet tramlines of the previous strokes.

"Jeeeeeeeeez. Sir, that really hurts. Yaaaar. Jeeez."

"Well, that's certainly good news. It would have been sad if you had said that you enjoyed it. I think Melanie can have her ten now while you suck up those last five."

He moved behind Melanie, running the tawse all around the large, trembling cheeks.

"Are you ready for your grand finale, young lady? Shall I give these beautiful darlings their final honouring?

Melanie's gulp was loud and desperate, her fear apparent as she burbled a shaky response.

"Yes sir, thank you, sir. Oh sir, I am so sorry, sir, and promise I'll never be in this sort of trouble again."

The tawse lashed down on the huge expanse of the red-striped bottom cheeks before him. Stones could see that the large width of the target minimised the effect of the split-ends as the blow went centrally and even spaced over the high crack of the buttocks' join. Melanie's scream he ignored; the point of the tawse was the double bite with the secondary effect of the split ends, and he was only interested in assessing how to deliver the strokes to get the full benefit of this particular punishment implement. Such his methodical approach to the delivery of the flagellation, at this point the recipient was largely irrelevant! He paused in his assessment; Emily met his eyes as she raised her head as much as she could to watch Melanie's taking of the wicked-looking tawse. He could see that she wanted to speak so nodded his assent.

"You were looking puzzled and very intent, sir. I was just intrigued to know why?"

Stones considered, then he decided to air his thoughts.

"Melanie's expansive but stunning bottom presents a real challenge to a flogger of my level of experience. The layering of excess fat absorbs the blows very well and for all the fuss she is making, she has been quite lucky so far. Shush, Melanie, now, you do not have permission to join in this conversation. So, Emily, what I am trying to do is to ensure that the next strokes wrap around her buttocks to whip the split-end delayed strikes against her less fleshy hip bone area, as I did with you to good effect. As you can see, I am just laying the tawse on her bottom to see where exactly is the most effective spot to hit on her right buttock so that the ends wrap around to provide the essential second impact. Now, watch and listen carefully, Emily, to see if I have got this right."

Stones drew back his right arm and brought the tawse down fast and hard. Emily's view was mainly of Melanie's screwed up features as she jerked her head up and loudly hollered into her face. The double slap was clear though as the split ends wrapped around Melanie's cheek to slap into her thigh at the bonier part of her hip. The wobbling of Melanie's immense buttocks gave a mark of respect to the stroke but the repeat in exactly the same spot gave Stones the ultimate acknowledgement as, although Melanie's scream was sensational, her physical reaction was to actually lift the punishment desk off the floor as never before. Her howling continued unabated for so long that Stones decided another stroke was the best way to interrupt it. This time he stepped back and, with an unerringly accurate stroke, landed the blow centrally on her left cheek so that the ends curled into her anal cleft, the very tip just brushing her anus. A slightly lower aim brought the same response: a bright red mark across her buttock and a real sting in the tail! The table seemed to have a life of its own as Melanie showed her strength by lifting and crashing it down. Stones went low for two quick strokes and, if Melanie thought she seen and felt the worst, then when the split ends caught her lower vaginal lips, she probably thought again! Stones played the remaining strokes straightforward across any remaining white skin that was visible, turning it a bright, glowing red and provoking further shrieks of agony.

"I think that may well have achieved my objective, Emily. So, just your final strokes and we are done. Relax, Melanie, try and control your caterwauling, it is actually all over for you, my dear."

As Stones laid the tawse on Emily's left cheek, she tightened visibly, having realised that the next stroke was going to be aimed to allow the split ends to whip round her under cheeks and into the valley beneath where her unprotected pussy and arsehole would be the obvious recipient of the leather lips.

The professor's taunting voice confirmed what he was sure she had already worked out.

"Of course, Emily, you must have known that this would be your fate. Just so you are prepared and you can judge how successful my aim is, one stroke should wrap round to tickle your anus and the second stroke should tickle your fancy, so to speak. Give or take a letter, I suppose."

He cackled with laughter at his own wit, his audience not joining in the merriment. One being too distressed still to care and the other concentrating on how she was going to deal with the next couple of lashes. Not that Stones intended to make her wait long as he drew back the tawse and watched the beautiful bottom before him as Emily tightened her muscles, causing the cheeks to go taut, her arsehole squeezing shut. He bided his time until she naturally relaxed and whipped the tawse down, watching with delight as the main body landed perfectly across her left cheek before the whiplash of the split ends followed the curve of her buttock into her cleft, the very top of one prong catching her anal hole centrally. Emily screeched, bucked and swore profusely. The action was repeated immediately as Stones went lower, the sensitive lowest part of her left cheek taking the main crack of the tawse a split second before the tip flicked round and down and Emily's pussy felt the sharp sting.

"Oh, fucking hell, no, no, no. No fucking more please, Professor. That is so painful. Sorry for the language sir but fuck me, that hurts! Ooooh! Ooooh!"

Her writhing and twisting added to the screams were a satisfactory response and he was prepared to overlook her crudity in the circumstances. He raised the tawse again and struck Emily's buttocks three times, once centrally and twice on her left cheek, with the split ends whipping her high on the side of the thigh. She screamed again but Stones was well aware that she had already taken the money-winning shots as far as they were both concerned and he was happy that she had paid her dues so he uncuffed her immediately, convinced that her recovery would be quicker than Melanie's.

"Wow, Professor Stones, that is a nasty little bugger, isn't it?"

She always had the ability to make Stones smile and she had done it again.

"Emily Govan, you really are my golden nugget, the gift that keeps on giving," he said as he knelt between her legs and found himself basically talking to her most intimate places mere inches away from his face. He noted the swollen labial lips and red arsehole with a nod of contentment. The rest of her buttocks were red and swollen but she seemed reasonably unconcerned as she stretched her body, now free of the shackles that bound her for the beating.

"Release Melanie and take her through to the ice bath in the bidet for ten minutes, then we will give her a nice, soothing massage with my special cream. *You* can bear the effect with no assistance, of course."

Fifteen minutes later, Melanie lay flat on his chaise longue with him massaging and working cream into one buttock while Emily did the same to the other, all three enthralled with the application of the cream. Stones enjoyed immensely the opportunity to fondle and massage the pliable and smooth layers of Melanie's buttock under the guise of showing care and compassion and could see from Emily's vibrant face that she was also enjoying herself. Melanie, meanwhile, was clearly as relaxed as she had ever been since she crossed his threshold and Stones had to remind himself that he was close to crossing the lines he had set himself when dealing with undergraduates.

"I think it is about time we looked at helping you with your issues, Melanie. Much as I think your bottom is a delight and a thing of absolute beauty, there can be no doubt that for health, as well as self-esteem and self-confidence reasons, you could do with losing a few pounds. So, let's have you on my bathroom scales, young lady."

Melanie reluctantly heaved her body from the chaise longue to follow Stones and Emily into the bathroom and onto the scales, bemoaning her weight and figure. Stones needed to prod her to make the step onto the weighing platform and her face began to colour immediately as he moved to see the digital display.

"One hundred and forty kilograms, Melanie. Own it, young lady, do not look so embarrassed. It is not a surprise is it, after all? You know you are carrying substantial excess weight, you know it is unhealthy and you know it is down to you to do something about it. So, it is no surprise, is it? You are clinically obese, but that is it, Melanie. It is your call, you are beautiful, your body is awesome and you are a lovely, kind and well-rounded young lady, but your weight is an issue. Now would you like us to be your supporters in tackling this? Because I think I could speak on behalf of Emily when I say that we will give you the encouragement required to guide you along the path you choose to take."

Emily was nodding along enthusiastically, her eyes alive with the idea of this joint enterprise, and Stones hoped that her heart was in the right place for the right reasons.

"Oh my, wow, sir. I mean that would be truly awesome. Do you mean that, sir? Emily?"

Stones just raised his eyebrows whilst Emily was carrying on with her manic nodding!

"You understand that what I am suggesting is a program that we will work out with Elizabeth, our head of health, which we will agree with you. My input will be to encourage you by using corporal punishment to ensure that you comply with an agreed set of rules regarding your weight loss. In fact, as a final piece of your punishment, you can both go and stand in the corner, noses to the wall, hands on head, red rosy buttocks on display while I set things up with Elizabeth. Move, ladies, move."

The two moved obediently and quickly to opposite corners with opposite demeanours, Melanie with apprehension and unease back in her expression, Emily with a skip in her step and a big smile.

A flurry of communication between Stones and Elizabeth resulted in a harumph of satisfaction and a clicking of his fingers to bring the two students back before him.

"Melanie, you have a meeting to arrange with Elizabeth and a nutritionist colleague whom she will invite to chat to you. In addition, you will commit in writing to follow a disciplinary route to encourage your compliance. I have agreed a set of figures that Elizabeth recommends, subject to the nutritionist's approval. Are you happy to follow our guidance?"

Melanie's pleasures and gratification bubbled over.

"I don't know what to say, Professor. Of course, of course, of course. No one has ever cared like this before."

She broke down, huge sobs racking her large frame as a grinning

Emily wrapped her arms around her.

The professor spoke into his computer console and a voice-activated program hummed into being.

"At your request, you will visit me once a fortnight on my command via email. Emily will attend whilst still in college and still under my management. You will arrive having done the necessary ablutions so you are ready for a caning if required. You will take your clothes off and present yourself naked to be weighed on the scales. If you have not lost 2 kilos since your previous weighing or a minimum of 4 kilos in the month, you will bend over and present your buttocks for, at the very least, a 12-stroke caning. You may request more if you feel that you have let yourself down and are consumed by guilt. You will never receive less than 12 other than zero for a successful period achieved. You may stop the arrangement, in writing, at any point. I would presume that this would be at a time when your weight has fallen to a level that you find acceptable. This is at your request and for your benefit. We will merely assist and encourage you in your aims. You will express your gratitude for the assistance of myself and my young capable assistant here. PRINT!" he commanded his equipment.

Handing the printed sheet to the still tearful student, he indicated his desk where paper and pen awaited.

"Separately, you still need to write and thank me for carrying out our remedial punishment today, as you do too, Emily, if you could unravel your naked bodies from each other. I assume that you wish to thank us for committing ourselves, our time, effort and dedication to your improvement, do you not?"

"Oh God, yes, sir, of course, sir. I am really grateful to you both. It just, er, it just bloody hurts, sir, beyond my wildest nightmares, if you'll excuse my language," Melanie said with the merest hint of a smile.

"I forgive you the swearing as the intent was to stress a point, with a little humour creeping in, I am pleased to see, rather than being blasphemous in anger. On the whole, you have taken your punishment well, your buttocks and legs are sufficiently blistered as to cause you a fair deal of ongoing pain and discomfort over the coming days. The punishment was delivered with considerable force, hence the requirement for my younger and more powerful friend to attend to help us out in this matter, due to having to combat the protective cushioning provided by your layers of surplus fat."

Melanie winced at his words and Stones stepped forward and raised her chin with a finger.

"No, young lady, do not shrink away from this. You are overweight, own it. It is your body and it is no business of anyone else if it does not affect them adversely in any way. I keep stressing that you are also a pleasant and intelligent young lady with a clear sense of right and wrong. You are charming, with a lovely personality, you have indicated a clear sense of personal responsibility and I believe you to be a kind and thoughtful young woman. In my eyes, that makes you beautiful. Your inability to accept a compliment without going bright red with embarrassment is also delightful but on the negative side suggests that we have some work to do in this college to ensure that you leave our care with your head held high and an inner belief and strength that we will find and nurture. Now, get over to the desk, sit your very sore and absolutely delightful bottom down, and get writing. I have total faith that you can put into words what you need to, so get scribbling and once you have fulfilled your obligations there to my satisfaction, we will discuss next moves."

Melanie was almost beaming with joy; her heart fluttered and love for her tormentor filled the air. Stones sighed but knew that this was an established pattern with some of his miscreants and there was little he could do to stem that yearning for now. He had ideas that he could improve her lot considerably and was happy to take her under his wing. He noted with interest and self-satisfaction the envy portrayed on Emily's face; he knew his crack about her position working with him would have hit home as much as the sting of the strap but it suited him to ensure that she did not get over-confident about her role.

"Emily, you let yourself down badly today but you have been punished severely and have made a genuine effort to make amends. You are Melanie's mentor, now, in her health program. I assume you are willing to accept that role?"

"Oh, what? Too right, Professor. Melanie is going to kick arse on this task and I'll be behind her all the way." She winked at a delighted Melanie.

Stones fixed her with a warning stare.

"As her mentor then you will, of course, receive the same punishment as Melanie if you fail at any stage. That goes without saying."

Emily hesitated for barely a moment but recovered very quickly to answer.

"Yes, sir, indeed. Goes without saying, as you said."

"Good girl, now park your bottom and get writing, please."

For once, Stones reflected later, he really would be pleased if he never had to take an instrument of punishment to a particular student's bottom again. Admittedly, the fact that the plan meant that Melanie would be displaying her – currently – considerable assets to him regularly was a definite bonus, he happily pondered. The beauty of it would be that, as he now had her completely under his control, she would undoubtedly be stripping naked for him most willingly and proudly. *A good day's work all round*, he thought.

CHAPTER 7

IN WHICH SARA MEETS

EL PRESIDENTE

Sara was pleased to hear that Jamie had agreed, without hesitation, to Professor Stones' suggestion that she should accompany him to the next meeting of the Bondage and Domination Society (BADS) and undergo the initiation process. As the final part of her punishment for her high-level rule breaking, Stones had intimated that Sara needed to volunteer to undergo initiation and put herself forward to being treated as a prospective submissive, and thereby become a sex slave for the duration of a forthcoming session.

Sara had already told Jamie that, despite the horrendous punishment and humiliation she had so far been subjected to, she would not feel forgiven by Professor Stones until she had fully atoned for her sins to his satisfaction. When pushed, she had admitted that the prospect of submitting herself to unknown degradation absolutely terrified her, however, the thought that Jamie and Professor Stones would witness whatever she had to undergo turned her on immensely.

The final part of her punishment was supposed to teach her how to deal with her sexual proclivities and desires by opening her mind to depraved behaviour in a controlled environment. Sara was not convinced that this was not a subterfuge designed by Professor Stones to both humiliate her and arouse him. She had seen the excitement in his eyes at first hand when he had thrashed her and Jenny, and was convinced that his punishment regime served a dual purpose in maintaining success through discipline, surely more severe than it needed to be, as well as satisfying a personal and deep fetish. However, she was prepared to do absolutely anything to win his approval, and gain some sort of redemption in his eyes for what had turned out to be a most monumentally disastrous sexual liaison with Jenny. At times, looking back, she found it hard to regret her actions as she knew that the relationship she had participated in with Jenny had helped transform her and open up her sexuality in a way that had brought her sexual enlightenment. Sara was convinced that without Jenny there would have been no linkup with Jamie, and as she believed that Jamie was the best thing that had ever happened to her, how could she regret it? She realised that the payback had been phenomenally distressing and painful, the loss of face and threat to her career notwithstanding, but Jamie had stood beside her, and both her line manager Dr Ford and the college mistress Professor Bellingham seemed keen on her retaining her college position. Sara had realised early on that there was a sexual undertone to the whole punishment ritual at the college but accepted that it appeared to be discreet and, certainly on the surface, a policy that had contributed to producing an outstanding and impressive success rate as far as high-level qualifications and future development of its graduating students went.

Sara and Jamie had spent hours talking about the circumstances that had led to her being in this vulnerable position and both of them had agreed and accepted that these strange goings-on and her reprehensible behaviour had pre-empted the gradual evolution and betterment of their developing relationship. Both of them were honest about their sexual proclivities with each other and their burgeoning love seemed to Sara to become more sealed and strengthened each day that they were together. Sara's thrashings had, in retrospect, been well-deserved and something that she viewed as part of her emotional and physical growth. She accepted that in the aftermath, and even during breaks in her chastisement, she had been monumentally aroused and turned on, so the consequences of that led her to accept that she had masochistic tendencies and an inclination towards submissive conduct. Jamie, to her relief, found this quite life-affirming and had opened up in response, telling her his own secrets and blending their emotions together in a way that she had never experienced with partners in her previous relationships. She had no false memories of the pain and distress that the individual strokes of Professor Stones' various implements of punishment had delivered. At the time, they had hurt, and hurt like hell, she acknowledged, but the sense of relief and freedom that the retribution had given her was immense, and so unbelievably uplifting that she regretted not a single stroke that had landed on her flesh.

So the day had come, as agreed, when she would attend her initiation ceremony at the Bondage and Domination Society, with a view to taking a role as Jamie's personal submissive at future meetings, the invitation to the next full day's party (only days away) being dependent on her successfully passing her initiation and winning the chairperson, El Presidente's, approval. Sara had been quick to reassure Jamie when he had privately told her he was unhappy and that maybe he had been too quick to support the professor's plan to further punish her through participation in the fetish society's activities.

"Look, my lovely," she had declared. "You really enjoy spanking and flogging female bottoms and I love watching and participating. You know I enjoy a good spanking and the thought and anticipation of a harsher thrashing excites me no end, even if the pain at the actual moment of the experience terrifies me to bits. Yes, it hurts like fuck but the feeling afterwards of being debased, humiliated and stripped bare of all defences and the total loss of dignity is like being on a wondrous and liberating emotional rollercoaster. It is strangely empowering and satisfying to be taken to the depths of your resilience and pride, and I am happy to share this with you, my love."

Sara could see that her words had moved her lover considerably and her heart pulsed fast as she moved towards him and into his arms.

"Whatever you have done in the past, my love, is history to me. You are mine now and I am yours. Let's see what excitement this is going to bring to our lives; if it is with you, for you or because of you, then I accept and welcome whatever we come up against ..."

Jamie found himself unable to continue as in seconds Sara had slid down his body and released his semi-hard cock from his trousers and was running her lips gently over his helmet as the large penis grew rapidly to its full and proud size. She gradually drew the massive column of flesh deep into her mouth, the tip of her tongue flicking along the complete length as his hands went to her head to urge her on. His breathing became heavy as he urged her head and began to thrust his hips as he started to fuck her mouth. She sucked harder, one hand snaking around his hips as her fingers delved into his tight cleft and sought out his arsehole; his hand joined hers, his fingers dripping with saliva as he opened himself to lubricate the way for her. She pushed a finger in deep as she sucked down hard on his thrusting cock, the fingers in her hair tightening as her face now thumped against his stomach. His pace accelerated and she felt the twitch as his cock discharged, the spunk flowing down her throat as he gave her his bitter offering, filling her mouth as his erection gave her his essence and he emptied into her. As his rapidly shrinking member slipped out of her mouth and his spunk dribbled down her chin, she looked up at his face and her heart melted as she saw the love and pure joy in his eyes.

Sara knew that, ultimately, she was a possessive person, twinned with her inclination towards a jealous heart, and so did not want to share him with anyone, let alone a roomful of deviants and fetish-lovers. But she had resolved to do whatever it took to satisfy Professor Stones that her absolution and contrition were complete. In addition to that, she was worried that if she forbade Jamie from spending time at this ruddy society then it could rebound badly on their relationship. She was confident that, as he had promised her, he would stop going rather than risk losing her, but she suspected it would be with reluctance, so she had taken the only course she could see that would satisfy them both. She accepted that she had to pass her "audition". Jamie said it was an initiation ceremony but Stones had made it clear that she would be virtually on trial, so she felt it was definitely a test that she must pass. It was tonight, and she was determined that she would not let the professor or Jamie down, and that there was no humiliation or pain she could be on the end of that she hadn't already experienced in the prolonged punishment sessions she had already had. Sara was well aware that if all went well tonight, then she would be going with the two men to a fetish party on Saturday afternoon and that she had agreed her repentance would be complete if she complied with the professor's less than subtle suggestion that she be taken as Jamie's trainee slave for the duration of their time at the country manor where it was to be held. In truth, she was as excited as she was apprehensive at the prospect of being put out to offers from other members of the club as part of her initial visit. Professor Stones had made it obvious to Jamie, deliberately in her hearing she was certain, that he had some unfinished business with three female members and that Sara might be a useful component for their denouement at some point during the weekend. It was clear that Stones called the shots and his intimation that Sara would be left in his hands while Jamie dealt with the three submissives to begin with had irked her but she had managed to quell any reaction. For a few hours she could put up with what they had to offer and she was well aware that there was a part of her sexual being that craved depravity, debasement and punishment. She suspected that the professor had recognised this in her very early on and now was enjoying making her face up to the reality of her perverse mind. Jamie had told her most earnestly that he would quit the society if it looked like causing difficulties with his relationship with either her or her career. Sara had not hesitated in saying that she would rather join in and enjoy the society with him than be the cause of him losing out on his sexual adventures. She had told him that she had no problem with his love of spanking and flogging and that she would enjoy watching and participating to a degree. Her caveat had been that he could save his extreme thrashings for others as long as she was aware of what he was up to and that he saved his cock for her. He, in turn, had said that he would love her to come to club events but only on the condition that her pussy and arsehole were to be off-limits to other members, although he had stipulated that this rule could only apply after Professor Stones was satisfied that Sara had paid her dues and her slate was clean as far as her college standing went. Sara had secretly felt that this was the opportunity to be the best of both worlds for the two of them, and much as the extreme punishment thrashings that she had received from the professor had distressed her and gone far beyond what she would classify as comfortable pain, she accepted that she had submissive tendencies and was sexually aroused by the thought of being punished. While she accepted that her role at the college meant that she would have generally a much lower level involvement in student castigation than Jamie, she could not help but be slightly jealous of his access to more dubious activities as far as the opposite sex went. His partnership with the college's venerable Dean of Discipline, Professor Stones, allowed him so much free reign to view and study young naked females, let alone whip their bottoms raw red, that she felt that membership of the society was a way of keeping some sort of equilibrium in their relationship as far as the more kinky practices took them on their joint sexual journey. So, the path had been set and now they were about to make their way to the room above the pub where Sara was to be presented to the society and to undergo the president's approval and initiation session. Jamie had talked her through his own trial evening and she had heard nothing to scare or horrify her. He had assured her that any beating, depraved behaviour or humiliation would fall short of what she had undergone and survived already! In truth, Sara was as excited as she was apprehensive and now just wanted to get things going.

Two hours later, they had arrived at the pub; essential introductions had been conducted and Sara had been escorted to the private room upstairs that the society used for its committee meetings, bi-monthly catch-ups and the occasional initiation ceremonies.

"Welcome to my lair, young lady." The formidable president of the fetish club, known by her society name as El Presidente, or Pres for short, ominously introduced herself.

"So, you have been put forward and recommended for acceptance into our little society by both our eminent former president, known here by his pseudonym Professor, and our young friend known here as Porter. In theory, then, it is a done deal, just the formalities to go through and you will be welcomed as one of us, and your invitation to our Saturday gathering will be rubber-stamped. I do understand that you have been nominated to go through a submissive's new entry session, the details of which are to be determined between myself, Professor and Porter, your owner, of course." Pres paused and looked deep into Sara's eyes as if challenging her to raise issue.

Sara had been well-tutored in the ways of the society by both Stones and Jamie, had accepted her role and knew that her compliance over the two days would supposedly absolve her in the eyes of Stones and the college hierarchy. She nodded eagerly in response and then dropped her eyes in a show of respect and obedience, in the manner that Jamie had tutored her.

"It will be my honour to be given these opportunities, El Presidente," she quietly responded.

Sara was fairly certain that this confident, intimidating and Amazonian-looking woman had the power to make her do anything she damn well liked and she most definitely was not feeling the slightest desire to contradict or open any sort of debate with her.

"In that case we had better give you the once over, then. I understand that your society name is tendered as Serf and I formally accept that as an appropriate and admissible pseudonym. Serf, you will remain here, as will Professor. Porter, please go and have a drink with our friends downstairs while I take a few moments to put Serf through her paces and fully initiate her into the club. Serf, remove your clothes please and let us have a look at you properly before we start proceedings."

Sara took one long intake of air and then disrobed quickly, folded her clothes and faced Pres with her hands on her head and her legs apart, trying to ignore the fact that she, alone, was naked.

"I hope this is satisfactory, mistress," she murmured demurely.

Sara was totally overawed by the substantial, imposing woman in front of her, who now proceeded to walk slowly around her, peering intently at her naked body from head to toe. Professor Stones had taken a seat at the side of the room and Sara was conscious of his eyes, too, running over her body. At least she had nothing to hide from him – he had had close contact with just about every bit of her body during the punishment sessions and had seen her howl, sob and beg for forgiveness, as well as expose every part of her most intimate places. She felt that she should be comfortable under his gaze but did not feel comfortable in the least!

She jolted as she felt the first contact of Pres's hands as they so gently ran over her bottom.

"Certainly looks and feels satisfactory, and these are nice too."

Pres moved her hands seamlessly up and around Sara's body, then cupped her breasts, engulfing her in a huge bear hug, her fingertips closing on her nipples, swiftly making them erect.

"Hello!" Pres exclaimed as she squeezed Sara's nipples hard. "Someone is horny already. Or should I more correctly say someone else? Because I can feel my juices starting to flow now I have seen the full beauty of you. I think we are going to have a fun time together, my little flower. Now I think we should get straight to get things underway with your spanking, so come with me."

Pres pulled Sara over to the large, oak wood high-backed chair in the centre of the room and settled her substantial rear down. With a jerk of her arm, she had Sara sprawling over her lap, fixing her firmly in position with her left arm. Sara grabbed at the chair legs, her face inches from the floor and tried to empty her mind and prepare herself for what was about to come. Instead of the expected hard stinging slap, she felt Pres's hands again as she caressed her cheeks, delicately running fingers around and over her cleft and then letting them slip into the valley, slide down to her exposed labia lips and tickle the damp surface. Sara sighed, relaxing, enjoying the intimate contact and accepting completely this turn of events. Pres tickled, stroked and aroused her for several minutes, her expert fingers working into her vagina as Sara lifted her flanks eagerly to allow Pres further and easier access to her sex.

"Oh, you are so wet, Serf. Now, I must not get distracted." Her hand suddenly came away from Sara's pussy and slammed down on her unprepared bottom. She jolted and bit down on her bottom lip, determined not to show any weakness this early on in the experience. Sara steeled herself as Pres's large hand proved to be almost the equal of Professor Stones or her lover, Jamie, and begun a full-blooded assault on her backside. The meaty slaps had soon turned Sara's bottom from white to pink to red, and continued as she resolutely held her dignity and kept her silence apart from a few stifled moans.

Thankfully the barrage stopped and Sara felt a large hand sliding under her flanks and a single digit tweaking her clitoris expertly as other fingers delved between the folds covering her vagina to her moist warm interior.

"Nice," whispered Pres huskily as she removed her hands and sucked at her fingers. "Lovely, lovely. What sweet juices you have, my dear. Oh yum, yum, yum."

Pres then wiped her fingers down the open cleft of Sara's bottom and fluttered and hovered over her arsehole. As Sara held her breath, a single fingertip tenderly stroked around her anal ring, just brushing the puckered rose and teasing the twitching opening. Sara was incredibly aroused; the spanking had been at the level that she found turned her on immensely, and the intimacy of a female hand impacting on her buttocks had made her so wet that she knew that she was already close to orgasm. She was unsure as to whether or not she was ready to have her most secret and private of places breached but she was determined that she would do her best to go with the flow, to ensure that she did not fail or disappoint the professor in any way. Pres, however, did not attempt to penetrate but just worked her finger gently around her ring, causing Sara to relax completely and allow herself to enjoy the pleasant sensations she was experiencing. As one hand continued to tickle and caress her arsehole, Pres's second hand slid under her stomach and fingers soon delved to work their magic between Sara's legs. She succumbed totally to her expert touch, the movement of a true exponent of the art, and her breathing quickened perceptively as she started to rock her lower body against the hand in her pussy.

"Oh, yes. Yes. Yes. Fuck, yes. Oh yes. Fuck! Yes. Give it to me. Yes. Yes. Yes. I am going to come. Yes. I'm coming. Yes. Fuck! Fucking fuck fuck! Here we go. Aaaaaaarrgggggghhhh!!! Yes! Yes! Ooooooooo! Yes, my beauty. Yes. Yes. Oh yes."

Sara's climax was explosive and long, her body wracked with pleasure. Her hands grasped at the carpet, her feet thudded rhythmically on the floor and her bottom arched high as she lost all control. Pres tightened her hold, struggling to keep her fingers ensconced in her pussy as Sara jerked and shook dramatically in her passion.

"Good girl. Was that nice, Serf?" Pres's voice was husky and Sara snapped alert, knowing that this was a very sexual beast holding her and she would have her own needs that might need tending to.

"Oh yes, thank you. Mistress, that was lovely, thank you so much for giving me such a treat. Please can I now do something for you to express my gratitude for the pleasure you have given me?"

Sara was very much relying on her experience with Jenny that had led her here in the first place. She was well-tutored in the words of subservience and put on her most coquettish and coy expression as she turned to face Pres, doing her best considering she was naked with a bright red, spanked bottom and having just orgasmed in her newly acquired acquaintance's lap. She desperately tried to avoid looking over at the watching Professor Stones; she really had no idea what he expected from her but assumed that anything that pleased Pres was ticking boxes for him as well. It was beginning to feel to Sara that this man had infiltrated every aspect of her personal life and she knew she should resent how exposed and unveiled she found herself before him. That she felt no such emotion towards him was a mystery that she did not want to dwell on for long. He had seen her beaten, shamed, humiliated, used and tormented, he had seen every private detail of her body, he had touched her in a way only a lover should, yet she felt no antipathy towards him, only a ridiculous desire to earn his forgiveness and approval. There was something about him that was magnetic and all-consuming and she knew that, like a lot of women who had gone before, she had fallen under his spell.

"Well," said Pres, after what seemed an age to Sara, who was aware that she was holding her breath, awaiting her answer with a mixture of trepidation and aroused expectation. "I'm open to suggestion. What exactly did you have in mind?" She released Sara who slid off her lap and knelt at the feet of the fearsome looking woman with an impassive face.

"If it pleases you, Mistress, why don't you remove those clothes and let me see what I can think of to earn your approval?" Sara hoped her tone was as respectful as she was aiming to be, and she waited with bated breath for the response. A quick glance aside at Stones was met with that penetrating impassive stare that she knew only too well.

"Nice idea but not for today. There will be plenty of time at Castle Hall during the weekend for you to undergo the full works so let us leave it until then. We do not want to do anything that might spoil the fun on the day of atonement that Professor has planned for you. I have been hearing what a naughty little girl you have been. I imagine your backside will be on fire by the end of the weekend, my love, so I will have first pickings before too much damage is done to these lovely sweet cheeks."

With that, Pres pushed her away and turned her back on her, before addressing Professor Stones.

"Take her away and get the formalities completed, Professor; she has your approval so this was a formality, anyway. She's acceptable – sign her up."

She grabbed Sara under the chin and kissed her deeply, her tongue probing around the inside of her willing mouth, before leaving her with the words that she would keep constantly in her mind as the days dragged towards the weekend.

"I look forward to having the full works from you my sweet; now get dressed and go with Professor to get you all signed up, then you can have a drink and relax for this evening."

Sara hardly relaxed but the evening at least held no further surprises or much in the way of conversation of a sexual nature; but she knew the landscape had been established and that what was ahead was going to test her resolve in many ways.

The weekend was only days away and she and Jamie had agreed that they would abstain from any sort of intimate contact in the build-up and would practise addressing each other by their club names. Jamie had talked her through the rules that they would need to play by, and the importance of sticking to their chosen monikers in front of other club members. Not that any of this talk prevented Sara from masturbating furiously in the shower on the Thursday evening as she fantasized about the thought of seeing Pres in all her naked glory. Much as she felt that in her relationship with Jamie she had discovered her one true love and that her indiscretions with Jenny, which had led her to the trouble she was in, were just a fleeting fascination with lesbian love, she could not deny that her desire was ignited by certain members of the same sex. The thought of feasting on Pres's substantial flesh kept intruding into her mind as she willed the hours to pass.

The drive to Castle Hall proved most educational for Sara, as Jamie attempted to prime and ready her for what he referred to her as an experience unlike anything she would have partaken in before or even imagined. Sara rather felt that her sex life with Jenny and then Jamie and the introduction into the world of college discipline would have surely prepared her for anything that this weekend had to offer, but Jamie was insistent that she listen to his words of caution and ready herself for a sexual world beyond her imagination.

The setting of Castle Hall was most impressive and Sara was almost lulled into believing that they were on a luxurious, romantic weekend break as they strolled in the grounds before lunching in a delightful conservatory amongst what appeared to be your everyday collection of reasonably well-to-do folk just enjoying their freedom and the facilities on offer. However, as they showered and dressed in the outfits that Jamie had brought along, Sara could sense his mood changing as 2 o'clock approached, the striking of which would signal that the 'occasion' was under way. Sara's outfit was a twin-set consisting of a leather, split-side, short skirt, a leather top with flaps hanging – barely – over her breasts, strapped at the back, and slip-on leather sandals; no knickers included. Jamie wore leather shorts with flaps cut into the back and front with a clasp underneath to enable total access; he too had leather sandals. His shirt had long sleeved cuffs with tight loops attached which, as he explained to Sara patiently, would allow him somewhere to sheaf any accessories he wished to carry. His raised eyebrows suggested to Sara that this was not really her concern and she would likely be soon enough aware of their exact function!

Sara allowed herself to be led rather meekly to the main hall. They were early so there was little going on. She quickly assessed the room: a large main floor with lots of alcoves and minor rooms leading off. At the end of the room stood a prominent stairwell leading down and a flashing red neon sign indicating that this was the way to the 'Basement of Baseness'. As they wandered through the room where little groups of people in various stages of undress, similar to themselves, were chatting, hugging or lightly petting already, a tug on her arm alerted Sara to the realisation that they were heading for the basement stairway. Her heart sank; Jamie had alluded to the basement area in hushed tones and she knew that this was where some of the most seriously depraved actions took place. In the gloom at the bottom of the stairs she could see arrows highlighting the way towards the punishment area and she sighed disconsolately as Jamie led her to a corner of the room where Pres awaited.

As Pres threw off the long leather cape she was wearing, Sara finally had a close up view of the woman's huge breasts and, as promised by Jamie during a period of teasing, the largest nipples and aureole that she had ever seen. Sara was mesmerised by the sheer size of her voluminous orbs before tearing her eyes away to sweep down, her eyes feasting on the forest of pubic hair that covered her pussy. Jamie had told her that she oozed sex from every pore and Sara was certainly aware of a body scent that was primitive and blatantly sexual. Sara could not stop herself was noisily breathing in the strong and erotic sexual aroma. Her words of welcome turned Sara's legs to jelly.

"My dear Serf, unfinished business I think. I get first dibs before the hordes get to ravage and savage your delightful body. Get that ridiculous garb off and let us get started. The day is long and I have a full agenda."

Sara felt a soft pulse of fear in her gut. Her nervous energy as they had counted the hours down to this day had driven them both slightly mad but thankfully Jamie had always been able to talk her through her anxiety and nervous energy. Her expectations of what would happen and how she would cope were very conflicted; sometimes her fear won out and she would almost beg Jamie to find her a way out of this absurd situation, but other times she was so excited, so turned on, so sexually ready, that it frightened her. Part of her had decided that this weekend might well define her and her whole future, something that both scared and exhilarated her.

Her reverie was broken as Jamie prompted her.

"Clothes off, Serf, you are a submissive due for punishment now. Do not shame me, please. Hands on head, eyes to the floor, you disgusting piece of filth," he ordered, instantly switching to his role as her owner. To Pres, he added:

"As discussed, thank you, Pres. Do what you will and let me know if you require my input or assistance at any point. Otherwise, I will collect her when she's paid her dues and satisfied the conditions agreed." With that, he walked away without a backward glance at the now rather terrified Sara.

"Right, let us get down to it, my beauty. First, fingers in your fanny and let's see how lubricated you are already." Pres's words were spoken very much like a conversational aside and Sara felt flustered and failed to respond.

Crack!

That failure to immediately obey did not last long as Pres's hand slapped her face hard.

"Immediate compliance is required, sweetheart. Fingers displaying your wanton shame, please."

Sara's hand delved and delivered rather quickly, her face reddening as the fingers she offered showed a wetness to illustrate her readiness for sexual action. For once she was thankful that her usual, bare, naked lust had conquered her fear and reservations.

"Oh lovely, now lick them clean, there's a good girl."

Sara did as she was told as Pres began to fondle her breasts and moved in to kiss her ears. Fingers scratched at her back as this forceful powerhouse of a woman pushed her backwards into one of the small rooms surrounding the main hall and soon had her pinned and spread-eagled against the wall. A knuckle pressed against her clitoris as Sara found her own hand being forced into the mass of Pres's pubic hair and into her wet, swampy fanny beneath. Sara felt helpless as the far stronger, dominant woman began to rub herself against her own unresisting body and was powerless to resist, even if she had dared, when she was thrust forward and bent over the stool in the centre of the room. In a moment, her legs were akimbo as Pres forced her face into Sara's groin and she felt the long tongue sliding into her wetness. Despite the anxiety the situation was causing her, Sara felt her willing body respond and involuntarily pushed herself back into Pres's face, her bottom crack opening to allow the nose of her controller to nudge into the dark, tight back orifice. A creaking noise snapped Sara's eyes open and she realised that a few people had quietly entered the room to watch proceedings. As Pres's lips clamped and sucked on her clit, two young men approached, having removed their scant coverings, and Sara found her head manoeuvred down to accept two erect cocks into her mouth. The act of doing so combined with Pres's expert cunnilingus was enough to start Sara's first orgasm and she sucked greedily on the fleshy swords that rubbed against each other in her stretched mouth. As she shuddered and groaned in the grip of her climax, her body was abruptly vacated and she was twisted around.

"My turn now," said Pres as she dismissed her recent accomplices with a dismissive wave and turned to present Sara with a first sight of her enormous bottom. As if by an unseen, magnetic force, her hands immediately grasped the surprisingly firm and beautifully rounded buttocks. Pres, unasked, bent over, opened her legs and clasped her ankles, proudly displaying her gorgeous buttocks at their best, now taut and parted, displaying a continuous growth of black, curly hairs with a pinky-brown arsehole just peeping out of the centre of her dark valley. Moments later, the giant buttocks were inches from Sara's face and as she placed tentative kisses on the smooth flesh of the mesmerising globes, she reached her hands round to fondle the colossal, hanging breasts. Sara understood in that moment the fascination that this woman held for Jamie: her sexual allure was so erotic and arousing that Sara found herself wanting to do whatever it took to make this wonderful person happy. She wrapped her arms around Pres's middle and began to lick the naked bottom before her, lips and tongue sliding up and down and round and round, exploring the sturdy but silky-soft, protruding buttocks. Buttocks that were far firmer than she had expected, buttocks that had Sara involuntarily licking her lips as she breathed her scent in, loving the pure ooze of sexual lust and readiness that came from her. Her tongue began to flick out and lick the dank hole that was offered so blatantly; her lips sucked and her teeth nipped little slivers of skin and pulled at the mass of black curly hairs surrounding her centre. Sara was enraptured, the size of the bottom at her mercy was almost overwhelming, and she found herself just wanting to bury her face into the fleshy paradise of the welcoming cleft. Dropping to her knees, Sara's hands moved to pull Pres's inner thighs apart to display fully the large wet folds of her pussy, her labial lips exposed completely and glistening with the juices of her arousal, the sweaty, earthy smell of her open orifices filling Sara's nostrils. She pushed her face into the darkness enveloped easily between Pres's thighs, her tongue lapping at the lower lips of the oozing pussy, her nose seeking out the dank, black hole nestling deep in her cleft. Sara felt a huge hand reach around and force her face deeper into the massive valley of her open buttocks. Suddenly, she was lifted clean off her feet by this immensely powerful woman and without really knowing how, Sara found herself on top in the classic sixty-nine position. Giant hands grasped her flanks and Sara found her pussy engulfed by Pres's open mouth, a huge hand forcing her own head down to the crater between Pres's legs. Knees came up to pin her head and force her face to be almost sucked into the sodden folds beneath her as Pres invaded Sara's own orifices once more, a long tongue deep inside of her pussy and Pres's nose plugging her arsehole completely. Sara automatically started to thrust backwards against her even as she fought to gasp whatever air she could as Pres's own thrusting motions told of her quest for her own satisfaction. Just as Sara thought that she was in danger of being suffocated, fingers grasped her hair and she was unceremoniously yanked her out of the cavernous lower regions of this forceful and fearsome woman, before being plunged down once again into the swamp of her sex.

"Come on, bitch, earn your keep. I want to feel those luscious lips and that slippery tongue on my arsehole. It is time to decorate the back door now, petal, a new lick of paint is required. Come on, mouth open, nice wet sloppy kiss and now give me that tongue. Don't tickle me, sweet, I want it in the letterbox, not knocking on the door. Oh yes, fuck it, that's good, in and out, come on, taste me. Fingers in my fanny, thumb on my clit, my dear. That's it, sweetie, tongue fuck my arse, finger fuck my fanny. Oh my, suck and fuck. Fuck! Fuck!"

Any initial reticence to enter the dark chasm between the woman's monumental buttocks had long gone as Sara embraced the experience and relaxed into the task set. Very much a novice as far as it went with anal play before her liaisons with Jenny and Jamie, she had come to realise and accept that this was a key component of sexual adventure within the new circles she had entered. She could not pretend she had not embraced the experience although she still felt a sense of shame, as well as shock, that her face could be encased between the bottom cheeks of a lover without resistance or hesitation. Sara increased the speed of her finger-frigging as she tried to get Pres to climax as quick as possible, fully aware that the restriction to her ability to breathe was becoming a drawback! With limited oxygen available, Sara was twisting her face to allow her tongue to ease right out of the bitter-tasting dark hole so she could gasp for breath. Pres, however, had a hand on the back of her head giving her limited options and Sara found her face rammed back between the massive dark cleft before her. Sara worked her hand frantically into Pres's pussy, fingers probing and rubbing everywhere they could. Just when she was beginning to think that passing out was a distinct possibility as she slavishly licked, sucked and probed for all she was worth, Pres screamed as her orgasm arrived and she yanked Sara's face from her dark recess.

With her body shuddering all over, Sara found that her task was not completed as Pres issued further instructions.

"I want something substantial in me now that you've greased me up. Fill me up, baby girl, fill me up."

Quickly pushing her thumb into Pres's rear hole while two fingers simultaneously plunged into the sodden pussy, Sara looked around desperately for something of substance to meet Pres's expectations. Her thumb had slipped so easily into the woman's private portal and her fingers felt so insubstantial inside the oozing wet hole that Sara knew she needed artificial help to satisfy this sexual goddess.

"In out, in out. Alternate the thrusts in my holes, come on, Serf, you little slut, fuck me properly. In my fanny and out of my arse, in my arse and out of my fanny. Go on, fuck me slag, fuck me!"

Sarah thrust the heel of her hand hard against Pres's pubic bone and bent and sunk her teeth into a meaty buttock. Her reward was the cessation of the foul language demands and their replacement by a series of grunts and moans. Sara reached up and grabbed a handful of hair as she wedged another finger into Pres's pussy, bringing her face up from her bottom with a smile of triumph, slipping her thumb out to allow her to force a fourth finger up to the knuckle into the sodden pussy. Pres's moans and groans turned into a strangled and guttural cry as her body shuddered and she gave into a climax that took over her whole body. Sara reveled in her growing sense of control over the supposedly more powerful woman. She pulled her hand from the spasming, warm pussy, twisted around and forced it into Pres's mouth.

"Right, bitch, lick me clean. All of them! All of them! Lick them clean of your fanny and arsehole drool, you dirty, smelly cow. Lick them, lick them. Who's the daddy now, bitch!" she chided.

Pres obediently sucked on Sara's fingers, clearly content and happy with the newbie's performance. She looked deeply into Sara's eyes and the penetrating stare had its desired effect as Sara visibly wilted and her sense of control drained away.

"So far so good, Serf," said Pres as she stared up at Sara. "You have done extremely well so far, and I will forgive you your insolence, but let's see what happens when the tables are turned back to where they should be, shall we?"

Sara gulped, fear and apprehension in her face and her wide eyes as Pres reached for her.

"I hear you are a bit of a fruit and vegetable lover."

Sara gasped, eyes now flashing around frantically.

"She told you. The fucking evil bitch Jenny told Professor Stones? That sodding bitch, that fucking mouthy cow. So Jamie knows does he?"

Pres appraised her for a moment before replying.

"The answer, sadly for you, is in the positive, I am afraid. The lesson for you is to be truthful to your loved ones; only deceive those who matter least, the peripheral nonentities not the important confidantes, more to the point. Name breech! Name breech!"

Pres's voice was loud and clear, stunning Sara completely. Pres virtually threw her off, onto the floor, and clambered over her, slapping her face hard. She froze in shock, flat on her back, legs splayed apart, her ears ringing from Pres's meaty slap. She felt a real sense of fear and shock as people from all round the room came over and a chant went up.

"Blaze! Blaze! Blaze! Blaze!"

Pres whispered in her ear.

"You used real names and not club ones. I am afraid that it is a massive offence here. Bend over and grab your ankles quickly to show contrition and invite your punishment."

Sara did not hesitate; she quickly realised that there was no way out of this, and she was going to be badly beaten at some point during the session and now seemed as good a time as any. She was annoyed with herself for her stupid slip of the tongue and could hardly deny that she had not invited this outcome. The chant swelled and, through her legs, Sara could see the crowd part to allow an extremely attractive, well-built man into their midst.

"What's your name, little one?"

Sara felt her heart melt at his silky, sexy voice.

"It is Serf, sir. Oh sir. I am so sorry, I inadvertently let a real name or two slip out. I beg your pardon, sir."

She trembled as he gently felt her buttocks, his hands soft and tender as he intimately stroked her parted cheeks.

"With your permission, Pres, I will deliver a short, sharp shock to remind her that she is guilty of a dereliction of duty. How many of my punishers would you like her to receive?"

Sara was delighted to hear Pres's response that three strokes would suffice. Little did she know that she was now in the hands of the society's foremost dominant, renowned for the sheer power of his strikes with his powerful, fibre-glass, leather-covered switch. She waited, reasonably relaxed, and she held herself still as she sensed him raise his arm behind her. A split second later she found herself crashing to the floor as a cutting strike seared the skin of her bottom and her legs collapsed beneath her. She screeched in agony as the effect of the single most powerful blow she had ever received fully registered. Her hands clasped her bottom cheeks as she wailed, floundering at the feet of her audience before Pres dragged her up by the hair, fiercely slapping the backs of her legs as she did so.

"How dare you besmirch and disrespect me by acting like a novice? Get back into the punishment position and apologise to Blaze immediately, you pathetic wimp."

"Oh oh oh oh. I am so sorry. Fuck! Fuck! I am so sorry, Pres, so very sorry, Master Blaze. So sorry. Oh my, it hurts, oh fuck. Fuck! Fuck! Sorry. Sorry."

Sara struggled back into position, her legs trembling and tears dropping from her eyes to the floor as she registered the tittering and enjoyment of her disgrace by the watching audience.

"An extra stroke to be applied for outright disobedience and outrageous response to punishment. Apply the next stroke sharply please, Blaze." Pres's words sent a fissure of fear through Sara's body but she presented herself meekly and gritted her teeth as she waited for the disturbance of the air behind her as the switch flew through the air.

"Yaaaargh! Yaaargh! Ah! Ah! Fuck! No! Fuck! Ah! Ah!" Sara held her position by a massive exertion of will power and stubbornness as the tears poured from her tightly clenched eyes and her body trembled and swayed in agony,

"Good girl, good girl. Now, hold on tight for the next stroke. Fire away, Blaze, actually let us have another three of those purple lines. Let's hear her truly scream and shout in her shame and sorrow," Pres egged on Blaze as Sara tried to compose herself for the next strike.

Sara screamed as Blaze applied the next three quick and vicious strokes, all met with her watching audience's approval and delight, a ripple of applause breaking out as Blaze took a step back after his final cut had landed. Tears were hitting the floor below Sara's bent over form, her hands grasping her ankles so tightly that Pres had to gently prise her fingers off.

"A thank you would be the order of the day, if you please, Serf. Up you get, retain a small shred of dignity and act in accordance of the rules you are expected to follow," said Pres, loud and clear to keep the watchers' interest.

A distraught and flummoxed Sara, hands squeezing her buttocks, turned to face Blaze, her mouth opening and closing but her brain struggling to provide the words, weeping and mewing incomprehensibly.

A stinging slap across her face from Pres brought her to full alertness and she managed with a supreme effort to blurt out:

"Waaah! Oh my word. Thank you, thank you, thank you, oooh. Ow! Ouch! Yikes! Oh my bottom, oh my, oh my word. Oh, thank you. Oh oh oh. Sorry, sorry. Thank you, Blaze, oh sorry, Master Blaze, sir."

Pres raised her eyebrows at Blaze in the orchestrated manner suited to their well-practised roles.

"Well, Blaze, is there anything that this vagabond can do to thank you further?"

Blaze's smile sent a shiver through Sara's body as thoughts of flight moved fleetingly through her mind.

Blaze walked around behind her, his fingers running along the raised welts on her bottom.

"Well, it has been a pleasure to stripe such a delectable arse; may I be allowed to kiss this gorgeous trophy?"

"It would be her pleasure. She's about to be put out for public usage and her ribbons will show her limitations and availability; she's top entry only, no low entry but everything else is allowed."

Pres referred to the coloured ribbon and wristband code as she now began to loop the bands around Sara's wrists. Sara acquiesced as she struggled to understand what Pres was referring to, her hopes rising that her beloved Jamie had been able and inclined to limit her availability. Clearly taking pity on Sara, Pres put her mind at rest.

"The colours dictate that no one can penetrate your pussy or arsehole without the permission of myself, Professor or Porter, but I hope you give good head because your mouth is designated 'open for business'. I may well have a little treat for you later but I will keep that to myself for now. Remember, you are adorned with blue ribbons to denote that you are owned but available with your owner's consent. For this purpose, consider Professor and myself to be your co-owners for the day, on loan from Porter. Food for thought, Serf, food for thought." Pres's chuckle as she spoke failed to enlighten Sara as to her plans, but she was somewhat preoccupied by the image that entered her head of the multitude of cocks that might be heading the way of her mouth!

"Obviously you are available for beatings so these beautiful cheeks are going to be rather ravaged by the time everyone is done," Pres continued. "Take my advice, Serf, give great head, take your time and make sure you loudly appreciate any tongues and lips that your holes accommodate. Quite simply, any distraction from a continuous pummeling of your backside will make your sentence far easier to bear. Unless, of course, you really are here to enjoy being flogged. I must say that it did not sound that way from the fuss you made when Blaze gave you a tickle."

Pres's peals of laughter suggested to Sara that she was not expected to contribute a response and she bowed her head submissively. She sensed that Pres was at the end of her session with her and she was soon to be turned over to the gathering hordes of interested and inquisitive watchers. Her fear was heightened, she gulped loudly and tried to control herself as she could feel the overwhelming need to hold onto Pres's presence.

"Oh my days, it is really happening, isn't it? Please do not leave me yet, Pres. Let me pleasure you some more, please. Sit back in the chair, I want to suck your nipples, please."

Pres stared at Sara, who was feeling butterflies from nervousness like never before, desperate to hold onto the contact and connection she had made with this woman whose power and protection she felt completely encompassing her.

A beautiful young black woman who had materialised beside Pres moved to position beside the chair as Pres sat her huge frame into it.

"Allow me to introduce you to Zoo, Serf. Zoo is one of the event maidens, here to assist in ensuring that the evening runs smoothly and on-hand to meet the requests of the senior members. She will oversee your time here and is basically on playground duty. She is available overnight, as she is a slave girl, so if she takes your fancy you may bid for her company later."

Sara's shock was plain to see. She assumed that however this went that, at least, come later her ordeal would end when Professor Stones was satisfied that she had completed this last stage of her punishment. Her thoughts of being in bed later on with Jamie, exchanging tales of their evening's experiences whilst he massaged and soothed away the results of whatever beating she had taken, were part of her focus to get through whatever was in store. Being involved in some kind of auction to win a night with this beautiful young woman, whose beguiling smile she was finding transfixing, had not been any part of that process. Dressed in a black and white apron, cut open to display firm breasts and long, very dark nipples with revealing slits at the front and back that allowed tantalising but fleeting views of her nakedness beneath, the woman oozed sensuality and coy wantonness. They exchanged long, searching gazes and Sara felt a frisson of sexual longing before Pres's bark broke the moment.

"I said that she was a possible option later, not now, bitch. I am waiting to have my tits sucked!"

Sara was quick to obey and almost threw herself onto Pres, her mouth locked onto one long, erect nipple as her left hand grasped the other nipple tightly, her right hand slipping down into the swamp-like, sodden engorged vagina below. It was not to be a long session as Pres began to thrust her groin up into Sara's face before fastening her hands on her head and upping the tempo to an almost violent level. No longer was Sara in control of an act of cunnilingus; her lower face was now just the tool that Pres was using to bring herself off. Completely under the control of the far stronger woman, one moment Sara found her nose slammed into the warm, dripping folds, the next her chin was somewhat rammed against Pres's pubic bone. Sara gasped in breaths when she could as the slime of her controller's juices were rubbed all over her face. It was a relief when Pres came and Sara slurped up as much of her juice as she could, sucking hard on the protruding clitoris as Pres shuddered and jerked in her moment of ecstasy. She pushed Sara to the floor in a disdainful manner, her words to Zoo sending little flutters of terror through Sara's body.

"Strap her down, Zoo. It's time for her to start seeing visitors, I feel. Time for you to be fully open for business, Serf!"

Zoo smiled kindly in support as she guided Sara over to the cushioned contraption that she guessed would be her home for the next few hours. A cross between a massage table and a gymnastic pommel, with supporting struts that held her face down, but with openings cut in allowing access to her breasts and stomach from below. Her buttocks and legs were forced apart and raised up, her ankles cuffed, her face and shoulders supported while her arms hung down, her hands not fastened but with handles to grip. She was basically helpless, her torso with limited movement as straps bound her down, her head propped up and her lower body basically prepared as though to welcome whoever so wished to take advantage, her bottom perfectly presented for beating.

"Have a nice day," were the parting words from Pres as she pulled her leather cloak around her shoulders with a flourish, patted Sara's cheeks gently at both ends and walked away.

Sara watched with fear and fascination as Zoo wheeled over a table containing sex toys and punishment accessories. She twisted her head as members of the watching audience began to move in to surround her, and fingers began to flutter at her pussy and bottom. Zoo had affixed more blue ribbons to the attachments holding her in place and Sara was relieved to hear some muttering of discontent that affirmed she was not to be penetrated vaginally or anally by any of the strangers, some of whom were seriously fondling her pussy lips already.

She tensed as she felt a dildo being wiped up and down her pussy lips, her body reacting immediately to the obvious approval of the group gathered behind her. A woman, dressed as Catwoman, came around to face her and started to place tender little kisses all over her face, before brushing her lips against Sara's own. What Sara did find surprisingly and slightly surreal was the woman kept purring as she nuzzled at Sara. Then a tongue began flicking her lips apart and probing around her teeth as Sara compliantly parted her lips to allow Catwoman to delve deeper inside. As Sara entwined tongues, the action at the other end was becoming more serious. Sara closed her eyes and gave into the sensations that were now coursing through her body as a small vibrator played against her clitoris and a finger rimmed her rear hole tenderly. Instinctively, Sara began to push back to welcome the invaders, her body opening up to accept the pleasures promised from deeper insertions, but to no avail as her assailants minded the instructions that she was off-limits as far as penetration went. However, she was swiftly taken to a climax as Catwoman bent down to nip and suck at her nipples and her accomplices expertly applied themselves to the manipulations that her clitoris, vulva and arsehole required to take her to her zenith. A long last kiss from Catwoman and she was gone as other fingers replaced those that had sated her, fingers being pushed into her mouth to be sucked clean as Sara once again tasted her own juices. She jolted as a large male hand began to slap her proffered buttocks, but held her position as she resolved to be compliant to whatever came her way. She held steadfastly onto the bar below her as the heat and stinging sensation grew and the blows became harder and faster. As quickly as he had started, it was over and her cheeks were tugged further apart as a saliva covered tongue slid slowly down her anal cleft before lips sucked once more at her pussy.

"Uh oh, here comes Cakeman."

Sara registered the words, but the meaning was lost on her although she was able to discern the amusement that seemed to be rising amongst the gathering around her. A plain-looking, bespectacled man appeared in her eye-line, naked apart from footwear, a pair of bright red boxers open at the front and a gold medallion hanging around his neck. A semi-erect penis, cock ring tight around the base, twitched as she stared, wondering what the presence of this mysterious man meant for her. With a big grin, he placed a large hand on the back of her neck and steered her face down towards his growing cock.

"Say hello to Herbie, Serf. He will be serving you your lunch soon." He roared with laughter.

The pressure on her neck rather suggested to Sara that there was not an option open to her and she dutifully parted her lips and accepted the cock just as it reached its fully erect state. She had only just started to twirl her tongue around it to begin the process of full fellatio, when the twitching prick was unceremoniously withdrawn from her mouth.

"Well, you are a keen one but Herbie isn't ready to serve up your treat yet so you will just have to keep your eagerness on hold until I have had my just desserts, so to speak."

The laughter that greeted this remark caused Sara some concern. Her audience clearly had experience of this member's proclivities that she was yet to discover. However, she did have to admit that the name Cakeman, his vocabulary and the fact that he appeared to have a freezer bag over his shoulder suggested that food items might be on the agenda. Sara was rueful, having already discovered to her great embarrassment that former lover Jenny had hung her out to dry with her full recounting of the sexual endeavours they had enjoyed a couple, and she accepted that she was probably fair game to any taunts and suggestions concerning the use of foodstuffs in this situation.

"Zoo, sweetie, I would like you round the front to ensure that her hands stay on the bar. Cuff her if she does not comply throughout. I am playing my gold coin so will leave it on your table here. Just in case you are not aware, Serf, I have paid for the honour of having your holes available to me for a short period. Hence the gold coin I am giving up in payment. Pres has accepted a fee and your owner has been informed and agreed the transaction. So, basically my dear, you are mine for the next hour, all access points allowed with the exception of actually putting my cock in your pussy or bottom at the request of your owner. However, anything else is acceptable, so I will be making use of both the back and front doors for my culinary fun. Hoorah!"

The words of this eccentric man were not particularly to Sara's liking. She was pleased that he had been forbidden, by Jamie, from fucking her, it was a great relief, but she was very much apprehensive as he had clearly been given permission to penetrate her otherwise. The unzipping of his freezer bag did not bode well and she was quite relieved when Zoo cradled her face and planted a delicate kiss on her lips before whispering in her ear.

"On the plus side, Serf, it does mean I will get to wash and clean you up after he has finished with you." The wink from Zoo was worth its weight in gold to Sara at that point as she suddenly felt her buttocks pulled further apart than they already had been, followed by rather podgy fingers from one hand prodding her arsehole while the other hand engulfed her pussy and fingers worked along her lips.

"Excellent, excellent," murmured Cakeman. "Not too tight in the grill area and the oven feels like it has been pre-warmed! I think we are ready to start baking."

Sara eyes widened as the feel of a thick liquid being squirted down her bottom cleft indicated that her ordeal at the hands of her new companion had properly begun.

"That's a layer of fresh cream to start you off," whispered Zoo.

Sara could not help but jolt as her arsehole was breeched by a plastic nozzle, and a familiar noise announced that a large deposit of instant cream was being projected inside of her. It was not actually an unpleasant sensation, mused Sara, but possibly not a route she would have chosen within minutes of being introduced!

"I guess you know what that is. Nothing makes that noise like squirty cream," laughed Zoo.

Not that Sara had time to linger on any one aspect of what was happening as Cakeman reached under her and she felt her breasts being covered in something thick and sticky. Seconds later, the distinct scent of honey answered her unspoken query.

"Honey, honey," smiled Zoo.

"Hope you like chocolate cake, my dear. Not that you are going to taste much at this end. Ho ho!"

His touch was no longer as delicate as she felt a thin slice of chocolate sponge rather forced into her pussy. Again and again his hand dipped in, as much slipping from her to the floor as staying put. Sara fought the natural urge to try and eject the substances filling both her orifices behind as Zoo held her hands tight to the metal rail.

"Just go with the flow, sweetheart," whispered Zoo. "Please him and you won't get beaten. He only harshly punishes the ones who don't play by his rules and, trust me, it is best if he doesn't get angry as he has a bit of a temper."

That warning was enough for Sara. Not being beaten for a while was surely a good result, she pondered. She was terrified that she would let Jamie down in some way today and was fearful that she may have a cracking point that could well be lower than most of the other attendees. Her enjoyment of corporal punishment was very much driven by the person wielding the instrument of her punishment and the sexual urges that they were creating. Cakeman was not turning her on in the slightest, primarily because she did not find him the least bit attractive, and she was fully aware that what he was doing to her was not the issue. She would have no objection to Jamie working his way through the contents of her fridge in this manner because she loved him and loved everything which he did to her. Cakeman was a different proposition.

Her reverie came to an end with a jolt as there was a sudden further intrusion, firstly into her arsehole and then the same sensation as his fingers opened her pussy up again and delved amongst the mush that she sensed the chocolate cake had become.

"Strawberries," Zoo simply stated.

"Whatever," sighed Sara in response.

Then his mouth was on her, tongue inside of her pussy, as he worked his lips to eat the cake and strawberry from her gooey sex. He sucked and slurped, Sara assumed deliberately making a disgusting spectacle of his endeavour. It was not unpleasant, and indeed was reminiscent of activities that she and Jenny had enjoyed, and Sara felt her arousal grow. This met with Cakeman's approval which he shared with the ever-growing crowd on onlookers.

"Oh lovely, she has decided to anoint my meal with some sweet juices of her own. Hoorah!" Sara found herself ridiculously pleased at the murmur of approval that met this announcement.

Then his mouth was on her breasts and Sara could feel that as much as he was licking and sucking off the honey, he was depositing cake remnants to replace it. She tried to imagine the picture she was presenting to the audience and found to her shock that this thrilled her immensely, and her nipples hardened noticeably, to Cakeman's delight.

"Rock-hard nipples now, everyone. She is definitely up for this, the little slut."

Sara could not help but be aware that all this activity had resulted in much clenching and unclenching of her nether regions and when Cakeman's mouth next found its way to her arsehole, she could already feel the strawberry juice and cream dribbling out. To her horror this was something that her companion felt the need to highlight! With his fingers digging in hard and pulling her cheeks as far apart as he could, he announced gleefully:

"Look, look, everyone. Sara has made a lovely strawberry and cream sauce for you all. I have brought little spoons, please take one and have a mouthful. Come on, come on quickly, let's not waste her effort. Tuck in, everyone."

As much as Sara tried to clench her buttocks tight in sheer shame and embarrassment, she was helpless as several of the group cupped their spoons in her crack and her congealed deposit eagerly taken as it dribbled out.

"Bet you never imagined that you would be doing this? Possibly not quite what you signed up for? You must have been a very bad girl, Sara." Zoo was holding her hands very firmly now as Sara struggled not to fight against the horror of the moment.

"Now, my little food-lover, it is time for your speciality. Maltesers,

I believe it is. Is that correct, Serf?"

Sara groaned. The professor had clearly passed on every morsel of Jenny's betrayal of their sexual activity and she closed her eyes, willing herself to relax and knowing that there was no escape from the further depravity that was to come. She then discovered that not answering a question from Cakeman was offensive to him as a fusillade of blows struck her backside. As she stifled her surprised yelps, the blows stinging without being too painful, she heard Zoo's quiet mutter.

"Rude not to answer a direct question, Serf. Now you get to have a taste of his rhubarb!"

"Sir," Sara immediately responded, "many apologies, sir. Yes, that is correct, sir. I love Maltesers in my holes, sir. So sorry, sir, for my rudeness. Thank you for beating my badness, sir."

The attack stopped and she felt Cakeman's mouth on her bottom as he licked up the rhubarb juice which she could feel trickling down her bottom, the forlorn-looking vegetable now discarded on the floor beside her to provide further evidence of ritualistic deprivation that she had opened herself up to.

Suddenly, his face was beside hers and she heard a yelp from Zoo as, with a fistful of hair in one hand, he thrust the two women's faces together.

"Stop the private, cosy little chats. You are not here to make friends and catch up on the gossip, nor are you here to help her out, Zoo. If I catch you guiding her again, I will find an aubergine to insert which should keep you more preoccupied. You remember how your associate Amazon enjoyed her experience, do you? Perhaps you could enlighten Serf here."

Zoo's face, so composed throughout Sara's ordeal, decidedly blanched as she directed a look of panic at Serf.

"I am so sorry, sir. I apologise for my behaviour and beg your forgiveness. If you would like to beat me, sir, it would be an honour for me to receive it as a blessing to help me behave. Amazon was a very naughty slave, Serf, and back-chatted Mr Cakeman and was punished by having an aubergine pushed completely inside of her pussy. She then had to run on the spot while Mr Cakeman kindly thrashed her bottom with his wooden serving spoon. Her punishment did not stop until she managed to evacuate all the mushy mess of the aubergine from inside of her. It was so messy, so disgustingly noisy and embarrassing for her with her fanny farts, and it took ages. Her lovely black bottom was a picture afterwards, so purple and bruised. Mr Cakeman must have given her about 200 blows with his spoon and she cried buckets. She is such a strong woman, Serf, but Mr Cakeman beat her into deserved submission because he was very angry. Please, sir, do not give me the aubergine, I beg you."

Sara could tell that Zoo's plea was heartfelt and with no sense of play-acting. Cakeman released her and delved into his freezer bag, returning with a thick, wooden serving spoon.

"This is my favourite salad spoon that I use to correct naughty behaviour from wretched wenches. Zoo, you will bend over and grasp your ankles in front of Serf so she can see what your little secret conversations have earned you. Legs apart, hold firm, girl!"

Standing beside Sara's head, so as not to obscure her view of the taut bent over buttocks directly in front of her, Cakeman drew back his arm and began to beat Zoo. A hardened slave and servant of many years with the BADS group, Zoo took the savage blows almost without sound. Her breathing quickened and her buttocks tensed and relaxed rather dramatically in turn as she absorbed the blows but she retained her position and her dignity throughout. Sara could not help but watch fascinated as the dark brown skin changed colour before her eyes, and to her mild consternation she found herself with no real sympathy for the young woman who was receiving punishment for trying to help her, a stirring between her legs giving the truth of her own sexual desires being foremost over all other emotions. Shamefully, she thought, that all she wanted to do was to cover the beaten flanks of the beautiful servant with kisses!

As Cakeman ceased his pummelling, having landed a good 50 blows, he marched behind Sara and without warning delivered six fast and hard strikes to her own lower buttocks. Unprepared and undoubtedly nowhere near as experienced a recipient as Zoo, Sara yelled wholeheartedly at the sudden inferno that tormented her bottom.

"Just a taster for you, Serf. Now stop that awful racket and have some pride, you pathetic creature. I expect better; please do not embarrass yourself like this."

Sara struggled to control her writhing, grasping the metal handholds as hard as she could, suspecting that to let go would bring down further wrath from her persecutor.

"Sorry, sir, so very sorry. Thank you for my strokes, sir," she replied meekly, the shock over, the pain absorbed.

"Accepted; now let us get those lovely little chocolate balls into your waiting holes, my dirty little one."

Sara looked deeply into the silently weeping Zoo's eyes as they linked fingers before she quickly moved her head forward to lick the tears from her companion's cheeks.

"You two can pack that in immediately. Zoo, come here and hold her open while I see how many we can fit in each tunnel." Cakeman's orders were obeyed instantly by Zoo, who clearly was not keen on another wooden spoon battering, Sara surmised.

Sara felt Zoo's more delicate fingers in her pussy as she gently pulled apart her wet folds to allow Cakeman to begin his fun. Although Sara was aware of the mild sensation of a presence that was growing inside of her, she was pleased that it felt very much like sex play rather than anything unpleasant. Her arousal levels were much higher than she would have expected from a not particularly friendly soul shoving chocolates in her pussy, but she put that down to the gentle manipulations, squeezing and stroking of Zoo's expert fingers rather than anything that Cakeman was doing.

"Now, how many do you think we have got in that cavernous cunt of yours then, Serf?"

Sara jolted at his crudity, which seemed a ridiculous reaction considering what she was going through, but knew better than to react in any way that was submissive.

"Oh sir, I do not know. Are there maybe 12 Maltesers inside of me?"

The laughter from the watching crowd gave her a hint as to how wrong she probably was!

"No, you stupid girl, there are 34 up there. Your cunt is like a volcano's crater!"

Sara was taken aback. Thirty-four ruddy Maltesers rammed up her pussy. This was insane! Her words, however, belied her inner turmoil.

"Oh wow, thank you, sir. That is wonderful. Thank you so much, well done." The pressure was evident but she did not feel any great discomfort and only intrigued as to how they would be removed. However, his next words caused her to tense somewhat!

"Now, let us see how many of these lovely little chocolate balls will fit in that gorgeous arsehole, shall we, my dear?"

Sara did not answer. She suspected that it was a rhetorical question. Unfortunately not, she soon discovered as what she guessed was the strap from his picnic bag landed three times in quick succession on the backs of her legs. Managing somehow not to expel any of the chocolates inside of her, she quickly corrected her earlier supposition.

"Ow, ow! Sorry, sir, Serf did not mean to be rude, sir. I think I can take as many Maltesers as Cakeman wishes me to up by bottom, sir. It will be my pleasure to accept whatever you decide, sir." Sara desperately hoped her obsequious attitude and compliance would forestall any further punishment for the time being.

"Apology accepted but no further lubrication for you to teach you a lesson, although you do seem to be leaking a fair bit anyway."

She felt a finger and thumb from one hand open up her arsehole as he quickly inserted the first of the chocolates inside of her, his finger following through deeply to force it firmly inside of her rather nervously constricted tunnel.

"Relax, dear, you will find it much easier if you embrace their presence rather than fight it."

All very well for you to say, thought Sara, but wisely confined herself to nodding.

One by one, the chocolates were pushed into her; she felt the urge to eject them increase as their presence became more and more unwelcome and intrusive. At last, the additions stopped and she sensed him stand back. There was a ripple of applause as he announced the total.

"Ten – well done, Serf, quite an impressive score. Not many take that. Perhaps you have had a lot of practice. From what I have heard, most of the contents of your evening dinner have been up there in the past!"

Sara blanched as he leered in her face, his captive audience chuckling away at the demeaning repertoire at her expense.

"I wonder what your favourite is. Do tell, Serf. What do you most like having in your fanny and arse?"

"Sir, Serf does actually prefer a hard cock and nice wet tongue but has to admit to having a penchant for bananas, sir." Sara gritted her teeth and went along with the role play, wishing that this would come to an end as the pressure of housing the Maltesers in her most private places was beginning to feel more and more uncomfortable. She became aware of the crowd moving around behind her and assumed that the next stage of her shame was about to begin.

"Excellent. I see you are all old hands at this. Just in case you are wondering, Serf, a queue has formed behind you, ready to relieve you of the contents of the sweet shop inside of you! Ha ha! Let the feeding frenzy commence."

To Sara's horror, for the next few minutes, mouth after mouth sucked and licked at her pussy as the melting Maltesers were removed one by one. The slurping and crunching was accompanied by much delight and amusement as the onlookers cheered and encouraged each new recipient of one of the chocolates. She received her loudest cheer when uncontrolled fanny burps accompanied her deposit of one and occasionally multiple chocolates into waiting mouths. The redness of her face as the belittling intensified also caused much merriment. Looking up into the reappeared professor's grinning face crowned her sense of total humiliation.

Her dismay was to be heightened as Cakeman announced triumphantly, "Those patiently waiting for a chance to get your Maltesers from her actual chocolate box, I am happy to pronounce that your time has come. Please take your fill. You may need to give them some help here, my dear. A bit of gently pushing might be required to urge the little sods out! Enjoy, Serf, enjoy!"

A last look at Professor Stones' jubilant face and Sara shut her eyes as she felt the first pair of lips seal around her arsehole and she willed herself to relax her sphincter and push the chocolates out. Thankfully, they were easier to expel than she had feared and she felt fingers holding them back as the feasters from her arse took their turns. As Cakeman counted them out and then procured the final one for himself, roughly biting her inner bottom cheeks as he did, her ordeal came to an end as he moved around to her face and gave her a very chocolaty kiss.

"Just my muffin to go now, Sara. A last treat for you."

Sara was beyond caring as to what manner of food stuff was to be rubbed, mashed or crammed into her orifices now. She was just focused on the fact that this belittling escapade was coming to an end as she felt the large, creamy muffin pushed hard against her pussy. To be honest, to her chagrin she did not feel that this was an unpleasant sensation, even when his hand swept around, and cream and sponge was squelched and rubbed up and down her bottom cleft. Then Cakeman was before her, covering her whole face with his cream-covered mouth, ensuring she had confectionery smeared all over. Now she could see that his cock was unleashed properly and was not surprised when he wiped cream around its tip and guided it into her mouth.

"Come on, slut, earn your keep. It's time for you to be given a layer of my special icing to top off my lovely cake. Time to appreciate Herbie now. Suck, bitch, suck."

Sara couldn't help thinking that of all the attractive men and women at this convention, Cakeman would have been a long way down the list of someone whom she would have fancied having oral sex with! His hand tangled in her hair, his protruding belly bumping into her face as he rammed his cock unceremoniously in and out of her mouth, the flakes of cake and chocolate dropping from his lips! However, she knew that much as her present lover was doing nothing for her in the desire stakes, the promise of Zoo cleaning her up after he had finished had definitely got her juices flowing. With those thoughts in her mind, she enthusiastically sucked and moaned as Cakeman increased his pace and she prepared for the jet of sperm that was surely due to be filling her mouth shortly. Sara was caught unaware when he pulled out, though, and with a quick jerk of his fist, he jettisoned his milky fluid all over her face, directing it in a circular motion to ensure she barely had a part of her face that was not dripping with his copious and very runny come. She managed to close her eyes in time to avoid that particular fate, but was then not best pleased to feel his offering hanging from her hair. A final, rather forcible, wipe of his cock end across her mouth and Cakeman moved away, rearranging his clothing. Zoo immediately moved in with a wet cloth, whispering into Sara's ear.

"Do not worry about the bastard shooting his load into your hair, Serf. It just means that you get to have me properly shower you and the more time spent cleaning you up, the less time left you have to be poked, fingered and beaten." As she moved her face away from Sara's, she planted a quick kiss on her freshly cleaned lips. Unfortunately for Zoo, and Sara, it would turn out, this was spotted by Cakeman and earned his ire.

"Oi, oi slave girl. Who told you that you could kiss the slut? That's most certainly an offence that I can order you punished for. Should you be punished, wretch?"

Watching the interchange with trepidation about the consequences for herself, Sara could tell that Zoo looked well aware that Cakeman was covering his back with the question. A punishment she requested appeared to require no further permission, but Sara, under Jamie's tutelage, had picked up on the intricacies that operated within the society's protocols and was intrigued to see Zoo weighing up her options before she committed to a response.

"Oh sir, Zoo is so sorry and Master Cakeman is totally correct that Zoo deserves punishment. Zoo is happy to place herself at Master Cakeman's disposal and under his disciplinary control. Zoo asks that Master Cakeman beat her naughty bottom and teach her the error of her ways, please sir."

With that, she turned her back to Cakeman and bent over, exposing her bronze, marble-like buttocks to the room and the riveted audience.

"Well, young Zoo, it will be my honour to have you beaten, but I do not feel I can conduct a caning when we have such illustrious company as Mistress Chloe in the room. Mistress Chloe, would you do me and Zoo the honour of giving her one of your toilet seat specials, please?"

Zoo, who had started to rise as he spoke, slumped down dejectedly as a tall black woman stepped forward, attired in a loose-fitting, thin leather outfit, her breasts encased in the black material, the dark nipples blending in as they jutted out through openings in the top, a loose, wrap-around skirt casually open to reveal a very bushy pubic area and, ominously, a long holdall attached to her waist showing black handles that boded ill for Zoo.

"It would be my pleasure, Cakeman. Hold still, wretch. It is time for you to feel the wrath of Mistress Chloe. I can see the perplexed look on Serf's face, Cakeman. I think you need to fill her in as to what my so-called toilet seat special is."

Gently stroking Sara's back, Cakeman explained, filling Sara with dread as he spoke.

"Of course. In fact, I think it is only fair that Serf also experiences the sensation that is such a speciality of yours Mistress Chloe," he leaned in to cup her chin. "It's called a toilet seat special by those of us who have had the honour of seeing it delivered because it is a six-stroke delivery all on the same spot on the widest part of the bottom, so that it gives much discomfort when the recipient places their beaten backside down on a toilet seat. You see what fun we can all have? Give her a sixer as well, please, Mistress Chloe. Let us see what she can take."

If it was not for the tremor that Sara could see coursing through Zoo's body, she might not have been too concerned about a straightforward six-stroke caning, but Zoo's obvious fear was sending warning signals. It was not long before she understood as Mistress Chloe slipped out a wickedly long cane from her sheath and began to practise fast sweeps through the air.

She tapped the cane against Zoo's bottom and Sara found herself transfixed by the slave's stunning, perfectly rounded, symmetrical buttocks. The cane rose high and then flashed down, finding the dead centre of Zoo's taut cheeks, Sara watching fascinated as the thin, bendy cane seemed to wrap itself around the target area. Zoo swayed and, apart from a small sob, remained fully composed.

"One; thank you, Mistress Chloe. Zoo is so sorry that you need to punish her and would like you to strike her again but harder, please."

Sara could not help but admire her calm delivery, secretly acknowledging to herself that she was a long way off being able to perform the role of a slave in this set-up! The thin red line was already vivid and Sara could see exactly how the flexibility of this particular cane had allowed a much wider impact line than a cane normally delivered. The second stroke landed as promised, directly on top of the first, but this time Zoo's legs trembled and her buttocks tightened perceptively as she absorbed the strike, although again without crying out or moving her body to any great degree.

"Two; thank you, Mistress Chloe. Zoo is so sorry that you need to punish her and would like you to strike her again but even harder, please."

The third stroke was unerringly accurate and landed on top of the rising, fiercely, red welt. There was a very small cry from Zoo which she immediately stifled, and Sara watched fascinated but in growing fear as Zoo's left leg developed a tremor that went on for several seconds.

"Three; thank you, Mistress Chloe. Zoo is so sorry that she has been so naughty and disrespectful and asks you to strike her again but harder still, please."

"Good girl," said Mistress Chloe in a husky voice that rather gave away her own rising sexual level.

The fourth stroke seemed savage to Sara and was as accurate as its predecessors. The whack of the cane striking was matched by a strangled scream from Zoo, her body now swaying backwards and forwards as she started quietly weeping. She took a shuddering breath and repeated her subservient mantra.

"Four; thank you, Mistress Chloe. Zoo is such a bad girl and needs to be properly caned to mend her ways. Thank you, Mistress Chloe, for helping me on my path to be a good girl and a better servant. Please beat me again, Mistress"

"As you have taken these so well I will give you the last two together so no need to acknowledge and count. You are permitted to move after the sixth stroke lands, but not before, and you may scream."

Without time for anyone to process what this meant, the last two strokes were delivered at breakneck speed and, of course, unerringly accurate. The strip of skin seemed to turn a multitude of colours before the spellbound audience as Zoo howled and collapsed to the ground in front of Sara, her hands grabbing her blistered cheeks as she writhed on the floor.

Mistress Chloe stood over the crushed and distraught Zoo, whose wailing wracked the room, before she managed to get herself under control with several deep, shuddering breaths. She crawled forward on her belly to kiss the feet of her tormentor.

"Zoo thanks Mistress Chloe with all her heart for showing her the error of her ways."

A loud throat-clearing noise from Cakeman behind Zoo caused her to spin quickly and crawl over to him. She slathered over his toes, her cringing words making Sara's heart feel for her and terrifying her even more at the prospect of being next in line.

"Oh Master Cakeman, sir, Zoo is so sorry if she was disrespecting her master, sir. Zoo thanks you so much for having her naughtiness beaten from her. Please forgive me my sins, oh sir, please. Zoo is so sorry and promises to behave better in future."

"Enough! You may go and hold onto Serf's face while Mistress Chloe gives her a good, hard six-stroker. I think that since you have caused her punishment you should have to watch closely while she suffers. As suffer you will, Serf. You are a novice compared to Zoo here, and you are about to experience an apocalypse on your beautiful backside. No comfortable time on the toilet for you for a while, Serf! Strike, Mistress Chloe, strike. Set those cheeks on fire for me, please."

Sara knew that there was no way out apart from using her safe word and she was determined that she would be beaten into unconsciousness before she would call quits on any punishment. Zoo was babbling words of apology into her face as she held her cheeks between her hands but Sara was concentrating on steeling herself as the long cane tapped her buttocks as Mistress Chloe prepared to unleash the torment. She heard the swish of the cane as it travelled through the air an instance before it landed dead centre on her buttocks, the pliable material wrapping around her cheeks. The pain came in stages and seemed to intensify as her brain acknowledged the agony that seemed to spread across her whole backside. It was like nothing she had experienced before and her scream was banshee-like as her head snapped up and the tears streamed down her face. In her agony she failed to register the kerfuffle around her until, through tear-filled eyes, she saw the sight of the professor, one giant hand around each of their necks as he dragged the figures of Cakeman and Mistress Chloe to the front of the room, his voice booming out.

"Guards! Guards!"

Suddenly, the presence of three strapping, muscular young men, hitherto unseen, seemed to dominate the room. Mistress Chloe, head bowed, submitted to the hold of one without protest and was led away without any fuss whatsoever. Sara watched, fascinated through her tears, glad of the distraction from the pain of her burning buttocks, as the other two guards manhandled a struggling and protesting Cakeman from the professor's hold.

"No, no, no. I have permission. I have the power. Let me go! Professor, stop this nonsense."

The cold, chilling voice of Professor Stones in response did not bode well for the distraught Cakeman, but a smile settled on Sara's face as she enjoyed the moment of her tormentor's downfall.

"You know very well, as does Mistress Chloe, who at least is showing a bit of dignity in her disgrace, that you have crossed a line. Zoo is a protected servant as you well know and Serf here has well-publicised limits and restrictions set that you were made aware of. You have been stretching the rules for a long time, Cakeman, and now it is the moment for you to get your comeuppance. Guards, double peg, stretch and slash for the pair of them in the central hall, please. Ball gags for both, I think; I do not wish to hear any more of his whining. But first, strip him and bend him over in front of Serf, please. I am going to give him a taste of his own medicine in front of her."

Within seconds, a gagged and clearly terrified Cakeman was naked and having his legs kicked wide apart, a strong hand on his head bending him right over before Sara's amused eyes. Stones now had Mistress Chloe's wicked-looking cane bent in his hands, his eyes focused on the skinny, taut buttocks of the crying Cakeman, exposed and helpless.

He flicked the thin bamboo between Cakeman's cheeks saying,

"Open up that cleft, man. Show these lovely people your sweet little anus. You know the score, man. That's better, point it at your waiting public."

With those belittling words, the bamboo was brought back and delivered swiftly across the dead centre of Cakeman's displayed cheeks, wrapped around the tender skin, as was its speciality, and greeted with a strangled scream that his gag just allowed.

"That is just a little extra for you on behalf of Serf. Now, take him off for his punishment, guards, please."

Zoo, who had been allowed wrap-around icepacks to encase her own beleaguered bottom, whispered to Sara that, as one of the special servants under the protection and ownership of Professor and Pres, she could only be abused in certain ways with her protectors' permission. However, she admitted to Sara, she had a bit of a thing for Mistress Chloe, and her submissive bent meant that she had enjoyed the experience if not the intense pain of the beating.

"If you can break away from your little spell of gossiping, you need to clean her up please, Zoo. Give her a shower and clean her thoroughly – there is cake and chocolate everywhere! Then get her strapped back down. There is still time for her to be given a couple more beatings and her mouth has not seen anywhere near enough action yet!"

That has wiped the smile off my face, thought Sara. But at least there would be a break from being abused as Zoo unbuckled her and helped her down off of the contraption. She led her into an attached room. *Glass walls and door, of course*, thought Sara. God forbid that you were allowed any privacy. Little cameras in the ceiling and walls blinked and flickered continuously to remind her that everything was being filmed and presumably watched somewhere in the building.

"Pee now if you need to, Serf, this is about as private as you will get."

Sara studied the see-through toilet and hesitated, although she could see the sense in what Zoo suggested as the toilets she had spotted for slaves were generally in open spaces and attracted small audiences whenever they were used. This, at least, had a modicum of privacy as they were alone in the room albeit a small crowd had gathered outside the glass doors to watch Sara's cleansing. Her first attempt to sit herself down found her squealing in surprised pain as the truth of Mistress Chloe's claim of the discomfort of her wrap-around cane strokes became apparent when the inside of the toilet seat rubbed against the red stripe. At Zoo's look of disapproval, she squatted and quickly emptied her bladder, aware of the chocolate-tainted colour of her pee, and she refused to look up and meet the eyes of the watchers gathered outside of the room. Looking for toilet roll, she sighed as Zoo moved towards her, folding tissue in hand.

"Yes, you're right. You are not allowed to wipe yourself, sorry."

Zoo was gentle and, to her horror, Sara felt a frisson of pleasure course through her body at this most intimate and delicate act.

"Come now, into the shower and let's get the gunk out of you." Zoo's eyes twinkled as she stood naked before Sara and took her hand and Sara's excitement levels increased.

"Face your watching fans, my dear. Spread your legs, bottom out. I'll leave your sweet cheeks until last but I think we will ensure that beautiful pussy is nicely cleaned up as I imagine there are still a few who will fancy a taste of that before your time is up."

Sara succumbed without response. As far as she was concerned, this private time with Zoo had to be preferable to being licked, fingered and thrashed by the gathering hordes and she rested her head against the glass wall and gave into the indignity of Zoo's fingers feeling around inside her pussy as she began the most intimate wash she had ever experienced. Zoo was using some kind of douche to spray little jets of water inside of her, while one finger delicately rubbed against her clitoris. A clitoris that was now rock hard and Sara's mouth opened to take quick, shallow breaths as the pressure increased. She blanked her mind to the fact that Zoo was providing a running commentary as the last vestiges of the inserted food assortment had clearly just been flushed from inside of her pussy, and concentrated on her growing, lustful thoughts.

"Please tell me that I am allowed to come, Zoo," she whispered.

A throaty laugh was the response from Zoo as her thrusting fingers inside her suddenly quickened and the finger on her clitoris rubbed harder and harder.

"What if I said no? Would you actually be able to contain yourself and not come, Serf?"

It was a question that was superfluous as, thumping her head against the shower screen before throwing it back, Sara's climax exploded inside of her and she screamed long and loud.

"I presume that's a 'no' then, you naughty little girl," Zoo chided her and Sara could not care less. Certainly, any punishment Zoo might offer would be gladly accepted as Sara knew that this younger woman had her completely under her control.

"Thank you, thank you, Zoo. Please do what you must and what you want. Oh wow, that was lovely. Am I allowed to give you anything back?"

"You most certainly are not. Now, pull yourself together while I soak your armpits and breasts before we sort out that rear end of yours."

Sara held herself in place as the soft hands massaged cream all over her body, enjoying every second of Zoo's hands touching her so tenderly. Her nipples were rock hard as Zoo tweaked them between thumbs and fingers and she almost cried out in protest when her hands left her body. Seconds later they were back and Sara found herself willing her body to relax as first she was manipulated around so that her bottom was facing the massed ranks of engrossed watchers before her buttocks were parted, and she felt the nozzle of the douche against her anal opening.

All the time, Zoo was quietly and efficiently guiding her.

"Just breathe slowly and give yourself to me entirely, Serf, and this will more pleasurable than you think. Do not worry about your audience; they will not be judging you harshly if you concentrate on what I am doing, pleasing them and putting on a show. Do not give in to shame and self-disgust. I will do this bit as quickly as I can but remember that you are here for the benefit of the members and I must make sure that we are keeping them engaged."

Sara fixed a smile on her face and tried hard not to grimace as she felt a warm jet spurt inside of her before she allowed herself to relax enough to eject it back out. The noise of the shower running was nowhere near loud enough to drown the drumming of the jet hitting the glass wall and her cheeks were bright red as she heard the loud cheering. The audience rattled the glass and gave their appreciation as the shower floor was covered, temporarily, with the remnants of Cakeman's confectionery and fruit deposits. Sara looked down fascinated as the debris of a chocolaty mess swirled around her feet before disappearing down the drain.

"Good girl, good girl." Zoo kissed her on the cheek as she thrust a soapy finger inside of her arsehole. "Nearly done now, well done, my love, well done."

Minutes later, wiped down and lovingly moisturised all over by Zoo before she was strapped down again on the contraption that advertised her availability, Sara realised to her horror that the bathroom episode had doubled the size of her crowd and there was much discussion going on around her as to who was going to do what to her and when!

Fingers probed her rear quarters and her labia was splayed open; her bottom felt like so many pairs of hands were touching her and pulling her open. Two erect cocks were offered to her hands and she obediently took hold and began to pump as a rather limp penis slipped into her mouth with the clear instruction from its pink leather-clad owner to "make me hard, bitch".

To Sara's relief, a tongue began expertly lapping at her pussy and with her own juices flowing she found herself very much engaged in bringing the flaccid flesh inside of her mouth to an impressively thick, if not particularly long, size.

"Ready to fire, Pink," said the owner of the twitching cock in her stronger right hand.

The thick cock withdrew from her mouth and was replaced by the longer, thinner version from her right hand, his thrusting speed increasing as Sara got ready to accept his offering.

"No swallowing, bitch," came the voice of the obvious leader of this trio, who Sara assumed was known as Pink.

"Green is ready to donate, bitch. Keep it in your mouth until you've drained all three of us."

Sara had no time to process exactly what this would mean as the man called Green took hold of her head in both of his hands and thrust deeply into her mouth as he came. In truth, she definitely felt some of the sour, stinging liquid slip down her throat but thought it would be wise not to be sharing that information. As one drained cock slipped out from between her lips, another one replaced it.

"Blue is going to add to your stock levels of spunk now, bitch. Do not dare swallow," Pink snarled at her as this smaller, stubby cock began to pump inside her mouth, which was now starting to ache! She did her best to be still and let this man, apparently called Blue, basically just fuck her mouth.

A guttural groan came from above as a smaller but very thick amount of liquid splashed the roof of her mouth, joining his companion's more runny deposit. Sara found herself musing about the differences in men's sperm as Pink now thrust his cock back in between her lips and urgently jerked his lower torso as he strove towards his own orgasm.

"Do not swallow, bitch, or I will tear you a new arsehole!" His threatening words bothered Sara not a jot. She had sussed out that this was a man intent on dominating her with his aggressive behaviour and the earlier episode with Cakeman had given her the confidence that she was protected from any excesses by Professor Stones.

Discreetly swallowing, she noted that Pink's own come was much creamier than the previous two and she rather shocked herself in judging it the tastiest of the three. No further time to contemplate as he now whipped his cock from her mouth and bent down to replace it with a swirling tongue as he licked and sucked the mixture of sperm from her mouth. Sara had to put this down as one of the most bizarre moments of a very bizarre day as Pink eagerly sucked and lapped away inside of her mouth. To her surprise, he then gave her a very tender kiss and murmured thanks into her ear before he stood up, slipped his cock back into his pink outfit and walked away without a backward glance.

She was not given long to contemplate that episode as a tap on her behind suggested that someone was lining up what she guessed was a paddle. The whoosh of air that followed gave her scant time to prepare as wood impacted against her lower cheeks and she could not contain a squeal of pain. A sadistic chuckle from out of her line of sight did not bode well and the second slap left her in no doubt that a fair sized wooden paddle was indeed in use. A further eight strokes had her yelling disconsolately into the air, her tormentor cackling rather terrifyingly as he applied the punishment. She had no time to pull herself together and as Zoo quickly wiped her face, an extremely overweight man presented his flabby buttocks to her, instructing her to bite him and mark him. As she sunk her teeth into the soft flesh, she took out the anger the paddle beating had installed in her and bit hard and long, repeatedly, until the man pulled away from her. Sara had a moment when she thought that she had overdone it as he seemed quite distressed and she could see the evidence of her fury in the very obvious bite marks, but seconds later he was covering her cheeks with tender, fluttering little kisses, thanking her and complimenting her on a job well done.

"Nice one," said a clearly impressed Zoo. "He is rarely bitten as hard as he likes. You did well."

Sara was amused at how proud she felt considering what she was being complimented on but came to the decision that, in the context of this very unreal and bizarre day, it did all make sense!

The next person requiring her services just wanted to masturbate in her arse crack and then lick up his own deposit which suited Sara perfectly. No effort on her part, no contact with her pussy. She didn't even have to see what was happening and crucially there was no pain involved. Her bottom and the tops of her legs were very sore and she was hoping that there would not be too much more in the way of beatings as Zoo indicated she had only a limited time left of her ordeal.

"You get a sort of treat next, Serf. Whether you like it or not, I have been instructed to take you to one of the cinemas to watch the highlights of what your Porter chap has been up to while you've been busy."

Sara's heart sank. Much as Jamie had warned her that this was about both of them fully engaging and interacting in the BDSM lifestyle, she could not help but wish that their time would be spent on shared experiences rather than individual ones. However, this was by necessity due to her own behaviour, which she fully accepted, and she had agreed with her lover that they embrace the weekend and see how they felt about where their relationship would go in the aftermath.

"However, before you leave, my little contraption, there's a couple of old friends just come to pay their respects. Or even to give you your last rites." Zoo's chuckles matched Sara's despair as Professor Stones and El Presidente appeared in her restricted view line.

"Hello, Serf, sweetie, how's it going? Time for you to be finished off and then your dues are paid, I believe. Is that correct, Professor? Has our little girl received her full desserts do you think?"

Sara waited with a growing sense of anxiety as Stones stayed silent and moved behind her. Zoo wheeled over a sturdy-looking wooden table and placed it directly in front of her face. Her concern deepened as she heard the swish of a cane and worsened when she felt a long, thick leather strap laid across her back.

Finally, the cold, deep voice of Professor Stones announced her fate.

"Twenty-five strikes of this bamboo will be followed by five hard lashes with this beautiful thick leather strap. Then, young lady, you will have paid for your gross misconduct and deception. I assume that you agree that this is fair, appropriate, and that you welcome and agree with my judgment?"

Despite her fear and apprehension, Sra did not hesitate, so keen was she to earn this indomitable man's approval. It had crossed her mind that he might fuck her as part of her humiliation and she had been quite shocked to realise that the possibility of this did not cause her any concern; in fact, she felt disappointed in having to accept that this did not look likely.

"Oh, Professor, sir. I most certainly do. You have been fair throughout and treated me far better than I deserve. I am happy for you to beat me thoroughly to help me improve and repent my dreadful and sinful behaviour. Thank you, sir."

Pres's laughter boomed through the room.

"Goodness me, Professor, what a good job has been done on this urchin. Sounds like she may have learned the lesson you required of her. I just hope that she is as good manually with her lips and tongue as she is at speaking supplicant words."

Sara was now very much aware of why the table had been placed before her, as Pres heaved her hefty weight on to it, her feet facing Sara's face. Slowly, she shifted her huge bulk down the table top, her legs straddling Sara's face, until her wet quim was just in line with Sara's mouth.

"Ready when you are, Professor. My fanny is rather on fire and needs an appliance of a wet tongue to dampen it down!" Pres's laughter caused her thighs to wobble dramatically and Sara found her nose embedded in the swollen folds before her.

The swish of air behind her had barely registered before the impact of the cane jolted her face forward, further engulfing her between the marsh-like pussy before her. Absorbing the blows as much as she could, her ability to cry out being much curtailed by her mouth's pre-occupation, Sara diligently applied herself to licking and nuzzling Pres's sex. Her fortitude served her well until the 13th stroke, as Professor Stones returned to aim the cane on the spot of the first stroke; her head bucked up from Pres's tight thighs and she screamed loud and long before two huge hands forced her head back down.

"You can come out when I come and not before, my dear, so I would concentrate on satisfying me rather than concern yourself with the pain of your sore little bottom. Two extra punishment strokes on her legs, please, Professor – we cannot go easy on her now, can we?"

Sara heard the guffaw from behind her and then suffered the anguishing sting of the two quick strokes on the backs of her legs. Her yells spluttered into Pres's saturated folds and she searched out her hard clitoris and fastened her lips upon the hard bud, sucking for all she was worth in an attempt to bring Pres the orgasm that hinted at an end to her torment. The beating was severe and made worse by the professor's exemplary aim as he duplicated the first dozen strokes exactly. Her bottom was on fire as Pres suddenly began to rub her whole face hard against her sex, her urgent grunts indicating that she had reached her zenith at last. A final tug of her hair and her legs fell away from Sara's trapped head; as she gasped in breaths of relief, the strap landed in a flurry of blows which ended her ordeal. Sara screamed long after the sheathing of the cane and strap, tears rolling down her face, before finally she realised that Zoo was wiping her face and that her cuffs and buckles had been undone.

"All done, my darling, all done. You have done so well,"

whispered Zoo. "You get twenty minutes of icepacks now, my sweet, so lay down on your front on my table and we will let them get to work to ease your throbbing. Then you just have to be paraded through the main hall and taken to meet Prof and Pres for your final little treat."

Sara's look of concern was enough to cause Zoo to quickly reassure her that this last part was most likely not to involve any sort of physical punishment and that she had to take her to one of the small cinema rooms. Sara surmised that she was probably going to have to sit through watching her ordeal with the two seniors and found that thought mildly exciting until the shock of the ice packs placed across her scorched backside brought her thoughts back to the present directly!

Thirty minutes later, feeling now returning to her bottom after her ice treatment and a quick application of body moisturiser by the sensual hands of Zoo, Sara was paraded by Zoo and a second slave through a throng of guests who applauded her as they manoeuvred to lean in to inspect her ravaged backside as she passed. As the path cleared and they went into the body of the main room, Sara was stunned to see Cakeman and Mistress Chloe naked in the centre of the main hall on a raised stage, both tied and spread-eagled in crucifixion poses in a metal framework that allowed limited movement. Sara could see exactly what the professor had meant when he had cited 'double peg, stretch and slash' as their punishment. Cakeman had several metal clamps attached to his nipples and all along his cock, hanging from a semi-erection, all tied with string which passed through a handrail and arranged with their ends looped, so that anyone could pull on the loops, thereby tugging all the clamps to cause extra pain to the recipient. Mistress Chloe was nipple-pegged as well, with a cluster of the clamps affixed to her labial lips that were fully swollen and bright red from the pressure. Both of them had what looked like a large butt plug inserted in their arseholes, presumably, mused Sara, the other half of being 'double-pegged'. The slash aspect of the punishment was in evidence as they approached, with the intention that Sara bear witness to their downfall. Clad in a black leather cloak and shorts, Professor Stones emerged from her right and, at a distinct nod from him, two leather-clad dominatrix appeared and immediately began to slash small, wooden-handled whips across the buttocks, legs and backs of the two incumbents. In not more than a matter of seconds, bright red lines were criss-crossing the duo's bodies and the screams of Cakeman rang out. Mistress Chloe, made of far sterner stuff, mused Sara, was far quieter but the look of agonised control on her face gave evidence that she too suffered for her sins.

Taking hold of Sara's arm and dismissing Zoo, whose discreet wink promised much for later, the professor led her across to a doorway where a caped Pres, topless and wearing open-crotch, leather knickers, was waiting.

"Maybe those two will think again before breaking society rules. Their thrashings will be severe. I think you have probably realised by now that this is not the arena for shrinking violets!"

Sara was not left wondering for long as to why she was joining the audience in the small room as the lights dimmed and the screen lit up, displaying a room where three naked females, bottoms pointing lewdly, open-legged, at the camera, were bent over and strapped down. Beside them, naked – apart from a front and back flapped, side-less leather skirt, which, Jamie had explained to Sara, was a very popular garment in the BDMS world due to the accessibility it allowed to what was enclosed – was her lover. It also barely disguised the sexual state of the wearer and Sara could very well see that Jamie was in an aroused state as evidenced by the tented front of the covering! Sara discerned that the three bound and displayed women were the submissives Jezebel, Isabel and Sloth whom Jamie had briefed her about.

The professor was giving Sara a running commentary, informing her that the three had been rounded up with no resistance to his orders and taken to the room for Jamie to have his pleasure with. As the film showed angles from all around the room, Sara was not best pleased to see that screens on every wall were broadcasting simultaneously what she had been going through. She cringed as she saw Jamie scowling at a screen showing Cakeman pushing Maltesers into her orifices before he picked up three parsnips and one by one forced them into the unwilling arseholes of the three captives. Thankfully, Stones was whispering to her that it was only the highlights she would have to sit through and this indignity was to be the final part of her punishment for her gross misconduct at college. She could barely contain her pleasure when Jamie took switch after switch to the taut buttocks of the screaming women but was not so enamoured to see him present his erect cock to their mouths one by one. The only consolation in her mind was that he appeared not to climax as a consequence of any of their oral actions.

Her shame was complete as she saw Jamie freeze, in his use of a small whip down Isobel's arse cleft, as the screens showed her taking Blue, Green and Pink's ejections in her mouth as another man licked her pussy from behind. The look of anguish on Jamie's face broke her heart but she saw it replaced by pure anger as he began to crack the whip down the open arses in front of him, with parsnip pieces flying off all round the room before Sara saw Professor Stones step in and speak to him.

"Close to going too far there, was your young man. Think he was feeling a tad jealous and possessive. Just remember that was down to you, Sara. Your lust getting the better of you. You have paid your dues as far as I am concerned but now I believe that you need his forgiveness."

Sara felt very conflicted and suspected Jamie did too. The sexual desire that her afternoon session had raised was evident between her legs. Her bottom may have been stinging incredibly but she was aroused by the complete sexual deviance that encompassed and surrounded her. Even now she was aware that Pres had exposed herself and was masturbating slowly as she watched the screen and the professor's shorts were not hiding the enormous ridge of his cock. There was no resistance from her as Pres's other hand slipped between her own legs and her fingers slid up and down her wet slit as on the screen Jamie pumped a huge dildo in and out of Sloth's gaping pussy as two young nymph-like slave girls appeared in the room. One girl took his cock into her mouth whilst the other opened his bottom cheeks and pushed her face deep into the dark valley. At Pres's urging, she pushed her hand between the woman's legs, being guided so that four fingers plunged deep into her sodden opening. As her arousal increased, she became only too aware that for the first time she was able to see the professor's cock while he openly masturbated at the same time watching the screen. The sight of the huge erection, certainly as big if not bigger than Jamie's in length and decidedly thicker, she thought, in his pumping hand both embarrassed and thrilled her. To her shame, this unexpected sight sent her lustful desires over the top and she climaxed along with Pres as the screen moved to a close-up of a slave girl's fingers frantically fucking Jamie's arsehole.

The lights flooded on and, with her legs still trembling from her orgasm, Sara found herself literally lifted from the room by Professor Stones, his erection once again covered, and deposited at the feet of

Jamie, who had appeared in the doorway. The shock that Sara felt by her sense of disappointment at being denied the opportunity to indulge herself, with her mentor, in gratifying his obvious sexual arousal, gave her pause for thought. Her mind was a whirl as she tried to process and understand the craven thoughts which had flashed through her mind. The fact that she had just envisaged leaning down and sucking the cock of Professor Stones to climax was causing her much discombobulation and mortification.

"We are done with her, Porter. Her sins are forgiven, the necessary punishment has been carried out, remorse and contrition have been shown, improvement is a given. We need speak of this no more." With that, Sara found herself being lifted up by her lover and carried from the room, her face buried into his shoulder, his soothing hushes stemming her stuttering apologies.

Back in their room, Sara was barely able to look Jamie in the face due to the shame and embarrassment at what she had done and the situation she had created. He seemed oblivious, however, pouring her a bath, kissing her gently each time she began another choked and heartfelt apology and cutting off any conversation to the point that she realised that he was in the role-playing zone and she decided to just go with the flow. Bathed, dried and creamed, she let Jamie put her to bed and, within minutes, she was in the deep sleep of the exhausted.

CHAPTER 8

THE EVENING THAT FOLLOWED

Sara had no idea of how long had passed when she awoke to see the dusky black maiden, Zoo, standing naked and proud before her. Solid-looking, large breasts jutted towards her, the deep, dark brown nipples standing proud and pointing, the legs parted so that beneath the forest of black hairs Sara could see the beginnings of very bright pink labia. Turning around, Zoo lifted her hands first to the nape of her neck, allowing Sara a full view of her beautiful, blemish-free, ebony-skinned body, her strong back tapering down to a narrow waist, rounded buttocks setting off muscular, but slender, legs. Then Zoo bent and grasped her toes, presenting Sara with tightly flexed buttocks and a dark mass of tiny curly hairs encasing the darker black crinkled skin of her arsehole, contrasting magnificently with the pick of her glistening vagina.

"Zoo can be beaten, Zoo can be bitten, Zoo can be sucked and Zoo can be fucked. Whatever Zoo's mistress demands or wants. Zoo can do all of those things to Mistress Serf if she wishes. Zoo is owned by Mistress Serf now, so Zoo is at your command."

Zoo straightened and turned to face Sara, then dropped her eyes to the floor. Sara knew that she now had to take control and assert her authority. To buy time to compose herself, she snapped at the maid.

"You smell a bit ripe to me, Zoo. Run a bath and I will scrub you clean before I give you a damn good walloping for being such a dirty slave."

Zoo complied immediately and ran a bath as Sara brushed her teeth and washed her own face to fully bring herself out of the deep sleep to which she had succumbed. Her nether regions still felt like a bonfire was taking place down there, but like the true masochist that she had to accept she was, she embraced the heat and throbbing, and felt her passion beginning to stir as she thought about beating her willing accomplice. Sara felt no qualms about Jamie's thoughts on this as she was now convinced that he was complicit in everything thing that was taking place. She climbed into the bath with Zoo, her mouth salivating as she moved her hands over the other's firm breasts and rock-hard nipples. The bath was of a size that allowed Sara to straddle and manipulate Zoo as she saw fit, soaping and rinsing her in intimate detail. Sara had to accept that Zoo was a far more experienced and knowledgeable member of this fetish society life that she had been introduced to so dramatically, and therefore Sara was well aware that any sense of control she had was probably paper thin. However, she embraced her role and once she had soaped and cleansed every inch of the slave girl's body, she turned her back to her, her legs either side of Zoo, and passed her the moisturizing soap.

"Clean me, wench." Sara kept her tone cold, maintaining the pretence. "Then we will see if you can start to make amends for your role in my shaming today."

"Yes, Mistress Serf." Zoo's voice had now become cringingly servile and Sara smiled at the prospect of what this promised for the evening ahead.

Moments later, her head was bowed, almost touching the bath water as Zoo's expert fingers soaped and teased her twin orifices, her blistered buttocks lovingly massaged, her breasts soaped and her nipples brought to solid hard erections.

"Rinse me off, dry me off and then, if you are a good girl, I will let you bring me off."

It brought a wide smile to Sara's face that this was exactly the sort of behaviour with Jenny that had led her to today's experience.

Rinsed off and then caressed dry with the most luxurious bath towels that had ever touched her skin, Sara pushed Zoo in front of her into the bedroom, slapping her firm, marked buttocks to hurry her along. The squeals in response were clearly of joy rather than pain and Sara took on board that this was a young woman who had probably been subjected to serious levels of punitive beatings in her role in the fetish club. She resolved that she would not tread lightly and that Zoo would receive what she deserved and what she almost certainly desired!

Zoo, illustrating without the slightest reservation that she was on a well-trodden path, opened the bedside cabinet and removed a wooden spoon and a small, whippy cane. A double-headed vibrator, a strap-on cock, a blindfold and a pair of restraints soon followed and were placed on the bed by the self-assured woman. Sara remembered that Jamie had told her that each bedroom in the establishment came with a package of sex aids; they might not be the most usual of goody bags, mused Sara, but it certainly suited their purpose.

Sara sat down on the bed, picked up the wooden spoon and laid it beside her, pulled Zoo down across her knees and abruptly began to spank the unresisting servant with an open hand. She tried to avoid the purple welt that Mistress Chloe had left although her stare was fixed in fascination at the expertly delivered wound. Soon realising that a hand spanking was doing nothing other than turn Zoo's bottom a slightly darker shade of brown, she switched to the wooden spoon and increased both her speed and strength of delivery. Aside from little squeals that acknowledged the slapping down of the wood, there was still little to show that Zoo was in any real discomfort. Sara decided to change her strategy and her target. The next 30 strokes of the spoon landed alternatively on the backs of the ebony legs and, at last, some reaction was provoked as Zoo began to twist and shuffle on Sara's lap and the squeals became more high-pitched and more in protest. This reward gave Sara a stamina-boost and she increased the tempo again as she worked the spoon across the top of the bouncing buttocks, mesmerised as the ebony skin turned darker, took on a more purple hue and became mottled. Discarding the spoon, Sara started anew with the whippy cane, slashing down randomly, creating a criss-cross pattern of bright thin weals across the writhing bottom and legs, with Zoo now clearly vocalising her suffering. Unrelenting, Sara caned on and on, delivering well over 200 slashes with the small whippy cane as the beleaguered submissive's bottom initially became a mesh of yellow-brown stripes which then turned a very dark shade of reddish purple before finishing as deep, black raised welts.

As Zoo lay dishevelled and breathing heavily across her knee, Sara slid her hand between her legs and fingered the slickness of the very full and bright pink wet lips below. Zoo's restrained sobbing turned to guttural moans as Sara delved into the moist, warm folds, probing fingers exploring and massaging the rocking and mewing woman's most private of places. Confident in her control but keen to bring only pleasure, she covered a thumb with Zoo's juices and moved the digit to gently rim round and round the winking, puckered anus nestling in the jungle of black curls before her. As her deft fingers went deep into the welcoming pussy, she pushed her thumb through the initial resistance of Zoo's tight arsehole, and then jerked it fully into the dark tunnel. Zoo's head jolted up as a loud groan escaped before she began to move and thrust in that way that Sara recognised as the search for climax and release. All restraint gone now, Zoo began to emit little yelps of pure pleasure as she writhed and rocked across Sara's legs and lap, trapped between pleasure and pain, her arousal increasing by the moment. Her flanks raised high and her legs opened further, she gave herself to Sara's pumping right hand as her left hand squeezed a breast hard between her fingernails, digging in as Zoo began to shake her head from side to side as her orgasm approached. Zoo's scream, as she came, gave Sara the most satisfying moment of the day so far and she pulled the shuddering body into her arms, collapsing back onto the bed. Within seconds, Zoo had laid Sara face down and climbed on top of her, her hands massaging Sara's shoulders as her head dipped to plant gentle kisses down her spine. As Zoo's tongue tickled the top of her anal cleft, she automatically opened her legs wide and raised her haunches, inviting her love to glide her tongue down her crack, which flicked at her offered arsehole before dipping into the wetness offered below. Sara's hands knotted the sheets in her fists as she gave into the experienced, long tongue and nibbling teeth.

Sara had barely registered the door opening and closing, nor the lights dimming considerably, whilst in the throes of passion but, in truth, was past the point of caring what happened to her now. This voyage of sexuality, of supposedly depraved and obscene behaviour, was all-encompassing, her whole world in an evening unlike any other she had experienced. Jamie's low voice speaking to Zoo slipped into her consciousness and her happiness reached a level never before experienced as she realised that her lover was joining them and that this adventure had not yet ended. She recognised the feel of his large hands as her body was manouvered into a position at his bidding, and she was placed in a position so her head now rested in Zoo's lap and her hips were raised above her bended knees. Zoo's legs opened and gentle hands guided Sara's mouth to her sodden pussy. Sara automatically lapped at the musky secretions and her tongue probed those lush, bright pink lips; she sucked and kissed the swollen gorged labial lips and, with Zoo's direction, she raised her hands to encircle the full, prominent breasts, her fingers seeking out the erect nipples.

The smack of Jamie's hand on her bottom forced her gurgling into Zoo's welcoming pussy. However sore and blistered her cheeks felt, she still found herself further excited at the feel of her lover's palm bringing the stinging sensations to the fore once again. Zoo's hands tightened in her hair as she guided Sara's mouth, embedding the hard ridge of her nose against the pubic mound of the maiden, and Sara felt the urgency as Zoo began the journey towards another orgasm.

She displayed her open arse without inhibition, inviting both the continuation of contact with Jamie's punishing flat hand and her once-taboo back hole which she offered as fully available and accessible. At the same time, she pushed back to fully engage the probing fingers of his other hand in her yearning pussy. Zoo's fingers reached under her and twisted her nipples harshly as the two worked her in tandem between them. Jamie's thumb finally probed her anal passage as he ceased the fierce spanking and she reached the point of no return. Suddenly, she felt his cock thrust deep into her welcoming, wet sex and he began to jerk his hips as he slammed inside of her. With Zoo jerking and shaking uncontrollably beneath her, she screamed into the other woman's pussy as her own climax came quickly and violently, arching her body in intense physical pleasure as she allowed the heady sensations to sweep through her. Her gasping and grunting as she eked out every last drop of her cum was animalistic and she accepted that she had passed the time of any behavioural restraints, especially as her lower holes spluttered and belched when Jamie pulled his cock and thumb from her body and it reacted and adapted to the voids created. As she felt Jamie lower his face to lick the droplets of her spend which dripped from her swollen sex lips, she came again, shuddering frantically at the light contact of his tongue on her clitoris. Zoo lifted Sara's face to meet her own and she held her gently as she placed fluttering little kisses all over her cheeks and licked up beads of sweat from her forehead.

Minutes later when Jamie tenderly turned her onto her back, she was able to see for herself that he was still firmly erect; she hadn't felt him come but her befuddled mind was long past worrying about such matters! She half-noticed the look that passed between him and Zoo, and, as the woman moved quickly to kneel with her legs either side of Sara's face, she realised that the two were following a previously discussed script. Zoo held her body above Sara's face and Sara instinctively licked her lips as she anticipated the lowering of Zoo's torso to bring her pussy into range of her eager tongue. Sara was vague on what followed as Jamie reached under her and lifted her legs up, her ankles lodged on his shoulders, his twitching cock resting against her open pussy lips. Jamie entered her without pre-amble as Zoo dropped herself onto Sara's face, her tongue and lips welcoming the swampy wetness of the other's sex while the tip of her nose slipped into the dark, smoky hole of Zoo's anus. Fingers reached to rub her hard clitoral nub: Zoo's, Sara guessed, as she felt the manly hand of Jamie rub against her when he performed the same favour to Zoo's sex, also slipping a finger into Sara's mouth. The movement above her indicated that her two lovers were kissing fervently but Sara felt no jealousy, only a desire to ensure that she played her part in bringing this congress to a happy conclusion. Raw and delicious sounds of rampant all-consuming sex filled the room as the three searched for their climaxes. Jamie's thrusts became more urgent, his groans more desperate as he plundered her pussy; Sara sucked hard and pushed her tongue deep inside the pleasure garden of Zoo's drooling pussy, struggling for breath as the woman above her forced her bottom down hard onto her face, her nose now fully submerged in Zoo's tight, but accommodating, back passage. Zoo's buttocks all but encased her as she ground her body hard against Sara's face. The finger that Jamie had wetted in her mouth was now forcing its way into her own arsehole as Sara found herself penetrated on all fronts. Zoo came first with a long, high-pitched scream as she bucked and jolted, Jamie followed, grunting loudly, and Sara could feel his cum jetting deep inside. With her hands scratching and pinching Zoo's breasts, her own climax hit, small electric shocks racing through her juddering body as she arched her back, her quaking legs kicking madly against Jamie's upper body. As Zoo slipped away from Sara, Jamie wrapped her up in a loving embrace as his cock's twitching subsided and her breathing began to calm. He kissed her slowly, his fingers stroking her forehead, murmuring endearing words of love into her ear. Sara felt herself slowly coming back to normality, and a sense of disappointment that the day had come to an end washed over her. She watched the divine backside of Zoo disappearing into the bathroom, her tongue instinctively licking her lips until she noticed Jamie staring at her with a big grin on his face.

"She's something, isn't she?" he smirked. "I would be happy to share you with her again."

Sara coloured, unable to deny the desire that had been clearly evident, the taste of Zoo's pussy still on her tongue.

"We could join her in the shower," she whispered. "She is undeniably luscious and I don't mind if you fuck her as long as I am with you, my love."

Minutes later, Sara was pinned against the shower wall, Zoo's mouth fixed to her right breast, most of her hand thrusting in and out of her fanny as Jamie rammed his cock into the black temptress's pussy from behind. It had not taken long, with both women's lips taking turns to suck and lick his cock, before he was fully hard and ready to perform once more. Now, with both hands twisting Zoo's breasts and squeezing the prominent nipples, he increased his rate and came again, biting the dusky-skinned shoulder as he slammed Zoo against an already screaming Sara, ecstatic in her latest orgasm. Zoo came as Jamie emptied, grabbing Sara's arse, his fingers delving into her bottom crack as Zoo jerked and twisted, sandwiched between the two. They slumped together in the shower, water falling over all three; heavily breathing, their sweating bodies entwined together as they came down from their combined ecstatic states.

After Zoo left, with a promise that she would always be available, to be bid for, at future BADS gatherings, Sara snuggled into Jamie's arms as they settled down for some much needed rest.

"The whole experience has been mind-blowingly wonderful and so much more intense and awesome than I could ever have imagined or dreamed. Oh my God, Jamie, today has been out of this world. Thank you, my love, thank you. I know this would not have been so bearable without you. I was so scared but aside from a few moments when my poor bottom felt as if it had been set on fire – and maybe I could have lived without the cake and Maltesers – it has been fucking wonderful! I love you so much."

Jamie acknowledged her words by a tightening of his arms, a twitch of his cock and a kiss to the back of her neck, and Sara slipped into the sleep of the exhausted.

CHAPTER 9

SARA'S SECOND DAY

WITH THE SOCIETY

Jamie and Sara used the free time set for the morning for a leisurely wander, stopping for coffee and an early lunch, knowing that at 1:30pm the final session of the weekend would begin. Sara was fascinated to learn, and relieved that she was not included in it, that the morning was set aside for anyone receiving long-term punishment. Many miscreants had spent uncomfortable long hours in overnight incarceration, having slept on padded benches, shackled by metal ankles chains and handcuffed, thus allowing limited access to a small kitchenette and basic toilet facilities. Sara watched in horror as the captives were escorted through to the outside changing rooms and shower block with their potties to empty before being allowed a breakfast consisting of slops in bowls which they had to eat like dogs before enduring a brutal exercise routine. They were, of course, naked at all times in the grounds, their beaten and bruised buttocks evidencing their earlier treatments. Sara thanked her lucky stars that the professor had not ordained that she should be treated likewise. Her own bottom was sore enough as it was, and she certainly did not envy the fact that, for these poor unfortunates, their ordeal was not yet over, albeit she knew that they were all here willingly and, presumably, playing their chosen roles.

Jamie, now *au fait* with the order of the day, had ensured that they both were following the general second-day dress code. Though bedroom slippers or sliders accompanied by shorts or skirts were very much encouraged, most females matched the menfolk and went bare-chested, most, if not all, without underwear.

"Professor did say that you should try out every experience on offer, so what do you say? I thought that you might fancy a little gay escapade. Or is that too tempting for you considering that the last lesbian tryst you entered into is what landed you here with such a sore bottom in the first place? Not that it is optional, actually, as this is a pre-booked experience and failure to attend once booked is an offence punishable by public flogging. That is not necessarily one of those experiences that I want to experiment with!"

Jamie's announcement caught Sara off-guard. Much as a female on female BDSM appointment sounded like a treat for her, she was very much surprised that Jamie would have signed up for a homosexual erotic experience for himself. As he led her towards the back of the room and the neon sign clearly indicating "A Gay Time", Sara could not help be suspicious that she was being set up. Jamie hesitated before entering.

"I am not sure how much we will be allowed to communicate once we step through the door, so just know that I love you with all my heart and I hope that this is an experience worth sharing, my love."

The genuine concern and adoration shown in his eyes relaxed Sara somewhat and with more confidence that she really felt, she encouraged him to go on.

"A shared sexual time with you, however deviant, different or painful, is always going to be worthwhile. Let's have fun!" Sara pushed open the door and the two stepped inside.

They entered a spacious room with various equipment and contraptions spread around. A young couple came towards them enthusiastically. Sara's eyes widened as she took in the appearance of the statuesque blonde, dressed in a white bikini-style outfit with an open-front, lace-up skirt which highlighted a lack of underwear beneath as Sara caught glimpses of a generously hirsute pubic bush. Jamie was welcomed with similar enthusiasm by a thin, bespectacled, small man wearing a beige T-shirt and boxers who introduced himself as Crossword. The contrast between the two was stunning. Conversely, Sara could see that at the back of the room, half-hidden by curtains, sat a small, frail-looking, elderly lady who was knitting alongside a giant of a man, rippling with muscles, sitting cross-legged and almost naked, reading a superhero comic! Their expressions as they glanced from one to the other were polar opposites. Jamie's relaxed attitude when confronted by the bespectacled and puny figure of Crossword betrayed his relief that his first gay experience was to be conducted by a man he felt completely unthreatened by, although briefly replaced by clear apprehension when casting a quick look at the well-built man reading. He appeared to show no interest in them at all although Sara felt a moment of something stirring as she discreetly checked over the impressive muscular physique.

"Hi, gorgeous lady," said the blonde as she bounced across to kiss Sara on each cheek. "Welcome, welcome. My name is Angel. Ooh, we are going to have such a fun time. Let us get those slippers and shorts off and have a look at the rest of you. If the tits are an indicator, you are going to be a fine feast to partake of!"

Sara found herself naked in a thrice as she was spun round to squeals of glee before Angel wrapped her in a hug. She could hear Jamie receiving a similar reaction from Crossword who had stripped him naked to sighs and expressions of admiration. The two naked lovers were taken over to pieces of equipment that Sara thought looked like a cross between a bicycle of the future and a steel horse!

"Pop on, my loves, and let us get you strapped down for the ride of your lives," exuded Crossword who was grinning from ear to ear, his wide eyes taking in every part of Jamie's body as he helped position him on the contraption.

Soon they were both ensnared to their respective devices. Like racing cyclists, their hands fixed by the wrists to handles, their feet bound in peddles, their torsos raised and bent so that their heads were forced low and their bottoms were raised high. Of course, Sara reflected, their legs were parted and the seats designed so that their bottoms were fully accessible and whilst she had a hole allowing full access to her pussy, she could see that Jamie's cock and balls were fed through the opening and fully exposed below. She noted that he was semi-erect and was relieved since her own sex lips had become moistened when the beautiful woman had handled her intimately while securing her.

"Oh dear," said a pensive-looking Angel. "You have taken a bit of a beating, haven't you? Never mind, we will try not to add too much to the distressed state of your lovely bottom. Certainly won't be putting any Maltesers and cake in these hungry little sex mouths."

Sarah immediately turned bright scarlet at Angel's words, let alone the feel of the fingers fluttering around the parts of her body being so brashly high-lighted. The professor had informed them earlier that Sara's session with Cakeman had been the most viewed film overnight by the guests, and that she had better be prepared for being recognised by most others members now.

"You'll probably be much in demand from now on if you would like to continue as a true submissive for the members to partake of," Angel continued, her fingers now stroking Sara's nipples.

"Uh, um, no, no. It was just a one-off. I am not sure that I will be continuing in a sub-role after today." She managed to get the words out rather breathlessly as Angel's fingers had now begun sliding up and down her vaginal crack and was well aware that she was not exactly supporting her argument against being a submissive.

"For now, my sweet lady, I am just going to be gently stroking and kissing your lovely body while we watch lucky Porter being given his treat."

Sara met Jamie's eyes, which now looked full of apprehension, as Crossword slipped beneath him and began to lick at his cock. The excitement she felt as Angel tenderly stroked her back and bottom combined with seeing her lover's eyes close as a man sealed his lips around his erection and began to bob his head in the time-honoured fashion was perplexing to Sara. Her sexuality had been taken on such a journey since she had joined St James' college and been introduced to the field of corporal punishment that she wondered what feelings had been latently inside her all this time. Her mind seemed suddenly so open to sexual adventures and experiences that she knew previously would have horrified her and sent her running for the hills! Yet here she was naked, bound, displayed completely, and basically offering herself up to whatever a bunch of strangers wanted to dish up. Part of her was appalled at her quickly attained, deep involvement in kinky and fetish sex scenarios, but she did realise that a much larger part of her was grateful that her sexual vision had been expanded like this. She knew that she was hanging on to a belief that maybe most women had these inner fantasies and that she was just the one lucky enough to be living hers!

From the corner of her eye, Sara saw the seated man rise and move over to a concealed cupboard from which he took a handful of canes, straps and whips. To her delight, he unclipped the leather cloth covering his midriff and groin and she saw his thick, half erect cock for the first time. This Adonis of a man: about six feet six tall, face as though chiselled from rock, deep blue eyes under dark, sleek, thick eyebrows, long, glowing locks of jet-black hair. As far as Sara was concerned, Hercules was anyone's, nay everyone's, she corrected herself, definition of handsome. She felt that giveaway increase of her heartbeat and the tingle of sexual lust between her legs, as she followed his naked figure to the extent that her bindings allowed. He turned his back to her for a moment as he kept out of Jamie's eye-line, the screens around the room focusing on her and Jamie's bodies. His taut, muscular buttocks caused her to lick her lips; his figure was that of a Michelangelo statue and every movement caused a muscle to ripple. Sara felt her nipples harden and inadvertently licked her lips again.

The slap of Angel's hand as it contacted ferociously with her face shocked Sara out of her erotic reverie.

"Take your lusty, slut eyes off Hercules; he is not even going to look at you, hussy. Clear those dirty thoughts from your head; he is not interested in the likes of you. He lives for cock, he wants your Porter's thick, long cock, not that scrawny, wet gash of yours. He is Hercules, the god of strength, and in a league way beyond the likes of a wretch like you. You are just a strumpet, here for our entertainment, a plaything, a piece of flesh to do with what we like. This is not a pleasure room for straight losers like you and this Porter specimen; you are here as our toys, for us to use and abuse as in whatever way our gay and queer inclinations take us. You are ours, bitch, you are a plaything for the Sapphic ones, so take your slutty eyes off Hercules. Look at the state of you, hussy, your fanny is dripping! What an embarrassment you are."

Sara yelped as Angel reached around behind her and pinched her sex lips harshly before slapping her bottom. As Sara was spun round to so that Hercules could move directly in front of Jamie, she saw Jamie's face register the implications of the other man's more active presence. Hercules took a handful of Jamie's hair and turned his head so that Sara had a full view as he offered his hardening manhood to her lover's reluctantly half-open mouth. Their eyes met briefly and Sara winked teasingly; Jamie's cheeks reddened as he broke contact with her gaze, closed his eyes and accepted the thickening protuberance into his mouth. Sara was mesmerised as Hercules held Jamie's face between his strong hands and his cock began to slide slowly in and out of her lover's mouth. Both of them were oblivious as Crossword moved behind Jamie, picked up and then swung the leather tawse hard against Jamie's buttocks. The loud slapping sound as the thick leather connected with Jamie's tight cheeks made them both jump. Although, Sara assumed, in Jamie's case it maybe was not the sound that caused his eyes to squeeze shut, as Hercules eased out of his mouth before slamming a now fully erect long cock back in as Crossword's arm swung down again. Hypnotised as she was by the sight of her lover giving a blowjob at one end while taking a strapping at the other, Angel diverted her attention by sliding several digits into her pussy as she hand-fucked her. Sara had no thoughts of sympathy for Jamie, particularly as his cock remained fully erect during this extremely homoerotic action. Much as she acknowledged that none of what she had endured previously, in the drawn-out punishment routine that Professor Stones had put her through, was of Jamie's doing, she had never sensed that he had harboured any doubts or reservations about what was happening to her. She very much suspected that her denouement had sat comfortably with his fascination with the BDSM scene and that he had been in favour of the punishment dispensed. She could not help by grin widely at him at Hercules spoke.

"Time to stop with the starters, Porter. I think you have me aroused and wet enough for your main course now," he said as he drew his throbbing erection from her lover's mouth.

"Oooh, let me just give him some grease, Hercules. I so want to get my fingers in that nice snatch of his." Flinging the tawse down, Sara watched with widening eyes as Crossword produced a tub of gel and slapped a handful between Jamie's buttocks. Jamie's eyes closed once more as fingers pierced his anal opening and Sara was moved to express concern.

"Darling, try and relax. If what I think is about to happen is correct, you need to help yourself take this by breathing slowly and willing your muscles to relax and accept what's coming."

Crack! Crack! Crack!

Sara screamed as Angel brought the tawse down on her inflamed cheeks.

"That's a reminder that you need to ask for permission to speak, Serf. You are very much mistaken if you are under the impression that you are in some kind of luxury spa on your holidays, wench. Your bottom may be extremely sore from your public humiliation yesterday, yes we have all enjoyed watching it slut, but that does not gain you any exemption from being well thrashed today. Please remember that you are in a punishment room. You do not speak again without asking permission. Do you understand?"

"Yes. Yes. I am so sorry. Ow. Ow." Until then, Sara had not taken on board just exactly how tender her bottom was, and was now entertaining serious doubts about what Jamie had signed them up for. Her discomfort eased as she focused on the distraction of watching Jamie as, after Crossword had tenderly slipped a condom over his cock, Hercules held his hips and guided his giant cock to the dark orifice before him. Jamie's eyes bulged and his breath escaped in a long, low-pitched moan as inch by inch Sara watched the prominently veined sex organ disappear between her partner's cheeks.

"Open up, sweetheart. It's time for your spit roast." Crossword was now easing his own cock into Jamie's mouth and in a couple of seconds the two had established what looked to Sara to be an oft-performed routine. Hercules eased almost completely out of Jamie as Crossword grabbed Jamie's head and pushed himself completely into his mouth. As he came back out to rest his tip between Jamie's lips, Hercules simultaneously drove deep into his rectum. With Angel's fingers back in her pussy, Sara could feel her arousal levels peaking and knew that she was going to climax soon.

"I am going to come, Hercules," announced Crossword to a look of horror on Jamie's face as Sara could see that it had just sunk in that he was going to be swallowing a man's semen for the first time.

"Yes, yes, yes. Fucking coming in your arse, scumbag! Coming! Coming! Coming! Ugh!" grunted Hercules as his pace increased and he began to slam back and forth into Jamie, convulsing as he reached his climax.

"Permission to speak, please Miss ... me too, me too, me too, coming ... aaaargghhhh!!!" Sara's body shuddered as she came. She saw Jamie struggling to cope as Hercules slumped over his back, still pumping frantically as he drained his cock deep inside of Jamie's rectum.

"Well done, Porter. You have learnt quickly. No teeth, lots of lovely tongue around my helmet and you kept those lips tight and wet. Good boy, Porter. I will not be long as you are a natural cocksucker. Now open up and let me cover you with my love juice, darling, open wide for little daddy now. Aaaaaargggggh!"

Sara nearly laughed aloud at words she would store away for an appropriate time to tease her lover with. She was transfixed as Crossword held his cock close to Jamie's open mouth, gave a quick flick of his wrist and suddenly the sperm came shooting out all over

Jamie's lower face. His cum spurted for several seconds, then the creamy semen ran down Jamie's cheeks and chin. Sara could hardly believe that she was witnessing her partner having a man's sperm wiped across his face before he obediently sucked on Crossword's offered fingers that dripped with his cum.

"Lick my fingers like a good boy, all of it. Swallow it down, good boy, good boy." With a last wipe of the final droplets forming on the end of his shrinking cock, Crossword knelt down in front of Jamie and moved to take his cock into his hand.

"Back to me, Serf, back to me, please. I will forgive you not waiting for my approval, Serf. But you can lick your sticky mess off my fingers now," said Angel as she thrust her hand into Sara's mouth.

Quickly doing as she was told so that she would not miss a second of the captivating episode playing out in front of her, she could see that Jamie did not look that ecstatic and welcoming when Crossword began to lick at his own still throbbing cock.

"Time for you to have your pleasure now, Porter. Oh and Hercules will help you on your way by giving you a few encouraging taps on that delectable backside."

Sara watched as Crossword slowly took the full length inside a mouth that looked way too small for the large appendage on offer. She pondered on the technique, assuming that this was an actual 'deep throat' experience and guessed, from Jamie's reaction and the smoothness of the process, that it was being conducted by an expert. Jamie's eyes bulged as Crossword began to nod his head and then they blinked rapidly as the strap landed on his buttocks with a resounding impact, wielded by the muscular Hercules.

Sara's gaze switched between the flaying arm of Hercules, the bobbing of Crossword's head and the contorted face of her lover as his expression veered from anguish to apparent ecstasy. She watched in awe as, with arm muscles bulging, Hercules began to truly thrash Jamie, the mirrored walls showing the deep red stripes now covering his bottom. With a sudden roar of release, Jamie announced his climax as Crossword pulled back, frantically sucking at the tip of Jamie's spurting cock. One last lash of the strap and Jamie's scream of pleasure turned into a howl of agony before Crossword scrambled up to his face and began to kiss him deeply. Sara could see that Crossword was transferring Jamie's cock juice into his own mouth and experienced a stab of jealousy that she felt excluded from this threesome as she watched Hercules drop down behind Jamie and bite and kiss his ravaged backside before finalising Jamie's homoerotic moment with a long kiss as his lips sealed on his anal opening.

Sara attention was taken now by the appearance of the old biddy from the back of the room as she wheeled a table in front of her head.

"Hello, sweet pea, I am Millicent, nice to meet you," said the elderly woman as she pecked Sara on the cheek.

"Um, hello, Millicent," seemed the only response to Sara who was just beginning to consider that now Jamie's threesome ordeal was over, there was a possibility for her to join in next time too. The thought that the woman looked close to 80 years old had meant that Sara had discounted the possibility that she would be sexually featuring but now she was rapidly readjusting her thinking.

"Ooo dear, you are rather transparent aren't you? I can almost see written across your face what you are thinking. So, yes, I am a part of this or else what the devil would I be doing in this building, let alone this room? Seconds out, round two. Time for you to be fucked and for me to be licked out. Mmmmmm." Sara automatically opened her mouth as Millicent slipped her tongue inside and started to French kiss her expertly.

With her head now held between Millicent's hands, she could only guess at the activity behind her as she could hear Angel moving around. As Sara's head was released, Millicent slipped her housecoat off and sat back naked on the table before her. Her attempts to contemplate that she was really about to have her face between this old lady's legs were interrupted by the feel of Angel's tongue on her pussy and her clitoris being nipped between sharp teeth.

"Now," said Millicent, "just so you have fair warning, young lady, any reluctance to give me cunnilingus of the highest quality to my satisfaction will be punished by a thrashing from Angel. Any reluctance to accept a nice good seeing to, with the 12 inches that Angel has strapped to her, will be punished with me taking over the strap-on and giving it you up your dainty derriere. So hopefully that's all clear and we can get stuck in. Head down, get licking, baby doll."

Hercules moved to wheel the table, on which Millicent now lay with her legs spread wide open, towards Sara's face.

Taking a breath and trying not to spend too long taking in the small breasts, wrinkled stomach and the greying pubic hair above the rather dry looking vulva below, Sara licked her lips and dutifully bent her face forward. Angel's administrations between her legs were making the ordeal far more palatable as her arousal had been stoked and she could hardly deny her readiness for sex. She tentatively licked the older woman's labia and was surprised to feel an immediate wetness as Millicent moistened quickly in response. As Angel sucked at her clitoris and she felt an orgasm approach, she mimicked the younger woman's actions and was rewarded by the obvious hardening of Millicent's sexual nub. Allowing herself to submit to Angel's expert tendering, she soon found that it was easy to lose herself in what was happening to her rather than what she was doing. She came quietly and discreetly but could hear from Angel's murmurings that it had not gone unnoticed as a tongue entered her, deeply lapping at the juices released. For several minutes the three worked perfectly in tandem, Sara barely noticing that Jamie was being wheeled around on his contraption so that he was alternatively given close proximity, and a very detailed viewing, to both ends of her! For a while, the only sounds in the room were the contented moans and sucking and slurping noises from the three women, and Sara was lost in a world that only months ago she could not have even envisaged existed. She failed to even consider the implications when Angel's tongue was replaced by fingers, and a wet thumb was now gently rimming her anus. Her focus was rather abruptly changed as with no warning her vagina was invaded and filled with the huge protuberance of the strap-on that Angel had driven deep inside of her.

"Careful, dear, no biting or the lash will be saying a big hello to that bottom," came the warning words from Millicent as Sara struggled to continue with her oral administrations to the saturated pussy her mouth encircled.

Going deeper even than the huge length that she had grown accustomed to, given Jamie's impressive girth, her bulging pussy tremored and spasmed as it adapted to the size of the intrusion into her body. Thankfully, her aroused state did mean that it slipped in rather easily but she was still forced to splutter out a long breath into Millicent's pussy as it reached places that had never accommodated a foreign visitor before! Not that Millicent seemed to mind the vibration of her lips and the long breath she breathed into the stretched open orifice most of her face now seemed engulfed by. Millicent's hands were now in her hair and her head was being forcefully used for the woman to masturbate with. The bridge of her nose was wedged against the other's clitoris, her tongue working frantically on the engorged labia as Millicent started a howl that signaled her coming climax. Simultaneously, Angel was now pumping her hard and fast, one hand now having reached around to pinch and rub at her own clit.

"Fuuuuuuuuccccckkkkkk!" wailed Millicent as Sara's face became covered in her glistening juices and she rammed her face against her during her quite violent orgasm.

"Yaaaaar!" yelled Sara as at last her face was free of the wet mush of Millicent's pussy and she gave vent to her own pleasure as Angel went as deep as she could and rubbed her knuckles hard against her vagina while she came, long and frantically. Her eyes opened to see Jamie's grinning face as he was steered right before her and close enough for them to share a desperate kiss before he was pulled away. Sara yelled, with the emptying sensation of the sudden void, as Angel snatched the strap-on cock from her pussy. Suddenly, Angel was before her, forcing the fake cock, creamy with juice, into her mouth, before withdrawing it. The next thing that Sara felt was her bottom cheeks being yanked apart, exposing her arsehole. Sara realised that the two women had changed position when she felt the Millicent's small, wet tongue penetrate her anally as Angel jerked her hips backwards and forwards, fucking Sara's mouth with the hard leather. Fingers slid inside her pussy, a thumb rubbing in small circles around her clit, as Millicent drove Sara towards yet another climax.

"Yaaar! Yaaar! Ugh!" an almost breathless and exhausted Sara managed to exclaim, her mouth free when Angel withdrew as her body went into the familiar tremors again.

"Say thank you to Millicent, slutty little Serf. You have just had the honour of the skill and beauty of her magic fingers. Not everyone gets that treat, so you need to acknowledge that you are suitably grateful."

Sara could hardly argue, having lost count of the number of

orgasms she had had in the room, nor, as she was well aware, would it have been wise.

"Oh wow, yes of course. You have both been awesome and I have had the most brilliant time. I hope that you feel I have deserved the experience and that you are both satisfied with my performance. It was a pleasure to be of service to you both." Seeing the smile that her breathless words brought to Millicent's face, Sara opted to ensure she kept in her good books, rather suspecting that when push came to shove she would turn out to be the senior of the pair as far as their partnership went.

"Your pussy was gorgeous, Miss Millicent, thank you so much for allowing me to drink and sup from your honeypot of love."

Millicent laughed.

"That will do or you will overdo it and I might think that you were taking the piss, young lady. Now, give me a nice kiss and then I am done with you.

The kiss was long and tender, Sara finding it so easy to indulge herself in the mouth of this woman twice her age. Their tongues entwined and encircled with relish and both had flushed faces when they drew apart, lips glistening.

"Good girl," said Angel, moving in to plant a surprisingly gentle kiss on her lips. "Hercules has just got wood again, so I think your boy here is in for another treat. Let's watch that and then you can go."

Sara could see the resignation on Jamie's face as Hercules appeared, showing that he had indeed "got wood" one of the porn film phrases that Sara had picked up just lately, that meant an erection had returned to the scene. His cock looked as thick and prominent as before when he steered it once more between the lips of her lover.

"Beat him with a cane, Crossword," instructed Hercules as he gently rotated his hips, causing Jamie's cheeks to bulge rather obscenely in Sara's eyes. "Let us see how many times you can strike him before he brings me off. Suck, you pussy, suck!"

As Millicent continued to kiss and nibble all over her bottom, murmuring the most obscene and complimentary entreaties, while Angel just stroked her hair, Sara watched Jamie's ordeal continue. She was certain that of the two of them, she had had the far more enjoyable time! Jamie's face was a picture of despair and he frantically tried to concentrate on working the big cock inside of his mouth in the hope of producing yet another offering of Hercules' spunk, however, the grimaces every time the cane landed illustrated no joy in the experience whatsoever.

"A third orgasm takes even a stud like Hercules time, however good your boy's technique is," commented Angel as the thwack of the cane announced Crossword's 50th stroke. However, with a nod from Hercules, he drew his arm back and continued with the onslaught.

Twenty strokes later, with a hearty grunt from Hercules, Sara could see from Jamie's reaction that his mouth was taking the latest creamy deposit from this hulk of a man. She would later admit to Jamie that if she had been given the opportunity, she would have been perfectly happy to have been the recipient instead of him. That news drew a promise from Jamie that once he had constructed a similar frame then he would replicate his experience from Hercules' perspective and that they could both see if that was true. Since Jamie had admitted that he would have loved to have been given the chance to fuck Angel, it seemed a little bit of an imbalance that she would supposedly suffer for her admission but the reality was that she would have been happy to watch that happening!

Jamie's final humiliation was to have Crossword come around to him to suck Hercules' cum from his mouth and swallow it himself.

Minutes later, the two were released and ordered to stand up straight while Millicent and Crossword wrote in marker pens on their respective backs. They were then instructed to read what was inscribed on each other.

"Been to the Gay Zone and had a gay time. I have been thrashed, sucked, fucked, rimmed and reamed, had so much cock and have loved every moment," said Sara solemnly, wondering if her back would read the same.

"Been to the Gay Zone and had a gay time. I have been beaten, fingered and fucked, my orifices explored, my face covered in pussy juice and I have loved being treated like the dyke whore that I am," said a distinctively subdued Jamie.

"In case you are wondering who will see that, well I can tell you that everyone will because you can put footwear on but otherwise you leave here naked so that everyone can see what fun you have had. You may collect your clothes from reception at the end of the day. Get out!"

Hercules and Angel unceremoniously manhandled them out of the door to the jeers of Crossword and Millicent.

They were greeted by a round of applause by the gathered crowd of over 100 guests and then subjected to the most intimate inspection with probing fingers and probing questions as their experience was completed.

As gradually the crowd melted away, Sara could see that Professor Stones and Pres were waiting for them.

"Hope that went well you two," said Stones, his eyes twinkling. "Might have left some of the detail out when I suggested this, Porter, old boy. Never mind, eh? I am sure on reflection you will agree it was an experience worth having. Have a bit of a treat set up for you next. Possibly more of a treat for you, Sara, since you have been on such exemplary behaviour. I think your punishment is complete now, so time for a bit of fun. But first of all you can go to the showers over there and wash that nonsense off your backs. I am afraid that you are not allowed clothing until the activities this afternoon cease but I doubt you have much left in the way of shyness anyway."

Freshly washed, Sara had laughed to see how pleased that Jamie was to discover mouthwash available. His expression when she teased him about the amount of manly come he had swallowed gave fair warning that her bottom was probably going to feel the repercussions of her comments at some point. As they returned to the main room, Sara could see that three naked women were on their knees but bent over a long bench with their head and elbows on the opposing side. There were wedges beneath their groins, their midriffs supported by the cushioned bench, which raised their haunches high, whilst a rod between their legs held them wide apart and manacled by the ankles at each end. The result was that they were faced with three sets of taut, raised and splayed apart buttocks, clefts wide open and orifices exposed to the room, shackled fast in place.

"Now Jamie will definitely recognise these three lovely bottoms but I do not think you have been properly introduced."

Sara, on seeing Jamie's broad grin, realised that she was about to formally meet the three submissive strumpets who had previously set their sights on her lover.

"On the right here, Sara, is Isabel. Now, as you can see, Isabel is a blonde, has neat, small breasts, trimmed, blonde, downy pubic hair which surrounds quite a discreet pussy slit. Her bottom is comprised of cute little cheeks with a nice tight little anus at the heart encircled by a clearly coiffured little garden of curly hairs."

Pulling Isabel's head up and taking off her mouth gag, the professor addressed the rather apprehensive looking woman.

"Say hello to Serf; she is Porter's girlfriend and she is going to get to know you in a way that I am sure you will enjoy. Serf, they are all yours, no limits, you can do no wrong."

"Isabel is pleased to meet you, Mistress Serf, and would first of all like to apologise for her sluttish behaviour towards Master Porter. Isabel is happy to make amends and would be most grateful if Mistress Serf was instrumental in assisting her to mend her ways." Isabel's eyes told a different story to the words that left her mouth, but Sara was well aware that Professor Stones' power and standing at these gatherings were not to be challenged.

Sara managed to keep a straight face and restricted herself to a safe and expressionless nod of acknowledgement.

Stones moved in front of the second woman, indicating to Sara to lean over beside her to get a close look as he spoke the words meant to taunt and tease the helpless submissive.

"Jezebel has shown definite designs towards Porter, Serf. Of the three, she is the one I feel that you might wish to bestow most favour upon. Favour, of course, is a word of my choosing. You may wish to think more of retribution or revenge. However, I think that she should have the opportunity to speak for herself. Say hello to Serf, you strumpet." Stones snapped her mouth gag out with no sense of gentleness whatsoever.

Sara found herself revelling in this role play. The three women that Jamie had described in detail as basically lusting after him at every turn were clearly being handed to her on a plate. She did not need much prompting from Professor Stones to slip into character. She could not think of anything that she would relish more than putting these three to the sword. Submissive or not, she welcomed the chance to cause them to suffer.

She poked and prodded at Jezebel as she moved around her. She knew from Jamie that she was the most vocal and forward of the three women. Sara ran her fingers through the black hair before sliding her hands underneath to encase the large, white breasts which, like her bottom, contrasted starkly with her otherwise tanned skin. The breasts felt full and soft, light pink aureole surrounding dark, jutting nipples which Sara pinched hard, rewarded with a small gasp from the slave girl. Putting her hands on the generous buttocks, Sara parted her anal cleft fully, inspecting the dark hole with its clearly defined ringed entrance, surrounded by a forest of dark pubic hair that grew abundantly all the way around her full, thick vaginal lips with its frame of silky black hair. She twisted a handful of pubic hairs harshly around her fingers, tugging and pulling as Jezebel gave stifled yelps of pain.

"Speak to me then, trollop. What have you got to say?"

"Oh Mistress Serf, Jezebel is sorry to have caused you to be jealous of her attraction to the lovely gorgeous Porter and his thick, hard cock. Jezebel meant no harm and is happy to face her punishment from his current mistress. Oh dear, your own bottom does look sore, Mistress Serf. Surely you have not been a naughty girl as well?"

Sara slapped her face hard and with real intent.

"You will pay for every word and every thought. Now, shut the fuck up, bitch, I will see to you soon."

Sara saw Jamie's eyebrows raise at her rather obvious anger and she reminded herself that she needed to be in control and that this was all a game. A game with consequences, yes, but a game nonetheless. Both Jamie and Professor Stones had briefed her in advance that this was not the real world and that the participants' behaviour here was a theatre production of which they were all bit part players. She took a deep breath and moved to the third of the exposed and bound women.

As Professor Stones snatched Sloth's mouth gag out, she yelped in pain and looked at Sara with no small amount of fear and apprehension. Reaching under, she massaged the small breasts and finding the petite nipples that slipped between her finger and thumb, she squeezed and pinched, digging her fingernails into the sensitive nipple tips as the woman moaned and struggled. Much smaller and slimmer than Jezebel in build, however, her bottom was out of proportion with well-rounded, prominent buttocks which stood proud and enticing. Even with her legs splayed, her cheeks were formed so that her bottom cleft was still tight and her arsehole was mainly hidden by small, brown hairs. Sara parted her cheeks with two fingers to totally expose her anal slit, tickling the tiny hole as Sloth tensed and clenched to deter her touch. Looking down between her legs, she espied the neat Brazilian landing strip consisting of tiny coiffured small curls, her labia perfect little interwoven, fleshy strips.

"You are a shy one. Are you sure you should be here, hussy? You do not look as though you will take much to break." With that, Sara ran a fingernail down between her buttocks, scratching along her arsehole and then twisting her finger sharply round the rim of the tight opening.

"Ow! No, I mean yes, Mistress Serf, madam. I am so sorry if I have caused you any offence. I meant no harm, and beg your forgiveness. Please have mercy on me."

Sara stood back, away from the three, looking at the bottoms that all showed signs of previous chastisement, recovering welts and minor bruises and mottled marks evident on each one. A maid had appeared with a trolley containing an array of implements, many for punishment use but others for pleasure-giving or pure entertainment, albeit some verging on the more perverse side of entertainment, Sara thought!

"Would seem rude not to start with a thrashing. Pass me a nice firm crop, please, Porter. I think that you can be useful to me if you just do what you are told, young man."

Jamie smiled and leapt to obey her as a murmur went up amongst their gathering audience in expectation of a floor show worth catching.

"I will start with you, Sloth, just to warm my arm up and get my eye in. I hope that you are going to show that you have a bit more courage than it appears. There will be a few markers to begin with, then be ready, as the rest will be rapidly delivered. Lovely tight bottom so these should mark nicely."

With that, Sara drew back her arm and lashed down with the leather-covered fibreglass riding crop. With her buttocks stretched over and open and her skin as tight as possible covering the jutting cheeks, there was little body fat to help cushion the blow and the resounding crack was followed by a yelp of pain from Sloth.

"Oh dear, how feeble. This is going to get noisy, I suspect." She swung again and landed the crop just below the first stroke. The response was identical and Sara swung down with a third, creating a perfect row of three straight lines across the protruding buttocks.

"Take a breath, trollop. Here comes hell." Sara was relishing the power and control, her senses heightened, and she became aware that her nipples now stood out erect and proud. Considering the performances and displays of her body that most of those present had been able to view over the weekend, Sara was not surprised to realise that she felt no self-awareness at all that she was naked, aroused and inflicting punishment to a helpless woman bound at her feet. She was not entirely comfortable in what had been unleashed from within her, but felt that was enjoying herself far too much to think too deeply about what this meant! She let loose the torrent of blows that landed randomly and haphazardly, which rather emphasised her lack of control and expertise with the crop. However, the effect was perfect as far as her supporting audience went. The buttocks before her were now criss-crossed with fierce red weals and Sloth was howling and thrashing – to the limits that she was able to move – in clear distress.

"You can thank your friend Jezebel for that. She has put me right in the mood to do this. Now shut it with your snivelling, you pathetic wretch, pull yourself together while I go and pay homage to Isabel's skinny little butt."

A sobbing Sloth still managed to stutter out words of apology and thanks as her training kicked in and, like most submissives, her agony turned to something approaching sexual satisfaction as the afterburn of her torment merged into a sexual buzz.

In truth, Sara was finding herself more and more attracted to the bottoms of naked females; she had certainly seen more than her fair share this weekend! Standing over Isabel's cute little bottom, the desire that had built up during her thrashing of Sloth was growing and she was well aware that she was now moist between her legs, and rather hopeful that this would not be obvious to others if her desire continued to develop. Unlike Sloth, Isabel's cheeks were spread completely and her cleft was wide open, giving a mesmerising view of her fine, blonde, tiny curls surrounding the neat little and barely crinkled anal slit above her labial lips. Sara shook her head to force herself to concentrate on the task in hand and much as she dearly wanted to drop to her knees and pay homage to the beautiful little bottom and pussy below, she raised her arm and swung down with force.

More resilient and experienced than Sloth, little more was heard from Isabel than discreet exhalations of air as the submissive used her familiarity of previous beatings to breathe in a controlled manner to aid in withstanding the stinging pain. As Sara increased her speed, the blows went into double figures, and she added to the developing sensation of the strikes landing on top of already suffering strips of flesh. Isabel began to cry out. Going alternatively to the more fleshy, lower cheeks then sharply across the tightly stretched skin across the top of her bottom crack, Sara found the submissive's breaking point, and with four strokes remaining, Isabel was screaming at full volume. Knowing that any show of mercy would not go down with her watchers, who were mostly agog, wide-eyed and relishing the breakdown of her victim, Sara laid on the last four strokes, one on top of the other, across the centre of the severely blemished buttocks as hard as she could.

Almost breathless, Sara stood back, cheeks aglow, lips glistening, her ardour in top gear, as she enjoyed the echoing screams from Isabel.

"Anything to say, strumpet?" she queried.

"Oh, Mistress Serf, thank you, thank you. Oh my, oh my. Isabel is most honoured to have received such a, oooer, my word, ow, sorry Mistress, such a fine beating. Isabel apologises for any offensive behaviour that has caused ire to Mistress Serf and earned her wrath. Isabel would be, in fact honoured, if Mistress Serf wished to lick her or fuck her. Isabel finds Mistress Serf most desirable and would feel very privileged if she wished to take comfort in her unworthy body in any way."

Isabel's soft and acquiescent voice was arousing Sara even further and after a sly look at Professor Stones, who just raised his eyebrows in response, she decided that as she needed to get her breath back before she thrashed Jezebel, a little sideshow as a break might be in order.

Sara found it hard not to be conscious that her body was on show for all to see and was too aware of the sight she presented to those behind as she dropped to her knees and dipped her head to Isabel's neat little pussy. As she looked up, she was relieved to see that most of the observers standing close had shed much of their clothing and were indulging in heavy petting sessions now. The distraction of spotting Pres's hand clearly masturbating Professor Stones's cock through the opened slit of his shorts, his cloak now on the floor, while he fondled her enormous breasts almost put her off her intentions. She wondered fleetingly whether any of those behind her were similarly reacting and found herself hoping that her open legs and exposed orifices were the cause of any activity. She began to lick up and down Isabel's slit, lips obligingly parting and swelling to accommodate her probing tongue. Sara loved the taste of pussy juice and was delighted that Isabel was a spurter whose inner juices suddenly appeared in globules of creamy liquid between her lips. She sucked and lapped at the enticing honeypot beneath her as fingers explored her own pussy. She hoped it was Jamie but in reality the thought that it might not be spurred her on to suck harder on the hard nub of Isabel's clit that she had captured between her lips. Sara was not sure who came first but both women shuddered and writhed as they groaned and moaned in their orgasms.

Jamie's hand beneath her arms took her back into the room mentally as he brought her to a seated position and gave her a glass of water. She hoped that the smell from his fingers was from her own wet pussy but it was not something that she found bothered her either way. She pulled herself together, relishing the fact that she had a waiting audience to entertain, and rose to her feet.

Sara picked up the crop and stood behind Jezebel.

"So, slut, your turn. Anything to say?"

"Jezebel thought that Mistress Serf must have forgotten all about her. Is Mistress Serf sure she is up to dealing with such a naughty little wench as Jezebel? Maybe Mistress Serf should stand aside and let one of the more experienced members take her place."

Sara almost laughed out loud at this woman's audacity, bound and exposed at her feet. She had to give her some respect, she felt, but decided that nothing so positive would be appropriate, much as she was in awe of Jezebel's confidence and courage.

"Oh no, sweet Jezebel, I have not forgotten you. Just making sure that I am ready to do these fine cheeks justice. Extra ten strokes for rudeness, disrespect and lack of humility would seem appropriate. We will see if you are quite so lippy and full of yourself after these." Saying that, she slammed down the crop and without pause unleashed a volley of quick, hard strokes. To Sara's dismay, as she paused after delivering the twentieth blow, the most she had heard from Jezebel was a few low moans and intakes of breath. A quick glance across at the impassive watching faces of Pres and Professor Stones was enough to restore her stamina as she prepared to give everything to the final ten. Jezebel, however, was not content to keep her triumph of silence to herself.

"Whoops, Mistress Serf. Seems like you are not up for the job. I have received a far more effective thrashing by novices that have just started their training. Do put some effort in, I don't like being tickled!"

Sara felt her cheeks redden and sensed the unease amongst the watching crowd. She met Jamie's eyes as he mouthed words of encouragement, having sensed her concern. She took a moment to compose herself as she was very aware that this had now became an extremely personal battle of wills between herself and the experienced submissive. She focused on the narrow strip across the top of Jezebel's buttocks where her bottom was at its most taut and less protected by flesh and swung her arm down. The clenching of her cheeks added to the satisfying crack as the crop landed and spurred her on to rain down six more strokes onto the same strip of flesh. Jezebel's breaths became audibly more rapid and prolonged but still she did not cry out as the beleaguered skin turned a purple colour and a thick welt rose high. With three strokes left to apply, she returned to the centre of the splayed buttocks and applied the three hardest strikes she could at the most prominent part of the woman's bottom. Jezebel's whole body seemed to tense, her bottom cheeks squeezing together as much as they were able and a scarlet line appeared where the crop had landed. Sara willed her to cry out to give her a chance of saving her face as the mood amongst the watching throng palpably darkened. No sound emerged from Jezebel, and Sara stood silent, feeling defeated and apprehensive as to any repercussions of her failure to cause Jezebel to break down and cry out. Sara sensed that this was to the crowd's immense disappointment and disapproval and was not at all surprised to find Pres removing the crop from her hand.

"Very poor show, Serf, very poor show. You have been bested by a sub, a tough sub to crack, I accept, but a nut that had to be cracked nonetheless. I now need to give you a lesson on how a punishment thrashing with this crop should be properly applied."

Sara stood back to allow Pres the space behind Jezebel before she was abruptly brought up short by Pres's next words.

"Oh no, Serf. I am not going to thrash her. I am going to thrash you so that you learn how a properly delivered beating with this fine crop should be applied. Now, move around in front of Jezebel and bend over. The professor will have your head between his legs to keep you still and your shame will be further enhanced by facing the minx that you have allowed to conquer you. After that, you will be allowed another attempt to break her with an implement of your choice. Now hurry along, smartly now. Legs apart, bottom up, head tucked down under Professor's groin. Thirty strokes delivered unsuccessfully – let us see how many it takes to make you holler, young lady."

Sara felt in a trance as her head went down, almost grazing the prominent erection of Professor Stones that tented the front of his leather shorts. The beaming face of Jezebel faced her, as she felt someone force her legs further apart. Jezebel licked her lips seductively, blew her a kiss and mouthed the word 'loser' into her face. Sara tensed as she heard the whistle of the crop through the air before it slammed across her still sore cheeks. The pain was ferocious but bearable and she gritted her teeth as she heard the second one approaching. On and on the beating went, Jezebel continuing to blow kisses triumphantly as Sara's face contorted in pain. Her desperation not to disgrace herself and retain her pride lasted until the halfway point of her beating when the crop flicked around her thigh and caught a piece of skin already badly marked. To Jezebel's obvious delight, Sara scream lasted for several seconds. This only seemed to inspire Pres, and Sara's resistance and dignity went completely as she writhed and twisted, attempting to avoid the fusillade of blows, wailing loudly with tears flowing down her face.

As Professor Stones pushed her face from between his legs, she could see Jezebel's sneering face as she quietly mimicked Sara's sobbing.

"Thank you, P-P-Pres. Thank you for c-c-correcting and g-guiding me," she stuttered out between sobs. "Please may I have the thickest strap and I will show you that I have learnt my lesson and punish this reprobate properly. Pres, she will howl and beg for mercy, I assure you."

Sara, trying to regain some composure, took some tentative steps across to the maidservant with her cabinet of articles and selected the thickest, longest strap from the selection. Jamie moved to her side and whispered into her ear.

"Hit lower and target the top of her legs; avoid that welt at the top of her bottom as breaking the skin would land you in more trouble than you would believe. Stand slightly nearer to her when you swing so that the tail end of the strap whips around the sides of her thighs and hits the tender skin there. Keep firmly in mind the whole time that if you fail to make her cry out, you will be receiving the same number of strokes yourself and I suspect that it will be Professor holding the strap. Trust me, my love, you do not want 20 lashes of the strap from him."

Sara resisted the temptation to tell him where he could put his advice, particularly as he was sporting an enormous erection again and she was not too impressed that this appeared to be as a result of her humiliating thrashing. The agony of the crop strikes did not appear to be diminishing but she realised that his words were wise and decided to try and win back some control of the situation. Taking hold of his twitching cock, she led him back to the still smiling Jezebel. Looking her straight in the eyes, Sara dropped to her knees before the woman's upturned face and took Jamie's cock deep inside of her mouth. To her relief, there was a ripple of approving noises from the onlookers as she took him deep down the back of her throat and began small, quick sucking motions. Jamie's moans added to the overall positive atmosphere as did the scowl that now appeared on Jezebel's face before she regained control of her expression and looked down.

Sara pulled away from Jamie. "We will return to that later. For now, I have a fat backside that needs a damn hard strapping."

She positioned herself behind Jezebel whom she could hear humming to herself in a totally unconcerned way, and brought the strap down from a much lower height that she had applied the crop and planted it with force on the backs of Jezebel's fleshy thighs. The humming stopped and Sara was pleased to see the tension form in the jutting buttocks. She brought down the strap repeatedly to the same area and, finally, as the skin turned bright scarlet, Jezebel began to moan and to Sara's delight she heard the words that brought her so much relief.

"We have some tears finally," came Professor Stones's voice, ringing out loud and clear.

Another stroke to the beleaguered thighs brought forth a wail and with renewed energy and strength, Sara struck the centre of Jezebel's buttocks, ensuring that the split end curled around her hip.

"Naaaaah!"

As though possessed, her energy levels restored and her feelings of vengeance enhanced by the response, Sara repeated the strokes.

Swish! Crack! "Naaaaaah!"

Swish! Crack! "Naaaaaah!"

Swish! Crack! "Naaaaaah! No, please!"

Swish! Crack! "Naaaaaah! No. No. No! Please, no more!"

With two strokes left to deliver, Sara took a breath and slammed the strap down to the highest part of the woman's legs that were still unmarked.

The howl was now much higher and prolonged.

With the thought that she had lived dangerously all weekend, she decided to take a chance and exploded the strap down across the top of her buttocks, catching the raised welt with a full-blooded, final strike. The screech was of banshee proportions as the welt flattened and sprang back, now framed by an angry-looking red surround. The skin held firm and Sara smiled triumphantly, congratulating herself on the chance taken with no comeback to be paid.

Jezebel was sobbing full on now, her punishment so severe that both Sloth and Isabel were trembling and weeping quietly. Whether in apprehension or sympathy, Sara did not know nor indeed care. She stood back as the applause rang out and enjoyed her moment.

Professor Stones moved in to take the strap from her and leaned over to inspect Jezebel's battered bottom, sparing her no mercy as he poked and prodded at the skin that was virtually entirely a bright red now.

"Took a chance with the last one. If you had broken the skin, your next couple of hours would have been an eye-opener, I can assure you. You have heard about The Torture Chamber, I take it?"

Sara gulped and nodded. Jamie had insisted on watching a few minutes of highlights on one of the screens over dinner and it had not been to Sara's liking. Secreted in the basement of the building, it was entry only for participants, be they givers or receivers, and no audience members were allowed to be present. Brief highlights shown on the screens had been a revelation as Sara had, for the first time, seen what true and dedicated sado-masochistic behaviour looked like. A selection of medieval torture equipment mixed with 21st century devices, extreme bondage situations and flagellations that had terrified her, electric probes invading all parts of the bodies, clips, buckles, pegs galore, enemas and water torture in abundance, and screeching and wailing that chilled her blood. Sessions were measured in hours, and were voluntary, albeit within the Society's punishment terms for rule breaking, and were the only option to expulsion, so there were degrees as to how voluntary the attendees were! Secretly, Sara was thinking that she would have accepted the expulsion option rather than be left for an hour with the masked sadists that she had seen on show. However, Professor Stones did not need to know and she suspected that it would have diminished her in his eyes if she had shared her thoughts. Like most of Stones's punishment subjects over the years, she still wanted his approval.

Meanwhile, the strap had been passed on to Jamie by Professor Stones.

"Porter, be a good fellow and give the other two a few with this. I fear they may be feeling left out! A nice rosy hue, please, there's a good chap. It will also allow Serf here to get her breath before she decides on the desserts that these three scallywags need to be served with."

There was no hesitation from Jamie and a big grin spread across his face as he immediately moved into place and began to lay long, swinging strokes of the strap down hard on the bottoms of Sloth and Isabel. He switched from one to the other after every two strokes and, within seconds, their screams rent the air to compete with the echoing cracks as the leather made brutal contact.

"A dozen will do. Give Jezebel an extra couple while you are there. Shame for her to miss out on your deliveries. Serf, have a rummage through the implements on offer and see if anything takes your fancy for your grand finale with these three wretches."

All resistance gone now, Jezebel's screams soon joined the companions in a choir of high-pitched, shrill renditions.

Sara had to her delight discovered a small, leather-knotted lash and was beaming with ill-intent as she took Jamie's place behind the three wailing women.

"I think it would be wrong of me to leave these three ladies with white patches anywhere on their bottoms. As you can see, they all have white strips between their buttocks although with such prominent, full buttocks Sloth's narrow crack is going to be a challenge. I think it would be nice to see matching red all over. In which case your final treat, ladies, is that I am going to use this perfectly proportioned knotted lash to thrash the insides of your bottom cracks. My audience seems to be in favour; what say you, wenches?"

Further sobbing from the three, with both Sloth and Isabel babbling apologies and begging for mercy. Sara was well aware that although the trio would know that the virgin pale skin between their cheeks would be very sensitive and the pain level would be extreme, their biggest concern would be that there was an inevitability that their arseholes and vaginas could well be recipients. She knelt down beside Sloth, facing in the opposite direction, and ran her fingers down the shaking woman's cleft.

"Not sure there is enough room here to properly decorate your inner cheeks. How I wish! I wonder if there is any objection to me releasing her hands to help me out?" Sara targeted the question at the professor and Pres but even as she hesitated, a maid was coming forward at Stones's nod.

With the woman's hands released, Sara bent her head down so that her forehead rested on the floor.

"Right, my dear, hands back on your backside. Fingers positioned where my fingertips are, now dig in and pull those fat cheeks apart, slut."

Sloth sobbed but with her bottom now raised high to an almost ridiculously subservient point, she proceeded do as instructed and yanked her cheeks fully apart, exposing her anal slit and its neat forest of surrounding brown curls. Her pussy was now fully on show for the first time, its Brazilian landing strip consisting of tiny coiffured, small curls trailing down to the neatly entwined labial lips. As she relaxed her tiny arsehole opened to present a dark tunnel to Sara and those craning in to see.

"Well, that's a surprise, looks like there's a crater down here waiting to be filled! I think I will be lucky not to lose the knot down there if I connect right," came Sara's laughing comment, amusing her audience but provoking a desperate clenching in response from Sloth.

"No, my dear, don't clench. The more open your valley is the more accurate I will be. Just in case you are hoping that these two holes here will be lucky enough to miss out, then do not waste your time. The last two strokes will be landing there on purpose, I can assure you. With the other ten, my intention will be to land them inside the lovely white bits of your crack. You should keep still and pray that my eye is in and that my aim is true, otherwise those fingers are going to get stung! Enjoy these last seconds of a pain-free pussy and arsehole, my sweet, here comes a living hell!"

With her elbow resting on the lower back of the trembling woman, Sara flicked her wrist down hard as she targeted the fleshy outer part of the opening. From the babbling for mercy of the three girls when they had heard what Sara was intending, she was convinced that the chastising of this sensitive area of their bottoms was going to be a new experience for all them. It was apparent that the fear factor had been elevated to way beyond anything she had witnessed from the trio so far. The first blow brought the perfect response as her aim was true, the knotted leather creating a perfect strip of bright pink with red blotches where the knots had connected. The narrow, splayed tip whipped down to the lower lips below, the screech of sheer pain and desperation her reward as she immediately landed a matching strike to the opposing cheek. With each following stroke, Sara carefully landed the small whiplash closer and closer to centre, Sloth's arsehole squeezing tightly closed with the result that the gap between her buttocks diminished and the impact caught the sensitive orifice unintentionally. With Professor Stones watching closely, Sara kept catching his eye to monitor his approval level; she was keen to do a good job and concentrated hard on the control and accuracy of her strokes. Stones's nodding head and beaming eyes, along with the wailing from her victim, were all the encouragement Sara needed as she placed the last two strokes, with slightly less force, down the centre of the crevice. Having deliberately aimed lower, her second stroke was perfection, one knot whipping down into the open, dark hole as Sloth relaxed her cheeks for a second, with the final two knots making contact with the labial lips below. The high-pitched scream in response confirmed Sara's accuracy and that the intended punishment had been as successful as she could possibly have hoped.

With the accompanying keening of Sloth, who rubbed at her stinging orifices, Sara moved to kneel down beside Isabel.

"Any more resistance, Sloth, and I will return and give you some more." The threat was enough to calm Sloth's actions, if not her loud wailing.

Sara ran her hands down the small cheeks of Isabel's bottom before tickling her pussy and arsehole.

"Hold still and hold tight. Here we go again."

The smaller buttocks were a bigger challenge with far less unblemished skin to aim for. The curl of the lash went under Isabel's body time and time again as she whipped her inner cheeks. The high-pitched screeching testified to the success of this as a pain-inducing punishment and Sara wondered, not for the first time, what exactly attracted these women to the role of submissives at these gatherings. Much as Sara had come to be comfortable with the knowledge that she enjoyed the sensation of being beaten and dominated in a sexual environment, she also saw it as a two-way street that was always jointly consensual in a role-play situation. Having once more been on the end of a thrashing from Professor Stones, she had a total appreciation of the difference between a full-blooded punishment beating where the intention was to cause distress, humiliation and anguish with no sexual undertones, and she had no doubt that there was a definite dividing line between the two forms. For these submissives there seemed to be little obvious pleasure, and not much choice or say in what they were put through here. She took a breath and thought *each to their own* as she whipped the knotted lash down the centre of the open cleft and completed her beating of Isabel with the last two strokes.

Both strokes landed accurately, the knots slamming against the proffered openings to frantic writhing and screeching from Isabel.

Feeling calmer and more in control that she had since she had arrived, she bent down next to Jezebel and began running her fingers up and down her cleft, tweaking her pubic hair and then sliding down her pussy up to the top of her bottom crack.

Sara was almost put off her stroke as she flicked nervous eyes towards Professor Stones, who had moved behind her, wanting to reassure herself that she was still meeting his approval. To her undisguised shock, she had chosen the moment when he released his fully erect cock and was guiding it into Pres's mouth as she knelt at his feet, her own skirt lifted as she masturbated in full view.

Aware that she was offering him a full open view of her own bare bottom, she automatically closed her legs tight to a guffawing laugh.

"No, young lady, keep them wide open. Enjoying the sight! Remember that you are on a punishment weekend, so legs wide apart. Let the room see your goods again. In case you had not learnt your lesson from the poor cropping that you gave Jezebel, and the repercussions you suffered, I ought to point out to you that unless you make her howl again then you will be receiving a corrective lesson between those gorgeous, if rather disfigured, buttocks yourself.

So, concentrate and let us hear evidence of a job well done. Beat her, Serf, beat her hard."

Gulping but forcing herself to comply, she spread her legs and pushed her bottom out before returning to her fingering of Jezebel's cleft. Sara enjoyed the moment of gently massaging the stark white strips of skin on either side of the nervous woman's winking anus and, with one hand still holding her as open as possible, she whipped the lash down for the first time. Harder than she had struck the others, there was a clear slapping sound as the lash made contact, followed by a yelp from Jezebel before she managed to stifle herself. As Jezebel unwisely took the second stroke with barely a sound, Sara's anger at her resistance, combined with the fear of the fate that would befall her if the courageous and stubborn woman continued to stoically endure her beating, gave her a determination that Jezebel would regret. Sara slashed down with force again and again until a full-blooded blow that whipped around between her labia lips drew a tremendous scream of pure agony from the, finally, broken-spirited young woman. Sara felt nothing but satisfaction; she acknowledged internally that she was being incredibly hard-hearted, particularly considering that Jezebel's stoicism had earned her deserved huge respect, but to her mind this was a battle and there could be only one winner. She slashed down again, slightly higher so that the lash was concentrated on the tormented woman's cleft, a knot landing perfectly on her open anus as she had intended. The scream became a banshee's wail, Jezebel reduced to shaking her head from side to side and begging for mercy.

"I am going to deliver a further six strokes across the lower part of your bottom now, just so that you will be reminded of me when you attempt to sit down for the next few days."

All fight gone now, each of the six blows was applied as mightily as Sara could manage and answered by more distressed howls from Jezebel. Her bottom was now just a sea of red; Sara's application had covered every part of her previously unblemished skin with a mixture of patches, raised weals, cane lines and blotches where the different implements had done their damage.

Sara was now in full flow and her passion fully aroused. She froze, momentarily, as she saw the face of Professor Stones screw up before he let out a long satisfied groan. Sara could see from the way that Pres was working her cheeks and swallowing rather noisily, with no small amount of drama, that she had taken his full deposit all the way down her throat. With a last, long suck, she pulled the twitching cock from her mouth and sighed, smacking her lips together in keeping with her show. A tongue flicked out and took a final drop of sperm from the tip of the wilting penis before a maid arrived with flannel and towel to obsequiously wipe him down. Sara was completely disconcerted as her eyes lingered on the sated penis of this most senior college academic, yards away from where her boyfriend stood with his fully erect manhood twitching in the air to the obvious delight of a middle-aged female club member who stood beside him. Conflicting emotions crossed through her mind as she tried to fully comprehend the surreal situation that she had found herself in.

"Please continue, Serf, we are all enjoying your performance. Do not let us distract you. You are doing a fine job of entertaining us all, please do not falter now."

His words sent a vibrating thrill through her. She felt vindicated, accepted and forgiven. She could hardly believe the acts that she had endured, partaken of and enjoyed but she knew that this was not the time for introspection. There may be regrets, and a fair portion of disbelief she was sure would come later but, for now, she was truly in the zone.

"It is not over yet, you worthless bitch, Jezebel. Wipe her face, please," she barked at a maid.

Sara strode over to the container that housed various, more natural, elements for carrying out a range of punishments and sexual rituals used by the Society. Looking through the root vegetables in one section, she beckoned the maid back over to her side. Flicking a glance at the professor and Pres, she was delighted to see both smiling encouragingly at her.

"Hand down to the bottom of the tub and scoop some loose dirt out, please. Now, young lady, you may rub it all up and down my bum crack, there's a good girl."

Sara, feeling in full flow as far as the theatrical roleplaying went, turned, bent over and put her hands around and spread her own cheeks. She could only hope that Jamie would see her performance for what it was and forgive her any over-indulgence as she turned to ensure that the display was facing the majority of her audience.

"Rub it in, girl. Get up that crack now, nice and muddy."

The sensation of the damp soil being massaged into such a private place (*well, it used to be,* Sara reminded herself) felt incredibly erotic but as she felt a fingertip invade her whilst another touched her moist vagina, she snapped herself back into her role.

"Stop, stop, stop. What a naughty girl, taking liberties. Can a volunteer take her into the corner and give her a quick 50-stroke thrashing with a whippy cane, please?" An eager volunteer, a young man who was naked apart from a crotchless jockstrap, his erect cock standing to attention, almost leapt forward.

"Take her away to a corner of the room and bring her back to me, in tears, to apologise, with a severely whipped backside please," Sara instructed.

"Now, Porter, time to sort that big cock of yours out again, I see.

Come here and stand right in front of the slut." Sara positioned Jamie to stand facing Jezebel, whose eyes betrayed that she was fully aware that she probably was not about to become the lucky recipient of the cock she had clearly lusted for ever since she had set eyes on Jamie.

Sara leaned down and pecked her on the nose

"Guess what I need, slag?"

Jezebel's doleful eyes indicated that had a very good idea.

"Yes, that's right, slut. I have a very dirty bottom and someone is going to wash it clean for me."

Sara dropped to her knees in front of Jezebel and moved to give her a perfect view as she lovingly took Jamie's huge cock into her mouth. She swung her hips around, spread her knees and pushed her bottom into Jezebel's face.

"Hmmmmm. Lovely," she whispered as she let Jamie's cock slip from between her lips.

"Your job, slut, is to completely clean me up to Porter's satisfaction by the time I have swallowed his cum. So, get that tongue out, your mouth open and start licking and sucking, bitch."

There was no hesitation from Jezebel and the slurping sounds from both women were soon holding the watching crowd in a respectful and intense silence. With her hands clutching his taut, muscular buttocks and Jamie's hands in her hair, gently massaging her scalp, the two fixed eyes on each other.

"I love you," he whispered as his breathing became quicker and he began to jerk his hips. Sara slipped one hand down to her dripping vagina and started to frantically frig herself, her fingertips catching Jezebel's chin as the slave girl slid her tongue up and down her arse crack. As Jamie spurted his cum inside her mouth, grunting loudly as his cock spat on her tongue, Jezebel took her cue, seized the moment and thrust her tongue into Sara's arsehole as Sara rubbed a knuckle against her clitoris to bring herself off. All three bucked and jerked as one for a moment, until Sara slumped to the floor. Jamie knelt down and pulled her bottom cheeks apart and turned to the nearest people in the crowd who weren't indulged in their own sexual activities, saying,

"Just check her out, friends. I think we can agree that Jezebel here has done a good job. Sara has a nice clean bottom, so well done, slut, you have done a good job."

Jezebel's smile, on her mud-smeared face, soon froze as Sara rose to her knees and took hold of Jamie's cock.

"Close your mouth, slut. Porter here is now going to smear my spit and the last globules of cum from his cock over your face. You'll stay that way, smelling of our congress, until you are released, whore." Sara wanted to take back the initiative, not over-impressed with Jamie's display of her rear quarters to everyone in such a proprietorial manner.

She had fully embraced her role and felt that she had mostly vanquished the beasts of envy and hate that had lain in her heart since Jamie had first told her about the three young women. However, she did not see any reason to let on that she had actually developed a real sense of respect and admiration for the way that Jezebel had just behaved. There was no reaction at all from her as Jamie smeared his dribbling cock around her face to mix with the smeared dirt. To Sara's slight concern, she was very aware that she had particularly enjoyed the abuse, humiliation and degrading acts she had put Jezebel through. She had relished allowing the bound woman access to her body, and had found the sensation of the woman's tongue invading her bottom as she had sucked Jamie off a real turn on. Luckily, Professor Stones jolted her out of her reverie before she did or said anything she might later come to regret.

"Let's hear your thanks and apologies, you horrible bunch of misfits!" snapped Stones as he walked around the stricken trio.

"Sloth!" he barked.

"Yes, sir, sorry sir. Sloth would like to thank Mistress Serf for her deserved punishment and is very sorry to have caused her any offence."

"That will suffice, I suppose," said Stones. "Isabel!"

"Yes, sir. Isabel would like to beg Mistress Serf's forgiveness, sir. Isabel is very sorry and most thankful and grateful to Mistress Serf for thrashing her so well. Thank you, Mistress."

"Hmmmm, Jezebel!"

"Oh sir, thank you, sir. Jezebel is so grateful to be given the opportunity to apologise profusely to Mistress Serf and to thank her for beating her, abusing her and degrading her in such a wholesome manner. Jezebel humbly offers Mistress Serf herself, in her entirety, whenever Mistress Serf wishes and would gladly make herself available for more chastisement if anyone thinks Jezebel has transgressed further or purely if Mistress Serf desires to inflict further punishment on naughty Jezebel. Please consider me at your service and disposal for anything you desire, Mistress Serf."

"Yes, thank you, Jezebel. That will be all. I think you have made your position rather clear, wretch." Stones's response was to raise his eyebrows theatrically and shake his head, and Sara quickly hid the smile that Jezebel's words had brought forth. Sara ran her hand across Jezebel's shoulders as she moved away and the look that passed between them sent a thrill through Sara's body. *Would there indeed be a second instalment?* she wondered.

Professor Stones and Pres now stood over the protruding sets of battered and beleaguered buttocks.

"A very good and efficient punishment appears to have been

carried out. Lovely rubicund cheeks with some excellent welts now fully formed, some very sore looking thighs and upper legs, always painful and so always recommended and approved of. An interesting and, as importantly, very entertaining element, performed with the beating of the inner cheeks, topped off by a laudable finale of a rather painful application to the anus and vaginas of all three reprobates. All three, especially Jezebel, should have learned valuable lessons today and I imagine that they are all most grateful for Sara's administrations. A damn fine job all round, do you not think, Pres?"

Pres moved across to Sara and hugged and kissed her heartily.

"Well done, young lady. You have been through one hell of a weekend. There are very few members who have not enjoyed sharing some aspects of your journey, either in person or on screen. You were certainly the most in demand person in the screening rooms and you have rather built up a fan club while you have been here. I hope you have found a few things out about yourself, as well as having paid your dues on Professor's instructions. You are most certainly welcome to join us again and I can think of a few more episodes that we could find that might take your fancy, judging by your performances so far. Good job, Serf. Your lovely bottom could probably do with some nice tender massaging with a moisturising cream. I would happily be the person to apply that cream if that would appeal?"

Although it was ridiculous, the joy she felt on hearing Pres's words made her beam with pride. Sara suspected that it would take her days to process exactly all she had entailed but, in truth, she was already coming to terms with her fantastical weekend and any sense of shame did not bother her for long. Given that this was the woman who had beaten her savagely with a crop, Sara thought it was rather incongruous of her to be feigning sympathy towards the carnage delivered to her throbbing behind. However, in keeping with the weekend and the continued opening of her mind, she responded in the affirmative and allowed Pres to take her hand and lead her off to one of the private rooms.

"Stay loyal while I am gone, my love. Just got to be attended to by this lovely lady. I should imagine I can probably be seen in a cinema near you shortly!" she threw back over her shoulder, seeing Jamie's inquisitive face.

With no reservations whatsoever, Sara climbed onto the double bed in the centre of the room, aware that the tiny blinking lights signaled the cameras filming from every angle. Any shyness or disquiet about her bodily flaws, real or imagined, had left her completely. She was well aware, if she had not been before, that the mirrors on each wall rather highlighted that her bottom was badly marked and possibly not at its most attractive, but this did not seem to be the environment to let it worry her. She dutifully parted her legs as Pres leaned in behind her, almost covering Sara's body with her own, and began the massage by rubbing in handfuls of very rich cream into Sara's shoulders and back. Sara wallowed in the most exquisite manipulation of her body as Pres displayed skills with lightness of touch and thrilling tenderness that her size and demeanour belied. All tension left her body as Pres's hands swept up and around, kneading where it was necessary and tantalising her in between. When finally the hands stroked her bottom, Sara was in a state of blissful serenity and she allowed Pres's knees to part her legs wide open and slide pillows under her haunches without the slightest concern. The cream was slathered around and around her sore bottom cheeks repeatedly before a finger trailed down the parted cleft, lightly caressing her anal ring as thumbs parted her cheeks fully. Sara swooned as she felt the tip of Pres's nose which probed her most secret place, and her head spun as a long tongue entered her pussy. As Sara raised her hips high to urge the tongue deeper, one hand slipped beneath her, fingers and thumb rubbing hard against her clitoris. Sara's orgasm was intense and extended as the embedded nose, long tongue and thick digits worked their magic in her orifices, and she bit down on the sheets as she tried to stifle the scream of ecstasy forced from her mouth. As she lay panting on the bed, Pres's hands once more caressed and massaged her body, gently soothing her as she recovered from her frantic climax.

"Probably time we joined the others. Not that there will be any mystery about what we have been up to," said Pres as she helped a breathless and exhausted Sara up.

"Did you want me to repay the compliment?" offered Sara in her huskiest voice.

Pres laughed. "No, love, you're alright. My treat."

They rejoined the others to knowing nods and a wink from Jamie, a glint in his eyes and, more noticeable, a throbbing erection illustrating that he had indeed been watching her latest session. One other thing she had learned, she pondered, was that her lover had quite impressive powers of recovery!

A light evening meal preceded their departure and Sara found herself the subject of much praise and knowing nods even before the highlights of the weekend began playing on screens all around the room. Once she had got over the embarrassment of her most private places being displayed close-up in high definition imagery, particularly having to sit and suffer too much catcalling and whistles as she ejected Maltesers from her body, she started to enjoy the attention. There were a lot of *oohs* and *aahs* at the finale of her treatment of the three submissives but they were noises of approval, albeit Sara herself was beginning to feel some guilt at the level of force she had employed and the pleasure it had given her.

Having not seen the trio since she had left them, they were still in Sara's thoughts when they checked out ready to depart. She was delighted, therefore, to see the three on their knees, naked and bent over on a bench by the exit with a sign inviting anyone leaving to inspect them and deliver a slap to their exposed behinds on their way out. Sara could see the full glory of her administrations as although much of the initial redness had diminished, the discoloured skin in certain places was producing a mosaic of shades of red, brown, blue and purple as bruising and healing began. The The vicious-looking weal across the top of Jezebel's crack had a beacon-like quality now, although her legs were by far the sorest looking and, with her knees wide apart, the stark redness of the marks littering the skin in her anal cleft were obvious to all.

As Sara moved to face them, she was not at all surprised by the differing reactions. Sloth looked cowed, apprehensive and visibly shrank from Sara's closeness to her; Isabel gave her a solemn and respectful nod before submissively lowering her head; whereas Jezebel grinned and gave a cheeky wink. Sara could not help but admire the woman's spirit as there could be no doubting the discomfort she was in. Jezebel beckoned her closer and as Sara bent down to her face, she whispered softly into her ear.

"Loved licking your dirt hole out, Mistress; we must do it again sometime."

Sara pulled back abruptly; she had expected something flirtatious and could see by the beam on Jezebel's face that she had enjoyed her triumph. Sara could not disguise her surprise at the woman's front. Unfortunately for Jezebel, Professor Stones had spotted the interchange and read the situation perfectly.

"Right, Sloth and Isabel, you may go to your changing rooms, get dressed and wait to be transported away. Jezebel has just volunteered to remain alone and has kindly offered to be caned and whipped by anyone still to depart."

Almost immediately on his words, a receptionist appeared, carrying the mentioned items and laid them beside the outspoken Jezebel, whose head was now down on the table top, and she looked as though she might be regretting her impetuous tease.

"Allow me to demonstrate as an example to you all," said Stones, addressing the gathering that the spectacle had attracted.

Whop! Whop! Whop! Whop! Whop! Whop!

He laid the cane, tightly gripped, across the centre of Jezebel's buttocks and passed it on to an eager, older and rather elegant looking lady who had come close to watch.

"Good afternoon, young lady. I am Lady Muck. I have not had much chance to deliver this weekend, having spent most of the time sucking cock and fanny and being shagged and beaten myself. I will therefore enjoy a spot of dominance. I am a renowned leg stinger myself. I find it returns a higher level of verbal reaction from these little imps. They tend to be not quite so keen on a proper punishment intended to hurt rather than to arouse."

The tension that appeared in Jezebel's body as she steadfastly maintained her supplicant position gave early evidence to the truth in Lady Muck's words. As the cane flashed through the air to strike the back of Jezebel's legs at mid-thigh height, the immediate cry of pain gave further support to the theory!

Chuckling away, Professor Stones led them out of the doors and away to their waiting cars.

"Always good to end on a high," he chortled as the sounds of a now screaming Jezebel followed them out. "That young lady does not know when she is beaten, so to speak. Ha ha."

It had been a momentous weekend in Sara and Jamie's burdening relationship and the journey home led to a lengthy discussion as to whether or not they would ever want to share their sexual predilections in such an open manner again. The actual travelling was quite problematic to both of them, very sore bottoms being hard to endure only hours after the treatment they had both experienced. Sara was well aware that Jamie, in particular, was suffering as not only were the weals on the outside of his bottom causing him discomfort, but also the spasms internally as his muscles continued to adjust to the pummeling he had taken in his arse by the well-endowed Hercules were a continuing sensation he was not enjoying. Not that this bothered Sara a jot. Whilst she was impressed that he had voluntarily gone through their mind-blowing time in The Gay Zone, she had little sympathy for his discomfort and was secretly pleased that he had been on the receiving end of an experience that she was well aware he wished to replicate with her, albeit from a different perspective! Admittedly, her jokes about needing to use a broomstick to turn him on and bring him to orgasm in future seemed to be wearing a bit thin, judging by his sour expression.

Within a day, however, they had committed to move in together, with Jamie agreeing to put on hold his attendance at the BADS meetings and events but Sara agreeing that he should continue with his support to Professor Stones when required for punishment beatings at St James'. Jamie was relieved that Sara acknowledged that it was a pleasurable hobby of his and that she could live with it, particularly as it perhaps would save her own bottom from his need to cane so regularly! Knowing that just being present in the room occasionally, when Professor Stones dished out his thrashings, aroused her no end so she could hardly quibble with Jamie getting his kicks in the same scenarios. *No secrets* was their mantra and the weekend had seen them exposed in a way that few couples would ever experience and it had solidified their love and sealed their devotion to each other.

CHAPTER 10

IN WHICH WE MEET DAISY

AND CASPIAN

Professor Stones fixed the young couple before him with his well-practised, most penetrative stare: Daisy Weaver, a second year Land Economy student, and Caspian Corlington, a Sociology student from the nearby Victoria College, one of the city's most revered institutions. Stones had worked diligently over the years to develop very close connections, at the highest level, in all of the 12 colleges that made up the collegiate body of the city's university and was aware that the young man would be in deep trouble if Stones pursued this matter with vigour. His presence in Stones's quarters suggested an opportunity that would be a first in his time as Dean of Discipline, and he was intrigued to see how this one would play out.

The scenario was similar to many other cases he had dealt with over the years; the themes and content might be different but the basis was the same: an act of poor judgement and undeniable folly, now regretted. The punishment to fit the crime was terrifying to the miscreants, the hope that sincere apologies, promises for the future and unreserved contrition would be seen as grounds for leniency and an opportunity to escape unscathed. That glimmer of hope, overlooking the heinous misdeeds, could be feasible and possible. That misplaced faith that somehow there could be a perceived lessening of the seriousness of the crime. That belief that forgiveness was a gift that the venerable Dean of Discipline possessed and felt enabled to use. Stones allowed all this to take place in the minds of those unfortunates before him, without them realising that he had seen and heard it all before. As part of the punishment, Stones was happy to allow hope to develop before he crushed it with his mighty fist: toying with his subjects was all part of the process. He had no truck with any of the reprobates who risked bringing shame on his beloved college. If guilty of the most serious misdemeanour, then they warranted the most serious chastisement in his eyes. They needed to be ashamed and contrite, terrified and humiliated, thrashed and improved. He saw it as his duty as well as his undoubted pleasure to carry out the sentence that he decreed. The option of being 'gated' and restricted to college, suspended and sent off site, or the ultimate punishment to be expelled or sent down in disgrace, was not an alternative that appealed to many as the repercussions for their future were almost inconceivable to consider, let alone the involvement of their parents or guardians in their ordeal.

Daisy and Caspian had unwisely chosen the college ante-chapel to escape from the cold and discomfort of a blizzard on a late winter's evening. Fuelled by alcohol, the empty bottle of wine left behind rather confirming their impaired judgment, they had commenced with a kiss and a cuddle, and, left at that, no major infraction would have occurred, but things had developed somewhat. The young couple were not to know that the CCTV in the chapel was discreet and limited so the actual detail of their behaviour was not recorded due to the use of a concrete pillar which acted as the backrest to their canoodling!

The professor's ace up his sleeve had been that, having watched the recording three times, there could be little doubt that fellatio had taken place and brief glimpses of the young man's body had shown his erect penis prior to the activity and a rather limp one a few minutes later. Combining that with the bobbing head and low kneeling body of his partner in the endeavour meant the explanation of their actions was almost unarguable. Daisy's rearrangement of her clothing, the pulling down of a sweater tucked up under her chin, the obvious movements of re-fastening her bra strap and the tugging and buckling up of her trousers as she stood up, all nicely captured by the camera as the two tidied themselves up afterwards, added to the evidence. Caspian obligingly and inadvertently flashed his rather white and slim, naked buttocks at the camera as he got himself sorted afterwards which all meant that Stones had the perfect amount of proof to engage the couple with confidence. Footage of a gentle finger touched to her lower lip suggested from her reaction that a drop of his semen had dribbled out of her mouth and was the subject of much mirth for the two of them as she made a show of seductively sucking the finger before performing a dramatic swallowing sequence.

When she had first stood before him a week ago, she had been more bewildered than concerned to have been called before him. He had patiently explained to the shocked and terrified young woman that the college deemed her behaviour as being of the highest level of rules breech, and that her future at the college was under discussion. A traumatised Daisy had broken down and confessed fully, admitting her act of fellatio on her boyfriend, but only because they were very much in love and that, in the moment and fuelled by alcohol, they had forgotten their location and had got carried away. She pleaded, in floods of tears, that this was a solitary aberration that would never be repeated, and could she do household chores, clean toilets or any similar duties to make up for her sordid act? The professor, unsympathetic of course to her entreaties, had given her the opportunity to select an option that did not involve her parents being informed. It had taken a lot of patience from Stones, and a final exasperated threat with his phone in his hand to call her mother before a weeping Daisy had written her note of apology, remorse and contrition with a request to be subject to a thrashing on her bare buttocks to atone for her sinful actions. At the time, he had suspected that there would be follow-up messages beseeching him to reconsider or offer alternatives to her agreed chastisement and that she would seek to avoid the punishment. However, he had heard nothing and had to accept that it was possible that the student had more backbone and acceptance of her guilt with the accompanying requirement for a just punishment. He now had cause to reassess once more as the appearance of Daisy with her partner-in-crime in tow rather suggested that she had a plan in mind.

Under his gaze, Daisy's mouth opened and closed, sounds were made but no discernible words were formed, tears started to seep from her wide eyes and run down her cheeks, her demeanour that of a frightened rabbit caught in headlights.

"Daisy Weaver, would you please pull yourself together. Young man, hold your tongue – I forbid you to speak on her behalf. Spit it out, child, come on spit it out!" Stones had a damn good idea where she was going with her entreaties, but was determined that she would at least find the words.

As the dithering and totally flustered student continued with her struggle to form any recognisable words, her mouth opening and closing as she failed to deliver, Stones went in for the kill.

"Spit it out, I said, or should I presume, with the evidence I have seen on film, that you do not understand that instruction, prone as you apparently are to swallowing?"

He managed to keep a straight face which he was delighted to see was more than Daisy could do as she burst into floods of tears, her cheeks turning a bright shade of red which swept down her neck to the skin displayed on her upper chest.

"Sir, sir, I am so sorry. Please don't hurt me. Caspian says that he will take my punishment for me, sir. Is that OK, sir? Please, sir? I can't do this, sir."

The professor's face reddened and his lips twisted into a sneer.

"Unbelievable, pathetic and totally unacceptable behaviour from a St James' student. How dare you stand before me and offer up another to take your just desserts. I have a mind to double your punishment, young lady. If your young man wishes to take your punishment alongside you, then that may be a plausible concession but it certainly does not lessen your own punishment. If Caspian's college is happy for him to be thrashed as punishment for his part in your disgusting actions in a place of worship, then I would consider it just and correct that he endures this with you. I will speak to your college, Caspian. I am, of course, on very good terms with the Master and the Dean of Discipline. I am sure that we will come to an arrangement that will see you punished appropriately and to the satisfaction of all concerned. Sadly for you, your feckless girlfriend has proved so weak of fortitude and responsibility that you also have to accept a higher level of punishment to that originally planned. However, I am so impressed with your duty of care and your clear recognition of the abominably wicked deed that you have been caught performing, that I am minded to allow a bit of leniency in your case."

His tone of approval vanished completely, along with his calm demeanour and his passive expression, as he directed himself to Daisy.

"You, however, are a disgrace. Your sexual needs and desires are of no concern to me, but I accept the fact that you were desirous, slightly inebriated and forced into close contact as you shielded yourselves from the appalling weather. What, however, I do not accept is any excuse or reason to justify your shameful use of a sacred building to display your wanton nature and need to perform fellatio whilst allowing yourself to be penetrated vaginally by your co-conspirator here!"

His thunderous diatribe masked the fact that he had little CCTV evidence that any such acts had indeed been proven to have occurred. It was true that their body and limb placement during the activity on recorded film firmly suggested that his accusation was correct, but the images were not conclusive and his intent was to illicit a complete confession without them realising his lack of concrete proof. His ruse was proved successful when, ever the gentleman in his gallant protection of Daisy, Caspian fell conveniently into the professor's trap.

"Oh, but that was all my doing, sir. I am afraid that I just took advantage of the situation and rather got carried away in seizing the opportunity."

Stones inwardly smiled but with a flick of his hand stilled Caspian's tongue. Daisy however was keen to speak.

"Oh my, I am so sorry, sir, I hadn't even remembered that. Oh God, I can't bear the thought that you have a recording of me doing these things, sir."

"Well, Daisy, if it is of any relief to you, I can promise you that there will be no recording kept showing your blow job and cock-sucking, to use the vernacular that you youngsters understand. Added to that, we have you swallowing the spunk from Caspian's cock along with the fingering of your fanny and sucking of your tits. All of this you clearly enjoyed, even if your memory has let you down on the detail! No recording kept of the incident is dealt with internally, I should add. Do you understand what I am telling you, young lady?"

Daisy went from pure shock at his crude language to a look of sheer panic as she appeared to assess her situation. She squirmed as she tried to compose a response, her mouth opening slightly then closing. Her face flushed red in shame, her brow furrowed in concentration and her eyes showed her fear.

"So," she began with some hesitation. "If I have my spanking, then no more will be said and no one will be notified as to what happened?"

Caspian's nodding head rather exaggerated his clear relief that Daisy appeared to be finally accepting the outcome but his face was to drop alongside that of his accomplice when Stones laid out exactly what their behaviour had earned them.

"Finally, the penny has dropped, albeit the acceptance of the seriousness of your crimes and the deserved severity level of the punishment seems not to have completely registered."

Daisy's forehead furrowed as she blatantly struggled to comprehend the cryptic word craft employed by Stones. As always, he was keen to ensure that his miscreants about to undergo physical chastisement fully understood that their punishment was to be of their own choosing, albeit rather led by their noses, to the conclusion that he deemed proper and correct. Any supposed impropriety was very much made legal and socially acceptable if the punishments doled out were at the students' (all legally adults) bequest and not accepted under duress. So, Professor Stones had learned to be patient and amenable to his charges' hesitation and slow-wits in coming to terms with what he felt was their destiny. He fixed his gaze on Daisy and spoke slowly and clearly.

"Daisy Cleaver, you have correctly acknowledged your guilt in your note of contrition and have accepted that a thrashing would be a suitable and appropriate punishment for your actions. This is commendable and I commend you for your foresight. However, I would be rather disappointed and frankly quite saddened to hear that you feel a mere spanking of your bottom would suffice in regard to a fitting punishment for the heinous crimes committed."

He paused deliberately to allow a crestfallen Daisy to interrupt, and, as he had anticipated, his beguiling words led her meekly into the trap set.

"Oh sir, sorry, sir. Of course we deserve far more than a spanking. I am sorry, sir, I have never been caught doing something this naughty before and I don't really know what I should be asking for. Oh lord, sir, am I to be c-c-caned, sir?"

Stones took a deep breath and continued with his resigned air as he continued his monologue.

"Casting your mind back to our original conversation, when your foul acts came to my attention, I believe that I told you that you would have the option of undergoing a three-stage castigation as an alternative to the shame and public disgrace of being suspended or, indeed, sent down for your behaviour. I informed you that the college would be prepared to be lenient on this occasion if you were to offer up an acceptable substitute that we could consider a viable option. You requested, and, indeed, put into writing here, that you wished to be given a severe thrashing to atone for your transgression and the college accepted your offer and graciously allowed that you be given this second chance. You pleaded that your parents should not be informed of your transgression, and accepted that a formidable punishment of the corporal variety was the appropriate sentence for the offences committed. Please do not make us regret the opportunity you have been given, young lady. I believe that we are already indulging you in allowing young Caspian here to take his just desserts alongside you. Now, enough of all this, I do not have the luxury of the time to waste that you apparently do. Do you want this damned thrashing or not?"

The mention of her threatened expulsion sent tremors through Daisy's slender frame and, prompted by the noticeable elbow nudging of Caspian, she duly delivered the words of acquiescence and humility that Stones had been directing her towards.

"Oh sir, sorry, sir. Yes, yes, yes, I must be beaten, sir. Er, um, oh no, yes, yes, with a cane, sir, beaten, sir. Oh please, no, no. Yes, sir, sorry, sir, please give me a thrashing, sir."

Stones sighed as though exasperated with the student's reticence and reluctance to name her dues.

"Acceptable risks have acceptable outcomes is the best way you should view actions such as these. Despite your pathetic performance and reluctance to take full responsibility for your actions and the repercussions that must follow, I am happy that a thorough spanking of your bare buttocks, followed by a 30-stroke caning and then a grand finale of six lashes of my heavy strap, would suffice as punishment in this case. Allowing for this being your first known offence, and your obvious remorse, I believe that this is a merciful, mild and positive outcome for you. Unless of course you feel that we should apply a harsher response to your actions?"

None of Stones's words were alleviating the obvious distress of the tremulous Daisy but by now she was spellbound and nodding assent to everything he said.

"Oh no! I mean yes, sir, thank you, sir."

Caspian looked unperturbed by Stones' judgement and seemed perfectly calm as the professor turned his eyes onto him.

"Young man, as Daisy wishes, you will also be spanked and caned although the strap will only be applied to her as she is the one I wish to suffer the greatest. Enough of this tiresome forestalling: I want you both naked and standing in separate corners of the room, please, while I make the preparations for the consequences of the disgraceful actions to which you have admitted."

As Stones quickly sent a text, the two students began to disrobe. Caspian was naked in seconds, although his face turned rather pink as his underpants came down to reveal a semi-erect cock. Daisy, with her back to both males, was attempting to be more discreet as she slowly stripped down to her shocking pink underwear before looking round to see her boyfriend's rather obvious protuberance.

"Caspian! That's disgusting! How can you be aroused? What is wrong with you?"

Stones brought her up short.

"His erect penis, sadly unsubstantial though it is, is less of an issue to me then the fact that you still seem to have bra and panties on. Now, off with them and get into the corner this minute or I will double your punishment!"

It was enough to ensure that Daisy was naked in seconds, giving Stones his first view of her pert little breasts and neatly trimmed pubic hair before she turned to the corner as they both obeyed and presented their rear views.

"Well, what a matching, sweet, little pair of bottoms we have here. Hands on heads unless otherwise directed, please. You are both in the punishment period so everything is now under strict observance of compliance rules and submissive posture. Not much of a target unfortunately with such slender bodies but jolly aesthetically pleasing to be sure. I'll be checking your personal hygiene shortly and then we can get this little issue resolved."

Stones was delighted to see both naked bodies tense at his words, with Daisy risking directing a fleeting face full of woe and fearful anticipation at him. Meeting his eyes, she quickly turned her head back to the bookshelves adorning her corner of the room. The tension had not left their upright bodies for long before a long buzz and a responding click of release from Stones was followed by his inner door gliding open and the sound of someone entering from outside became apparent. Again, Daisy's head spun around and she took a step away from the wall before turning and bringing her hands down to cover her breasts and groin as third-year student Emily Govan rather danced into the room. Emily's pink cheeks and wide eyes rather signalled her eagerness to be part of the scenario she quickly took in, the inadvertent licking of her lips sealing the excitement she displayed much to Stones's amusement. Not that any sense of being in a good humour was shown on his facial expression as he moved towards Daisy and took hold of an earlobe to assist in dragging her unceremoniously to a side table.

"Welcome, Emily. I'll do the introductions later but first of all we have to deal with this young terror's inability to follow clear instructions. Hold your position, young man, as I am debating as to whether, in the agreement Daisy has made with me, you need to receive her punishment for disobedience as well."

Daisy was blubbering rather incoherently, pleading for mercy and apologising, but to no avail as she was forced to bend double over the table.

"A leather paddle from my cabinet for the backs of her legs, please, if you could be so very kind, Emily. Now, Daisy, compliance and obedience at this point will limit this little additional punishment to a quick six of the best to the tops of your legs. Any further resistance or poor behaviour and the extra strokes coming your way will be far more severe. Do you understand, young lady, or do I perhaps need to give you 20 with the paddle rather than six?"

The struggling and rather bewildered burbling from Daisy dried up as quickly as it had started as she processed what Stones had said. Bent over his desk, one giant hand in her back flattening her, she stopped struggling.

"Oh no, sir. I am so sorry, sir. I just was not expecting anyone to see me. Please, sir, I don't need the extra punishment, sir. I'll be good, sir. I was just surprised. Oh no, don't hit me with that. Aaaaaaarrrrgggghhhhh!"

Stones took the paddle from Emily and with one smooth movement slammed it down flush across Daisy's thighs, just below the dimples of her bottom. Emily slipped around to the other side of the desk and grasped Daisy's hands tightly in her own as her arms flailed helplessly under the firm pressure holding her down. The six blows came fast and hard, Daisy's upper legs glowing a bright red after the completion of this unplanned addition to the scheduled and agreed castigation.

Stones decided to allow her no opportunity to recommence her reluctance to acquiesce to further punishment and within seconds he had forcefully dragged her over to his chair and flung her over his knees in the traditional spanking position. Emily was quick to take her place at Daisy's head and grasped her firmly with one hand on each cheek, her eyes piercing into the stricken and flustered student's face which was filled with hope and desperation. Emily, primed by the professor, disillusioned her by slapping her hands sharply against either side of Daisy's face.

"Stay still, accept your punishment and try to retain some dignity. I will do what I can to help you through your ordeal but you must be strong and let me be your guide and comforter. Behave yourself, Daisy, and take what you are due; the professor is going to spank you now, sweetheart, so look at me and take a deep breath."

Stones smiled as Emily's rather bewitching words seemed to calm

Daisy down and he took the opportunity to land several blows on her buttocks which she presented as an unmoving target. The barrage had not reached double figures before the impact finally registered fully and reached Daisy's consciousness, and she began to howl and fight his hold on her. Emily's grip on the younger and smaller woman's head was firm as she continued to whisper soothing words that now failed to have any effect as Daisy reached that stage of most resistance and fought with a strength that belied her small frame. Stones, however, was well practised in his art, and understood the phases that his sufferers went through; and he knew that he needed to break through Daisy's resolve as he held her firmly and continued his thorough spanking of her small, hard cheeks. It was about 70 slaps in when defeat registered, the fight went out from her like a light, her body slumped and the defiance dissipated, the final spanks delivered to a passive body, small cries, yelps and copious tears being the only accompaniment to the torrent.

Stones allowed Emily to wipe the tears and continue with her quietly spoken words of comfort as he stroked the bright red cheeks, parting them to peer at the dual openings.

"You really have the cutest pair of little slits imaginable, my dear. What a pretty and cute anus you possess, so tidy, sweet little silky blonde hairs running right down to your labial lips. Lovely, lovely, lovely. Oh no, dear, do not tighten, do not be shy, it is a delightfully pretty anus, please display it proudly."

The professor was well aware that many of his victims would probably be happy to accept further actual physical chastisement than be put through his humiliation by word rituals but that very fact made him all the more determined to turn the screw and add to their feelings of shame, belittlement and disgrace.

"Must not have too much of a good thing too soon though and

spoil our fun, eh?" he chortled away to himself as he slipped Daisy from his lap and quickly rose and led her to his twin desks. She was bent over, and with Emily's willing assistance, had her wrists and ankles cuffed, her legs spread, her groin raised by the rubber mound below and between her legs, ready fastened in position for further admonishment before she seemed to register her position.

"There you go, my dear, all set for your caning soon. Have a rest to contemplate your shortcomings and we will give your young man his requested spanking before we move on." Tenderly running his hands over the blazing cheeks of the sobbing student one last time, he returned to his chair.

"Oh Emily, in all the excitement I have forgotten to check their hygiene. Better late than never; you know the ritual: armpits, vagina and anus. Please give them a quick once over for me."

Her face aglow with pleasure and excitement, Emily leaned her body completely over Daisy, whose body had stiffened in tension all over, to the limit of her bindings, at the professor's words. As Emily laid her head alongside of Daisy, she grinned in her face, blew her a kiss and dropped her head to sniff loudly under first one and then the other stretched armpit beneath her. A gentle kiss was applied to the stricken woman's forehead before, amid much whimpering from Daisy, she slid herself down her back until her face dropped between the young student's parted buttocks, her nose rubbing up and down from Daisy's arsehole to her pussy, making exaggerated sniffing and snuffling sounds as the defenceless woman tried in vain to squeeze and hold her cheeks together to avoid the inevitable denigration of the inspection, mewing pitifully in her disgrace and anguish.

"This one is lovely and lemon zingy fresh, sir. I wonder whether Caspian has been so thorough with his cleaning? We know what dirty creatures little boys are, don't we, Professor?" she said, turning to

Caspian. "Turn around and face me and keep your hands on your head. Hello to you too! Oh sir, he does seem rather pleased to see me!"

With a fingertip, Emily flicked the tip of the hardened cock that rose proudly from Caspian's groin as a deep red blush of embarrassment spread down his body.

"Yes, a sweet little hard rod indeed, Emily, but is it clean, my dear? Have a good look and sniff around that groin for me. I am not having a dirty, sweaty boy over my lap. If he needs cleaning, then you will have to take him into the bathroom for a good scrubbing."

Caspian's face was a perfect picture of shame, bafflement and denial as he stuttered in response.

"Sir, honestly, sir! Please, I promise you that we both thoroughly cleansed ourselves in anticipation of the possibility that you might accept my offer to be beaten in Daisy's place, sir. I can assure you that I do not need this intrusive inspection. Uuurrrgghhh!"

His words dried up as, with an encouraging nod from the professor, Emily encircled his cock with her fingers and moved it aside so she could bend in and run her nostrils around his genitals. With Stones watching her intently, Emily was careful not to overplay her role and while he was sure that she was gently applying and releasing pressure to the manhood grasped in her hand, it was done subtly enough for him to allow her leeway. Emily maintained her hold as she twisted him round, pushed his upper body forward and pushed her face between his buttocks.

"Results, please, Emily; let me have the verdict. Remember that this is just an inspection not a sexual adventure for you." Stones's voice brought Emily on to her feet as she manoeuvred Caspian back to his position facing the wall.

"Without doubt I can confirm that they have shared beauty products, sir. Overwhelming identical scent and flavour of lemons all round, sir, so no concerns on cleanliness sir. Pits, cock, balls and arse all nice and fresh, sir. All clear to proceed, sir. Would you like me to bring him over to you for his spanking?"

Stones had to hold his amusement in as Caspian's face, chest and shoulders had all turned red in his embarrassment, and his forlorn look at his twitching cock illustrated his recognition that it had taken on a life of its own!

"Yes, my dear, thank you, let us continue. My hand is about ready to perform again. Since he has helpfully provided a handle for you, I think you better oblige and use it to bring him over. Take a firm hold and walk him slowly over. Are you watching, Daisy? Your young man's penis is an obstinate little beast, is it not?"

Stones chortled away, adding insult to injury for the two reprobates and causing Emily to giggle rather vivaciously as she was clearly delighted to take a grip on his erection once more. Following the professor's request to the letter, she inched her way over to him, each step taken accompanied by a seemingly innocent and inadvertent sliding of her hand up and down his shaft, Caspian's eyes and mouth both wide open. Stones noted that he ignored the fixed and disapproving glare of his girlfriend, her head twisted round to allow her to focus on his walk of shame.

Emily completed her task and reluctantly removed her hand as Caspian's cock twitched and swayed on release. The young man stood before Stones, his beetroot red face a picture of despair, his cock still firmly erect despite the humiliating experience that he had clearly just undergone.

"Well, young man, let's see if you can maintain that level of excitement once the spanking begins. If you could be so kind as to lay yourself across my lap, legs apart, bottom raised, I will commence your punishment with a damn hard hand walloping on these sweet little dimples of yours." He ran his fingertips lightly over the tight cheeks of Caspian's arse before taking his arm back and swinging down with force.

The slap was loud and the handprint on the small bottom almost covered a cheek as the pink outline formed. Other than a minor flinch and intake of breath, there was little reaction.

"If you could try and keep that throbbing little member still throughout, please. Any grinding of your penis against my groin will not go well for you, young Caspian, however much it arouses you to be doing so."

The snigger from Emily was as if scripted, causing Caspian to raise his head from its fixed point on the professor's carpet and meet her taunting stare. His face turned a similar colour to his left buttock and he quickly dropped his gaze. A wink from Stones assured Emily that she was playing her role perfectly.

Slamming his hand down on the other buttock, Stones continued the verbal assault in the suffering student's pride.

"Disregard of rules, disobedience, humiliation, desolation, contrition, remorse and improvement."

Each word was accompanied by a swing of his arm and a stinging flat hand as Stones increased the speed and was rewarded by frantically tightening buttocks and little yips of pain in acknowledgment. He continued the mantra, alternating his strokes on the reddening cheeks as sobs from below were greeted by a very unsympathetic, grinning Emily. She released his hands and wiped his face as the tears and saliva flowed, indicating that the professor had broken through Caspian's resistance and reduced him to rather pathetic sounding, blubbing mess.

Stones was mildly surprised to discover the sexual thrill he was experiencing as he spanked the young man on his bare behind. It no doubt helped that the bottom on display was such a good example, owing more in appearance to the female form than to some of the more padded, hirsute and frankly blemished male buttocks he had had close encounters with at his fetish club, BADS. He could still feel Caspian's cock hard against his thigh and with fears that his own arousal would become obvious he reluctantly applied a final flurry of slaps.

Stones flexed his fingers; his palm stung badly after the double spanking and he was glad that the next part of their punishment would be with the cane. He reflected on whether or not he may have been misguided in not calling upon Jamie to deliver the canings but was content with the decision that with this being a first-time thrashing, the severity level that he intended to deliver was appropriate for the misdemeanour and that he would leave summoning Jamie for when the need was of the highest status.

"There, there, young man, hush your fuss. Emily, wipe his tears. Nothing to be ashamed of, you youngsters all break down and cry when your bottoms get sore enough. Your sweet little cheeks are very sore after all, hush now, shhh."

Stones gently stroked the inflamed cheeks and gradually they relaxed and the snuffling and sniffling came to a halt as Emily wiped Caspian's brow and smiled encouragingly at him. She laughed out loud, however, when his eyes filled with horror and shock as the professor parted his buttocks and, with a wink at Emily, he described the view.

"Oh he has got a charming little anal opening for a man indeed, Emily. You are so correct, good enough to frame, I would say. What a treat, no need to tighten up, young man, we are just appreciating an *object d'art*; do not be shy of such a beauty."

With that, he rose and tipped Caspian to the floor at his feet.

"Put him in place please, Emily; we will have a little break, maybe a cup of tea, and leave these two to contemplate what has happened and, more importantly, what is to follow. Thirty each with my medium cane is the agreed consequence for you both; think on, think on. Maybe we can finally cause you to lose that little protrusion, though I'm quite impressed that it is still so erect, young man. You must have very much enjoyed yourself on my lap, then. Come through when you have him ready, Emily, no touching his penis and no talking between any of you, unless you require additional strokes, of course. I include you in that, Emily, you must not be tempted to take advantage of your position, please. This will be your only warning so please do take heed, there is always room and time available for another bare backside that needs to be taken in hand."

Stones went through to his kitchen, leaving the chastened Emily binding Caspian down so that the two lovers faced each other, bent over, legs splayed and buttocks raised.

"Help me, talk to him. Please do not let him cane me. I do not want this, make him stop, please."

Crack!

"Ooooowwweeee!"

Emily's hand slapped across Daisy's upturned face without a moment's hesitation.

"Rule number one is do not speak, unless spoken to. Any further word from you and you will find that extra strokes will be added. I will help you take your punishment but any more nonsense like that and you could end up with a bit more than six with the strap, and trust me, Daisy, six is more than enough of that bastard, I can assure you!"

With Daisy's face now frozen, a red handprint on her right cheek, and Caspian transfixed by her dominant handling of him, Emily joined Professor Stones in his adjoining kitchen.

As she entered the room, Emily had good reason to be grateful that she had followed his instruction as Stones sat before a screen, watching the scene that she had just left.

"One sweetener in your tea, my dear, and thank you for that. All carried out to my satisfaction, especially that powerful and lovely reminder to Daisy to learn a bit more acquiescence. Well done, well done."

Emily beamed with pleasure at his complimentary words. Stones, as always, ensured that he had her under his complete control. He chatted away to her about trivial college happenings for a few minutes, Emily doing her best to keep up her end of the conversation although Stones was well aware of how surreal she found it. As she finished her tea, he rose, and as if they had just finished a work break, he took a sigh and turned to return to the main room.

"Needs must, my dear, jobs to be done, errant bottoms to be caned."

Emily laughed at his casual and offhand way of referring to what was to come, which possibly was not the ideal sound to greet the motionless, bound twosome. Caspian's raised cheeks tensed quite dramatically to greet them as they entered.

"Oh, you can relax for a while, young man, and perhaps concentrate on holding Daisy's hands in your own while I give her the whipping she has requested in payment of her dues."

Stones moved around behind Daisy, her whimpers failing to move him one jot, her unprotected buttocks exposed to his gaze as he leaned in and studied her intimately.

"Looks completely dry down there to me so at least one of you realised that this is a punishment and not a sexual adventure, eh Caspian? Emily, just have a check and see if that penis has still got blood pumping through it, please."

Emily kept her face in Caspian's eye-line as she slipped her hand under him and wrapped her fingers around his erection.

"Oh yes, indeed, Professor Stones. His little soldier is still standing to attention. He's probably quite excited at the thought of being able to watch Daisy getting her bottom caned, don't you think, sir?"

Stones ran his hands over Daisy's flanks, every word and action intended to increase her discomfort and add to the dread of what was to follow.

"These buttocks should suit my medium thick cane, please, Emily, if you can tear your fingers off her young man's penis, please."

A guilty look was thrown back at Stones, but he could see the glint in her eyes that rather broadcast her excitement and growing lust. The thought of any requirement to admonish Emily aroused him in a way that having these two youngsters strapped down and nakedly displayed could not match, and he shook his head to concentrate on the job in hand. Emily was a distraction at times, often welcome, he admitted to himself, and Stones realised that it was not beyond her to try and manipulate a situation whereby she would join the younger students on the receiving end of his castigation.

"Where would you like me, sir?" The coquettish blonde handed Stones the desired cane, her eyebrows raised, a contrived innocent expression on her face.

"Wiping brows, noses and eyes, my dear. I think young Daisy may well be one to present a runny nose and a tear-filled display. Take a deep breath, Daisy, your atonement is about to get closer. Help is at hand. The road to improvement lies before you."

The cane was in its way as he ended the patronising words and as the stroke bit into the taut little buttocks, the screaming commenced. Stones allowed Daisy time to truly absorb the impact and collect herself before he continued. It wasn't compassion or sympathy, he was not much given to those feelings. No, he felt that multiple strokes would be wasted if applied while the initial response to the earlier blows were still underway and he waited patiently until her frantic writhing and high-pitched screams subsided. As silence gradually returned, Daisy's buttocks tensed immediately she heard the swish of the cane and her skin tightened to its limits in anticipation of the strike. The compressed target, already with barely an ounce of fat to protect her, meant she presented a small landing zone even with her legs spread wide apart, and the cane landed for the second time with a loud crack across the centre of her taut cheeks.

Stones viewed the reddening line dispassionately as she howled in pain. He counted to ten in his head before slashing down again; he found her a poor target with no flesh to spare and her prominent-boned buttocks, albeit her pretty anus and vulva, and small, neat slits certainly met with his approval. He methodically tapped her cheeks with the cane several times between strokes, waiting for her to fully appreciate the punishment and keen to ensure that the beating would live with her for a long time. He aimed lower, targeting the more fleshy lower buttocks and tops of her legs. He could see that Emily had her hands full in keeping her face becalmed amidst the manic threshing of her head and banshee-like howls. It was one of the more lenient canings he had ever administered, but possibly one of the most impactful as Daisy suffered intensely and with much remorse and begging for forgiveness. Even so, her legs and bottom had blistered badly by the time that the cane had whipped down for the 30th time and he moved away to rest his arm before he started on Caspian. He watched as though he was an unattached observer as Emily soothed the beaten young woman's brow and held a handkerchief to her nose, whispering words intended to calm.

Stones, however, was not one to waste words with sympathy or support.

"Stop this nonsense please, young lady. I was lenient with the cane but the strap will be applied with full force and no favour, so take this time now to pull yourself together while I share the fun with Caspian, and prepare for the true hell the strap will bring to these little cuties."

His hand stroked her battered cheeks as he spoke, the purpose purely to add to her shame and dishonour as he deliberately allowed a fingertip to rest lightly beside her anal ring, twitching at its centre as she tensed her muscle in a pointless response to his intrusion. Stones was pitiless as far as the miscreants he chastised went; he rarely felt any regret as he had total faith in his mantra of punishment to bring atonement, remorse, contrition and improvement. He had faith that his actions only had positive outcomes – there was no evidence to counter this, indeed any feedback he did receive tended to be gushing praise and thanks retrospectively, often many years after the deed had taken place. Never had there been repercussions, never had there been recriminations and never had he been called to account years later. As he pondered on the past, he viewed the perfectly stilled, rounded buttocks of the young man who awaited his turn under the lash.

"Are you ready for the cane, Caspian?" Stones queried, tapping the cane nonchalantly across his bottom.

"Emily, could you please check again the state of his penis. Is he still aroused and hard, even though his love is crying her heart out in agony and despair before him?"

Emily's delight was evident to all as she slipped her hand underneath Caspian's body, her eyes meeting an aghast Daisy as she wrapped her fingers around his throbbing erection.

"Oh, indeed, sir. A decidedly firm and proud hard-on to be sure," she giggled as she deftly ringed his helmet and moved her wrist to add to his embarrassment and desire as his eyes bulged and he tried to stammer an apology to Daisy.

"Don't speak, boy. Extra strokes for any disobedience. Thank you, Emily, return to your position and be ready to wipe this young man's tears."

With those words, his arm swept down, drawing a gasp from Caspian as the blow cracked across the centre of his raised bottom. Stones was impressed with his stoicism as the first dozen strokes were greeted with nothing other than expansive realises of air. With such a petite bottom and no real trace of excess fat to pad the target area, Stones had assumed that he would reach the student's pain threshold much quicker. He whipped the next six strokes hard and fast, concentrating on the fleshier patch of skin where Caspian's cheeks met the tops of his legs. The gasps became louder, watery sniffs indicating a tearful demeanour, and Stones was pleased to see that Emily finally needed to move in to wipe his eyes and nose. A change of target led to a more vocal response as the cane bit into the top of the stretched buttocks, the thinner skin providing little protection, and strangulated cries now filled the air as Caspian's body thrashed about in his restraints. The next three were directed to the backs of his legs before the following six centred on a small strip across the middle of his buttocks, all pretence at showing forbearance or maintaining an ounce of dignity being entirely gone as the young man screeched and begged for forgiveness.

Stones hung up the cane, picked up his heavy strap, walked directly behind Daisy and with no words of warning slashed her cane-welted cheeks with a powerful blow. Daisy's head rose for a moment and froze in place before the impact of the strap registered fully. The sound of the still sobbing Caspian was drowned out as a piercing shriek from Daisy rent the air and she began to bang her forehead down on the table top before Emily was able to envelope her face in her hands.

"I know, sweetheart, I know. It's awful but it will soon be over. Count them down, darling. Just five more to go,"

That five became four and then three in quick time as the leather landed lower down and Daisy repeated her frantic reaction to the appalling suffering brought upon her by the strap. Stones waited, unmoved, of course, by the howls of the young woman; he had never regretted the severity of a delivered punishment and was well practised in his dispassionate response to the despair and agony he brought to bear on his miscreants. He allowed a minute to pass, and again, with no indication to warn Daisy, delivered a fourth blow just above the earlier three and with the same savage intent. It was so successfully delivered to the extent that Daisy's wail surpassed the volume of her previous reactions and Emily had her hands full in trying to stop Daisy harming her head and face as she flailed in her torment. Again, Stones waited until Emily had talked down and soothed the despairing Daisy before unleashing the fifth tempest to her ravaged buttocks.

"Just the one to go, young lady. Please compose yourself so that you are of the correct mind-set to appreciate the message that I am delivering with this thick piece of leather. I would like your full attention to the future rather than the past. So perhaps I will wait until you are ready enough to request the last stroke. Yes, yes. Let us take a moment to savour what has gone before and prepare ourselves for the grand finale, the blow to end all blows. Although not too long as I could always start again at the beginning if you appeared to be uncooperative in any way. I do so enjoy the effect of my favourite leather strap. Look at those cheeks – so very red. I call it The Glow!

There's nothing like it, a beautiful sight created by a beautiful implement. So gorgeous, such beauty. What a delight!"

If his intention had been to cause Daisy more turmoil, more shame and more fear, he appeared to succeed as she sobbed loudly and pitifully.

With Emily whispering words of encouragement into her ear, the tormented girl finally raised her head and blurted out the words that would earn her the final agonising moment of chastisement.

"Please, sir, oh my, oh no. Oh please, sir, can I have my final one, please? Aaaaaarrgggghhhhh!!!!!"

Stones had not waited for Daisy to settle as she finished her forlornly spoken request. The strap landed exactly on top of the first stroke, the red stripe turning purple as the skin blistered and swelled, her bottom now an array of raised welts, deep red bands and fingerprints. Daisy's reaction was perfect, bringing a huge smile of satisfaction and victory to Stones's face as her howl echoed around the room and tears flowed down her cheeks.

"Excellent! Good show, job done. Release her please, Emily."

Any vestige of modesty had long gone and Daisy sunk to the floor as the last cuff was unstrapped. Presenting her raised bottom to the room, she grasped her battered cheeks as she knelt, howling in despair and suffering.

"Take her into the bathroom, put her on the bidet, leave her there and shut the door, please, Emily. The iced water should be the perfect temperature by now. It will calm the throbbing and help with any bruising, along with removing her from our company whilst she is making that awful din. Daisy, you will stay on the bidet until you are collected by Emily in a few minutes. Do not move from there unless you wish to suffer further consequences. I have another job for you, Emily, so on with it, please, and remove this noisome creature from my hearing."

With Daisy out of sight and more importantly as far as Stones was concerned, out of earshot, Stones instructed Emily to take a seat and Caspian to bend over her lap.

"Not sure if you deserve this little treat but you have taken your dues with some dignity, and Emily will now apply some soothing cream to your stinging buttocks to give you some respite."

Stones was perfectly aware that he was putting temptation in her path but he was confident that Emily would realise his intention was to test her and, as far as he was concerned, the game was afoot! His own arousal heightened at the scenario he had set as Caspian dutifully settled over her lap, his erection still proud and clearly signalling his enthusiasm for his promised treat. As Emily scooped out a dollop of the moisturising lotion, Caspian raised and fully presented his sore and swollen cheeks, evidently keen to receive the feel of Emily's fingers on his beleaguered skin. Stones watched as she tossed her hair, raised her eyes to his, as though to challenge his authority, and swept her hands over his bottom, the cream being smeared plentifully over the reddened flesh. Still holding his gaze, she allowed a creamed hand to slip under his body and Stones remained impassive as Caspian gasped to signal that her fingers had found her target. With her visible hand over his cleft, Emily had a smile on her lips as she rimmed his arsehole with a fingertip and made clear her intent to breach his hole. The surprise to all three was Caspian's resilience to the activity already undertaken was suddenly surrendered, as frantic movement underneath and a squeal from Emily was matched by a guttural groan from the young man that signalled his loss of control.

"What exactly have you two got up to?" Stones knew full well but he was never one to miss an opportunity to belittle those under his control and add to their embarrassment.

Caspian struggled to his feet; Emily now had both hands at his groin which he in turn attempted to cover with his own hands.

"Hands away, both of you. Let me see what state you are both in," Stones thundered.

Caspian stood looking at the ground, cheeks red, his cock now losing its erection, his cum still dribbling from the tip. Emily kept her hands cupped together, and Stones could see her total concentration focused on not allowing any of his ejaculation to seep between her fingers.

"Emily, do not let any semen drip onto my carpet or you will be sucking it up while I thrash your bare backside!"

Without a moment's hesitation, Emily dropped to her knees, swallowed the contents of her hands and took Caspian's cock into her mouth, a very unladylike slurp accompanying her administrations.

Caspian was frozen to the spot as Emily withdrew, licking her lips as surreptitiously as possibly but her fleeting, wry look at the professor rather signalled that she was well aware that she had transgressed badly. Stones's look of fury in response confirmed that!

The professor marched the two of them to the bathroom by the scruffs of their necks.

"In here, you two! Up from there, Daisy. Grab a towel, get back in the room and dry yourself down. Caspian and Emily have disgraced themselves and need to clean themselves up."

Daisy was out of the room before she could see the evidence and Stones saw that she was perplexed and unsure of what had occurred.

"Dry yourself off quickly and hang the towel over the back of the chair. Hands on head and turn round and bend over, and I will have a look at that thrashed bottom to see if the job has been done as it should."

His delivery was as offhand and presumptuous as always and

Daisy automatically obeyed and as he had requested, presenting her temporarily despoiled bottom to his eyes without hesitation. He ran his fingers over several of the marks, murmuring in satisfaction,

"Yes. Very pleased. I hope you are satisfied that you have been appropriately dealt with? You may turn and answer."

Daisy faced him, her cheeks red but she seemed composed, taking into consideration her earlier demeanour.

"Yes sir, I suppose so. Does this mean that the matter goes no further, sir, and no one else will know?"

Stones stared at her for a few seconds until he saw signs of her newly found composure slip.

"You may wish to write me a short essay, detailing how you have been punished as agreed, accepting full blame for your actions and total appreciation for the methods used to take you on that journey from guilt, remorse, contrition and improvement. Then, if I find it to be satisfactory, I believe that I can pronounce that the matter has been dealt with, to the agreement of all parties and move on. We do have the issue of your young chap depositing the load from his testicles into Emily's hands, to deal with yet, though. Yes, my dear, I am afraid that his self-control let him down and encouraged by vulgar conduct from Emily, he ejaculated before me into her hands. You may wish to contemplate whether you feel that any action should be taken as far as that goes for both of them."

Daisy's eyes blazed for a moment.

"Did she toss him off? Is that what was going on?"

At that moment, Emily and Caspian re-entered the room. Stones's eyes, and Daisy's, were drawn immediately to his groin and the limp, rather forlorn looking cock nestling there.

"Did you let her toss you off? Did you bloody well pull my boyfriend off, you bloody slut!"

The next noises she made were yelps of shock and pain as Stones lifted her clean off her feet with one arm and deposited her face down across his lap as he moved swiftly backwards onto his chair. The cascade of blows echoed loud in the room as the professor's giant hand slammed down on her already sore cheeks a dozen times before he pushed her from his knee, leaving her crying and distraught once more before him.

"Daisy, if you learn one thing today, you do need to take away from this room that you need to think before you speak!" Stones was scornful in his dismissal of her as he pulled her up by one arm and led her to his writing desk to compose her words for her official act of acceptance of her punishment.

"However, you do have a point concerning the errant behaviour of these two. I particularly have an issue with someone acting as my support assistant taking sexual advantage of one of my reprobates being chastised."

Emily coloured but held his stare and Stones waited her out until she broke the long silence.

"Sir, I do apologise, my action was unwise and unacceptable. I do believe that I should receive a reminder of the standards I need to bring to your service. I am happy to take a caning as an aide memoir for the future, sir."

"Indeed, young lady. I believe that would suffice. Twelve strokes of my thick cane should be an apt reminder to you to behave better in the future."

He stopped in mid-flow as there was a buzz from his front door and with a quick glance at his computer screen, Stones gave electronic access to his caller. Dr Celia Ford, the Senior Tutor, burst into the room which caused both Daisy and Caspian to shield their intimate areas.

"Apologies, Dean, got here as fast as I could but as you know I was quite tied up. Looks like I have missed most of the fun, eh?"

Stones noted a sullen look appear on Emily's face as she realised that her role was now threatened by the professor's recognised deputy on hand and her decreed punishment would have an added viewer.

"Daisy, on your feet, hands on your head! Caspian!" Stones did not need to say more as both students immediately adopted their positions.

"Both of you can turn and bend over so that Dr Ford can inspect my work. Come on, turn and present. Move yourselves!"

Stones's tone brooked no argument and, hands on ankles, Daisy and Caspian once more found their thrashed bottoms being handled and peered at.

"Excellent, excellent. So sorry not to have been here to be a part of this. I can see that the thick strap has been at work. What a shame to have missed that."

With a final pat to Daisy's tender bottom, Celia indicated the two should return to their former positions, but as Daisy sat back down to write her piece she raised her hand. Stones granted her an affirmative nod as he allowed her to speak.

"Sir, Doctor Ford. Could I suggest that Caspian and Emily should be given six each with that awful strap as punishment for their disgusting behaviour? Emily should get that on top of the 12 with the cane don't you think, sir?"

Stones quickly brought Celia up to date as Emily squirmed in shame before a knowing, intense look from the Senior Tutor.

"Oh indeed, that sounds like a fair result, Professor Stones. In fact, as you have been so busy would you like me to deliver the prize? It would certainly be my honour to do so." Emily wilted before her challenging gaze and Stones could see that there was an anger in Celia's words that did not bode well for Emily. He was fully aware that Celia's presence in the room would add to Emily's chagrin and could see the self-recrimination in the student's eyes. Caspian's mouth had fallen open at Daisy's suggested punishment; then, his eyes welled up as he struggled to come to terms with the repercussions of his inadvertent moment of pleasure.

"Good call, Dr Ford. Yes, yes. But six strokes will suffice for Caspian. Emily, however, does need and deserve to be dealt with more severely. You may apply 12 hard strokes with the strap to her bare buttocks, we will leave the cane for now. Of course, if we have any further disobedient behaviour from you, my lady, then that punishment will come back into consideration. Once Daisy has finished her little bit of written work, we will commence with Caspian's thrashing. Emily get those clothes off, please, you should be naked and in the corner for the time being I think."

Emily started to remove her top. Stones could see that the thought of 12 strokes with the vicious, thick strap had knocked the life and light from her and she looked defeated and quite fearful. He was as aware as Emily was, that as much as she had a penchant for the bite of the cane and the stinging sensation it wrought, the strap delivered a different outcome and her earlier introduction to his thick leather favourite had not brought forth much in the way of pleasure for her.

Daisy raised her hand again.

"Sir? Would it be possible for Caspian to have his beating and leave before she takes her clothes off? I don't want him seeing her naked, please, sir."

Stones looked at Daisy until she began to almost shrivel before him.

"Hmmmm. I have given your, unasked for, proposal due consideration and believe that it has some merit. However, it is me that calls the shots in this room, young lady, and not you. I may just overlook you speaking out of turn this once, though. I have taken on board your concern and my decision is that Emily will for the time being stay partially clothed in front of Caspian, but will of course not be allowed to retain any form of protection when being strapped. However, Emily, top off, drop your trousers and put your hands on your head."

Turning to Caspian, he instructed the young man to bend over and put his hands on his ankles. Stones took his time, as though in great thought, as Celia took the strap and began to slap it against her palm with obvious impatience.

"Bear with me, Senior Tutor, bear with me, there is no hurry. Emily, shuffle over. Oh you do look ridiculous with your trousers around your ankles, ha ha! Come and stand behind Caspian please. Now bend over, firm hands on his hips, nose in the top of his cleft, bottom up. Excellent. This is known as a tandem beating. Dr Ford, please pull Emily's knickers down. Now, no one is to move until the first stroke has been landed and fully experienced but, when instructed, you will change positions, albeit Emily will pull her knickers up to comply with Daisy's expressed wishes."

Unwisely, Daisy stamped her feet in petulance.

"No! No! No! She's putting her face in his bottom. No! I don't want this."

There was a heavy silence in the room and Daisy's outraged expression turned to one of apprehension and then concern and then fear.

"Er, sorry, sir. But I don't want her touching Caspian. I don't ..."

Stones kept his face blank while the others waited. Emily, who without doubt was relieved that Daisy had taken attention away from her, froze in the act of compliance and stood half-bent, with her hands on Caspian's flanks, her head poised inches from his bottom.

"We now appear to have a volunteer for a tricycle! Daisy you do not quite seem to have learnt your lesson today. You will now take your place in front of young Caspian and you will remain there for the first round of punishment. Before you open your mouth and talk yourself into further trouble, I will give you this warning once. You do exactly as I say and you will receive this one additional stroke. You put one foot, one gesture, one injudicious word out of place, young lady, and you will stay in this cosy little threesome for all six strokes that Dr Ford is about to dispense for the benefit and improvement of your young man and the errant Emily. Your sweet little buttocks look rather disfigured and rather painful, Miss Weaver, so I would advise that you take your place as directed, and bend over. That's my girl, that's just the job. Now shuffle back, legs apart, until you feel Caspian's nose and forehead. That's it, that's it. Emily, head down, nose in his cleft, excellent, bottom up for Dr Ford. Enjoy the sandwich moment, Caspian, people would pay good money for what you are experiencing for free, ho ho! All in place, Senior Tutor. Wield the strap, wield the strap! Hold tight you three, positions to be maintained until instructed otherwise."

Celia swung the strap from high above her shoulder and landed the thick leather perfectly across the centre of Emily's waiting bottom cheeks. Stones was not surprised to see all three bodies shunted forwarded by the force of the blow and he heard Emily's muffled screech into Caspian's backside. All three held their position before Stones instructed Emily to pull up her knickers and move round to the front of the trio to reposition herself in front of a rather subdued Daisy, whose reluctance in putting her face towards Emily's bottom proved secondary to the fear of earning further consequences to her actions.

Stones rested a hand on Caspian's bottom, now fully exposed and in line for the next slash of the strap.

"Oh you are trembling, dear boy. Is it the excitement of having your face pressed between the gorgeous buttocks of your enchanting young lady maybe? Or are you just plain terrified of the strap? Perhaps Senior Tutor needs to put you out of your misery, eh? Some say that the feel of waiting for the stroke to land is as bad as the pain of the actual impact. It is nonsense, of course, as you are now about to find out!"

Celia's aim was true again and the leather thwacked against the tender cheeks already clearly displaying the effect of the earlier cane strokes. This time, the three almost broke their contact as Caspian's fingernails dug deep into Daisy's thighs and she in turn reacted by biting into Emily's right buttock, causing a yelp of pain from the front of the threesome. After 30 seconds, Stones tapped Caspian's back to indicate that he should now move round in front of Emily. Daisy, bottom now exposed for the next savage blow, was weeping copiously, her head and nose sliding on her tears, pitching her face halfway down Emily's crack, whose panties had rucked up, much to Stones' amusement, giving him more opportunity to belittle the vexed woman further.

"Now, Daisy, leave Emily's anus alone, please. This is a punishment, not an opportunity for you to partake in analingus!"

As her head shot up and Daisy opened her mouth to object and deny, Stones grabbed her around the neck and forced her head down into Emily's cleft, the panties forced even lower by Daisy chin.

Celia, as ever, was totally in tune with his thinking and swung down hard with the strap. The blow landed on top of one of the strokes received earlier and Daisy screamed into Emily's bottom, her hands going to her own stinging buttocks, her knees buckling as she dropped to the floor, one hand dragging fingernails down Emily's left buttock.

"Of dear, oh dear. Have not taken that well, have you, my little one? I think you rather owe Miss Govan an apology. Nasty scratch marks indeed. Perhaps Daisy should be swapping places with Emily. Would you like it if Daisy was to take your share?"

Emily was quick to speak up.

"No sir, I'm fine, Professor Stones. No problem. I am happy to take my dues, sir."

"Seems like you have had a change of luck, Daisy. Pull yourself together and take your seat again; you may watch the remainder of the punishment being carried out as long as you can retain a sense of detachment and keep that silly mouth closed. Understood?"

Daisy scrabbled to her feet, apologising to and thanking both the Professor and Emily as she jumped onto the chair, her pitiful sobbing and burbling continuing in relief as much as pain.

"As Daisy has insisted on pulling your underwear down, Emily, I think we can dispense with them totally now. Unless Daisy has any further objections? No?"

Daisy kept her head down and the lack of response suggested that painful lessons had been learnt and there would be no further input from the sobbing and cowed young woman.

Celia, with a smile on her face, delighted at Emily's further belittling as she flicked away her tear-soaked knickers. Emily obediently retook her punishment pose and Celia swept her arm down again, landing a second ferocious strike across the tops of her cheeks. Emily's whole body seemed to go stiff before she let out a stifled cry as she buried her face as deeply as possible in Caspian's cleft.

"Well taken, Miss Govan. Back in front of Caspian, please, this time without those annoying panties so he can get that face fully into your cleft."

The two shuffled around again, Caspian grabbing Emily's hips and leaning his forehead against the base of her spine. Seconds later, the strap landed and his face became all but embedded between Emily's cheeks. Stones could see Daisy's unease but she remained quiet, her eyes glued to the back of her boyfriend's head.

"Switch around again, please. Emily, let's have that bottom up high, show us how you take a beating, nice and proud!"

Celia slashed down, catching Emily under her fleshy cheeks at the tops of her legs. The slapping sound echoed around the room, soon joined by a full-blooded screech from the stricken student as her head jerked clear of Caspian's cheeks by the force of the blow. At the professor's, command she managed to gain control and staggered around in front of Caspian once more. She flinched as his fingers touched the sore redness of her leg but held position when he pushed his face once more into her arse crack. The strap landed with velocity but this time Caspian's knees buckled and he began to howl, tears pouring down his face. Stones pulled him up and manoeuvred him back around in front of Emily once more. He took hold of her neck and pushed her face back between his bright red buttocks as the stricken young man began to weep uncontrollably, all resistance broken, reduced to a beaten boy in total misery.

Celia allowed Emily no time to prepare herself as the strap whistled through the air once more and cut into a white band of skin between deep red tramlines. Emily howled the howl that the professor's thick strap induced in all its recipients; her head rocked, her legs trembled and tears flowed from her eyes in anguish.

"Come along now, Emily. You know the rules, no slacking,"

Stones barked as Celia pushed her forward in front of Caspian. Caspian had little interest any longer in Emily's nakedness and was so clearly intent on his own survival of this intense strapping now, his cock now shrivelled to a size as though to hide itself deep into his groin. The strap lashed down across his ravaged buttocks for the fourth time and only Emily's hands that reached back and grasped his wrists firmly kept him in place.

"Yes, good call, Emily. Let us have that replicated for the last two – both of you assist each other by holding on like that. Yes nice, nice. It looks as though the two of you have bonded. Isn't that sweet, Daisy?"

Stones taunted the subdued student, whose face quickly lost its expression of belligerence as the professor turned toward her. She passed his test, though, and he found her silent nod satisfactory evidence of her broken spirit.

Caspian reached back as Emily had done, as she presented again and awaited Celia's next swing.

"Eeeeeeeeaaaaaaaaaaaaaiiiiiiiii!" There was no muffling of her screech as her head whipped from between her co-recipient's bottom crack and she writhed dramatically, grabbing frantically at Caspian's hands as he returned her supporting clasp of sympathy and desperation.

No words were spoken as the two automatically changed places as though programmed. Stones saw Emily wince as Caspian pushed his head against her tender skin across the top of her bottom but still reached back and entwined her fingers with his as he reciprocated by taking her hands. His member remained shrunken into his compact balls and Stones felt that the punishment had become king and that the sexual element of the naked coupling between the two had become a partnership intent on helping each other through their joint torment. He was impressed at their co-operation and total acquiescence, and thus made a decision that he was sure would meet with their approval although he was intrigued to find out how Celia and Daisy would react.

"Make this the final round, please, Celia. They have both behaved exemplary and the teamwork is a joy to behold. Every good boy and girl deserves a favour, don't you think, Daisy?"

Stones could see the dilemma in Daisy's eyes; there was no doubt she particularly wished to see Emily suffer but her rage towards her boyfriend seemed to have left her as she gazed at his badly marked bottom that awaited the strap that Celia was eager to deliver.

"Emily is still going to get her extra six, though, isn't she, sir?"

"I bloody well hope so! She damn well deserves it, Professor Stones. I really hope you are not going to go soft on her." Celia's strident words drew a sharp look from Stones and her rather comic gulp suggested that she was well aware that this show of petulance was not the best display that she had ever put on!

"Thank you for your non-requested and non-required input, Dr Ford. I have noted your response."

His stare had the desired effect of reddening her cheeks and Stones was delighted to see her flick a glance at Daisy, the discomfort that the exchange in front of the student had caused her obvious.

"My decision is that there will be one further stroke of the strap for these two now, and indeed Emily will receive a further six, once Daisy and Caspian have left. Celia, you will have the honour of delivering those. The 12 strokes of the cane will be put aside for the moment but actually I will have it to hand as I may have a use for it later. If you could fetch it out of the cabinet for me, Dr Ford. Place it on the desk over there, please."

Celia's facial expression gave clear signs that she had understood the message and the threat towards her hung in the air. Daisy was too preoccupied looking at the rising welts on Caspian's buttocks to take note of the interplay between the senior academics.

Celia picked up the strap once more and, as Caspian's buttocks tensed dramatically, her embarrassment from the exchange translated to anger with the strap's delivery and it flew through the air in a wide arc before it slammed onto the target area. Caspian screeched in pain as his body's violent reaction thrust Emily to the ground and he tumbled on top of her.

It required Emily to take control as Caspian was now totally occupied with the pain from his rear and she placed the distraught student in – vaguely – the correct position to enable her to bend over and present herself with her face pushed in between Caspian's gyrating buttocks. Stones watched Celia's face as the college's senior tutor licked her lips, her eyes blazing as she drew her arm far back before striking the leather strap with a resounding slap across the top of Emily's cleft. To Emily's credit, and Stones was pretty sure that it was as much a determination not to give Celia the satisfaction as a sign of her resilience and strength of character, she squirmed and whimpered but stayed in position.

"Thank you, Senior Tutor." Stones moved to assist Caspian to his feet.

"When you have managed to pull yourself together, you will please add your words of gratitude to Daisy's on the bottom of her script, please, young man. Your time here will then be at an end and you two may dress and get ready to leave us."

Stones took hold of Emily by an ear, marched her over to the punishment desks and bent her over.

"You, young lady, will stay here in position to be beaten further while we finish business with Daisy and Caspian."

Celia had brought Daisy over to stand before the professor's desk, having quickly read the student's script and handed it on to a chastened Caspian. Celia's nodding head suggested approval of her words as she handed the document over to the young man and met Stones's stare. Her command to Daisy was to cause the defeated student yet more grief.

"I suggest you turn around and bend over, legs apart and present your bottom to the Dean of Discipline for a final inspection."

Stones awarded her with a knowing smile, Celia performing a mock curtsy to acknowledge their meeting of minds and mutual understanding of the shared venture.

Daisy, her obedience and submission fully apparent, did exactly as requested without hesitation and Stones drew up his chair close behind her and placed both huge hands on her ravaged buttocks.

"Sad to despoil such charming buttocks but so very necessary in the case of such filthy and disgraceful behaviour, I am afraid."

He prodded and squeezed the blistered cheeks before him.

"An excellent outcome, though, and if your words of remorse and gratitude meet my approval then you and your accomplice can get dressed and leave my quarters. Emily's final denouement will take place without an audience."

Caspian passed the document to Celia to present to Stones and the two students stood before him, side by side, their expressions giving full evidence of their trepidation as they awaited his verdict.

"Yes, this is suitable, you may get dressed and get out. Hopefully this has been a lesson learned and the two of you will not be brought to my attention again."

A prompt from Celia had the two apologising profusely to the professor and thanking him for their rehabilitation and correction. Seconds later, they had scurried from his rooms and the focus turned again to the prostrate figure of Emily.

"Right, Emily, turn around and sit yourself up on the desk facing me, please. Now lean back, legs in the air, hands under your knees and pull your legs back towards your shoulders. That's it, you know the position, pull back so your bottom is up and you are completely exposed and open to facilitate my next intentions."

Emily obeyed, without hesitation, the only look of concern was when she espied Celia running the thick leather strap between her fingers as a look of sheer malice crossed her face. Stones was fully aware of the simmering feelings that the two drew out of each other and knew that he had to keep Celia's possessive nature under control.

"Dr Ford will now deliver two hard strokes of the strap to the insides of your legs which I hope will be sufficiently painful and memorable to need no repetition. I will finish off your chastisement by applying a further four strokes to your bent buttocks. So, please take a breath and keep very still to ensure that the senior tutor's aim is accurate and we avoid any unnecessary unpleasantness with the stroke hitting your labia."

Stones cold and detached voice appeared to unsettle Emily more than the content of his announcement; she closed her eyes tightly but held still as the strap was raised high.

Celia whipped the leather down, the stroke hard and true, landing on the very sensitive unblemished skin of her inner left thigh, close to her pussy.

Emily stifled her scream, her body juddering on the desk before she opened her eyes to stare at the professor, her face set in a show of defiance. With a scuff of annoyance, Celia slammed the strap down viciously on the opposite leg, barely avoiding Emily's sex. An unladylike grunt and a curse as air escaped from her held breath was Emily's stoic response as, with eyes full of tears and an expression that highlighted the painful sting she endured, she met Celia's gaze and winked at her. With a furious yell, Celia raised the strap and swiped down with the strap, aiming directly between Emily's legs. Emily was to feel nothing, however, as Stones's thick forearm suddenly appeared and took the full brunt of the blow. Stones did not flinch but just removed the strap from Celia's hand as her face froze in horror, the full realisation of what she had just done, and had intended to do, hitting her consciousness.

"Oh dear. I do believe that you may have miscounted, Senior Tutor. That would be three strokes and we had clearly agreed on two. How unfortunate. Go and stand in the corner, hands on your head. If you behave like a spoilt child in my room, you will be dealt with likewise."

Celia did not hesitate or waste words in apology; she walked quickly to the corner, her shoulders slumped, and adopted the position of shame as he directed.

Emily's face was transfixed as the scenario unfolded: one moment frozen in fear as the strap descended, the next relief and amazement as Stones blocked the savage blow and saved her from the unimaginable anguish that the impact would have caused.

As Stones met her eyes, she whispered her thanks as she slid from the desk and turned to present her bottom as previously instructed.

"Ready to be beaten, Professor Stones. Please strap me as I deserve."

Stones smiled as she spread her legs wide and pushed her bottom up, her arsehole winked lewdly at him in such a manner that he knew that she was doing so deliberately.

He brought the strap down hard across her buttocks, her gasp in response a mixture of pain taken and pleasure given. He laid another on top of the first, her cry and long low moan satisfying him that he had inflicted a pain beyond her comfort zone. The third stroke on top of the first two drew a long howl and she began to sob uncontrollably, the sting once more testing the limits of her forbearance and ability to withstand the extreme bite and long-lasting sting of the thick leather. The advantage of never being troubled by bothersome pangs of mercy and clemency meant that Stones was very consistent with his punishment delivery strokes. He raised his arm above his head and landed the final, full-blooded blow directly on top of the previous three. The resulting scream from Emily suggested that he had surpassed himself, her fingers scrabbling around the desk top and her legs trembling uncontrollably as she raised her body and gave full vent in clear torment.

Stones took her hand and led her over to his chaise longue, assisting her to lie face down. Within seconds, he had placed ice packs wrapped in cloth on her buttocks and was stroking her hair and wiping her tears.

"You just lie there for a few minutes, my dear. It is all over, well done, well done."

Stones may well have spoken the words to Emily but his target was Celia, whose body showed distinct signs of muscle tension and rigidity, his intent to emphasise his total control of their relationship boundaries.

"Celia, perhaps you could come and apply some of my lotion to Emily's poor bottom and legs. I think she could do with some nice soft, soothing hands on her sore skin."

Celia spun around, her chin set and lips pursed, but complied, to Stones's amusement and expectation. As her experienced fingers massaged the cream into and between Emily's bottom and legs, the sexual tension in the room heightened and Stones was fully aware that the two had unfinished business.

"Now, we do not want to move this into dangerous territory, do we, ladies? Your fingers are straying close to areas that require no treatment, Celia, so I hope you are not planning on taking liberties."

Celia grinned and ran a fingernail harshly down the raw swollen red stripe on Emily's inner left thigh, which prompted a yelp from the student and a furious glare back at her tormentor. Celia ignored the look and responded to the professor in an obsequious voice.

"Oh, not at all, Dean. Just trying to go a good job and enjoying the sight of a naughty girl, well thrashed as deserved."

Emily, never one to hold her tongue when her ire was roused, was quick to fire back with her own dig.

"I think the senior tutor, with her wandering fingers, is keen now to receive her own flogging. You are going to beat her, aren't you, sir?" The words may have been directed at Stones but her eyes were fixed on Celia.

As Stones kept his face passive, he smiled inside as the two women, a clear generation apart, fought and jousted for his attention and approval. He was conscious that Celia leaned in to whisper in Emily's ear as she rose.

"I am afraid that I did not catch that. Emily, what did the Dr Ford just say to you?"

Emily's face was gleeful as she repeated Celia's whispered words.

"Sir, Dr Ford was very rude and told me that, unlike me, she will get to have your cock deep inside of her and she told me to dream on, sir."

Celia froze and shot a look of malice aimed at Emily before her eyes dropped and she turned to face Stones.

"Right, well, playtime is over, ladies, and I am rather disappointed in this juvenile behaviour. Dr Ford, you will return to the corner of the room to, as Emily correctly assumed, await your own thrashing.

In preparation for that, you can lift your skirt, tuck it into its waistband and drop your knickers to your ankles. I see no reason now why you should be treated any differently to a misbehaving student. If you dare to produce any words of argument from that open mouth, I will consider asking young Emily to stay and assist with your correction."

Celia's wince and immediate compliance suggested that she had finally realised the most prudent path to take. Her bottom was now exposed to Emily, though whether for the first time she did not know as it had never been confirmed that Emily was one of the attendees at a previous denouement when she had been wearing a blindfold.

Emily had gone into a rather trance-like state as her eyes fixed on her senior tutor's naked bottom and Stones was not at all surprised to see the tip of her tongue wet her lips subtly. Her recovery from a severe beating was impressive and proved once again that she was a clear future candidate for rather more personal attention once the young woman was no longer under his care. For now, though, he needed to wipe the smug expression off her face.

"Emily Govan, you seem to have still not quite learned how to control your quick-fire remarks in my room. Climb back onto the desk, back to me, head right down, bottom right up, hands back to grasp your ankles, legs wide apart. That's it, a set of nice taut buttocks, an open cleft, ready for two more stripes from my strap. Keep still as I am going to deliver them vertically and any movement from you may cause me to lose my target and you really don't want to feel this coming down between your cheeks."

As she settled into the submissive position, he waited for the reaction of her squeezing her cheeks tightly together to pass, and, as she unclenched, he lashed down hard. She yelled loudly but held her position as the second stroke laid a fiery red tramline down her right buttock. The blow was as hard as Stones could deliver and he was pleased to see the force knock her off balance and her body fall flat across the desk as she continued to cry out in pain.

"Get up and get out, wretch. Come along, clothes on, get out of my sight you blubbering worthless item. Get out, and I expect an email illustrating your shame, your thanks for your just punishment and an apology to all concerned for your behaviour, within the hour. Hurry, get out, get out."

Tears pouring down her face, all sexual thoughts driven from her head, the distraught Emily found herself bundled out of the door, barely dressed, without ceremony.

"I think we both know what happens now, don't we Celia?" His voice was stern and brooked no disobedience. Celia offered him her most servile look, and without a word, she swiftly removed the rest of her clothing and walked to his main punishment desk, bent over, legs apart and buttocks displayed to perfection.

"My apologies, Professor Stones. I believe that I let you down and that there are 12 strokes of the cane with my name on them and my bottom awaiting their delivery. You probably want to keep the strap handy to ensure I suffer as I deserve. Please punish me accordingly."

Stones truly appreciated the love they shared at that moment. Celia had transgressed, both of them acknowledged that this could have only one outcome, but her submission was absolute and he could not fail to admire her faithfulness and loyalty to his cause. He picked up the cane and flexed it as he feasted his eyes on her glorious naked bottom. The age difference between her and Emily may have been three decades but her bottom was comparable to the beautiful young student's. He had no doubt that they were both aware of his obsession and desire to do whatever he pleased with her smooth skinned, full cheeks and the prize deep in the divide.

He was a master of his craft, an artist with the cane, deft and assured. The repetitive sound of the rattan striking flesh was consistent in application both in force and timing. This was no white-knuckle fury but a controlled, ruthless and remorseless thrashing that brooked no argument in its quest to deliver a lesson. Celia held her stoicism for three strokes only before the searing sting of the harsh strokes broke her resolve and a strangled cry escaped from her mouth. Eight strokes in, all will to resist had been broken and her full-blooded scream rent the air in the room. Stones's focus on his intent to make Celia realise her error in crossing him warranted a ferocious response. He knew that she had been on the end of a beating from him on enough occasions to recognise that there was a harshness and cold focus to his delivery that signalled that this was pure punishment and not any kind of sexual foreplay as they had experienced together on so many occasions.

As Stones laid the final stroke of the cane across the tender tight strip of skin on the top of her cleft with all of his might, Celia's hands flew back to clutch her beaten cheeks. The tears flowed as she howled disconsolately and directed eyes at the professor showing deep pain and misery as she sunk to her knees, her distress plain to see.

"What do you say?" his words were delivered in such a cold tone that Celia shivered in her misery.

"Oh, Edward, I am so sorry. That girl is the cause of so many mixed emotions in me, I must admit. But, of course, you are correct in saying that my behaviour was poor and juvenile and therefore so deserving of such a severe thrashing. Thank you for showing me the error of my ways once more, Edward. I am so sorry that I am often a disappointment to you and you are forced to have to beat me. Please forgive me, my darling."

Stones kept his steely gaze on her and allowed her to work out the next move in this latest instalment of their long-lasting liaison. Even with her bottom ablaze on the end of one of Stones' heartiest canings, she never faltered in her love and dedication of his supremacy and total domination of her.

"Put your hands against the wall and lean forward. Push that bottom out. What do you need to say now?"

Celia's gulp before she spoke was just reward for Stones as he picked up his leather strap with savage intent in his eyes.

"Please, Professor Stones, I would like you to flog me with the strap for being such a naughty girl. I am so sorry, Professor."

The first stroke landed vertically down her back, the thick red stripe forming instantly from between her shoulders to the small of her back. As painful as it was unexpected, Celia screamed long and loud but held her stance. The next five strokes covered her bottom over the length of her crack, all the individual cane marks now lost in the crimson mass. He tossed the strap aside, knelt behind her and leaned in to place gentle kisses on the inflamed cheeks as she sobbed and struggled to contain her distress. He moved back as she thanked him for her punishment before turning a tear stained face towards him.

His erection was obvious, his trousers tented, and still with a wet face, she moved towards him. Stones watched as even in her torment she licked her lips while she moved to put her hands to his erection. Within seconds, she had released his protuberance and there was no countering her devotion and passion as she engulfed his cock with her welcoming mouth. Stones held her head as she began to rock on her knees and heels, her burning buttocks suddenly a minor concern, it seemed. As his arousal increased, he pulled her upright, twisted her round, pushed her over the desk and sank his twitching, eager cock inside her.

Celia laughed out loud in her delight at receiving him deep inside her inner, sodden cavern of love. That she loved him intensely at that moment he never doubted, and they both recognised that part of her pleasure and happiness was driven by the jealousy of his association with Emily Govan, although how ridiculous it was for Celia to be envious of the 21-year-old student! A beautiful woman with the world at her feet and men in countless numbers at her disposal. Stones knew that, in reality, Emily's feelings towards him were nothing more than a youngster's crush, and that his long-term relationship with Celia could withstand any fleeting distraction, however glamorous and available. In truth, he admired her natural inclination to assume that anything she had was hers to have to fight to hang onto, and over the years she would have been well aware that he had not only a wandering eye but dabbled in areas that she had resisted the temptation to become involved in. Her desire for him was both exhilarating and frustrating, her passion sometimes dampened by his relaxed manner towards their relationship, the unease she often felt heightened by his distant manner and arrogant dismissal of her. Her sore and throbbing bottom was now a reminder of the trouble such jealousy and possessive behaviour brought to her door.

As his hands lifted her up, a finger found her arsehole and penetrated her welcoming portal as she once more gave herself entirely to his wants and lusts. She was already close to coming and was almost in tears in her delight at his double penetration and total mastery of her willing body. She twisted to find his mouth and kissed him passionately, her tongue delving deep in his mouth as she almost tried to merge her body into his. As their mouths broke apart, his grin and sex-eager eyes melted her heart and with a push of her pubic bone against him, she felt her first climax exploding inside of her. Celia's second orgasm was to follow shortly as he began to build up the speed of his pumping cock and two fingers rubbed hard against her clitoris, the digit buried in her arsehole twitching continuously and probing deep. His moment came and his spunk gushed inside her as she cried out, while the pain in her beaten body merged with the pleasure of every frantic, heaving thrust of his groin. He whipped his finger from her arsehole and pushed it into her mouth as he bit down on her shoulder in the juddering finish to his climax. The combination of his excitement as he emptied, the musky taste of her inner being on his finger and the pain of the bite were enough to bring Celia off again before her exhausted, trembling body finally collapsed beneath him. Their lust and passion sated, his softening cock slipped from her, and they stayed coupled together as one, minds and bodies combined in their shared ecstasy, their arms entwined.

Less than half a mile away, Emily was on her own bed, positioned in front of her wide dressing table mirror, on her back, legs splayed apart, her head propped up on a pile of assorted pillows and cushions. Between her legs one hand was active, fingers sliding backwards and forwards, side to side, across her hard, clitoral nub. Her other hand grasped a breast, an erect nipple squeezed hard between knuckles; her head shook as she lost focus on her reflection in the mirror, beads of sweat appear on her brow. She was seconds away from the climax she had longed for during the time in the professor's study. Her buttocks were raw, swollen and throbbing, but this was of no consequence now. The marks left by the loathsome strap stung and she got no pleasure at the memory of the thick leather impacting her flesh but it was done and she was comfortable with the lasting sensation now that the beating was over. Admittedly, she had been outwitted yet again by her mentor, always ahead of her thinking; he had seen through her plan and desire to earn herself a punishment session, known her wish to be naked and bent over, her arse in the air ready for the lash and bite of his cane. The thick strap most certainly had not been in her plans, the intense pain of its weighty slap and deep, long-lasting sting even too much for her and her wanton lust to be beaten and dominated by him. Celia's appearance had not been considered a possibility at any point, although the physical attraction between the two of them could not be denied despite the obvious antipathy. Ever since the senior tutor had ill-advisedly let her sexual needs get in the way during one of Emily's earliest thrashings at the hands of the professor, Emily had known that Dr Ford had feelings for her. Being beaten by both her and the professor was not far off being a perfect fantasy and although the strap's lash was never something that she could think back on with a happy heart, once a beating was in the past she never regretted it, even though she could still feel the heat of the accumulated strokes and was well aware that she had days of discomfort to come as the bruises developed and the tenderness increased in an area that one could hardly avoid using! None of this mattered as her fingers fluttered and her mind replayed at speed the feel of Caspian's cock spurting into her hand, the taste of his spunk as she had injudiciously sucked down the hanging drops, and the lewd display as she had held her legs apart and bottom raised in preparation for the thrashing. The glorious after-sting, the amazing pain that Dr Ford had induced with her strokes to the insides of her legs, and the fearsome burn of her strapped cheeks after Stones had applied the final cutting lashes.

The fantasy of the professor falling to his knees before her and sinking his face between her legs was the image that pushed her over the edge. Emily reached her pinnacle at last, screaming out in her ecstasy, her body floundering uncontrollably as her climax rocked her whole being. Her body writhed and twisted for many seconds as what seemed like electric pulses worked their way up and down her body. Her pussy felt like a burning cauldron, her fingers now plunged deep inside as she imitated the thrusting of a man's prick burying itself deep in her gushing hole. She came frantically, jerking her body, her face flicking between expressions of pure anguish to the sublime pleasure as she experienced the most tumultuous orgasmic relief. She finally slumped, her passion sated, her body and mind exhausted, her sore body throbbing all over.

She can smell the air, sweet and ripe: her masturbatory indulgence has scented the room. Her hand is wet and sticky, her pussy moist and red from her frenetic frigging, a nipple throbbing from the pressure applied, her stinging buttocks adding to the overwhelming exhaustion as she stumbles to the bathroom to wash away the evidence of her self-abuse. For now, she is spent. Her longing will return, though, as her mission to make love with the Dean of Discipline remains an unfulfilled dream. Emily feels thwarted but not defeated. There will be other times, she thinks, other opportunities ahead.

The following is an excerpt from the next book in the series, due early 2023.

The Dean of Discipline 4
With Kisses on the Bottom

CHAPTER 1

THE GRADUATION OF

EMILY GOVAN

Another year, another graduation ceremony, thought the professor as he stood on the vast lawn of Central Court while the graduate students mingled, drifting in and out of the huge marquee with their beaming, proud parents, guardians and close relatives, the year's cohort having returned for the three-day event as the city celebrated its cerebral success by default. The university had turned this autumn event between academic years into a massive occasion and a huge economic boost for the area and its hotels, hostelries, guesthouses and private lets. The retail sector likened this to the Christmas shopping period, rammed into one week in September, as tills everywhere rattled in celebration of academic achievement. For many of the students, their hour of glory in the graduation ceremony was just a minor formality in this final hurrah that most dragged out from Monday to Saturday as they held onto clouds of love, memories, friendship and success. The next week really was the start of the rest of their lives, when reality would bite, careers would need to be developed, new relationships would be formed, and adulthood would truly begin.

Several young ladies approached him with their parents, always an entertaining moment for Stones as often the students who had suffered the most from the college's specific, and nowadays highly unusual, method of applying discipline and adherence to rules, were, oft unbeknown to them, offspring of mothers whose unfrocked derrieres he had also known close encounters with.

Stones's face failed to register the emotions he felt as Emily Govan and her eminent parents passed civilities. Emily was due her graduation at tomorrow's final ceremony, her parting shot and her final, formal act in college. As her parents drifted away to chat with some past associates they'd just spotted in the distance, Emily turned to Stones and spoke quietly.

"So, Professor, once I have received my degree from the chancellor of the university I have graduated and therefore I am no longer a student member of college?"

Stones looked at her knowingly as he answered.

"That is correct, Miss Govan, you will become alumni, a lifetime college member, but your undergraduate days and terms and conditions of that status will have come to an end."

Emily looked at him coyly.

"So, in theory you could no longer punish me for something I had done?"

Stones sighed; he could see where this was going and could not resist playing along.

"Correct, Miss Govan. I will be powerless to impose any punishment or take disciplinary action against you once you pick that certificate up. However, as I believe that I have told you before, I do get requests for assistance from occasional ex-students who call on me for my input in what I like to term as 'life coaching'. You have something on your mind, young lady, so get to the point, please."

Emily's face was now pink and she was clearly aware that he had already seen where this was leading.

"Sir, in my first year, I once stole bottles of expensive wine from a crate in the catering store. I think that they assumed it was an internal theft by one of the staff because there was never any fuss or public announcement, and I have worried that someone might have got into trouble over it. I am very sorry, sir, and feel that you should know as you have been so good to me during my time here. I am sorry that I had failed to come clean about this disgraceful act before and wanted you to know in case you feel that this deserved to be dealt with before I graduate."

Stones resolved not to allow any sense of amusement or interest to show in his face or in his voice as he contemplated her words.

"Excuse me, young lady, but you have just admitted to theft of college property, on today of all days, and apparently feel that this will be expunged from my memory if you offer up your scrawny backside for a seeing to."

Emily blanched, giving him the reward he had been looking for.

"Um. Er. Well, sir, sorry, sir. I know, sir. Um. I am sorry, sir," she muttered, her rather incoherent apologetic response gist to his mill.

"Presumably in your plan was me just happening to be free at the correct time to be able to punish you this evening, and no doubt there's a plan that involves your parents having alternative arrangements!"

Emily nodded. "Yes, sir, they are out for evening dinner and I told them I would be meeting up with friends, sir. Oh shit! I've screwed up again, haven't I, sir? Sorry, sir."

"Emily, you are a disrespectful and disreputable woman and you do make me despair sometimes. As it happens, I am free this evening before meeting the Mistress and the Senior Tutor for drinks and dinner with some rather important donors to impress. You will be outside my rooms with an essay admitting your guilt and your request for justice to be dispensed. You will volunteer what form that punishment will take and you will arrive in a freshly showered and fully prepared state. Oh, for goodness sake, you know the drill! Be there at 17:30 hours, fully ready for a final thrashing on your bare backside. Now be off with you, and be thankful that this issue will not be officially reported as it would not have been too late to stop you from graduating. Go!" Stones fairly barked at her, causing slight concern to nearby guests and more than a mere tremor down the spines of one or two students in earshot. A red-faced Emily scurried away.

As he expected, Emily reported to him at the agreed time, her essay in her hands. Stones barely glanced at it; he could see words *such an irresponsible, theft, rule-breaking, criminal act*, and then, quite predictably, the apologies and remorse followed by a plea to be punished severely to help her atone for her guilt and find improvement through chastisement.

"I suppose I should be grateful that it does not say that you are in love with me and want me to fuck you!"

Emily's mouth dropped open on two accounts, Stones suspected, the first being that he had actually spoken those words out loud, and secondly because he had used the F word in her presence.

"Oh close your mouth, you look ridiculous. I note that you have failed to stipulate which instruments of chastisement you feel should be used, but I accept that you have asked for a severe and thorough punishment to take away from this institution as a reminder of how bad behaviour has repercussions, and I commend you for that. Please remove your clothes and bend over, legs apart, hands on ankles for a hygiene check."

If he needed any confirmation that her presence in his room was prompted more by lust and passion than a genuine request for contrition, then Emily's smile told Stones conclusively so. With minimal clothing actually on, it took Emily seconds to divest herself of everything and with a rather flamboyant twist she presented Stones with her bottom, clad in a white string, before slowing pulling the panties down her legs and bending with her legs wide apart.

"Would you like my cheeks pulled further apart so you can inspect me properly?" Emily's voice was husky and quite breathless and Stones realised that she was extremely turned on already. The point of the hygiene inspection was twofold, initially to avoid any unpleasant aroma in dealing with unwashed and unprepared students, but far more importantly to immediately put his misfits on the back foot, confusing them, horrifying them, disgusting them and ultimately causing them massive humiliation, degradation and embarrassment. He knew that none of this applied to the confident and forward Emily Govan, and decided that he needed to take control of the situation.

"Actually Emily, I am so sure that your preparation for this session will have been of the highest level in terms of service cleanliness and hygiene standard that I will pass up the need to get close and personal with you. However, you do unaccountably appear to be damp between your legs, so perhaps you could take a tissue and dab your wet labia dry, please."

Emily spun round and up, clearly annoyed at being thwarted and basically ridiculed, grabbed at the proffered tissues and folded them between her legs. He watched as she struggled to control her renowned quick and fiery temper, knowing full well that he had bested her yet again. She marched over to the bathroom, giving him a perfect view of her bottom in motion, and flushed the tissues down the lavatory. She hesitated before washing her hands and then returned to face him, hands going to her head, her breasts thrusting prominently, her neat and obviously recently coiffured pubic bush displayed in all of its glory.

"Would you like to select the first two implements from my cabinet that you feel would be most appropriate articles to use for the beginning of your thrashing? Remember that this may be an historical act that you have confessed to, but it still theft and as such I do need to ensure that you pay the cost in pain and suffering."

She spun around and marched to his cabinet and returned within seconds holding the riding crop and his bat-shaped wooden paddle.

"I think a bloody good whipping with the crop, excuse my language, sir, after a quick hard hand spanking and then twenty firm slaps with the bat should set me up nicely for the grand finale of your choice, sir. I would hazard a guess that the wicked thick strap is going to make an entrance, it being your favourite application, sir. Thank you for your consideration and time, sir. I hope you approve of my selection?"

Stones could hardly say not; she had indeed chosen well and had slipped in that she was expecting to go over his knee as well.

"Fair enough, Emily. Take down the paddle bat and the thick strap then as we both have agreed that we will finish with that. I think you can go over to my cupboard and fetch one of the bamboo canes. About time that you experienced one of those again, I feel. The one with the red taped handle, please, it should look familiar as it is the bamboo used on you by Chloe and Zoe that memorable evening. The braided knotted lash I will hold in reserve for now."

Emily collected the cane from the selection of long bamboo canes that stood in his cupboard, along with the spanking machine and dreaded table that he had designed, with its strap and pulley system to configure how he saw fit to expose his victims when delivering the ultimate thrashing experience. Seeing it now still sent a shiver of fear coursing through her body, Stones was delighted to see.

"I hope I don't find the need to use my contraption again with you, Emily. It is clearly for the most severe punishments, however, the spanking machine could be a different story should our paths cross again."

The light returned to her eyes with those last few words as Stones's inference of future meetings added a spring to her step. She reverently handed him the bamboo that had wreaked havoc on her bottom a year ago.

Stones settled down on his sturdy wooden chair that he had bought years before, chosen purely on the grounds of the design being perfectly suited for over-the-knee spankings. He patted his legs.

"Over you go, young lady, assume the position, please. Put the paddle within my reach in case I opt to move onto that straight after. Good girl."

Emily obeyed immediately and holding on to the bottoms of the chair legs, raised her bottom high.

"Like this, sir?" she asked in her most coquettish voice.

He didn't answer but released an avalanche of slaps to the backs of her legs. Apart from the tiniest of yelps, Emily suffered in virtual silence. Stones progressed to her buttocks and began concentrating on the creamier white skin on either side of her bottom crack that had obviously been bikini clad. Once he had turned the visible area red, he placed one hand on her left cheek and gripped hard, pulling her cheek aside and unleashed well-targeted blows to the normally hidden crack line skin. He switched hands and repeated on the inside of her right buttock. With her arsehole twitching open and closed and her breathing heavy, he was not at all surprised to see her labia moisten again. He ignored her lust as he then went to work on the tanned skin framing her bottom. He was well aware that he had become erect and that she was trying very subtly to move her groin to rub against his hardness but decided that at this point in their strange relationship he would allow them both to enjoy the moment. After a hand spanking of 200 slaps, he picked up the cricket bat shaped paddle and brought it down hard across the centre of her seat. Her grunt of pain was satisfying and he began a slow, methodical stinging beating, his eyes riveted to her bottom, and he was well aware that she aroused him in a way few students ever had. He loved her rebellious character, her humorous quips and her fortitude in taking a very hard thrashing. That, in combination with her stunning athletic body and striking attractiveness, with her pretty face and long blonde hair, made her a joy to be with for a man of his tastes. Of course, her stunning breasts and very reactive nipples, the very neat bush and full labial lips of her gorgeous vagina helped. To have, in his eyes, the absolute perfect bottom with an arsehole that he felt was a work of art, worthy of his worship, topped it off. He had never succumbed to the charms of a student in all of his disciplinary days but Emily was definitely the one to have caused his temptation to waver the most. In truth, he rather adored her, but that was an emotion which he vowed he would not share with her. One hundred times his arm rose and fell, the heavily varnished wood meeting her porcelain cheeks with a resounding slap every time, her bottom a deep glowing red all over, her quiet whimpers, occasional sobs and haphazard breathing, all signs of her hurt and discomfort. She continued to gently grind against him throughout her ordeal and he

DEE VEE CURZON

suspected that without that sensation she would have been in much greater distress. He cast the paddle down and with his large hands on either cheeks continued to move her body against him. Her yelps of pain turned quickly to a mixture of signs and grunts of lust and pleasure. He spread her cheeks further so that her arsehole and vagina were inviting holes in front of his eyes, one a dark spider web of neat crinkles amongst little off-blonde curly hairs around her dank hole, a bright pinkness just showing within, the other a moist haven of interwoven, plump lips moulding into one another amidst the trimmed blonde pubes, the layers glistening with droplets of her secretions. He could see how much she wanted his touch and gently ran a finger along the wet crack and up into the crevice where her dark hole twitched open and closed at him. He leaned down and put his fingers in her face; she automatically knew what he wanted and she sucked them enthusiastically, covering them with her saliva. The wet fingers went straight to the neat, entrancing arsehole and as he ran one finger around her rim, she would have felt him drip her spit into the relaxed opening. His thumb slid into her pussy and she jerked her body but held onto his calves as she retained her position of surrender and subjugation. Stones switched and Emily now had two fingers in her pussy and his juicy wet thumb rimming her arsehole. He knew that they were in tune with each other and that she knew that he was biding his time, working her open to accept intrusion. That she wanted him so much was obvious as she was able to relax herself and his thumb was suddenly welcomed in through the tight opening with little resistance.

"Oh yes, oh yes, oh yes! Do it, sir, do me, sir, please do me with your thumb, go on, sir, please fuck my arse!"

Stones was aroused by the pathetic, pleading note in the voice of this strong and independent young woman. He knew that she wanted

316

him embedded in both of her intimate holes. He imagined that it was just the thought of what he was about to do that gave her an immediate, shuddering orgasm as she bucked her body up to force his thumb firmly and fully into her most private and personal place. She flinched as he spat phlegm into her bottom crack as she climaxed. He slowly eased his thumb out to allow his spittle to slide into the open hole before his thumb slid back inside of her wanton darkness and his fingers started to frig her pussy more deeply. His other hand now tweaked a nipple and she howled in her ecstasy and he felt her push her groin down to rub hard against what felt like a rod of steel in his trousers. She was leaking into his lap and coating his trousers as his fingers increased their motion in and out of her sodden sex, the squelching sound adding to both of their excitement and her total and abject surrender. Her orgasm repeated and it seemed to him that she had entered a long, non-stopping climax. Her head shook from side to side, her body bounced, her guttural screaming primal and without reservation. Finally, she slumped exhausted and his dampened hands moved back to stroking her throbbing buttocks, the pain of which he hoped was now coming back into her consciousness. There was more to come and her lustful behaviour would not distract him from his main focus.

The screaming changed tone as the paddle suddenly came down savagely on her cheeks …

PREVIOUS BOOKS IN THE SERIES,
AVAILABLE THROUGH AMAZON:

THE DEAN OF DISCIPLINE1 : DEGREES OF PUNISHMENT (2020)
THE DEAN OF DISCIPLINE 2: STRAPPING STUDENTS (2021)

ABOUT THE AUTHOR

Dee Vee Curzon was born in May 1976 and is a widow and the mother of two grown up young ladies. Working in academia for many years, she has an insight into the machinations, idiosyncrasies and vagaries of day-to-day University life but has never, ever delivered a spanking to a student!

Printed in Great Britain
by Amazon

87684193R00190